EMBERS
&
ICE

ISABELLA MODRA

FOR THE PEOPLE WHO FEEL TRAPPED IN THIS WORLD. FIND YOUR OWN ESCAPE, AND LIVE IT.

ALSO BY ISABELLA MODRA

ACKNOWLEDGEMENTS

This sequel would not exist if it weren't for the amazing support I received for *Rouge,* so I'd like to thank everyone who read, reviewed, purchased, stored away for the winter or mentioned my first novel to their distant relative of some sort – every ounce of encouragement fuels me to write. I am humbled by the praise, and I thank you for that.

Mum. Thank you for your gift of gossip and all of the books you helped me sell in your salon. Yes, I know, you *made* me. That deserves some gratitude.

And, as always, a HUGE thank you to my Heavenly Father, for the brainpower, persistence and heart.

You are the greater love.

'THE NOIR HERO IS A KNIGHT IN BLOOD CAKED ARMOR. HE'S DIRTY, BUT HE DOES HIS BEST TO DENY THE FACT THAT HE'S A HERO THE WHOLE TIME.'
- FRANK MILLER

PROLOGUE
HUNTER

Everyone is wrong about hell.

They think it is buried thousands of feet below the earth, a dungeon of demons and iron gates and endless, burning flames. If that were the case, hell wouldn't be so bad for me. It'd just be like having a vacation and picking the wrong hotel. If hell is *really* as hot as they say, then they haven't met me.

But this place I'm in is not warm. This prison is cold. And I have never known such cold.

It is emptier than a chasm between two canyons, where only the wind blows harsh and bitter. It is lonelier than a single iceberg bobbing on the deep, blue waters. This cold is so dark and endless that I've begun to wonder whether warmth exists any longer. Is there still a fire burning within me? Where is the flame? Where is the passion and fury and love when all I feel now is this hollow, bottomless, sickening, inescapable cold?

That's when I know I've arrived in hell.

I am lying on a mattress thinner than a slice of bread and splashed with stains. The mattress is placed upon a single bench just wide enough for me to lie on my back and long enough for my feet to hang over the edge, tucked tightly beneath a blanket that I'm sure couldn't keep even the devil warm. Around me is a cell no bigger than an average bathroom. It's the color of tea with too much milk. Paint crumbles from the walls and large cracks in the cement floor spider out around me like channels in the

1

Amazon River. The only part of the cell that looks even remotely modern is the toilet beside my head and the giant glass wall at my feet that doubles as a cell door. If I sit up now, I can see a corridor outside running left and right and an empty cell opposite mine. Identical.

It's dark now. Not that I would know, since I have no windows. But the lights are off.

A part of me wants to get up. To start smashing things. To find an escape. But I can't move at all. My limbs have turned to jelly. I'm tired, I ache, and in my mind, all see is Eli.

As I drift in and out of sleep, I wonder if this place is a part of my nightmares. Perhaps I am so consumed by grief and bitterness that I've somehow retreated into my own conscience and this is all a front for my harsh reality. Because surely I would have been more careful in the outside world and kept hidden from the Agents. Surely I wasn't so blinded by the pain of losing the only person in this world who calmed the fire. If I had been more careful, maybe I wouldn't have managed to get myself captured and thrown in this prison worse than hell. In hell, at least I'd be warm. Here, there is nothing but cold.

The soft hiss of my glass door sliding open wakes me from my thoughts, but I'm too terrified to roll over. Several footsteps on the linoleum floors pad towards me and hands remove the sheet from my body. The sleeve of my white jumpsuit is yanked up and a sting in the crook of my elbow makes me gasp. I flip over and blink at the bright lights from outside my cell. Is it day now?

I see three men standing before me. They look the same in this bright light; all wearing white with blurred faces and no eyes. They look at me like I'm a piece of science, like a solution in a test tube or a fungus sample in a petrie dish.

There are people out there who would want to do you harm if they knew what kind of power you possessed, Joshua once said to me. What would he think of me now? Would he care? Would he be worried? Or would he just laugh with that sadistic chuckle I still can't erase from my mind and tell me I'm a stupid girl, that I brought it on myself?

Whatever the men in the white uniforms have injected into my blood works fast. My heart begins to pound. A new kind of energy ignites in me as hands haul me to my feet where I waver unsteadily and my vision finally clears.

I stand between two men who appear rather like guards or orderlies; stoic and emotionless. A thirty-something guard leans against my doorway. He is tanned with wispy brown hair that droops over blue eyes. On his neck I see a tattoo of a weeping angel with wings that curl around his throat.

"Time for breakfast," he says and his mouth curves into a smile.

"What did you inject in me?" My voice is a low croak.

"B-12. We give it to all the newcomers who don't have the drive to get up. It gives you just enough energy to walk to the breakfast hall and join the others."

"Others? What others?"

He turns in the doorway, his eyes glimmering with a secret I am most likely about to uncover. "The others like *you*, Fire Girl. You're not in Kansas anymore." He chuckles as he leads the way.

I should have argued or hit someone or unleashed the anger inside me in the form of a deadly flame. But I can't, and for two reasons.

One; the fire is caged inside me. I feel panic rise as I summon the flames and push with all my might to release them, to form a ball of fire and hurl it at these men who grip me tightly. But it won't break through my skin. I look down and notice a silver band around my wrist. It glows blue around the edge, and black veins spider out beneath my skin, as if the accessory is poisoning me. The cold sensation comes from more than the chilly air around me; it is ice, seeping through the fire, dousing it down to dying embers. I know without having to guess that this restraint has stripped me of my powers.

And two; I have no idea what kind of trouble I'd be in if I disobeyed this man. I have to be smart, to wait until I know more about my prison before I stand up and fight.

So I let them lead me out of my cell and deeper into imprisonment, where I would dine with other mutants like me.

– PART 1 –

WELCOME TO DEATH CAVE

ONE

Jack always hated the rain. He hated how wet it made his clothes, how it always seemed to slide like a slippery snake down his neck and against his back. Most of all, he hated that it soaked through his shoes and into his socks and made his feet eternally cold.

But as Jack stumbled out of the warehouse, bloodied, bruised and aching in every part of his body, he found he cared more about making it to a hospital before he passed out than he did about the downpour. As he limped towards the sidewalk and down a path that led to one of the more occupied areas of the suburb, Jack shot a glance back at the warehouse that towered above him. Rain washed over the roof and it looked almost like a scene from a horror movie. *The Warehouse of Doom.* That'd be a bestseller.

Making jokes seemed to be an easier way to deal with what Jack had just been through, and what he'd discovered about himself.

He had a power. A real, slightly confusing power. Some kind of... destruction. Destruction of objects. *Hey, that could be useful,* he thought. *I could get a job as a demolisher. I'd make a ton of money in the trading business. Or maybe the President would hire me as a bodyguard. I'd kick all kinds of ass with this power.*

Jack distracted himself as he stumbled about in the rain, letting every fantasy he'd ever had come to life inside his mind. He could feel more blood oozing from the slash in his ribs as he walked.

Half of his thoughts were on the pain, but he also worried about Hunter. She had been in terrible shape after he fell off the rack and freed himself, but she changed. She softened. It was something in the rain that turned the fire off, and she just gave up. But had Joshua killed her? Was she safe, alive even?

A part of Jack wanted to go back and help her. She needed back up in case the psycho Iceman tried to kill her again. But she seemed capable, and she wanted him gone, wanted him safe. He needed to respect that.

So the next thing to do would be to contact Clare somehow. He wasn't at all looking forward to explaining to her why he'd been missing for a week and why he was so beat up. But Clare was his only family and he loved her more than anyone. She was his only chance at survival. So Jack searched through the rain for a payphone.

Once he'd limped a few blocks, the rain stopped and he came to a more developed area with houses and little cafés. He spotted the silver-blue box and limped hard towards it. Hurriedly fishing out quarters from his filthy pockets, Jack dialed home.

"Come on Clare, please pick up!" He drummed his fingers on the phone box and tapped his foot impatiently. If she didn't pick up and he passed out, would anyone find him? How could he survive?

A dirty black van whooshed past him on the road and a great puddle of water splashed against the plastic wall of the payphone box, making him jump a mile in the air. Then, after a few rings, the message machine beeped.

Jack swore. In a spontaneous rush of anger, he threw his fist into the phone box. Power he didn't know he had surged through him and immediately, the box exploded. Jack was blown back by a burst of sparks and smoke, landing painfully on the sidewalk. He coughed and winced and felt dizzy again as he peered up at the phone box. It looked as if it had been run over, smoke climbing up into the dark night sky.

Once more, Jack sat on the wet sidewalk, amazed at his own abilities. That was, until he became so consumed by pain and exhaustion that he just couldn't stay awake anymore. Finally he collapsed, wondering just for a split second where he would wake up. Praying it was back at his apartment with Clare by his side, he fell into darkness.

TWO

Joshua stood between the two steel tables, gazing down at the pale, frozen bodies that lay upon them, and knew without a doubt that this would not work. It was impossible. Science wouldn't allow it. The revival of complete long-term memory, personality and identity had not yet been proven in cryonics. Only cell structure and muscle tissue have healed within the body.

Joshua checked the temperature gauges, loosening his collar and taking deep breaths. Even though he did not sweat, he suddenly felt very claustrophobic in the freezer behind his laboratory.

I'm only a geologist, he couldn't help but think. *The only thing I'm good at is finding rare stones and researching the shit out of things. Can I actually perform one of the most complicated procedures known to man, when I have absolutely no experience at all, or am I basically just wasting time, money and energy on already dead bodies?*

He leant over Jennifer Smart, watching with intense fascination the way her skin throbbed and froze. He wasn't sure how long he stared at her sweeping eyelashes, at the freckles on her forehead and the small scar on the corner of her jaw. It must have been quite a while, for when he straightened to check her vitals, his neck had cramped up.

When Joshua initially decided to preserve Jennifer Smart's body, he was in a panic state. It was just after the high school fire, and Jennifer knew too much about Hunter's identity for her to safely walk away. Now that he looked back on it, killing her would have been possibly the stupidest thing he'd ever attempted. Jennifer would never have acted on what she knew.

She was a teacher; a scientist at heart, but an innocent teacher nonetheless. Putting her into a coma and freezing her at sub-zero temperatures was completely irrational, even for him. He really had no idea what he was doing, but something told him it was right. A voice.

And then he had to go and do the same to Eli as well. Joshua tried not to beat himself up over his choices, because he was possessed. At least that's what he told himself as he stared down at the boy. To kill him would break Hunter's world apart. But then, she believed him to be dead anyway.

Joshua pinched the bridge of his nose and felt heavy sobs rise in his throat. *God I've made such a mess of everything. Hunter is gone, drowning in grief that I caused because I was stupid and I let the Iceman control me and screw us both over. Now I'm responsible for two innocent lives that I might never get back.*

In his frustration, Joshua stalked over to the wall and threw his fist against the steel. Blissful pain shot through his wrist like fifty daggers. He cradled his throbbing arm, grateful for the distraction. But the bodies were still there, a constant reminder of the terrible mistake he'd made.

But what can I do? What risks am I willing to take to get them back?

You want them back for answers, said a chilling voice and Joshua stopped and glanced up. The Iceman – an illusion of his schizophrenic mind – had appeared, sly and comfortable as he leant on the storage unit near the doorway. *You need Jenny to help you understand Hunter's ability to overpower you. And you need Eli because you're guilty. Bring them back.*

"How?" he moaned, gripping fistfuls of his greasy black hair. "How do I do that? I've spent the last month and a half researching this and *nothing* has woken them up. Nothing! I'm not a doctor, I'm a geologist."

You're a scientist, the Iceman said shrewdly. *You've done well so far to find the answers. How else did you discover the physics behind your power and Hunters? How did you make that contraption to keep the fire inside Hunter? Because you adapt, you have the motivation, and it's in your blood.*

"Things like that don't just happen overnight. It takes years of study to learn this craft. It's impossible."

The Iceman seemed to chuckle at his stupidity. *Impossible? You're standing here talking to a figment of your imagination, a voice inside your head, the voice of your ability to wield and control ice, and you're telling me that it's impossible to wake two people up from a frozen sleep?*

"I have to give up," he sighed. "Nothing has worked."

The Iceman rolled his eyes and said, *Nothing of* this *world.*

Joshua halted in his tracks and spun, his heart racing. He faced the giant glass tank and a light bulb brightened in his mind. "Nothing of this world? That's it."

Finally, the Iceman groaned.

Joshua ran to the tank and raised the sealed compressor lid. Liquid nitrogen fog oozed over the tip and spilled out around him. Joshua reached in and pulled out one of the sample rocks. It was freezing, but it would soon heat if he kept it away from the cold. He brought ice to his palms and tried to cool it.

In a last minute attempt to right his wrong, Joshua placed the rock under the bright florescent light of his microscope and stared down at it. The stone that began it all. It started as a wonderful mystery, turned into a killer and had now become the greatest scientific discovery Joshua had ever and would ever make in his entire existence.

Now, this supernatural stone was going to help him bring them back. Their memories, their personalities and their identities included.

Most importantly of all, Joshua prayed for the safe awakening of their souls as he sat down to open the stone.

THREE

The dancing streaks of blue light through the water had drawn Hunter into a trance. She lost track of time sitting on the damp wooden stool in front of the giant glass tank, watching the dolphins circle each other and listening to their clicking sounds. A door not far behind swung open and Tom, the manager of the aquarium, limped up to her and sat down, his fingers clamped around a dirty mop.

"I'm sorry Lass, I'm gonna have to ask you to leave," he grumbled in a thick Scottish accent.

Hunter didn't respond at first. She was rubbing her fingers together, her mind still deep in a place she couldn't escape from. Watching the sea animals twirl together in the water was just about the only place Hunter could find peace and almost forget...

"Hunter?" Tom nudged her and she sucked in a gasp.

"Sorry, Tom, I wasn't... I'll go."

Tom readjusted his knit cap and pursed his lips. "You can use the back door, I've already shut up the garage. And we're closed tomorrow for the holiday, so..." He walked off to fetch a bucket.

Shoving her hands deep into her pockets, Hunter smiled once more at Rose and Halle. Hunter spent a lot of time wishing she could swap lives with Rose, so that the only person she needed was her mother, always by her side. She would give anything to have a mother, even just to tell her that everything would be okay. That she wasn't alone.

Hunter headed out into the warm, summer weather and felt nothing but a slight breeze as she walked to the subway. New York was beginning to darken, telling Hunter it must be later than she thought. The subway was crowded with men and women returning home from work, with their faces pressed into books or their eyes wandering. Hunter sat beside a woman chewing gum as though she were trying to exercise every muscle in her jaw. It didn't bother Hunter though. Nothing did.

A strong, sticky blast of wind picked up when Hunter left the station and hurried down Collins Street to the fourth apartment building. She was far south in Manhattan, a neighborhood she was only familiar with because of the Chinese restaurant she no longer worked at.

After punching in the code and jogging up the flight of stairs onto the first floor, Hunter fished out her key and unlocked the apartment. Inside, she could smell fried chicken. The television was playing an early episode of *90210*.

"Hey!" called someone from the kitchen and Alex Dempsey peered around the corner, her mouth stuffed with carrot and her blond hair tied up at the nape of her neck like a stumpy tuft of grass. "Did you pick up milk Hunter? And also, we're out of smokes."

Hunter dumped her bag by the door and collapsed on the beat-up sofa. "So?"

Alex threw down her spatula and leaned over the bench separating the kitchen from the living room. Hunter rolled her head to the side and met the same frowning face that had been staring at her for weeks now.

"It's your responsibility to get the cigs, Hunter, since that's *all* you consume these days. And milk. I told you this morning."

"Yeah. I forgot."

"Babe," Alex began in a soft tone that always alerted Hunter to another one of her friend's 'I think it's time you picked yourself up' speeches. "I know you're hurting, but-"

"Please don't lecture me for the billionth time. I've had a rough day."

"Oh please, *you* had a rough day?" Alex started. Hunter rolled her eyes and walked to her bedroom, but Alex followed her anyway. "Kin screamed at me more times than humanly possible and I had to work an extra hour because Ash went home sick. Then, I coughed up rent for the month because you were out watching fishes swim around in their tanks and *not making a living*. Hunter-" She threw out her arm against the door frame and stopped Hunter from running back into the living room. "I know what it's like to lose someone. I don't have parents either and I broke up with Michelle a few months ago. Now I'm on my own. I've been there too."

Hunter sighed, stripping off and shoving on shorts and a band T-shirt while Alex drawled on about how difficult it was dealing with her sexuality whilst trying to get an education, but she wasn't listening. She'd heard it before. And she couldn't take another minute of it.

But where could she go? Who else would offer her a room, even if it could only fit a rusty single bed and a cupboard they found on the road a few weeks ago. Who else in the world could she turn to?

It had been just under a month since Prom. Since Eli died. Since Joshua killed him and nearly destroyed her. And since then, she hadn't heard a word from him. Nor had she any luck in finding Jack.

At first, Hunter wandered around debating what to do with herself. Suddenly the life she once had felt like someone else's. School no longer mattered. She couldn't bring herself to return to the apartment to gather her things and move out. She couldn't even think about Joshua without breaking down in tears.

Hunter had thought long and hard about why she'd been able to grasp the fire. She should have given in to it. She was angry and terrified and fuelled by grief. Why did it not consume her like it consumed Joshua? Was it the voices of those she loved? Was it love itself? There had to be another element to her powers, an explanation as to why it had a mind of its own. The volcanic stone could not be human.

However, she had no room in her mind to explore this theory, not when she had to find Jack. The very night of Eli's death, after she had turned her back on Joshua in the warehouse, Hunter went looking for him. He was in more danger now than ever. Joshua's perception of science and all things abnormal were never incorrect. If he was sure Jack was special, he was most certainly right. Which meant that not only would Joshua be hunting him; the Agents would be on his back as well.

But Jack didn't return to his empty apartment. There was no trace of him. She went back a few days later, but Clare had vanished too with all their belongings. The apartment owner said that Jack never came home, and Clare moved in with her friend to finish school. The only place left to look was the very last place she would ever venture. There was no way, not even if her life depended on it, that Hunter could bring herself to search for him at Eli's house.

"Hunter!" Alex screamed and Hunter snapped out of her reverie and blinked at Alex in the doorway, who was practically yanking her hair out in frustration. "Where the hell do you go?"

"What?"

"I was talking for, like, ten minutes – I *swear* – and you didn't move an inch." Alex looked exhausted, no longer her usual lively, mischievous self, and for that Hunter felt terribly guilty. She didn't want to be a burden on her friend, not when her life was so screwed up. *The sooner you find Jack, the sooner you can go into hiding and get out of her hair.*

"I'm sorry that you and Eli broke up. I know you want to hide out here, believe me, I'd be doing the exact same thing."

Hunter looked down at her toes, guiltier still that Alex didn't know the truth. But it was safer for her.

"And I really hope that things get better for you," she continued, "but you need to wake up. You're not focused, you quit the restaurant and you dropped out of school before you could even sit your SATs, and all because of a break up. What the hell do you plan to do?"

With a sigh, Hunter shoved her hair up in a ponytail and slapped her hands by her side. "I'm sorry Alex. I'm a mess at the moment, and I swear I'll pay you back one day for letting me crash here. I just need... I need a little longer to get my head screwed on. Then, I promise, I'm out of here and on the road to recovery."

Alex's face softened immediately. Her eyes even glistened with tears. She pushed herself away from the doorframe and wrapped her long, skinny arms around Hunter's neck.

"No, I'm sorry. I don't have any right to tell you how to run your life." She pulled away and kept a firm grip on her shoulders. "And hey, what do I know? I'm a twenty-two year old lesbian studying media at a community college and living by myself."

Hunter gave her a warm smile and squeezed her elbow. "That's not true. You have girls here all the time."

Alex scoffed and ruffled Hunter's hair until she slapped her away. "Yeah yeah. Come on, the chicken is probably burnt, but I have leftovers from work."

"Great," Hunter said sarcastically, smiling all the same. "Just what I wanted."

They sat down with their microwaved noodles and dim-sim and watched Alex's favorite movie – *Mean Girls* – while Hunter tried to think of anything but Eli, who was forever on the forefront of her mind. Every breath felt like a deep ache in her chest, an ache that couldn't be cured no matter how many aspirins she wolfed down or how many hours she spent watching the dolphins play.

So many times she caught herself getting to her feet and almost walking out the door with the intention of catching a cab to Eli's. Countless hours she spent erasing the last memory she had of him; lying motionless, blue and dusted with icicles on the floor of room twenty-three. How long would it be before she forgot him completely, before she lost his scent or the unique color of his eyes or his cute, boyish laugh or his strong hands as they skimmed her neck and brushed her hair away? How was this fair? Why did Joshua take him away from her? Did he enjoy it? He sure seemed amused when he held her in chains of ice and laughed as she squirmed.

Hunter's fingers tightened around her chopsticks until they cracked in half. Alex was laughing so hard that she didn't hear her gasp. Sick of the movie, Hunter stormed into the kitchen and threw down her plate, grabbed some cash from the fruit bowl and crossed the apartment to the entryway.

"Hey, where are you-"

"Out," she snapped and wrenched open the door. "We need milk."

The wind outside was nasty and hot and the streets were empty. The convenience store was at the end of the main street, and she planned on taking no detours. Not after the last time she ventured into the dark night and killed a man.

When did my life become a pit of endless death? she asked herself. She couldn't remember a time when things were normal, when she didn't have the ability to walk through fire or draw it from within herself and shoot it at people – people, meaning Joshua. She couldn't remember living with Joshua, growing up in that empty apartment or going to school and sitting alone in the cafeteria where everyone pointed at her and hissed the words 'slut' and 'skank' behind their hands. Her freshest memories that didn't make her stomach clench were of Eli. Of kissing beneath the veranda at *Raoul's*, or under the bleachers, or on his bed. Of dancing at Prom and feeling blissfully happy before the walls crumbled and chaos erupted.

A car she didn't see sped past her and drove right through a puddle made from a drain leakage, splashing dirty water over her back. She gasped and squeezed her eyes shut. A memory washed into her mind of the night she met Eli, when they ran from the boring University benefit and saw a silent film. Hunter had fallen for him right then and there, but not until now had that become clear to her. He was the only person who saw her for herself; as a lonely girl who just wanted to love and live normally. If only he hadn't loved her back, he might still be alive.

The fire burned inside Hunter, as it so often did when she thought of Joshua. She almost didn't notice a couple taking an evening walk with their dog. When she looked back over her shoulder, she could hear them whispering about her and frowning, as if they knew her.

Hunter couldn't escape those people. Since she put her face on television and every news broadcast channel the night she ran into a burning restaurant to be a hero, everyone seemed to recognize her. But doing so only saved one life. The consequences were far greater. Not only did the little act of kindness put her identity at risk, it killed Eli. Because after that night, Eli knew her secret. And that was why Joshua killed him.

With fresh tears burning in her eyes and her chest heaving, Hunter stopped against a gate to a local elementary school, breathing in. For a moment she wondered if she'd ever be okay.

It was then that they came for her. Hunter somehow sensed the danger even before the black Mercedes van sped down the street and skidded to a halt on the road only feet from her. For a moment she was so frozen in fear, like a rabbit caught in a hunter's line of fire. Then men in black suits holding weapons like hand guns spilled out of the van and the flames burst to life inside her.

She would not go down without a fight.

FOUR

The elevator could not have been slower, but Joshua was in no hurry to get back to his apartment. With his arms full of groceries and the irritating jazz music in his ears, Joshua was regretting giving up his luxurious suite to move into room fifty-seven and the lab. It wasn't as if he couldn't afford the apartment upstairs. It just felt so empty without Hunter living in it. There were too many touchy memories.

Besides, living in the trashy room outside his lab – where the furniture still smelled like damp carpet – was the best way to keep an eye on Eli and... the *teacher*.

Joshua held his breath as he entered room fifty-seven against the pungent smell of age. It had been over two months since Prom, and still the apartment didn't feel like home. It was, after all, only a front for the lab that lay hidden behind it, just in case the Agents followed him home. No one would think to lift the picture frame on the mantelpiece of the fireplace where the hidden lever was that unlocked the secret coded door revealing his sound-proof, impenetrable laboratory. No one except Hunter.

Still, it was strange to be living in this room, especially when it was so uncomfortably homey. Joshua hated anything comfortable. If it wasn't stiff, it was cold or modern or disgustingly expensive. That was how he liked it.

Joshua dumped his groceries on the vinyl kitchen bench, gazed at the small apartment and sighed.

God. I'm living in Paul McCartney's bedroom.

In spite of the smell, Joshua lingered in the apartment for as long as possible, unpacking the groceries and making dinner for two. Yes, for two. Joshua plated up a salad and cold chicken for himself and microwaved a quiche – because he hated using an oven – and stood behind the kitchen bench, trying to force himself to open the lab. Truth was, he didn't want to face her. Not after yesterday.

Joshua took his time preparing for the cryonics process, and after combining his old research with the new formula from the stone, it took another few weeks for Jennifer Smart to unfreeze. Joshua didn't expect it to take so long, nor did he expect to actually succeed. He spent countless hours researching, re-researching and then doing so again until he was sure it would work. Even then, he didn't know for certain.

It was messy at first. As with any revival from cryonics, very advanced bioengineering and molecular nanotechnology was needed. Fortunately, Joshua saved well and had very good connections. Not to mention he could be very persuasive at times.

The worst part of the revival was repairing Jennifer's tissues. After the fire in the school, her skin was littered with burns, burns that made it that much more difficult to heal the tissue beneath the skin as well as on the surface. He worked very hard to balance the temperature and help her cells regenerate. It would have been easier if the technology was available, but – like always – Joshua was ahead of time.

Jennifer soon awoke. The moment her breathing became normal again and her words formed actual sentences, the screaming started. Some cursing and gibberish that Joshua neither knew nor cared to know was involved. Joshua deflected her attempt to punch him with a flick of his wrist and a spray of ice that froze her arm stiff, but that only made her scream louder. He hadn't been able to get a single word in to explain why he had frozen her in her hospital bed. She wouldn't allow it.

Since he couldn't get a word in, he also couldn't ask her if she felt any different. He feared she had lost some part of herself, and he didn't know her personally, so he couldn't determine whether anything had changed. So far, she wasn't speaking in Spanish or behaving like a gorilla, so that satisfied him well enough.

He hoped that by bringing her dinner and approaching the situation guardedly, she might actually calm down and listen.

He was very wrong.

The moment the door to the lab slid smoothly sideways and Joshua stepped into the bright environment, a female body collided with him from the left and he, the female body and both plates of carefully prepared dinner went crashing to the floor.

Joshua had no time to suck in even a breath before Jennifer was on her feet again and stumbling towards the door to freedom.

"No!" He gasped, rolled over on his stomach and shot his hand up.

A jet of ice burst from his palm and suddenly Jennifer's feet were frozen to the floor, as if she'd stepped in fast-drying cement with one foot in front of the other. She wobbled for a moment, then became still.

Ignoring the throbbing ache in his hip, Joshua ducked around Jennifer where he could close the door and lock it behind him. Then, he turned to face the woman who stood with her arms folded, her lips pursed tightly together and her chest heaving up and down.

Joshua would have felt sorry for the woman and even a little guilty for locking her up for almost two months, had he not been so shocked – not for the first time – by how closely Jennifer Smart resembled Liz. It wasn't her looks, per say, but more her stubborn and feisty nature. She glared in the same fiery way Liz used to. Her eyes were narrowed to slits and a string of hair was stuck to her lip in a way that made Joshua desperately need to flick it away. What's worse, she wouldn't say a thing.

For some reason, Joshua preferred the yelling.

"I know you're still angry," he said very slowly with both hands raised in calm surrender. "But if you let me, I will explain *everything.*"

Jennifer didn't flinch. "You want me-" she hissed through her teeth, "-to stand here and *let* you explain why I'm locked in some laboratory after you *kidnapped* me and did something really disgusting to my body? You've got to be joking."

"Uh, see, I'm actually *not* joking," he replied. "I owe it to you, and I made you dinner-" He did a double take at the splattered mess that was his quiche and salad, and then bit his lip. "Well, that *was* your dinner but I can make you another one. Anyway, my point is that I would not have done what I did if there wasn't a very logical reason behind it."

"Logical?" she spat. "This is not logical, this isn't even-" Jennifer froze with her mouth half open, and then her walnut-brown eyes widened. "Wait. Oh my God."

"What?"

"You're Joshua Harrison, aren't you?" Her smile widened, but there was no humor in her expression. "Hunter told me you were weird, but she never said you were freaking *psychotic.*"

Joshua opened his mouth and snapped it shut again.

"Yeah," she nodded, her tone poisonous. "I know all about *you.*"

"Wh-" he breathed, feeling suddenly faint. He didn't like being caught off guard, much less by a woman. "What did she... what did she tell you exactly?"

"How long have I been here? How are all my burns suddenly completely healed? What have you *done* to me?!" she shouted, her voice finally reaching that high-pitched tone Joshua hated. *It's like nails on a chalkboard.*

Joshua pinched the bridge of his nose and brushed past her, swooping to the floor and gathering the ruined meals back into their bowls. "I'm going to make more food. Do you... do you want anything in particular?"

Jennifer was about to snap back at him – he could see the sarcastic comment forming on her lips – but instead, she crossed her arms again and nodded. "I'd like something hot and a really big cup of coffee. Make it a bucket."

"Fine."

"Joshua?"

With his fingers hovering over the keypad, Joshua halted but didn't turn.

"You didn't... did you do something to me, to my genetics? Because I feel... different."

He turned quickly, his heart leaping. "Different how?"

"Uh... I guess I just feel... clean. It feels like all the bad stuff has been flushed from my body. I wonder if I'm okay."

Joshua looked at her thoughtfully. "I can't tell you that. If you have everything intact, like your memory and your personality, then you're going to be fine."

"That's reassuring."

"I'm sorry," he sighed. "I tried everything I could to bring you back. Your body is functioning. If you feel like yourself, then I've done my job."

She dipped a sharp nod. For a moment he saw something like relief in her eyes. Then she fixed him with a small smirk and said, "I look forward to hearing how exactly you managed to pull this off, by the way."

"I'll get right on it." He turned back to the door.

"Wait, one more thing. Where is Hunter?"

An ache far worse than his throbbing head burst inside Joshua's chest at the very mention of her name. He couldn't bring himself to answer. After punching in the code, he hurried into the safety of his mold-smelling apartment room, away from Jennifer Smart's questions that felt like a stake through his heart.

FIVE

The only downside to being woken from a cold slumber with a shot of B-12 was that, after the energy started to fade, things came back to Hunter worse than they were before. Fortunately she was so distracted by her surroundings that the aching grip of fear and loss was momentarily forgotten.

The inside of her prison was exactly how she expected it to be: still the same milky-gray walls, blinking fluorescent lights and claustrophobic feel, as if she were buried hundreds of feet below the earth.

The guards marched her down a corridor lined with cells just like her own – all empty with their blue blankets folded perfectly at the end of the mattress – and took a cement flight of stairs down to the floor beneath. There, they faced another corridor. The stairs took them down again and Hunter wondered how she'd ever find her way back to her cell without feeling as if she were in some sort of dream.

At the bottom of the stairs were two doors. The guard with the tattoo who led the way opened the right and stepped back to let Hunter inside. She had only a moment to catch her heart that leapt into her throat at the sounds of mumbled voices in an echoed room before she was shoved inside.

Dizziness overcame her for a moment as the giant space almost swallowed her whole. She blinked in the bright lights, the buzzing of voices and the clatter of plates on steel tables.

She was in a room bigger than the gymnasium at her old school. Like everything else, it was blindingly white. Tables spaced throughout the room were mostly occupied. On the left was a cafeteria where people were lining up to collect breakfast on little plastic trays. They, too, wore white jumpsuits.

Hunter peered around and caught some of them staring. They were all of different ages and race, some angry and some curious. What they had in common, however, was a look of sickness and defeat. It made Hunter want to retch.

The two guards that escorted her stalked off after the tattooed guard clicked his fingers and shoved her towards the cafeteria line. Hunter noticed other guards in the same tight suits stationed like palace soldiers around the room, their feet parted and their hands firmly clasped together.

"I'm not hungry," Hunter said to the tattooed man. She lined up behind a girl who could be no older than eight or nine with ratted blond hair.

The guard chuckled. "You'll need it. There'll be no more of those energy shots for you, so how else will you get out of bed in the morning?"

"I won't," she hissed through her teeth. They were clenched tighter than her fists at her side.

"You will," he said back just as harshly and left her in the line.

Hunter stared at the crowded room and wished she could shut her eyes and make it go away. Suddenly, her cell didn't seem so bad anymore compared to the looks she was getting from almost every other child in the room. She should be used to it after years of torment from her peers at school. But this time was different. She was the new girl now. She had no powers and no charisma. She probably looked like she'd been left out to dry in the desert. Not to mention her detached emotional stability.

She couldn't hide. She could only keep her head down and get it over with.

The line moved forward and Hunter gripped the thin, silver bracelet attached to her wrist, trying desperately to burn it off. Something about the bracelet stopped her powers from escaping. Blue ice dug into her skin and faded into her blood. The most frustrating thing was that the fire raged inside her, but could not get out. It was worse than no fire at all.

Hunter stared ahead as the line moved silently. Her stomach rolled over at the sight of what bubbled in the hot trays. This was certainly not a luxury resort. This was a prison, where the food looked like the worms that birds cough up to feed their young.

"Would you like the last piece of bread?" asked the girl in front of her.

Hunter glanced down and felt her heart drop with sadness. Big green eyes rather like Eli's gazed up at her with an open and welcoming expression. Looking down at this girl was like seeing someone with a disability on the streets and trying to avoid eye contact with them. A silver wire much like a head-brace was wrapped around her forehead, digging into her temples as though someone had drilled it into her skull. Much of the blond hair on the side of her head was shaved, and a deep scar lined her cheek. There was a strange airiness to her tone as though she wasn't quite... there.

Hunter didn't have the heart to decline, so she took the bread and smiled. "Thank you."

"You're welcome. It tastes a bit funny, but the ice-cream will wash it down. The ice-cream here is gooooood!" With that, she skipped away cheerfully.

Hunter glanced back at the counter of food and saw no ice-cream. Dumbfounded, she began to wonder whether she was not in an institution for mutants, but a madhouse.

With no intention of eating her breakfast, Hunter tried not to look at anyone whilst searching for an empty table. No tables were empty, so she found a long one where a small group sat at one end. She placed her tray as far from them as possible and sat down.

Her food didn't smell the least bit appealing, but she didn't want to sit still and do nothing. She picked up her fork and swirled around the gray mush. *If I put my face in it, maybe I'll drown.*

She was just about to attempt it when someone from the end of the table slid down the cold bench and sat directly opposite her.

Hunter looked up.

The boy was just younger than her, maybe sixteen. He was not at all what she'd call attractive, with a mop of mousy brown hair, a crooked nose and chubby features. His eyes were dark and glistening like a bronze coin as he stared at her with an expression of deep thought. On his wrist, Hunter spotted a bracelet exactly like hers.

The boy waited for at least thirty seconds before he pointed a pudgy index finger right at her face.

"Let me guess," he said slowly. "You're... an earth wielder."

"What?"

"No no no, that's not it." He shook his tousled curls away from narrowed eyebrows. "What about superhuman strength? Or x-ray vision? Oh! Oh! Are you one of those freaks who can like… turn into lizards and shit?"

Hunter said nothing, her mouth open. The boy laughed at her expression and shook his head. It was the first remotely pleasant gesture she'd seen in a while.

"Okay, in all seriousness…" He leaned forward, clasped his hands together and raised one eyebrow. "Are you a fish?"

Hunter made a face at him. "Do I *look* like a fish to you?"

"Well." He frowned and waved a hand at her. "You are channeling a bit of a mermaid vibe with… you know, your hair and stuff."

"So if I'm a mermaid… that makes you a moose, right?"

"Ha!" Hunter jumped in surprise. He shook a finger at her. "I like you. You've got some serious attitude. I suppose it's the hair. Gingers are notorious for their tempers."

"Leave her alone Zac," said someone from the other end of their table. Hunter glanced down and saw a beautifully thin girl with golden hair. Her accent was European, maybe French. Hunter noticed small indents on her cheek like faded scars. Around her neck was a silver collar and black veins like spider webs splayed out on her skin as though she'd been poisoned. It was just like Hunter's bracelet. "She does not want to talk."

"God Chantal," Zac sighed. "When did you become such a buzz kill? You'd like to know what Red can do, wouldn't you Benji?"

Zac was talking to the only other person at their table sitting opposite Chantal. He had skin whiter than her own and hunched shyly. His blond hair was shiny and short, and he had dark purple rings under his eyes.

"W-what?" he stuttered in a youthful voice. If they all had names and stereotypes, he would have been stamped with 'Super Nerd'. "S-sorry I didn't hear what you s-said."

"Forget it, I'll just keep guessing. Hmmm." Zac made a loud, irritating humming sound as if the answer to his riddle would come through meditation. Hunter groaned and clicked her fingers at him.

"Stop! Seriously stop it, you're giving me more of a headache than I already have." It wasn't exactly the truth; Hunter found she actually liked talking to them. It took her mind away from all the terrible thoughts that were swirling around in her head. Plus, getting her questions answered –

however horrific they were – was better than finding out the hard way. "What's the matter with that girl over there?" She nodded at Fearne.

Zac cast a glance over his shoulder and turned back to Hunter. "She's gone nuts."

"Zac!" said Chantal.

"It's true! She's been here most of her life. The scientists love messing with her brain."

Hunter felt a chill go through her. She watched Fearne, the young girl whose mind was permanently spiked by a metal brace and who had so much warmth in her empty green eyes. Was she really crazy? Had years in this cold prison driven her to insanity? Hunter's eyes dipped back to Zac, whose foot was tapping loudly on the floor. There was a twitch in the right corner of his mouth. She glanced at Chantal swirling patterns in her goo and Benji, who never looked up from his plate. Hunter was beginning to feel sicker by the minute.

"Hey, what's your name?" asked Chantal.

"Hunter."

"I'm Chantal, this idiot is Zac, and that's Benji down there but he doesn't really say much."

Hunter nodded. "Have you guys been here long?"

"Five years."

Zac threw up his hand. "Ten! Ha, I win."

"Wow," Chantal spat, "what an achievement."

"Wait, how old where you when they brought you here?"

"Eight," he said. "Like most of the sad kids in this place, our parents gave us up because they were told this was a rehabilitation center. Now they'll never get us back, and I'm not sure they even care. We are aliens, after all."

"We're not aliens," said Chantal. "We're just talented."

Zac snorted.

"And anyway, I'm sure Hunter's parents will miss her terribly."

"My parents are dead," said Hunter.

"Oh," said Chantal. "Well, you must have someone then, right? A boyfriend maybe?"

"Dead too."

Chantal went pale and Zac bit his lip, smiling at her. "Nice one."

"It's okay," Hunter lied. "I won't be getting out of here anytime soon, so it's probably a good thing that there's no one out there looking for me."

"Yeah," Chantal nodded. "That's one way of looking at it."

"Is this… it?" Hunter asked, waving her hand around at the room.

"Well…" said Zac. "I think some of the little ones are showering… Will's probably still in surgery…"

"There aren't many in the world with powers like ours, or at least ones that the Agents have caught," said Chantal. "So tell me-" She propped an elbow on the table and rested her head on her hand. "What generation of iPhones are they up to?"

"Uh…"

"Have they invented Terminators yet?" asked Zac.

"Um, no-"

"Who's president now?" asked Chantal.

"What? You guys don't know?"

"We don't know anything," said Zac, "except what all the new kids tell us. The guards don't exactly give us the daily news."

"What do you do then?"

Chantal let out a long sigh. "Well, we-"

"I'll explain," Zac interrupted.

"Fine."

"Okay." He shimmied closer to Hunter, glancing left and right at the tables with other kids like her. They weren't staring so much any longer. "Basically, the scientists call this place the Institution for Convalescence and Experimentation, but to the public it's just known as ICE Institution. Although, I'm not sure many people actually know it exists. Anyway, us kids sometimes call it Death Cave. The name pretty much speaks for itself."

Hunter swallowed her fear, and it tasted bitter.

Zac opened his mouth to continue when movement in the doorway caught his attention. His expression darkened instantly. Chantal raised her head and was staring as well. Hunter twisted around and saw two Men in White march through the doorway, dragging someone in their arms.

He was very tall. That was the first thing Hunter found distinguishable about him. As he half stumbled into the cafeteria, guided by the guards whose rough hands hauled him onto the table beside Fearne, Hunter became aware of the second thing that made this boy so different from the rest.

His brown, messy hair was parted in the middle and he hunched his well-built, muscular exterior. He had no collar or bracelet or entrapment that she could see. He appeared much older than he probably was. Fearne muttered something to him and he nodded gently, then he raised his gaze and looked directly at Hunter.

Doe brown eyes trapped her and she felt a sudden shock in her chest. He was so unnaturally pale. Dark, purple rings circled his eyes. He slumped as though he had no energy in his body. But his gaze was strong and dark and tormented and full of unspeakable pain. It was a different pain to that of the others. Hunter had to look away or she might be sick.

"He came out early," Zac muttered to Chantal.

"I know," she replied. "Ryo told me this morning that they want to drag him out for breakfast or he faints during procedure too quickly."

"That's what happens when you don't eat."

"Who-" Hunter began, but it was then that someone squeezed themselves opposite her on the very edge of the bench, shoving Zac aside. She looked at the boy with silky black hair, eyes the same color and a clear thirst for a fight and instantly wanted to be as far from him as possible. His very presence made her uncomfortable.

"Hello," he said cheerfully. "I'm Jet."

"Jet, piss off," Chantal glared. "No one wants you here."

Jet winced. "Oo, someone has their period."

Two more people had joined Jet. One was a girl of her age with long brown hair, tanned skin and beautiful features. But her face was a permanent scowl and she stood behind Jet as though she wanted to claim him as her territory. The other addition was a shorter, stockier boy with the same eyes as Jet, only not as wicked.

"If it's okay with you," continued Jet, "my brother Marcus, my girlfriend Mikayla and myself wanted to ask: has anyone like us … 'come out' yet?"

"What?"

Jet glanced around at the Men in White guarding the door. They were too far away to hear their conversation, but they were watching.

"Does the world know about our powers? Or is that why you were brought in? Did you try to save the world?"

Hunter crossed her arms, trying to think of anything but the fire in the restaurant and the explosion it caused in her life. "I don't know what you're talking about."

Zac was peering at her, looking eager. "Come on Red, tell us!"

"Stop calling me that!"

Zac put his hands up and his jaw quivered at the effort it took him to hold back laughter. At the same time, Mikayla bent down and whispered in Jet's ear.

"We're cut off, Hunter," Jet continued. "We just want to know if there's any hope. I mean, no one knows we're here. Even our parents haven't come looking for us. If there's more like us, maybe there's a chance we can get a message to them and…" he leaned closer, whispering. "And *escape*."

Hunter's stomach squirmed. She remembered the warning given to her by the guard with the tattoos. She couldn't afford to say anything, not when she didn't know what the punishment might be.

"So?" he pressed. "Is that how you got here? Or did things just get *steamy* with your boyfriend?"

Hunter's heart jolted in her chest, the words hinting that he knew exactly what her power was. But how? They'd never met before. In a mix of fear and anger at his words, the fire roared up inside her as if lit with gasoline. Hunter stood so fast that the table shook and her plate of goo toppled over. The fire raged, emotionally unstable and eager for a fight.

So, it seemed, was Jet.

"Oh, I hit a nerve did I?"

"Jet," Mikayla warned. "Don't start-"

"Shut up."

Hunter wanted more than anything in the world to sock Jet in the face, but she needed to be smarter than that. As much as it killed her, Hunter unclenched her fists and stepped out of the bench.

"Speak to me again," she growled threateningly, "and I'll introduce your head to the floor."

Benji, Zac, Mikayla, Chantal and Jet's brother Marcus were all gaping, open mouthed. Jet was thoroughly enjoying himself, but Hunter had had enough. She made to walk away when his words stopped her dead.

"I bet he likes it," Jet sneered. "I bet it's *warm* down there. What does it taste like, Hunter? Cherries? Or how about-"

Jet didn't get to finish his sentence, because Hunter spun and threw her clenched fist at his face. The sick crunch was louder than Mikayla's scream as blood spurted from his nose onto their trays of breakfast. Jet staggered back and Hunter went to jump on him, to keep smashing in his stupid, grinning face, but the Men in White caught her just in time. One of them snatched her arms and pulled them so tightly behind her back that she was afraid he was going to rip them off. The other threw his hand across her cheek in a slap that left her vision dancing for at least five seconds. But the sight of Jet's face dripping with blood was well worth it.

And it started something in her.

Suddenly, Hunter couldn't control herself. Her mind switched off and she started to go mad. All she wanted was more of Jet's blood on her hands, to cause someone else pain and not herself. She wanted to stop feeling so sick and so lost and start feeling the heat of an angry flame again.

With hidden strength, Hunter wrenched her arms from the guard that tried to pull her away and managed to grasp Jet's collar. His face went white as she drew him closer, her fingers closing around his throat, squeezing as he gasped.

But before Hunter could go any further, a sharp pain burst inside her hip. She knew that pain; it was the last thing she remembered the night the Agents collected her. Jet slipped from her grasp and before she knew it, her body was limp.

Then Hunter fell instantly into an empty sleep.

SIX

The strong smell of antibacterial ointment crept into Hunter's mind as she slept, and suddenly she was waking up shivering and clammy.

She lay on an adjustable bed covered in plastic, slick with her own sweat. Her hands and feet were strapped to the bed like a mental patient in an asylum. She began to panic. A bright light beamed down on her. The rest of the room was dimly lit and lined with cupboards and tools and machinery.

There was a man standing beside her. Hunter had never seen someone so unearthly and sick-looking in all her life. It appeared as though he'd been on a long journey battling Leukemia. His cheekbones were hollow and his eyes glinted like slimy oysters. His bald head shone brighter than the florescent lights around her, dotted with age spots. Blood splattered his coat and he wore black gloves over his hands. When his eyes fell upon her, they brightened instantly and Hunter was hit with déjà vu.

Oh God. I know him from somewhere.

"Hunter Harrison," he said with a grin as though she was someone he hadn't seen in a long time. "I am so delighted to have you here."

Too afraid and uncomfortable to move, Hunter stared at him with her lips pursed shut. She knew she had made a huge mistake when she attacked Jet. Her moment of satisfaction would surely not be worth the punishment, not after all she'd heard that morning.

"I apologize," said the doctor, "that I could not meet with you sooner. I have a morning appointment that I hate to miss, and I wanted you to have something to eat before we were introduced. Though I didn't expect it until later in the morning, and was quite disappointed to hear of the attack in the breakfast hall."

Hunter's throat went suddenly dry. She wanted to defend herself, but the very presence of the doctor made the fire cower so deep inside her, she could feel no warmth whatsoever. Beads of sweat dripped down the side of her head and she squirmed uncomfortably on the table, clenching her fists.

"Never mind that for now," he continued and pushed himself away from the desk, walking closer to her. "I suppose you're wondering who I am?"

Hunter managed to nod.

He rolled back on his heels and clasped his hands behind his back. "My name is Dr. Winston Elroy Wolfe. I was born in the wonderful countryside of Northern Ireland, just outside of Belfast. I moved to England when I was a lad and travelled around with my father and three brothers. I studied well at the University of Oxford, surrounded by great writers and minds and dreamt of becoming a chief surgeon at a hospital in America. When I graduated with an Advanced Diploma in Surgical Anatomy and Medical Science, I worked for many companies but mostly hospitals and laboratories. I soon stumbled upon unique DNA and genetics in a very select few, and set about researching them. I became aware that I needed a place to study their biology in private, where no other doctor or scientist would be able to discover what I was doing. This institution was my starting point. From the very bottom, I built it up until it became this, what it is now-" He spread his arms out, gesturing to ICE as a figurative whole. "I have done many great things for this company, and my research into genetics such as yours has opened a door to a world no one knew existed. I plan to document the life and genetics of every mutated being in this institution, and those who are still trapped in the wild. For you, my dear, are the future of science. Does that answer your question?"

Hunter's mouth hung agape. This man was possibly more insane than Joshua. Dr. Wolfe talked about experimentation and imprisonment as though he were explaining the itinerary of his next vacation.

"I presume your answer is yes," he said. "Now. I've reviewed the information we *had* on you here in our system, and Joshua's files as well, and it seems-"

"Wait," she croaked, finally finding her voice. "What files? How did you get information on us?"

Dr. Wolfe had his back to hers and she could hear him fiddling with instruments on a tray. "He never told you? Well, I suppose you were only young."

"Told me what?" she pushed, pulling on the restraints.

Dr. Wolfe's face was shadowed from the lamp when he turned to smile wickedly at her.

"Why, you've been here before Hunter," he said. "You and Joshua."

SEVEN

It suddenly felt as if the small surgery room Hunter lay in was shrinking around her. Hunter gazed up at the doctor with the knowing smile and felt like laughing and crying at once. It couldn't be true. Even at a young age, she would remember being in such a horrific place. Joshua always warned her about institutions like this, but never did he confess that she'd actually been imprisoned in one.

"Allow me to explain." Dr. Wolfe started to circle the bed she lay on. "It was a long time ago, but I still remember it clearly. Joshua Harrison was young and somewhat naïve, though he was clever enough to create a formula for your powers. Joshua miscalculated and... well you know what happened next, right?"

"He gave himself the power to manipulate ice rather than fire," she said.

"Ah, so he has told you? What a shock that must have been."

"You have no idea."

"After your birth," the doctor continued, "he was sloppy in covering his tracks. We were soon aware of his gifts and asked if he might let us study him, and you as well. He refused."

"Well it's not exactly a picnic in the park here," said Hunter bitterly.

Dr. Wolfe chuckled as he rolled up the sleeves of his white coat.

"You were only a few years old, Hunter, when you were brought here. I can't imagine you remember anything. Joshua certainly did. It's a shame, because he could have been one of the greatest scientists we've ever

35

employed. But he refused to cooperate. All he wanted to do was protect you. So he took you and escaped."

Hunter's heart dropped and she felt the cold steel beneath the plastic cover grow colder. Even that long ago, Joshua still put her safety before his own. All along she thought his obsessive nature was just a figment of his schizophrenic imagination, but he had been the same since her birth. He had always put her life above his own, and she never truly appreciated that.

Was he really crazy, or did he kill Eli to protect her? For love?

Hunter didn't want to feel anything for the man who took away her best friend, but against her will a small amount of guilt leaked from her heart.

"Yes, Joshua was a true man of courage, but he was always an unstable soul," said the doctor as he removed his gloves and sat down on the swivel stool beside her bed. "I'm sure you've experienced the possessive nature of your powers already. Joshua certainly struggled with it for many years. Tell me; when you first discovered the truth about your powers, was it difficult for you to keep control of them?"

Pursing her lips, Hunter didn't answer.

Dr. Wolfe clicked his tongue in disappointment and his bony, icy hand closed around her wrist where the bracelet was bound. "You will need to cooperate Hunter, or I will gather what information I need through other means. And those means will be far more painful than harmless chatter."

The very tone of his voice made fear bubble up inside her. She'd never before been so afraid in her life, and when she was afraid, she would turn to Joshua. But Joshua was miles away, alone and broken, just like she was.

"I'm not afraid of you," she blurted out. But her tone was lying, and Dr. Wolfe knew it.

He released her wrist. "You might want to talk to some of the other subjects, if you're so confident. They will have some thrilling stories about me I'm sure."

As Dr. Wolfe turned away and busied himself with clinking metal tools, Hunter took deep breaths to get her confidence back. The fire argued with her, telling her it was pointless to be brave when she was strapped to a medical bed about to be operated on by a mad scientist. But she needed to distract herself.

"Why are you doing this to us?" she whispered.

Dr. Wolfe looked down upon her and his bushy eyebrows furrowed. "I just want to understand how you work. I'm doing this for science, Hunter.

For the future. Do you know what this world will come to if children like them, like *you*, are allowed to roam the earth? Can you imagine the chaos, the domination, the wars? Not only are we discovering incredible genetic information in our research here, but we are protecting the public from menaces like you. And we're protecting *you* from the judgment the public will rain down upon you if your secret gets out."

"You're imprisoning us against our will."

"So you don't disagree that you're dangerous? Tell me, have you ever killed a man Hunter?"

She sucked in a breath.

"Just as I suspected. You couldn't control the raw power within you any more than Joshua could."

Wrong, she thought. He might have been right about her power in the beginning, but Hunter had stood the ultimate test. As much as she wished she could strangle Joshua, she had his life in her hands and she walked away in that warehouse. She said no to the flames, and they listened.

"But that is irrelevant now. I have some follow up questions I'd like to ask you." He sat down once more and faced her. "The formula for your ability is one of a kind. Where exactly did its ingredients originate?"

Hunter frowned up at him. "You don't know?"

For the first time, there was the smallest of sneers on the doctor's pompous expression.

"Wow," she smiled, the fire flaring up in triumph, finding its confidence again. "The all-knowing Dr. Wolfe doesn't have all the answers."

Dr. Wolfe smirked, and although it was definitely a grimace, it was still threatening. "You don't want me as your enemy, Miss Harrison. Joshua made that mistake when he wouldn't give up the location of the formula, and I won't let you slip out of here as quickly as he did. We have far more security now and I have all the time in the world to wheedle it out of you."

"What do you mean?" she asked, and instantly wished she hadn't.

"Oh you'll find out very soon, unless you tell me what I want to know. Now-" Dr. Wolfe wheeled the tray of glimmering silver instruments over to her bed, placing them right by her shoulder in plain sight. "-Are you going to cooperate, or will things be getting messy?"

Hunter swallowed hard, but did not break eye contact with Dr. Wolfe. As much as he frightened her, as much as her entire body shook in fear, the fire still blazed through her blood. It was protective and it didn't want this maniac to break her. Hunter thought of the boy from the breakfast hall dragged in by the guards, of his drained body and anguished, fierce eyes. Had Dr. Wolfe tortured him to get information as well? Was that the purpose of this institution, or was it to experiment on the weak like Fearne, who was barely sane?

Hunter had never hated anyone as much as the man leering down at her. Even Joshua couldn't compare, and he set the standards pretty high when he killed the love of her life. For the first time in… well, ever, Hunter knew without a shadow of a doubt that if she didn't have the bracelet on her wrist, the fire would have burnt Dr. Wolfe to crispy black bones, and she wouldn't have suffered a shred of guilt over it.

Which was why Hunter didn't give in to his threats. If Joshua could resist his torture, she certainly could as well.

"I'll cooperate," she replied. "If you take that tray of utensils and stick them up your ass."

Dr. Wolfe sighed deeply. "I thought it might come to that. Well, Miss Harrison, I gave you a choice but you wouldn't listen. No matter." Dr. Wolfe pulled a clean pair of rubber gloves out of the drawer and slowly slipped them over his hands, releasing the elastic with a sharp *thwack*. "Tomorrow," he said, "we will begin your check in procedures; things like genetics tests and DNA sampling. Tonight we will monitor your sleep so we have all your updated details on file. If the sleeping pattern is anything like what I just witnessed before you woke up, I'd say you've been through a very terrible ordeal recently, which will certainly have an effect on your testing."

"And what is this appointment for?" Hunter muttered, ashamed at the panic in her tone.

The light from above cast shadows across the doctor's dented cheeks, making him look like a skeleton whose skin was melting away. He gently pushed Hunter's stray curls away from her eyes, lifted a strap that hung down beside her head and secured it tightly across her forehead so she couldn't even look away. "Oh, I am always the first to evaluate a new – or in your case, old – patient. Rules are rules, and here we follow rules adamantly." He bent down so that his face was just inches from hers. Hunter managed to move her head just an inch back. The stench of his breath was enough to make her throw up, but her stomach was empty. "And I was so looking forward to seeing you again. Let's begin."

Hunter tried not to regret her decision to keep quiet. *You're tough, Hunter,* said the voice of her mother or the fire, she wasn't sure which. *You can resist. If not to protect the secret of the stone, then at least do it to make this bastard squirm.*

But Dr. Wolfe wasn't the one strapped to a table with a mad scientist bending over him, holding a syringe in one hand and a metal rod in the other.

Nope, she thought. *That unfortunate sucker is me.*

EIGHT

od please, Jenny prayed as she sat inside the freezing laboratory after possibly the worst day of her entire life. *Make him stop talking.*

She had swallowed a total of five cups of the strongest coffee Joshua could handle making – *apparently he can't touch things that are hot, the freak* – so she was running purely on an insane amount of caffeine. And still, she was falling asleep.

"I just don't get it," Joshua moaned, rubbing his forehead for the thirtieth time as he paced the lab. "How did she do it?"

Jenny sighed loudly, hoping this strange human being would find the answer soon, or she might literally go bananas. But he was oblivious. He had finished telling her everything she needed to know – even a little more than she wanted to about Hunter's mother and the fact that Joshua hadn't *ever* been with a woman, which didn't become obvious until she went to comfort him and he fell backwards in fright – and now he was trying to figure out Hunter's secret with figures and hypothesis.

He's got this all wrong, she thought. *Does this man have any humanity, or is he some sort of alien?*

"Maybe the secret lies in the mountains," Joshua whispered, his pale eyes wide. He was clicking his fingers as if he could summon the thoughts that way like a dog. "I've never even come close to figuring out where Ravenadium came from-" He tapped the glass tank and she peered at it from her chair. "It's not even from Earth, it's-"

"Alien, yeah, I know." Jenny dragged herself to her feet and over to the tank. "You mentioned it several times already. All these years and you've never tracked down its origin?"

"Of course I have, I lived beside the mountain for over a year."

"No, I mean its *original* origin."

Joshua snorted sarcastically. "Yes, as a matter of fact I talked to the alien king on Skype last night."

Jenny ignored his comment. "Then you're in a bit of a pickle, aren't you?"

"I'm aware of that, thank you. That's why I need your help."

"So you freeze me and kidnap me and keep me locked in your lab? Why not just tap on my classroom door at school and ask for a favor?"

"Sometimes I… overdramatized a situation just to avoid conversation. I blame my powers."

"Why isn't Hunter nearly as insane then?"

The room fell instantly colder than usual, and Jenny knew that it was Joshua's doing. Her heart sank.

"That's precisely what I'm trying to figure out," he said through his teeth.

"Well–" She tried to be brave and avoid eye contact at the same time. "I think I might have an idea as to why Hunter was stronger than you."

"What is it?" he asked eagerly, taking the other chair and placing it opposite her.

Jenny bit her lip. "Would you make me another coffee first?"

Eyeing her suspiciously, Joshua took the empty mug. "You're sure you want another? Your pupils are very dilated."

"For your information, I'm trying to stay warm. I'm not a tea person and it's not exactly balmy in here."

Joshua's face dropped. "I… I'm sorry, I wasn't aware… my body temperature is naturally cold, so…"

He fumbled around with the air switch by the door and for a moment, Jenny's heart softened. As much as she knew this man was insane and very awkward and malicious enough to fake hers and Eli's deaths just to prove how protective he was of Hunter, she had already seen his softer side. It was naïve and somewhat gentle. She was so interested in how this man functioned, that at times she forgot he had put her to sleep and was holding her prisoner in his tiny laboratory, and that he had the power to manipulate ice.

As much as their powers fascinated her, Jenny was sure she was getting herself into deep trouble. She was, after all, just a physics teacher. She may have braved the science years ago, but that all went away when the laboratories in Sweden were destroyed and all traces of Feucotetanus were lost. Apparently that was Joshua's doing. Was this her second chance to change the name of science, or should she turn away from it for real this time?

Jenny already knew the answer. She was there for a reason, she was alive for a reason, and she was whole and healthy for a reason. Before the fire, before all of this began, Jenny had nothing. She was a teacher living in a rented apartment with her cat, a dull future stretching ahead of her. Most of all, she was alone and felt there was something missing in her life.

And suddenly the fire happened. She believed her life was at its end. She thought her sickness would kill her. She was blessed to have Hunter, even in her final week, and she was satisfied with what she discovered, willing to let go and move on to... whatever else was out there. But then Joshua came for her on that cold night in the hospital wing and everything changed. She had a sort of... out-of-body experience while in her deep sleep. And when she awoke, she felt like a changed person. A new person.

Joshua returned with another cup of coffee, his expression young and hopeful. He truly believed she had the answer. Of course, Jenny knew nothing about this volcanic substance, nor was she as gifted scientifically as Joshua. But he and Hunter were completely different. Joshua had developed great skill with his powers, but Hunter's will was stronger and Joshua didn't know why. He believed she was fuelled by rage, but it was clearly something else. Something with pure strength.

But he doesn't see it, she thought, sipping her coffee as Joshua answered his phone to someone named Barry. *He can't understand the key ingredient, the very thing that pulled Hunter away from the dark side and gave her the courage to walk away.*

The thing that is alien in itself to Joshua: Love.

"Barry, I'm sorry, I'm swamped with work at the moment," he said and hung the phone up abruptly before turning to her. "So, you were going to share your views?"

Jenny clasped her hands together firmly. "Joshua I think there are more important things to focus on. Like whether Eli will wake up soon."

Joshua ran a hand through his hair. "I'm worried about the kid. He should have woken up first. I'm trying to move along with the process but it's taking longer than I expected."

"Well Hunter needs to know he's okay. She can't live like this believing he's dead."

Shoulders slumped, Joshua shook his head. "I have no idea where Hunter is."

For the first time that night, Jenny's stomach dropped. "What do you mean?"

"She hasn't come back to the apartment."

"Well have you looked somewhere else?"

"Of course I have! You don't think I care about her whereabouts, especially with the state she's in?"

"Uh, can you blame her?" Jenny raised an eyebrow. "You *did* just kill the love of her life."

"He's not dead," said Joshua stubbornly.

"You can't be sure of that Joshua. Cryonics is a dangerous science to mess with. Have you considered how lucky it was that I turned out fine, that I didn't suffer fractures from thermal stress or even permanent brain damage? It was a miracle I even woke up. You need to bring him out of it before the coma falls through. He's on the brink of death."

Joshua pursed his lips, too obstinate to argue.

"Where else could she be?"

"I know a place, but I'm terrified to think of it."

"You're talking about this ICE Institution? The one the Agents work for?"

Joshua nodded, and his silence made her skin prickle.

"How would you know if they've taken her? Has she contacted you at all?"

There was a moment in which Jenny swore she saw Joshua's eyes tear up. But of course, he didn't show her. "I will set up a proper bed for you and check on the kid," he said. "I'm hoping he'll wake up in the next few days, and he'll need you there to comfort him."

Joshua punched in the code to the door and stiffly marched back into the living room, leaving her alone again in the laboratory. Jenny glanced back at the freezer door and sighed. If only she could get a message to Hunter, to tell her that Eli wasn't dead. She could come home and explain everything to Joshua, and he would let her go and they would live happily together again and...

And she would go back to being a lonely girl with nothing to live for.

Jenny sipped her bitter coffee and stared at the wall across from the desk where the photos of Hunter and her mother were pinned. She wandered to the door and then to her right, where the giant glass tank hummed dully, filled with plants and the very volcanic substance Joshua was so puzzled about. Her research on Feucotetanus was only half of what information was needed to complete Hunter's formula, and suddenly all those years felt like a complete waste, as though she were hiking up a small hill only to come to a gigantic mountain soon after.

That stone is not of this world, he'd said. Of course, that was why Hunter could produce fire from within her body and why she reacted with deadly flames to whatever emotion she was feeling. But was it really alien? Was that even possible? Or was this rock, this 'Ravenadium', from somewhere else?

Jenny didn't know, but she wanted to find out. And the only way she could uncover the truth was to investigate the stone's origin. It would be just like her research on the drug, only now it was a paired project... with a madman harboring an evil personality as well as super-human abilities.

Sighing and taking another large gulp of the hot coffee clasped in her hands, Jenny tried to relax in her chair and think on the bright side.

Well, came the same voice from before. *At least you don't have to teach ignorant teenagers any longer.*

"Good enough," she muttered with a happy smile.

NINE

Hunter was escorted directly from the laboratory to the bathroom upstairs. She desperately needed a shower and actually started looking forward to it, until she was taken through an iron door into a long room with tiled floors, slimy mold and a single bench running down the center. Along the walls were shower heads with taps spaced at intervals above grime-stained mirrors. There were drains everywhere and soap scrubs hanging from chains for washing. Hunter presumed the water – like the rest of the juvenile prison – would be cold.

When she turned back to the two Men in White who were guarding the door, they shoved a dirty towel, fresh jumpsuit and shoes into her arms.

"This is the bathroom?"

One of them tried to hold back a smile. The other just rolled his eyes. "Does this look like a five star hotel, Princess?"

She shut her mouth instantly. They chuckled and stepped aside as someone else squeezed between them as they shut the door.

"You get used to it," said the girl with the brown hair Hunter knew as Jet's girlfriend. Having forgotten her name, she merely gawked by the doorway.

"I'm Mikayla, by the way." She was already unzipping her jumpsuit.

Hunter avoided looking at the naked girl as she shoved her dirty clothes down and turned on a shower head.

"Where are you from?" asked Mikayla.

"New York," she replied, adjusting the icy temperature and shivering beside the flow. She kept imagining she was standing on a damp forest floor, green moss getting stuck between her toes. *Don't think about it, don't think about it.*

"I knew you were a New Yorker. My mom lives there with my stepdad."

Hunter slipped under the chilly flow and gasped. Only her skin was cool; the inside of her body burned with raging fire. The water stopped her feeling so dizzy.

After her consultation with Dr. Wolfe, Hunter was lightheaded and an air of fear still swept through her bones. But the rest of the session wasn't as bad as she expected. He took at least three pints of blood and went over her body with a strange torch device that scanned her skin. What he was looking for, she had no idea. He worked in silence. She tried not to let her head be smothered with fears and thoughts of Joshua lying on the same bed.

"Is that your natural hair color?"

Hunter stared across the room at Mikayla as she scrubbed her legs with the moldy stick. Her initial impression of the girl was bitchy-cheerleader-with-a-dick-boyfriend. Those were the girls she despised. But maybe she'd rushed into it. Mikayla was obviously making an effort to get to know her.

"Yeah. It comes with the powers," Hunter replied.

"Right. Your fire."

Hunter pushed her wet hair out of her eyes and swallowed disgusting sewer water when her mouth dropped open. She remembered the way Jet hinted at her power that morning before she broke his nose. *Was there some kind of announcement at breakfast before I arrived?* "How'd you know?"

"Comes with *my* powers," she smirked. "I absorb other people's abilities and render them powerless, so I can sense what people do. They don't have bracelets like that for me. My power isn't that much of a threat."

"It's still a power."

Mikayla snorted. "Well until I figure out how to steal people's powers and use them myself, it's pretty much pointless."

Hunter looked away from the girl and pretended to scrub dirt from the bottom of her feet. The look of desire in her eyes like a thirst for power reminded her of Joshua's psycho moment in the warehouse. Hunter already knew that some abilities have the power to really mess with people's heads, and Mikayla was becoming one of those victims. What *would* happen if she could someday take other powers?

For the first time since she arrived at ICE, Hunter started wondering how it was that the other kids actually had abilities. Her powers were an occurrence of chance, a complete accident that would never happen again. So how did all the other kids have such a variety of abilities? She would have to make a mental note to ask Dr. Wolfe in her consultation tomorrow. If she could form a sentence that didn't end with a nasty curse.

"So anyway, have you met anyone else besides Barbie and Shifty the Sloth?"

"Who?"

"You know, the fat guy you were sitting with at lunch and his anorexic friend?"

"I'm sorry, who are you calling anorexic?"

Mikayla smiled and ran her soapy hand over her shoulder. "Just wait, Fire Girl. You may have some meat left on you, but a month in this place and you'll be a skeleton too."

Swallowing, Hunter tried to act like that didn't scare her. "If you're all skeletons, why is Zac so… pudgy?"

"He's a Shape-shifter. When they brought him in, that was what he looked like. He'll stay that way till they take off his bracelet."

Mikayla ran her fingers through her wet hair and switched off the shower. As she dried herself, Hunter found her mind wandering to the others in the breakfast hall.

"What about your boyfriend then? What's his deal?"

"Jet?" She threw her a cheeky grin. "I knew him in the outside world. We started dating in high school, then two years ago the Agents found us. Now we're locked in this prison and it's driving him crazy. He's always starting fights, especially with Marcus. I'm pretty sure he'll be in the Orb any day now."

"The what?"

Mikayla's grin widened. "You haven't heard about the Orb?"

I'm not sure I want to know, Hunter thought and shook her head.

"There's two places you're sent for bad behavior here. The first is Solitary, where you're locked in an empty room like a madman for forty-eight hours with no food or anything. They wrap you in a strait jacket just for kicks."

Hunter shivered under the cold flow from her shower.

"Solitary is only for the little things like answering back to one of the scientists or refusing to come out of your cell. But for other things, like trying to escape, there's a far worse punishment. We call it the Orb. It's an arena blocked by impenetrable glass. A small stadium surrounds it. Anyone who's done wrong is released from whatever binds their powers inside them and left to fight another person."

Hunter's mouth hung open and cold, bitter water ran into it. *What kind of sick place is this?*

"Yeah," she sighed. "It's pretty intense. I haven't seen a real fight since Jet went in there with Fearne."

"What happened?"

"Jet was teasing her about her head brace. It wasn't even the first time, but she just… snapped. Kind of like you did today."

Hunter switched off her tap and didn't meet Mikayla's eyes. That didn't stop her from wincing at the bite in her tone.

"The fight was relatively clean, anyway. Fearne didn't look so psychotic in the Orb without her head brace. In fact, she looked happy to have her head clear again. Jet was much the same. I've never seen him so blood thirsty. It was messy at first. That scar Fearne has down her cheek was from the fight. That was all it took before she cracked. She turned around and suddenly Jet was shrieking in agony and clutching his head as though his brain was melting."

Hunter shuddered. "So she did something to his mind? Is that her power?"

"Telepathy," Mikayla nodded. "That girl might look like a pretty little princess, but she's bonkers. And in the Orb, she turned into a complete monster."

"What did she do to him?"

"She flipped his evil switch," she said. "Jet's always been pretty cold-hearted. I just think she brought out his true personality." Mikayla smiled as though the thought turned her on. Hunter was liking her less by the minute.

"And what's Jet's power?"

"He's Telekinetic."

"Telekinetic?" Hunter snorted. "Like he can make things float?"

Mikayla's face morphed into an ugly scowl in less than a millisecond. "Suddenly I'm wondering why I'm standing here talking to you."

She stormed to the door, leaving Hunter with seconds to cover herself before it was flung open.

"Oh, and Hunter?" Mikayla called. "Jet isn't the only one you should be scared of. There are things ten times worse in this place. That psycho with the head brace is one of them." A look of sincere bitterness flashed in her eyes before slipping away in her wicked smile. "See you at lunch."

When the door locked and she was alone, dripping and freezing in the empty bathroom, Hunter found she couldn't get the look on Mikayla's face out of her mind.

TEN

Y ou know you don't have to sit alone anymore," said Zac as he slid in beside her at the table in the breakfast hall, his tray stacked with the same steaming gray goo they ate for breakfast. "We're friends now."

Hunter rolled her eyes at him. "Really, I wasn't aware."

"You're funny," said Zac, shoving a spoonful of lunch into his mouth. "So what punishment did they give you for your little spat this morning?"

"I saw Dr. Wolfe."

Zac's eyes went wide. "Ooo. Creepy guy, isn't he?"

"That's an understatement."

Chantal sat down beside Zac, her blond hair pulled up high in a twisted knot. She looked exhausted.

"What happened to you?" asked Zac.

"Show and tell," she grumbled.

"What'd they make you do?"

"Convince a trained hypnotist to take off his clothes and dance the Macarena with a sheet of glass between us."

Hunter's mouth dropped open. "That's your power?"

"Yeah," she said.

"How did you know you could do… that?" She scooped food onto her fork with no intention of eating it. Her stomach growled against her will.

"I told my ex-boyfriend to go jump off the Eiffel tower. And…"

Hunter felt suddenly queasy. "He did?"

Her jaw ticked. "The Agents caught me soon after I started stealing cars and clothes and going off the rails, but I really wish it was the police instead."

"The Agents would get you even if you were in prison, Chantal," said Zac. "That's how Marcus got here. He was arrested for stealing computers he wanted to use for a gaming competition, because he's a Technopath and he's pretty much a legend in the geek world, or so I'm told. The Agents came to him in prison and offered him a ticket out of his sentence."

"Yeah, and he practically signed the consent form," said Chantal.

"I know," Zac chuckled. "What an idiot."

Zac then proceeded to showed her the bruise that was forming from when one of the guards caught him mucking around and slugged him in the ribcage.

Hunter stared at the other poor kids surrounding her and wondered how long it would take before she looked like them – colorless and sick and drained. Years in this place would be enough to drive anyone mad, and Hunter had only been there a day. *They have so much potential and they're stuck here, in the best years of their lives.*

Suddenly something occurred to her. "Hey, guys, why are there no adults here with powers?"

The grin on Zac and Chantal's faces disappeared instantly. Neither of them looked like they wanted to answer.

"They uh... it all depends on the situation." Zac stared at his plate as he spoke and his oily curls covered her view of his eyes. "Some of them survive for a while, but others..."

"Just tell her Zac. She's gonna find out sooner or later."

"Fine." There was no humor in his gaze anymore. "There's no adults because no one gets to live past their twenties. Their bodies start to die."

"But... how?"

"How do you think? All of the testing, the constant chemicals jammed into our skin, the filth in some parts of this place... it's not good for kids in such a weak state. There's no sunlight or good food, there's just... sickness and gloom and death. We don't have any fun here Hunter. Even if you're the happiest, most optimistic person in the world, the cold eventually sinks into your soul."

"Speaking of," said Chantal. "Did you hear about Ted and Elena?"

"Of course I did," he muttered, averting his gaze. "Ryo said the scientists took them deep into Death Cave, and they never came back out."

"Let me guess," said Hunter, "they were old and deteriorated too?"

Zac shrugged. "Elena was completely fine, physically. But about three months ago, she stopped speaking. Nothing could make her move from her cell – the guards had to drag her everywhere she went. Eventually, Dr. Wolfe gave up on her. Ted... he couldn't handle seeing Elena so lifeless. They were brother and sister; they grew up in this place. He went crazy. He managed to kill one of the guards with a plastic fork. It was seriously messy."

Hunter's stomach turned over inside her.

"The other day, they were taken down for testing and... I guess they went wherever all the others go when they get too old or too loopy to be of any use to the scientists."

If Hunter thought her day couldn't get any worse – especially after that speech – she was wrong. At that moment, Jet and Mikayla entered the breakfast hall for lunch. Mikayla whispered to Jet and the both of them stared at Hunter with glimmers in their eyes. As they passed, Jet ran his tongue over his upper lip, reminding her of the reason she slogged him that morning. The fire roared to life inside her and she clenched the cold bench beneath her to keep from attacking..

"God, he makes me want to stick this fork in my eye," said Chantal as she shot them a loathsome glare. "Sometimes I wonder how he can be so sadistic in a place like this."

"Better than being a nutcase," Zac replied, his eyes watching Fearne as she sat at a table with two younger girls. They were staring at her and giggling behind their hands, but Fearne didn't seem to notice and continued to yap away.

Feeling not too hungry herself, Hunter flipped her legs over the bench and stood.

"Where are you going?" asked Zac.

"Anywhere. I can't take much more of this cruelty."

"But you-"

"See you later," she snapped and stormed towards the door.

No one had yet told her she couldn't roam around the hallways without consent, so she was almost nervous when she passed two Men in White standing stock still beside the doorway. A small girl with thick auburn curls bumped into her as she left and Hunter turned to say sorry, but the girl was already hurrying away from her.

The corridor was empty, and Hunter knew that if she went left and up the stairs, she would come to the cell level where she and the others slept and showered. She had no idea where the elevator would lead her, so the only other option was the door opposite the breakfast hall, which stood slightly ajar.

Hunter entered cautiously and found herself in a small room with a low roof. Around the interior were random objects; sofas, chairs and tables. It was something of a common room, and the light was dimmer, giving it a comforting aura. Hunter instantly felt more at home there than in her cell.

The immediate bank of couches on her left were occupied by several children playing on an old chess board. Down the way, at a round table made of light wood, Benji was hunched over a tattered book, his face engrossed. He didn't seem to notice her enter. The Men in White stationed in the room were watching closely, but didn't make a move to urge her out.

After a long look around the room, she decided she'd rather sit with someone than be alone and pulled out a chair at Benji's table.

"What are you reading?" she asked.

Benji's eyes glanced up and his face immediately paled. *Jeez, am I that scary?*

"Oh, it's u-uh…" he stuttered. "It's c-called–"

"It's *Peter Pan* by J. M. Barrie," said a voice from a deep maroon armchair beside their table and Hunter almost jumped in fright when a young Asian girl with a black concave bob and bright eyes popped up over the back of the chair and nodded to the book. "I've read it eight times, when this kid here hasn't got his nose buried in it."

Hunter stared at the girl with her mouth agape, feeling just as speechless as Benji whose jaw was clenched in frustration.

"I can t-talk for myself, R-Ryo," he said stubbornly.

The girl's grin turned to the side. "I'm sorry Benji, I guess I'm just impatient."

"How old are you?" Hunter blurted out. *Seriously, the girl looks ten but she talks like she's sixteen. Her English is immaculate.*

"I'm twelve, same as him." She shook her head in Benji's direction. "How old are *you*?"

"Uh, eighteen."

"And what do you do?"

Hunter cast a glance at Benji and caught him staring before burying his head back in the tattered book.

"You first," she replied.

Ryo nodded, a glimmer in her eyes. "I can manipulate the space-time continuum."

"How'd they catch you then?" she asked.

"Uh uh," Ryo tutted. Their entire conversation was like a game to the girl. "My turn. What's your power?"

Hunter told her about the fire. Benji put his book down slowly with his lips parted in awe.

"It must be frustrating to have a raging fire burning inside of you and not have the ability to set it free," said Ryo almost sadly.

"What's your story Benji?" Hunter asked, craving a change of subject.

"I'm f-from Sy-Sydney, in Australia." He dog-eared the already creased page in *Peter Pan* as Ryo climbed over the back of the armchair and took a seat at their table. "I used to live with my f-family outside the city in a place called Liverpool. M-my family was big and my parents worked two jobs to k-keep us fed. They didn't care that I was being b-b-bullied in school. One time I was walking h-home and… this group of year six kids started chasing me. I was running and… I don't know h-how it happened but suddenly things were flying past me and then I was… home. My legs ached, b-but I'd just made five k-kilometers in fifty seconds. I outran the bullies." Benji was smiling at the memory, until he dropped his head and all joy was lost in his tone. "That's actually when my parents started noticing me. 'Wh-why don't you have any bruises on you Benji? Wh-why are you home so early Benji?' So I t-told them. They didn't know what to do. My d-dad started telling people at the office, and pretty soon the Agents arrived. My p-parents sent me here on a contract basis of one y-year, meaning they could v-visit me when they needed to. I was six."

"Did they come back?" asked Hunter.

Benji fiddled with the corner of his unbuttoned sleeve. Hunter had to lean forward to hear what he was saying. "Once I was g-gone, my parents found it easier to live. They didn't have to pay for my education or f…food or other things. They saw it as a b-blessing. So no-" He looked directly into her eyes and whispered in an empty tone, "They haven't visited me since."

"I'm sorry," said Hunter almost automatically, her heart breaking for him. Benji's soft blue eyes were wide like a small child needing hope. "Your parents will realize what a big mistake they've made leaving you here, if they haven't already."

Benji started to smile, but then his shoulders slumped. "I wish I knew somehow."

Hunter wanted to be honest with the boy, to tell him that she wasn't psychic or that his parents might not even miss him at all. They were all abandoned, just like her. But Benji was young, and that meant he still had innocence and joy hidden somewhere in his heart.

And for the first time since the rain in the warehouse fell upon her and washed away the angry fire, Hunter heard her mother's words fresh in her mind, almost as if she had finally stepped away from darkness and into the warmth of the sun.

"Just have a little faith," she said to Benji gently. He clutched his book tighter, his eyes brightening even more so. "For when there is nothing else, there is always faith to cling onto."

Benji glanced down at the book in his hands. "Faith… like Peter?"

She nodded. "Exactly."

As both Ryo and Benji smiled, and the cold, empty room around them glowed just a little brighter, Hunter felt the comfort of her mother's words. It made the terror of the institution that much more bearable.

ELEVEN

I'm dead.

Holy shit, I'm dead. No matter how many times I repeat that in my mind, it still doesn't seem real.

This is what death feels like: stiff limbs, stinging skin, rasping breath and interminable cold. The world is black, so I'm either passing through to the 'Great Beyond', or I'm waiting to be cast into hell.

So what will it be, Eli? Eternal darkness or burning?

Darkness, definitely. Burning would be horribly painful. But then... would the loneliness be more tormenting?

Eli lay there, battling with his conscience about which choice to make, when a blinding pain slashed through his body from the tip of his head down the length of his spine. He would surely cry out in agony, but his throat was so dry that only a gasp escaped.

Wait a minute. Did I just gasp? Am I breathing? Is this still death?

Eli listened, his body throbbing with pain as though he were bleeding through his skin, and prayed for release. He much preferred lying in cold blackness than this new writhing. Perhaps he didn't get a choice, and he was already in hell. Stars of red danced in the blackness, making his head throb. After a few more moments, the pain started to dissipate and Eli almost smiled. *Well, that wasn't so bad. Actually, that wasn't terrible at all. Hell is quite nice and warm if you-*

Eli stopped thinking at once when he noticed something strange through the darkness. A light was blinking just out of reach, very soft and in the shape of a… wait, a human? There was a man, but Eli couldn't make out a proper form or even a face. And it flickered, like a candle about to burn out.

Eli lifted a shaking hand and reached out to the man when a shocking jolt exploded in his chest. Suddenly Eli was gasping for breath as if he'd just surfaced from the bottom of the ocean. White light blazed around him and he blinked – yes, blinked – against the rays that threatened to blind him. His chest ached, his body stung like sunburn and his throat begged for water. But despite the agony, he was alive. And being alive was better than ten years of torture in whatever hellish place he'd been lying in.

For a moment, nothing but the sound of his thumping heart could be heard. Eli heaved in air and waited for his hearing and sight to return. Shapes danced around him like alien blobs from his comic books. He heard a woman's voice, then a man's voice, and it was all he could do not to squeal in delight.

Finally the pain subsided and a tube-like object was placed in his mouth. Blissful water dribbled down his throat and he coughed and spluttered in his haste to consume it. *Get me to a lake, I'll drink it all,* he thought. The tube was taken from him and an eerie voice said, "More later."

Eli's vision came back slowly and the blurred shapes fused together into actual objects. The first thing he noticed was that the blinding white light came from everywhere he looked. He was in a small room made of some kind of shiny steel, with fluorescent tubes lining the walls and ceilings. Strange technology surrounded him; machines he'd never seen before with complicated dials and wires and blinking lights. He lay on a frozen steel table encased in some kind of clear sheet attached to more tubes. Eli forced himself into a sitting position and bravely looked down at his body.

Oh thank God, he breathed in relief. *I still have legs. I thought they'd been ripped off.*

He wore a thin white hospital gown, and the rest of his body was flawlessly pale. Usually this would alarm Eli – who was used to the olive tone of his skin – but he was too thankful that his body was all in one piece to care.

"Eli?"

The soft voice of a woman startled him and Eli's head whipped to the left where two people stood guardedly watching. The woman was younger than the man, with brown wavy hair and eyes wide and concerned. She bit the corner of her lip nervously and moved an inch closer to the man. He didn't seem to notice.

The person beside her was tall and quite thin, wearing a creased, buttoned-down shirt. He had hair as black as a raven, slicked back like a Hollywood actor. His eyes were so pale, they were almost frightening. He had sharp bone structure and a cautious expression.

They were both watching him as though they expected him to explode, but Eli wasn't even sure he had a voice at all.

The woman tried again. "How do you feel Eli?"

He said nothing, his mind completely jumbled. *Am I in a hospital?*

"How did *you* feel?" the man asked the woman and she shot him a harsh glance.

"I felt like I'd been thrown into an icebox and chartered off to Japan, no thanks to you." She rolled her eyes and stepped around the empty table, cautiously approaching Eli. He was too frozen in shock to move. "Eli, I know you must have so many questions for us. Let me first assure you that your vitals are completely in check and your tissues have healed miraculously well."

What? What the hell is this?

"We just need to know if you *feel* like yourself. Can you tell me that?"

Her eyes were so warm that Eli felt almost compelled to answer her. He shot a nervous glance at the man standing against the wall, his pale skeleton fingers touching the cuffs of his shirt, his eyes narrowed and waiting. So he tried to remember where he was before he woke up. Maybe it would explain who these people were.

Suddenly, he was drawn back into a memory. He wore a tuxedo his father had ordered for him. Sounds of clinking glass and loud chatter blared around him. The world was tinted golden and glimmering with faces. Somewhere in the distance, a violin was playing. He recognized the piece and longed for the instrument he'd played almost all his life. He attended the benefit for his father's sake, but he didn't want to be there. He'd rather be anywhere else, in fact.

Through the haze of glamorous people, he saw her: The girl with the red hair. She passed him, her arm looped through another man's. Eli stared closer at the man with the pale eyes and realized it was him; he was the one she came with. The girl locked eyes with him and his whole body tingled.

Her eyes were golden like a glowing flame. Then, she was swallowed by the crowd.

Eli breathed in slowly, stared at the man and woman, and suddenly felt a terrible fear rake through him. What had happened at the benefit?

"Eli," the woman pressed. She hesitated, her frown deepening, before she asked another question. "Do you know who I am Eli?"

He shook his head. "No. I don't know either of you." The man and woman exchanged worried glances, causing Eli's heart to thump. "Wait, should I? Who are you?"

"He doesn't remember us," said the woman. Her voice wavered. "Did something happen to his memory during the revival? What did you *do*, Joshua?!"

The man called Joshua moved not an inch, his pale eyes wide as he gazed down at Eli. A chill spread through the room. He opened his mouth and closed it again. An eternity seemed to pass before he spoke.

"Tell me, Eli, what is the last thing you remember? Can you recall Prom?"

"Prom?" he hissed, and started coughing. "That's – months – away. It's still January, right?"

Joshua pursed his lips. "Answer my first question."

Eli thought back for a moment. "I… I went to my father's benefit for Colombia University. It's like… a week before school goes back."

The woman put a hand to her mouth, her eyes glistening with shock. "Oh God…"

"What? Where am I? What day is it? *What did you do to me?*"

Joshua pinched the bridge of his nose and let out a long sigh. "If he doesn't remember who we are, Jenny," he whispered, "and his last memory is the benefit… you know what that means, right?"

The woman nodded. She looked about to burst into tears.

"He doesn't remember Hunter," she said.

– PART 2 –

REMEMBER ME

TWELVE

C heck mate."

Ryo sat back in her chair, her grin wide like a Cheshire cat, leaving Hunter completely flabbergasted.

"A twelve-year-old beat me at *chess*."

Benji was chuckling to himself in that cute way only nerdy kids do. And then Hunter was thinking about Eli and how much she missed his laugh.

"What's wrong?" asked Ryo.

"Nothing," she replied. "Rematch?"

"I could beat you with my eyes closed."

Hunter scoffed good-naturedly. "So... what else is there to do here?"

"Not much. I mostly hang out here, or in my cell, and I go down to the labs when I need to. There's the fitness room, but only Marcus and Mosi bother to use that."

"Can you show me?" Hunter asked, eager to keep moving and wanting to know more about the prison she was in.

Ryo jumped up. "Sure! You coming Benji?"

"Uh, n-no I think I'll just stay h-here..."

Without caring, Ryo grabbed Hunter's wrist and they went marching to the door. Out in the corridor, Ryo led her behind the stairs to a smaller door with a wonky handle. As she entered the room, Hunter was hit with the smell of cement and stale sweat. It was somehow refreshing in comparison with the salty, bacterial smell everywhere else.

Jet's brother Marcus was lying on a bench press lifting weights, with a very large figure that looked to be about thirty spotting him. Only his features gave away his youth. The tortured look in his dark eyes from across the room hit Hunter in the chest. He had dark, almost black skin and the broadest shoulders she'd ever seen.

"That's Mosi," whispered Ryo. "He hasn't been the same since he accidentally killed another kid in the Orb."

Hunter glanced down at her, shocked. "He killed someone? How?"

"He crushed a boy. His power is Terrakinesis – he controls geological matter, and he has diamond-tough skin. He worked in the mines in Africa." As they watched the two boys, Ryo lowered her voice. "It was an accident, and a very unfair fight. Most fights in the Orb are unfair anyway. One thing you should know about this place: it's not separated by age or the level of your powers. There are kids here who can rip people apart with their bare hands or kill you with a single spark of kinetic energy. But there are those with a power not even worth their imprisonment."

"Why do they do such horrible things?"

"To maintain authority and fear. To give the scientists a way to study us in action. You'll get used to the fact that the men here are monsters. They have no regard for humanity."

Hunter watched Marcus and Mosi in silence with Ryo, wishing she could close her eyes, go to sleep and wake up anywhere else but there. And if she could choose, she'd choose to wake up in Eli's arms.

"I have to go," said Ryo suddenly. "I'm due in the labs for my daily tests. Are you staying here?"

Hunter eyed the punching bag and suddenly had the irresistible urge to beat someone up. There was only a torn yoga mat and a rusty bike left in the corner. "Yeah, thanks Ryo."

"Have fun." She smiled and was gone.

Some of the strength she lacked after losing so much blood that morning had returned after eating and sitting down for a few hours. In order to keep herself fit, she needed to remain active even when it hurt. After what Mikayla had said in the bathroom, she couldn't bear the thought of looking so gaunt.

Hunter approached the punching bag. It was easy to imagine Dr. Wolfe or Joshua's face in the center. Mosi watched her, his black eyes deep and sharp like a hawk. She found herself thinking that he and Marcus were the most unlikely friends, but there were a lot of things that didn't make sense in ICE Institution – or Death Cave, as Zac had called it – so Hunter saved her thoughts for more important topics.

Like escaping.

Deep down, she knew it wouldn't be possible without her powers. The fire cheered its approval inside her, more excited than ever to escape, but Hunter scolded it. *You're not much use inside me, are you?*

Her fists pounded into the punching bag, pain zapping all the way up her wrists, but it felt real and not numb like the rest of her body. She broke out in a sweat and was so consumed in her thoughts that she didn't see someone sneak up behind her and stand on the other side of the bag. His hands curled around it and held it steady for her.

"You are holding your fists wrong," he said in a deep voice, his accent thick and as powerful as her punches.

Hunter stopped and breathed heavily, peering around the bag. Mosi wasn't wearing a shirt, and immediately her eyes found a device that stuck out of the skin on his left peck. It flashed 35, then 39, and back and forth. It was measuring his heart rate.

"How am I... s'posed to hold it then?" she asked defensively, dizziness breaking down on her again.

He grabbed her wrist and before she could yank it back, his calloused hands were curling her fingers and bending her thumb over the top. She was surprisingly frozen, feeling as though he might scatter away like a frightened gazelle if she moved. He was much bigger up close, and more muscular than a heavyweight wrestler. Hunter wondered if he preferred living as a prisoner in the institution to living outside as a slave.

"Punch here," he said, "and you won't hurt your knuckles as much."

She flexed her wrists and shot a glance at Marcus, who was sitting on the bench with his hands clasped between his knees and his face impassive as he watched her.

She turned back to Mosi. "Where'd you learn that?"

"In my home country, there is much fighting. I learn a lot of things because I listen and watch."

"Well thanks for the tip," she replied, not sure what to make of his cryptic talk. Mosi backed away from her slowly.

"You are welcome." With that, he sauntered to the door, Marcus not far behind him.

THIRTEEN

I f you show me another picture of this girl, Jenny, I'm going to strangle you."

Jennifer Smart bit her lip and clicked out of the photo viewer on the computer screen. Eli sat back in the swivel chair, his face in his hands. A long sigh fell out of his mouth.

"I'm sorry Eli, I thought that one of these might jog your memory."

"Why do you think showing me pictures of this girl will help me remember her? Why is she so important, anyway?"

"Because–" Jenny stood and walked over to the tray of coffee, pouring herself her sixth cup and ignoring the buzz throughout her body. "That benefit was the night you met. Hunter told me all about you when she visited me in the hospital. You went to Prom together."

"Remind me again how this happened? How did I suddenly fall so in love with this girl, I mean she's not my type at all. Guys fall all over her at school. We're nothing alike."

Jenny turned off the computer and put a hand gently on his knee.

"A girl like Hunter needed someone like you. You were a nice change. Trust me, Eli, Hunter would have done anything for you."

"Then where is she? Does she think I'm dead or something because that freak put me to sleep and took away my memories?"

Jenny fiddled with her fingers. *I am* so *not the right person for this conversation*, she thought.

Eli stared up at her through narrowed eyes for a long time. "Did you ever see a man while you were asleep?"

Jenny's heart started beating fast. She thought the figure was just part of a dream. In a hollow voice, she whispered, "You saw him too?"

"I saw something. It was a man I think, but he flickered… I never got to see his face. That's when I woke up. I thought it was just my imagination."

Jenny wiped her hands down her face. *None of this makes sense. I'm healed, Eli has no memory, and we both saw the same figure just before we woke up here in the lab. Could it be an angel, or was it just… a dream?*

"I don't know who it was Eli, but I think that's what brought us back. You have no idea how completely rare it is that we survived cryonics; it's near impossible to recover all emotions and mental characteristics. If you ask me, Joshua just barely got by with us. But," she added in a small voice, "he feels terrible about it."

"Are you guys in love or something?"

Jenny looked at Eli and laughed. "Not even if hell freezes over."

"Then what's his deal?"

Jenny really didn't want to attempt to describe Joshua's deranged actions to someone who hardly knew him at all – even she couldn't say she understood Joshua – but the poor boy was helpless without his memories.

"He… he loves Hunter. More than anything. But there's a part of him that isn't exactly human. It comes with his powers."

"Right, the… ice thing. Doesn't that freak you out? I mean if it weren't for that door, I'd be outta here in two seconds flat."

Jenny looked at the door, wondering if she would leave as well if she got the chance. She definitely wanted to when she woke up, but she was afraid and knew nothing. Things had changed.

"I guess everything's complicated now," she said to him. "And-"

Eli's hand whipped up suddenly. "Do you hear someone?"

Jenny froze, listening. Sure enough, muffled sounds were coming from the other side of the door.

"Joshua's home," she sighed. "I hope he has take-out."

"No," said Eli in a whisper, "Jenny. There's more than one voice."

"What?"

"Shh!" Eli got to his feet and lightly crossed the room. He waved her over, and Jenny shakily followed. "Listen."

With her ear pressed against the steel door, she could just hear soft male voices coming from the room beyond.

And neither of them were Joshua's.

FOURTEEN

The sound of the booming gong woke Hunter from a particularly terrible nightmare, but she felt worse awake than asleep. She rubbed her eyes and winced at the bright light in the corridors. Her head thumped as though she'd fallen out of bed in her sleep. Her nightmares worked her so hard that she was drenched in sweat and heaving. If she hadn't been wearing her bracelet, she would have set her entire cell on fire.

Hunter needed to shower before she went to breakfast, but the moment she lifted herself from her hard mattress, her cell door opened and the guard with the roaming eyes and creepy tattoo – Jamison, his name was – stood there to greet her.

"Let's go, Harrison."

"Give me a break."

"Couple more days and you'll get used to the routine," he said with a smirk. "Besides, you're not having breakfast. Dr. Wolfe wants you down in the labs for testing."

Hunter walked beside Jamison to the stairs, her empty stomach in knots. She'd completely forgotten that Dr. Wolfe had plans to inspect her even closer than he had yesterday.

Speaking of close inspection; Hunter felt Jamison's eyes on her as they walked. When she shot a sideways glance at him, his eyes were hungry. Getting looks from guys at school was one thing – having a sleazy man rake her up and down was ten times worse. *Are the guards that deprived that they have to perve on mutants like me? Do they live here, away from women and booze and bars and the real world?*

The corridors were starting to fill with kids waking up and heading down to breakfast. She and Jamison avoided a bunch of girls crowding around the bathroom door, pushing their way in. Despite the grime and awkward open space, Hunter longed for a shower.

They marched straight for the elevator and took it down two levels. The doors opened to reveal a small entryway and a sliding glass door. Past it, she found herself facing a long corridor. Windows lined the entire right wall through which she could see a busy science lab almost the size of the breakfast hall. Low cubicles by the dozen were scattered throughout the room. Men and women in white lab coats went about their work, testing and typing on computers and fumbling with papers. Jamison yanked on her arm and she nearly slipped on the linoleum floors. She made a point to keep her eyes straight. A scientist with a brown scruffy beard passed them, but did not look twice at her.

Her nerves were starting to build. It didn't help that Jamison led her through a door marked 'Surgery Rooms'. Like the room she was in yesterday with Dr. Wolfe, this one also smelt like sickly anti-bacterial ointment. It was completely dark, but for the light that shone down on the stretcher and the many blinking dials on the machines.

"Dr. Wolfe and his assistant will be here shortly," said Jamison. He picked up two items of clothing – a thin, lycra sports bra and matching bike shorts that would work better as underwear and were almost see-through – from the chair beside the door. "In the meantime, he's instructed you put this on."

Hunter fumbled with the flimsy set he threw at her. Jamison vanished and the door was locked behind her.

Using the privacy of the surgery room, Hunter stripped off. Her eyes roamed the empty space and caught site of a pin-up board on the far wall. Immediately and without thinking, she went over to inspect them. Amidst pages of information, there was a mix of children's drawings that made Hunter frown. Dr. Wolfe didn't seem to be the type of man to care about a child's messy pictures. Hunter peered at the closed door and then started rifling through papers, even though she was sure he wouldn't be stupid enough to leave important information out on display.

Hunter lifted up a graph and found a glossy image of Dr. Wolfe on a busy street in New York. He was getting into a yellow cab. The photo was taken in the middle of the day from a distance, like something a detective might snap for a case.

And as she gazed at the photo, it hit her. She *had* met Dr. Wolfe before; they shared a cab on a windy night after she almost set Eli on fire. The man on the other side was Dr. Wolfe. She recognized the smell in the lab and those oyster-gray eyes.

He was watching me even before Eli knew. How long was he watching me, watching us?

Feeling sick, Hunter stepped back and ran to the door. It was locked, as she expected. Hunter looked around for some means of escape, unable to rid herself of the image of Dr. Wolfe in that dark coat sitting beside her in the cab. *He saw the fire in my veins,* she thought as she recalled their conversation. *What did he say, that I had a blood deficiency? Then he said something about... being different. Urgh, he knew!*

A key turned in the lock. Hunter's heart rate picked up speed. Dr. Wolfe strode in, followed by an older woman with ratty brown hair and wrinkly skin. She couldn't have been more than forty.

"Good morning, Miss Harrison," said Dr. Wolfe. He placed a tray of steel utensils on a bench beside the surgery bed – laced with straps like the other – and turned to face her. They both wore the standard white lab coat, hospital shoes and mask around their necks. The woman had absolutely no emotion as she stood beside the doctor, and in the light from the surgery table they looked like Dr. Frankenstein and his robotic wife. "I trust you slept well."

Almost in spite of herself, Hunter smiled. She pointed to the wall where the photo still hung. "You were watching me, weren't you?"

The doctor rested his cool, all-knowing gaze on hers. "I've been watching you for a while now. Joshua did well to hide you away for most of your life, but not many can escape my watchful eye. I know how to find people like *you.*"

"But you took your time, didn't you? When I shared that taxi with you, it was months before the Agents came. Why?"

He shrugged and crossed his legs, leaning back against his chair. "I was interested in the way you lived your life. You had just recently discovered what you could do, after all. I wanted to observe you from an outsider's perspective. To see how you reacted to your emotions, to see whether you acted the hero or stood back as I'm sure Joshua instructed you to."

"I don't regret my actions."

"Oh but I'm sure you waged a war with yourself about rescuing that girl locked in the freezer, am I right?"

Hunter frowned at the doctor's elated expression. *How did he know that Kate was locked in the freezer? Wait...* Hunter recalled the moment she heard the young girl's screams and saw the padlocked freezer door, remembered the wonderful heat and the adrenaline. She never questioned why Kate had been locked inside, nor did anyone else. Not until now.

"It was a test," she breathed, gazing in horror at the doctor. "You locked Kate in and started the fire, didn't you?"

"I may have initiated the blaze," he said smugly. "And you needed a challenge, my dear. It's a part of discovering what kind of hero you want to be."

Feeling suddenly sick, Hunter eyed the door.

Dr. Wolfe tutted. "We have work to do this morning," he said. Then he indicated to the woman. "This is my wonderful assistant and colleague, Dr. Hosking. Today we're going to hurry through the basic check in procedures and hopefully have you out by lunch. We'll start immediately with the X-rays."

As Dr. Hosking marched over to the large and harshly modern X-ray, Dr. Wolfe opened a screen that seemed to pop out of nowhere. Hunter couldn't even see the monitor. The image was as clear as life itself, the calculations and numberings so small she could hardly read them. Was this some kind of new technology she hadn't seen yet? *I've only been here a few days and look what I've missed out on. It's a freaking scene from* Iron Man.

Dr. Wolfe grumbled. "Yes, I see you didn't have much luck sleeping last night."

Hunter cautiously approached the screen beside Dr. Wolfe. The image she saw was her cell from a camera in the top right corner of the room. She was tossing back and forth rather quickly, as if the tape were on fast-forward, but the time went by as normal. Letters and numbers and heart-rate lines squiggled beside the images. Dr. Wolfe remained very thoughtful as he watched the screen.

"Do you remember any of your nightmares, Hunter?"

Though she couldn't bear to talk about it, she wasn't sure she had enough energy to think of a convincing lie. Dr. Wolfe didn't know that Joshua killed her one reason for living – at least, she hoped not. Her nightmares were of Eli lying in a blanket of snow while Joshua stood by laughing wickedly like a villain in a cartoon movie. Though that was not the same as the broken, desperate man she walked away from in the warehouse, it was the only way she saw him in her dreams.

She shook her head.

"Hmm. But you slept through the night – a whole fourteen hours, I see – without waking?"

"Yes."

Dr. Wolfe nodded thoughtfully. "Right. Well we'll keep an eye on that and see how we can improve it. For now, let's begin the X-rays."

Hunter turned her eyes away from watching her jerking form in the dark room. She couldn't decide what was worse as she was forced to lie down on a bright, cold table like an animal in a veterinary clinic: seeing the one she loved die over and over again in her dreams, or living a horrific reality in a mutant museum as a permanent lab rat.

Hours later, she stumbled back upstairs to the breakfast hall, starving, light-headed and feeling as though every inch of her body had been poked, inspected and photographed for a file she'd never see again. Dr. Wolfe had taken every kind of sample of her DNA he could without removing any vital organs. Her fingerprints, skin cells, hair strands, bone construction, regular body temperature, heart rate and blood type were all in Dr. Wolfe's system. But for now, she didn't care. All she wanted was food.

The breakfast hall was almost empty. She assumed it was the very beginning of lunch. A group of kids about half her age were chewing their food like cows; slowly and unenthusiastically. She hurried to the line-up and gathered whatever the women behind the glass could give. Then Hunter sat down at a table and started stuffing herself.

She let her mind wander to escape her surroundings and the fact that her food tasted like vomit. Lost in the moment, Hunter didn't realize she was being watched. She met and locked gazes with two brown eyes under thick-set eyebrows, glistening with pain and emptiness. They were the same eyes she remembered from her dreams last night.

He sat a table-length away, not eating and staring at her intently. Something in his eyes sparked a strange feeling in her stomach. She couldn't translate the look he was giving her.

"That's Will."

She jumped almost a mile in the air and started choking on her food. Fearne was gazing at her dreamily from right beside her on the bench. Hunter washed down her food with a swig of water.

"Sorry," she puffed, "you scared me."

"I didn't mean to. I just noticed you sitting alone and thought you might like some company."

Hunter looked down at the young girl – who didn't seem so crazy now – and smiled.

"Thanks."

"That's Will," she said again. It seemed important to her that Hunter knew his name. "He always stares at people, so don't take it personal."

Her southern accent was more definable now that she wasn't living in the land of the fairies. Hunter wondered where she came from. Though, after hearing some of the other abysmally depressing stories, she wasn't sure she wanted to know.

"He looks quite sick."

"He always looks that way. That's because Dr. Wolfe chops him up every day and then puts him back together."

Whatever was in Hunter's mouth was immediately spat back out on her tray. Fearne giggled behind her hand and as Hunter wiped her mouth, she thought she caught the ghost of a smile on Will's face before it vanished.

"He *chops him up?* Why?"

"To see how his bones and skin and stuff regenerate. That's Wills power; he heals himself."

"Why does he have a scar then?"

A light appeared in Fearne's eyes. For some reason, this pleased her. "You noticed that?"

"Well… yeah. A lot of you have scars."

"We do," she said.

"I've heard that not many here live past their twenties. How old is Will?"

"Twenty," she replied. "He's very developed for his age because of his cell structure and rapid growth. He's practically immortal."

"Practically?"

Fearne's face fell. "Well… no one's immortal. But Will's as close as anyone. It comes at a price though. They pump a ton of medicine into his veins, stuff that makes him really weak all the time from being under anesthetic. And they've tried *a lot* of things."

"That's awful," said Hunter for what felt like the billionth time. *Note to self: expect many more horrible things and try not to get squeamish over them.*

"Uh-huh. He's been here longer than all these kids. When I was little and afraid growing up in this place, Will helped me get through it. Sometimes I returned the favor. He's like my big brother. He keeps to himself mostly and doesn't like to get into trouble."

Suddenly Hunter remembered what Zac said yesterday and felt her heart shrink in fear for the poor doe-eyed boy across the room. *There's no adults because no one gets to live past their twenties. Their bodies start to die.* Was that what was happening to Will?

With her appetite suddenly missing, Hunter pushed away her plate and tried to look everywhere but at him. She focused on a grimy stain on the table and listened to Fearne.

"…Eventually your body gets used to all the surgical procedures and what-not, sort of like someone who has cancer and has to battle through years in hospital, only… well we're here for a lot longer. And the kids aren't so bad. At least—"

Fearne stopped speaking, her face forming a blank stare. The expression left Hunter speechless.

"Even in death," Fearne whispered hoarsely, "it never leaves you."

"What?"

"It never leaves you."

Hunter glanced around to see if anyone — besides Will — was watching, and clicked her fingers in front of Fearne's eyes. She didn't blink.

Back to crazy mode. Hunter released the girl's wrist and pretended to eat her lunch, but the odd feeling in her stomach wouldn't go away, and neither would those words that played over and over in her mind like a haunting melody.

It never leaves you.

FIFTEEN

There was something very terrifying about the sounds coming from the room outside the lab. Jenny and Eli stood frozen in fear, listening to the thumps and the footsteps and the muffled voices and wondered what to do. Joshua had been gone only an hour, and there was no way to tell when he'd be back.

"Jenny-"

"Shh!" she hissed and Eli shut his mouth with a snap. Her eyes roamed the lab, praying they were safe and the room was protected. The door had a code, and she was sure there was something hiding it from plain sight. Whoever was out there must have no idea there was a laboratory behind the wall.

Then suddenly, there came a familiar creak and the voices were louder.

They found the entrance.

"We have to hide!" she mouthed to Eli, whose face was paling quickly.

"Who is it?" he replied, staring at the door. "Is it the Agents?"

Jenny hoped to God it wasn't, because Joshua said the Agents only hunted people with powers. What would they do if a couple of regular people got in their way?

It wasn't long before Jenny found out. Those behind the door had some sort of machine that roared to life, and in seconds Jenny and Eli were scrambling to the back of the laboratory and hiding under the desks; the only place they could find that would conceal them, if only a little. Jenny's heart shivered in her chest as the door broke, scattering sawdust and stone across the floor.

She closed her eyes and covered herself, hearing footsteps and male voices. A hand grabbed her elbow and dragged her out from under the desk. Eli shouted at them to let go. Dust was everywhere, clouding her vision, making her cough and splutter as she was hauled to her feet.

"Find it," someone directly in front of her ordered. His voice was low and calm. Jenny looked up into a face she would easily forget if she had passed him on the street. But the situation was different. His eyes were big and blue, brighter than the ocean. His hair was gelled back and his lips were abnormally large and red.

"What do you want?" she asked.

"Where is Joshua Harrison?"

Jenny glanced at Eli who struggled in the grip of two other men of Asian origin. They all wore black suits. They looked like smart business men. How did they find them?

"He's not here," said Eli.

The man turned slowly to face him. "Thank you for pointing that out," he spat and clicked his finger. "Keep looking."

One of the men standing by the glass tank where Joshua kept the Ravenadium made to open it. If the Agents got their hands on it, Joshua's life would be over. Her life, too, might be over.

"Wait!" she shouted and they turned to her. "I'll tell you where he is."

The blue-eyed man smiled, showing perfect teeth. "Go on."

"He just left, I think he was going to the... store. But he mentioned something about stopping off at his apartment upstairs first."

Jenny thought she'd actually sounded quite confident in her lie, until the blue-eyed man smiled wider and stepped closer to her. She felt the need to hurl.

"I have always been very good at picking out the liars," he whispered. "But it's okay, because the both of you are not my priority. Joshua is. You're worthless until you provide me with the correct information. Since you failed on that part, this conversation is over, and so is your life."

It all happened so quickly. Two of the men drew their weapons. Jenny had never seen a gun before. It felt just like a James Bond movie as the men aimed the guns at her head and Eli started to panic. Jenny, however, found herself frozen. She didn't understand why she had been given a second chance at life after the fire, only to die so soon. How was that fair?

Just as she was sure her question would never be answered, there was a bang that did not come from a gun. One of the Agents collapsed, and Jenny looked down at her feet where a man lay on his back with a foot-long icicle stake sticking out of his chest, coated in blood.

This time, Jenny screamed. There was a blur of action; shots were fired and she was released only to fall to the floor and pray it would be over soon. Amidst it all, she looked up and saw Joshua. Ice sprayed from his hands as he twirled and kicked and dodged every move the Agents threw at him. One of them tripped and fell a few feet from her. He locked gazes with her and an idea formed in his mind. Jenny scrambled backwards, but the Agent was already closing in on her, his hands reaching for her throat, dragging her to her feet. She screamed out Joshua's name as he pulled her in front of him as a shield. Joshua stopped fighting.

"I'll snap her neck if you make one more move," said the man against her ear. Jenny's entire body seized up in fear. She gazed at Joshua.

He slowly raised his hands. There were no men left conscious – or alive, she didn't know – and Eli was still on the floor.

"What do you want?" asked Joshua calmly. "You want me? Then let her go."

The Agent's grip tightened. "Not likely. I want the formula."

"I don't have it," he replied.

"I don't believe you. You have ten seconds to give it to me, then you're going to come with me quietly, or I will shoot her."

A cold metal barrel was placed against Jenny's upper back and she sucked in a breath, clenching her fists and gazing at Joshua in fear. A part of her wanted to tell him to run, to not give in. And in a split second, she wondered why she was suddenly so willing to risk her life for a man she hardly knew. A man who once intended to kill her himself.

"Ten," said the Agent. "Nine."

Joshua moved swiftly to the glass tank and opened the compressor lid. Liquid nitrogen seeped out with a hiss.

"Eight."

He reached in carefully and pulled out a spherical rock the color of charcoal, perfectly shaped. He held the rock out for the Agent.

"Is this what you want?"

"That's the formula?"

Jenny couldn't see his face, but she could hear the confusion in his tone.

"Yes. It's a special stone containing a supernatural element that, when applied with the correct substance, creates a formula for my powers. But," he took a step towards them and the Agent flinched. "It can be very temperamental. And if it breaks, this entire room will go up in flames."

"Put it in the briefcase," ordered the Agent. His hand around her neck was becoming very clammy. "Now, or I *will* shoot her!"

"Okay, okay," said Joshua. He turned slowly towards the steel table where his briefcase lay. The tension in the room thickened.

Then, quicker than the Agent could react, Joshua spun back, yelled "Catch!" and threw the stone at Jenny's head.

Any normal person would have reacted in the exact same way. It's instinct. The Agent knew that his job was at stake if he did not catch the stone. His fellow Agents were all dead, and his life depended on safely securing the formula. He released Jenny, reached out and caught the rock as it soared towards them. The gun clattered on the ground.

That was his mistake, and as soon as he knew it, there was an icicle through his heart too. He collapsed on the floor with a clang. The rock rolled out from his grip towards Joshua, but he wasn't concerned for it. He was rushing to her side, grabbing her shoulders and shaking her.

"Are you alright Jenny?" he asked.

She couldn't move.

"Jenny?" His voice bordered on hysteria. "Answer me!"

"I'm alright. I'm fine."

Joshua's pale blue eyes were so full of fear that Jenny wished she could capture his expression and hold it forever. He released her, breathing heavily, glanced at Eli and then at the rock and got to his feet.

"I can't believe they found me." He paced back and forth, going through things that weren't damaged and stuffing them in a bag. "We need to leave, there could be more coming."

"Leave?" said Eli. "And go where?"

"I'll figure that out once we're away from this building, but we don't have a choice."

"But I can't-"

"You must," Joshua snapped. "Jenny, could you help me with this?"

Nodding, Jenny assisted him with removing the other rocks of Ravenadium and placing them very gently in an airtight container which then fit into a briefcase. She had no thoughts at all in her head, only buzzing, and was all too happy to follow Joshua wherever he wanted to go. She tried her hardest not to look at the bodies on the ground that were bleeding out across the floor.

Oh God. Her breathing increased and her hands fumbled with the papers in her arms. *Oh God, there's death everywhere. So much death.*

"Jenny?" Joshua was snapping his fingers in front of her eyes. "Stay with me."

"Hmm? Oh, I'm f-fine," she muttered. "Yes, completely fine."

Joshua didn't look at all convinced. "Please just breathe. You can freak out later once we're in the car."

"Okay."

"Uh, I'm fine too by the way," said Eli as he stood idly by. "Almost got shot, but no biggy."

Joshua grabbed the last of his items and handed Eli a bag to carry. "Make yourself useful and take this bag."

"Sure," said Eli lightly, nodding as though everything in the world was fine. "And uh, what do you propose we do about the five dead assassins?"

"Leave them."

He handed Jenny a bag and ushered them out. She didn't even think about the fact that this was the first time she'd be leaving the lab in what felt like forever. It was enough just to get away from the heavy smell of death and the cold.

"Joshua, I-"

He stopped at the door and turned back to her. "What?"

"Thank you. For saving us."

Joshua looked at Eli, who shrugged, then back to her. There was just a little bit of light in his eyes as he turned the handle and gave her a nod. "Of course," he said.

Then they ran.

SIXTEEN

I n the days that followed, Hunter climbed out of her grief and depression and fell deeper into the cold fear that swarmed the institution like angry bees. Though she eventually became used to the routine and the testing and the morbid atmosphere, she still felt it clinging to her soul. At night, when the lights were off and silence danced around her and her blanket didn't warm her enough, she felt it the most.

The fire became like a dog deprived of taking walks: it grew lazy and hid away. Often she felt so empty of warmth that she feared the fire had diminished completely. She practiced circling the flames through her skin, from her toes right up to her scalp. After that, she felt better. And then she would become cold again.

Things about the outside world she took for granted were now in her thoughts constantly. Things like sunlight. It would be coming into winter soon in New York, but even to see the sky would be glorious. She missed take-out, movies, even school. She missed her freedom.

One other thing she felt ashamed to miss was Joshua. Yes, she hated him with every fiber of her being, and whenever her thoughts strayed to his despicable acts, the fire raged. Perhaps it was the familiarity of a guardian that she missed more than Joshua himself. But then she remembered the small things. Like his snow globe obsession, or checking to make sure he hadn't left the ripped tissue on his face after he cut himself shaving. And despite all he did, Hunter regretted taking him for granted, disrespecting him at times, and especially not realizing just how much he sacrificed for her.

And it took the death of a loved one and an abduction by scientists for her to grasp that.

Every now and then, she wondered about Jack and if he was safe, or if Joshua had killed him too. But the one person she yearned for and would never see again was Eli. It didn't pack quite a punch as it did the first few weeks after his death when he never left her thoughts, because now she was far more distracted. But the ache still remained and it would until she found something to be happy about. Sometimes, in spite of the awful and nauseating feeling in her stomach, Hunter tried to remember things about Eli. She remembered never feeling so happy than to be with him, a normal girl if only for a little while.

Until Joshua ripped him away from her.

Hunter tried not to let her anger cloud her mind and stop her from keeping focused on her present. Not much happened after her first couple of days in ICE, but she preferred to stay sane for as long as she could. And wallowing in either grief or anger didn't help.

She spent most of her time in the breakfast hall and common room with the others she'd 'made friends' with. That included Zac, who was consistently cracking jokes or speaking sarcastically or asking annoying questions that Hunter always ignored. Chantal often grilled her about fashion in the outside world – something Hunter couldn't care two hoots about. But she felt bad for the girl, so she made it up. Benji and Ryo were just happy to sit around and listen to the conversation, and Fearne was there from time to time. Hunter had no idea where she went otherwise. As for Jet and Mikayla; they kept to themselves after Hunter's falling out. She wondered if Dr. Wolfe really scared Jet after he was sentenced to Solitary for provoking her, because there were no more suggestive smiles or winks in her direction.

The other kids waved at her sometimes, or otherwise left her alone and stopped staring. Once she was no longer 'the new girl', they treated her like one of them. It felt nice to be in a place – however horrible it was – in which Hunter truly belonged.

It was around the four week mark, and she decided to hit the showers before dinner. Grabbing a towel and fresh clothes from her cell – where the

Men in White left them each day – she ran to the girl's bathroom and was relieved to find it empty.

She took her time, scrubbing herself and rinsing out her hair, pausing every now and then to glance at her withered reflection in the grimy tiles. After a while, she couldn't handle the cold any longer. She switched off the tap and patted herself down. The bathroom felt eerie and in the back corner, a tube light twitched like a scene from a horror movie. Hunter, however, had seen too many horrors there to be afraid of anything.

She was just dipping her toes into her jumpsuit when the bathroom door creaked open and shut tightly.

Hunter was used to other girls seeing her naked in the showers by then, and so she didn't even bother to shy away when she heard someone enter. But a moment later, there came a sense of heated male testosterone in the air and Hunter looked up to see not a female striding towards her but a guard, fierce determination and a crazy gleam in his roaming blue eyes.

Jamison.

Hunter's heart dropped. She started backing away as he came closer. His shoes splashed in the fresh puddles. He didn't say a word, but his eyes screamed desperately at her. She knew that look. She'd seen it in the hungry and wanting stares of two men in an alleyway.

"What are you-"

Jamison lunged for her. She stumbled backwards and slipped on the wet floor, nothing but her cotton underwear to cushion her fall. Her bones cracked painfully against the tiles. She was just about to usher out a scream when he fell down upon her and pressed his hand over her mouth. It smelled of sweat and metal.

"Don't speak," he growled. His blue eyes were glittering with a desire she'd seen countless times in many of the guards. He pinned her down hard on the cold floor, keeping one hand over her mouth as the other reached down for the zipper on his pants.

Hunter's heart was pounding in her chest, desperate to be free. She was lost in a spiral of memories of that snowy night in New York, the night she found out about her past and her powers, the night she was so out of control that she killed a man. Back then it felt like she deserved to die, that her powers were demonic and she was out of control. But they had saved her. And there, beneath the strong and vicious man, she was weaker than she'd ever been.

What's worse; she didn't have her powers to protect her.

For the first time in forever, Hunter felt truly helpless. She had absolutely no strength to pry him off. Punching bags did nothing when it came to having a two hundred and twenty pound muscled man pressed down upon her. She wriggled furiously, but it did no good. She screamed as loud as she could, but no one came. And even if they were stumbled upon, would anyone care? She knew Dr. Wolfe certainly wouldn't.

"Ever since I saw you Fire Girl," he hissed, his face buried into her chest, "I wanted to get my hands on-"

Hunter bit down on his palm and he cried out, releasing her mouth from his grasp. Hunter let out a shriek before he threw his hand across her face. The slap was so hard that her jaw rattled and tears blurred her eyes.

"You little bitch," he growled. His grip was so tight that it bruised her skin instantly. "Oh you'll pay for *that*."

Hunter struggled to keep his hands from pinning her down again. Jamison only laughed and forced her down harder.

And then a miracle occurred. Two large hands wrapped around Jamison's throat and yanked him backwards with so much force, his neck nearly snapped. Hunter choked on a gasp and pushed herself up in time to see Will standing over the man, his entire body rippling with rage, hunched but still huge and menacing. He thrust his foot into the guard's chest, causing him to cough harshly and double over on the floor.

"Will-"

"Get out," he growled at her. "Go!"

Hunter scrambled to her feet and snatched her towel and clothes. Her instincts begged her to do as he asked and run, but another part of her longed to join Will standing over the guard and kick his teeth down his throat. Will turned to her, his doe eyes urgent, pleading her to leave or they'd both be in trouble. The grit and torture had vanished from his expression and his brow was creased with worry. "Hunter, leave!"

She couldn't.

And as Will turned his back, Jamison clenched his teeth and crawled to his feet.

"Look out!" Hunter screamed, but Will was too slow.

Jamison rammed into Will and knocked him to the ground. Will's head smacked against the tiles and he blinked and gasped for air. The guard sat on top of him with his knees pressing into Will's stomach. Pinning Will's free arm, he raised his fist and threw it across his jaw. Once, then again, then again. Blood spurted out of his nose and a gash opened on his cheek. Will wasn't strong enough to fight back – the punches alone would have knocked him out. Instead, he turned his head and vomited blood.

When her body finally decided to act, Hunter dropped her belongings and ran to Jamison. She couldn't do much else but throw herself on him, wrapping her arms around his neck as Will had done, only this time she squeezed. He actually laughed, tossing her against the wall like a rag doll. Hunter's head hit the tiles and the world started to tip.

Get up, she ordered herself. Tears falling from her eyes, Hunter forced herself shakily to her knees, but she was so frail that she couldn't make it any further. Words could not describe the frustration she felt at the fact that her withered body could not fight her own battles, that she couldn't so much as damage Jamison. She had lived so long in ICE that even her hair had begun to lose its color.

Get up! the fire shrieked inside her, blazing and swirling, desperate to fight, to be released, to burn. *GET UP!*

I can't.

Her vision blurred and she swallowed to try and stay conscious, but her eyes were closing. The last thing she saw was the guard beating down upon Will, smashing his bones into broken pieces, a pool of blood dribbling through the cracks in the tiles to the drain next to her hand. The door of the bathroom was blown open and voices were yelling, but that was all she remembered before she fell under.

The noise was gone. The cold, wet bathroom floor was gone. The flicking fluorescent light was gone, replaced instead by a blinding white light everywhere around her. She was definitely lying on a hard surface. It was a moment before Hunter could actually move, much less turn over, stand up and see where Dr. Wolfe had put her.

Hunter could hear nothing but silence. Her eyes were burning from the glare. Honestly, she didn't think that the institution could get any brighter than it was, but apparently she was wrong. The space around her went on forever.

She wobbled to her feet. Someone had dressed her in a jumpsuit. The throbbing ache of a bump on her head reminded her of being thrown against the wall. *What happened to Will? Is he alright? Did they bring him here too?*

Those questions would be answered as soon as she knew where she was. *Solitary?* But she wasn't wearing a strait jacket. Before Hunter could even consider the second option, she noticed a figure standing in the distance, maybe ten meters away. Despite her thumping headache, dizzy vision and wobbly legs, Hunter started running towards the figure. He was familiar, his back to her. Six foot something. Strong shoulders. Long, brown hair. Blood-stained white jumpsuit.

Somewhere between them, Hunter ran straight into a solid surface and went tumbling backwards on the white concrete floor. Her head thumped and she brought a hand up to touch her skull when she noticed something that flattened her stomach like a pancake.

Her bracelet was no longer blue and tight against her skin. It hung like a regular band of silver slipping up and down her arm. For a moment Hunter almost smiled, the fire dancing excitedly beneath the surface, but then it dawned on her. About that same time, the figure turned and Will met her gaze behind the giant glass wall that separated them, disappearing high above their heads. His expression voiced her own fears. His eyes were sad and almost whispered to her words of regret. He looked around them at the sphere-shaped stadium.

Hunter found that if she stared long enough at the impending wall, she could just make out around the edges of the glass little faces peering in at them. Kids, scientists, Men in White. Everyone had come to see the show.

A single spark of fire burst from her fingers like a firecracker and suddenly, she knew exactly where she was.

The Orb.

And Will, her knight in a white jumpsuit, was sentenced there to fight her.

– PART 3 –

THE NOIR HERO

SEVENTEEN

A wise man once said–" came the monotone voice of Dr. Wolfe over an intercom system and both she and Will whipped around and searched for the source, "–that when the sentence for a crime is not quickly carried out, the hearts of the people are filled with schemes to do wrong. Hunter Harrison. William Evans. You have both broken a very important rule we follow here at ICE Institution; respect all authoritative figures. Your punishment... is to fight. I will decide when it is over. And please–" He chuckled low and it sent shivers down Hunter's spine. "–Fight fair."

The glass wall rose very slowly, severing the boundary between them. Hunter straightened up and stared around at the glass, the figures so far off and so foggy that she couldn't make out any faces at all. Her heart rate accelerated and she clenched her fists tight as she turned and faced her opponent.

They stared at each other for a long time. She could feel the anger radiating from Will's taut body. He squinted soulfully at her, his doe eyes shadowed by brown hair messy around his face and neck. She couldn't look at him without remembering what he'd done for her in the bathroom. Why would he risk it knowing this was their punishment?

Hunter remained still, waiting. She knew that Will couldn't beat her with his own power, but even the thought of burning him made her stomach curl. Not even if Dr. Wolfe commanded it, she would not attack with fire.

"Might I remind you," the doctor's voice resonated, "that this is the only time you will have to use your powers, Miss Harrison. I suggest you have at it."

Hunter looked down at her fists and let the flames creep through her skin. The sensation was… heavenly. The tingling warmth felt like rubbing her skin with soft soap after being dirty for a very long time. It was soothing and velvety and the flames danced around her fingers and up her wrists and arms. For a moment, she smiled at the bliss.

And then the fire started to get really angry.

For all the times Dr. Wolfe had prodded her with needles or sucked out her blood or shot her with X-rays, Hunter drew the fire out of the cage it had been trapped in for weeks and unleashed it. Like fire from the mouth of a dragon, flames burst from Hunter's hands. They were so strong that they kept going, twisting in the air like giant snakes, surprising even Hunter herself with their magnitude. The flames were beautiful, woven and intertwined with each other like dancing eels, bright and angry. The snakes twisted high into the air, brushing the glass ceiling that didn't burn or break. She launched them again and again at the glass, but it could not be penetrated.

"Please, Miss Harrison," said Dr. Wolfe over the raucous noise, "not on the impermeable glass. You are both in the wrong, and this is how we treat misbehavior. I'm afraid you must suffer the consequences, and if you do not comply, I will make things interesting."

As he spoke, a strange grinding sound erupted in the Orb. Hunter felt her heart pound against her chest and she stepped subconsciously closer to Will. Holes started appearing in the walls, spaced at intervals, all around the exterior. Hunter knew it would be something horrible, and she had no time to prepare before there was a sound like water from a hose. Then, fire appeared.

It shot straight at them, a ball of flames with so much power that it looked like a planet, like the sun. Hunter spread herself in front of Will just in time for the fire to hit her in the chest. She stumbled backwards against him.

"Are you o-"

Will did not get to finish his sentence before another fireball blasted from the rockets in the walls, this time from behind them. Hunter deflected it, but only just. And then another appeared, and she was too slow to protect Will. The fireball slammed into his back and he collapsed on the floor.

Hunter dropped to his side and sucked the fire into her arms, feeling another fireball shoot over her head. The contents of her stomach crawled up into her throat at the sight of the burns appearing on his skin. His flesh bubbled and blistered and his jumpsuit was scorched. Only his brown eyes remained rich and unscathed. They gazed up at her in agony.

"Let it burn me," Will rasped. "Again."

"What? No!"

"Do it." With immense effort, he managed to raise his quivering hand and clasp hers. As she watched, she saw that his skin was already reattaching itself, closing over the burns on his back. "I'll heal, just let me up… so they can see it."

A fireball blasted into her, but it was nothing but a breath of air. Another hit Will's legs and he screamed. Hunter diminished the fire quicker that time.

"No," she said firmly. "I will *not* be that sick bastard's entertainment."

Will looked defeated. "You'll just make things worse. Please, get it over with."

"I… I can't!"

"Just do it, Hunter, or I swear I'll-"

"I hate to do this," said Dr. Wolfe over the speaker system, and both of them froze. "But I can see the repetitive nature of this battle and I'm finding it rather dull. Let's try something different."

Hunter prepared herself for a lion to be unleashed into the pit or something horrible like that, but instead large funnels sprouted from the roof, and then it began to rain.

She dragged Will to his feet and they stared around, wondering if this was some kind of trick. Hunter supposed Dr. Wolfe was only doing this to see whether her fire would still burn even if she was soaked through to her skin. She lit her palms and angry, white-hot flames burned through the rain, sparking like fire crackers. That was how powerful her rage had become. She imagined Dr. Wolfe was impressed, and the scientists who were watching would be scribbling furiously on their notepads. As much as she hated that this was all just a presentation to them, she almost liked the challenge.

And then Will cried out through the rain.

She spun and stared. He stood there in his tattered, wet jumpsuit. The drops of rain on his skin were starting to burn through. Hunter lifted her palm up and watched as the water trickled over her skin. It didn't harm her, but Will's flesh was sizzling. As if the rain wasn't water, but-

"Acid rain," said Dr. Wolfe, a smile in his tone. "Of course, it isn't powerful enough to burn you, Miss Harrison, but poor William doesn't have the wonderful immunity your skin possesses. Though he will heal in time... he still feels the pain."

Will collapsed again, writhing, the rain burning gashes in his skin right through to the bone. He curled up in a ball and the acid poured over his back. A moment more and his screams almost drowned the sound of Dr. Wolfe's voice.

"Stop!" Hunter shrieked. She fell beside Will again.

"I told you how to play the game, Miss Harrison, but you had to be stubborn. Someone must suffer the consequences."

He can't do this to people, she panicked, covering Will's body but only managing to shield his upper half. He was so tall. The flesh on his legs was almost on fire. He was fading away. *This isn't fair, Will was only trying to save me from Jamison! Why are we being punished for defending ourselves? Why is he being punished at all?*

So great was her rage and so strong was the fire inside her, that in a moment of clarity, Hunter had an idea. With her body shielding Will's upper half, she lifted her hands and formed a wall of fire around them, dome-shaped and strong. *An orb within an orb.* The acid rain hit the dome and dissipated into gas around them. It didn't burn through, and Hunter grinned in relief.

"Ha! Who's laughing now, Dr. Wolfe?" she shouted.

Will stirred beneath her, his skin fusing back together. It was incredible. She understood now why the doctors were so fascinated by Will's biology. His skin was slowly reforming and within the space of a few minutes – though it felt like an hour – he was right again.

"It's not going to end," he said through gritted teeth. He looked more exhausted than he had the day the guards carried him into the breakfast hall. "He'll keep going until he's satisfied. Until we've both learnt our lesson."

Hunter held her dome, sweat pouring down her brow from the effort. Gazing into his eyes helped distract her. She couldn't read his thoughts at all. The defeat, however, was gaunt and sullen in his pleading gaze.

"So we just give up then?" She shook her head firmly. "No. He's seen what you can do, he's seen what I can do, that should be enough for him."

"That's not the point of this arena. The point is to teach discipline, to maintain order and to keep fear alive in us. It won't be over until we're both out." He pushed himself up on his elbows, his face inches from hers. The long scar on his right cheek went from the corner of his eyebrow to the joint at the back of his jaw. She had no time to puzzle over it then. "You know I can't beat you; there's nothing offensive about my powers. You're just going to have to put me out."

"What? Why the hell would I do that?"

"Because it's what he wants. Just do it."

"No, I-"

The fire dome dissolved in her panic, but fortunately the rain had ceased. Silence loomed around them. Hunter looked up at the roof and around the Orb, hoping to catch a glimpse of Dr. Wolfe standing behind the glass, his expression one of malice and authority.

I won't let him win, she decided. *Not today. Not with Will. In fact, never again.*

Hunter turned back to Will and – on impulse – shoved him in the shoulder. He fell back on the floor hard and stared up at her with wide eyes.

"Why did you-"

"Hit me," she hissed.

"What?"

"Come on, they've had their show of fire and water, and they know you can heal. Just knock me out and we both win."

"I can't-"

"You afraid to hit a girl? Come on, DO IT!"

Will grit his teeth, pushed himself up and shifted his weight from foot to foot. With a look in his eyes that read 'I can't believe I'm doing this', Will raised his right arm and drew back. The balled fist collided with the left side of Hunter's face, sending her spinning backwards. Despite his size and incredible muscle capacity, the punch itself wasn't powerful enough to knock her to the ground let alone knock her out. But it did hurt like hell. Spots danced in her vision and then a red-hot pain throbbed in her jaw.

She turned back to Will and spat blood on the clean floor. He grimaced, perhaps at her face or at the fact that he'd just punched her.

"You can't hit a little *harder*?" she groaned, trying to make it sound like she was teasing him. He only shrugged.

"Hey, I may look strong but it's kind of exhausting having to regenerate your own skin over and over. Cut me some slack."

Smiling only slightly, Hunter twisted her shoulder and kinked her neck as though she were preparing for a fight.

"They just want a show," she said.

Will nodded.

Hunter threw herself at him and they both went sprawling to the floor. As much as she didn't want to hurt Will – especially after what he'd been through to get thrown in there with her – hitting him was better than burning him.

Will rolled out from under her before she could get a good swipe at his face. She swung her knee and thrust it into his stomach. Will blew out a gasp of air and doubled over. As she pushed herself to her feet, she pretended not to see Will's leg as it whipped around and knocked her ankles out from under her, sending her to the ground. She hit her elbow hard but managed to roll back onto her feet. She took her time straightening, lighting her hands on fire for good measure, and met his gaze. With one last apologetic look, he clenched his teeth hard and threw his fist against her jaw. Hunter's entire head jarred and then she was out.

EIGHTEEN

Will wanted to catch Hunter before she hit the floor, but his reflexes were slower than they used to be. Her head made a terrible crack and her red hair spilled out around her like rose petals. He dropped down beside her, scooped her head up in his hands and tapped her lightly on the cheek.

She was completely out. Only her chest rose up and down. It was over.

A heavy sigh of relief fell out of Will's mouth. Never, in all his sixteen years imprisoned in the institution, had he ever been forced to fight in the Orb. He'd seen countless kills and witnessed horrible fights. It always made him that much more determined to stay away from trouble. But Will knew what he was getting himself into when he burst into the girl's bathroom. He knew that the justice system Dr. Wolfe enforced would have him punished for his heroic act.

But Will couldn't walk away. Even though every fiber of his being begged him to put his head down and go back to his cell, Will was drawn to the sound of Hunter's scream. And the sight of Jamison pressed against her squirming body still made his skin crawl with fury. Perhaps it was just in his nature to be protective over complete strangers.

Only, Hunter was no stranger. Will gazed down at her soft eyelashes that fluttered as she breathed, at her full lips and the already sunken shape of her cheeks. Asleep, she looked somewhat peaceful, but Will had been around enough pain and grief to know that she was hurting from something. He'd seen it in her amber-gold eyes the very first time he caught her gaze across the breakfast hall. Will could still remember when Hunter was free of pain and young and innocent. When she was his first and only friend in the nursery all those years ago, until one night the tall man with the pale eyes took her away and she never came back.

Hunter deserved to know why he defended her against Jamison. She didn't know how many other girls that filthy man had taken advantage of. But... why her? The question was one even Will himself could not answer. He only knew that he could not stop himself from entering the bathroom.

Crouching over Hunter, Will didn't see where the guards came from, but he heard their footsteps behind him. They took him roughly by each arm and dragged him away. After the guards escorted him through a door that had appeared in the Orb, which led to a dark corridor and a glass exit, he was taken in stiff silence to a room on the right. He'd never been in this part of the institution before. Inside the room, there was nothing but blackness. Black walls, dark mahogany furniture, several chairs with padded armrests made of leather and a single lamp on the desk that cast eerie shadows all over the room. The guards left, locked the door and Will sat in darkness for only a few seconds before the door opened again and Dr. Wolfe himself strode inside. His hollow cheeks were flushed from the excitement of the Orb. He undid the button of his white lab coat and sat opposite Will with his hands on the desk. A small puff of dust blew around his arms.

"Hello William," he smiled. "How are you?"

"Fine," he replied. He'd long ago become used to the doctor's sick optimism and sense of humor.

"You healed rather quickly after the acid rain. I presume you were trying to show off for your childhood friend."

"Your acid rain must not be as poisonous as you think, Doctor." Will wriggled on the chair and became aware of how shredded his jumpsuit was. He put his hands between his legs to cover any holes. "What will you do to punish Jamison?"

Dr. Wolfe stroked a finger down the gray stubble of his chin. "You know what it's like to have urges, don't you William? My guards are a bit like soldiers, you see. Deprived of natural cravings and homesick and needing something to quench that thirst."

"He was about to rape her," Will said through gritted teeth. His nails dug into his palms, the pain completely numb as anger swallowed him whole.

Who am I kidding? This man doesn't care what kind of abuse we take, especially when given a chance to punish us.

"Yes, well, I will deal with that small matter later." He waved a hand and met Will's gaze with cold, heartless eyes. "I'm interested in you William."

Will's eyebrows shot up. "I didn't know you swung that way, Dr. Wolfe."

The doctor's grin widened and he slapped his hand down on the wooden table with a *snap*, making Will jump and grip the armrests. "Ha ha!" he cried with glee. "Now there's something I haven't seen in you in a very long time. Humor! You must have the urge to laugh every once in a while. I can't have cut it out of you yet, have I?"

Will had never seen the doctor so enthusiastic. Was it Hunter? Was he excited to have her back, did it bring him closer to finding her guardian? Or was there something else happening in secret that they had yet to discover?

"Now," the doctor continued. "As I said, you've made me curious. Your infatuation with Hunter is reminiscent of your childhood, am I right?"

"I suppose I was angry," he admitted. "I didn't want that filthy man taking advantage of her in just her first month here."

"The world is a cruel place," Dr. Wolfe replied flatly.

"I wouldn't know."

"Oh, but you remember your father don't you?"

At the mention of his father, Will's muscles tensed. "How could I forget? The man beat me to death."

"Not quite. We brought you back, and as an added bonus you woke up with powers. You should really be more grateful."

"Grateful?" Will snorted. "What kind of life am I living here? If given a choice, I'd rather be dead."

They stared each other down for a very long time before Dr. Wolfe put his hands together and leaned forward on the table.

"I am curious," he said, "about your connection with our little Fearne."

"She's my friend," was all he could say. It came out jagged and harsh.

"I'm aware. I only wonder why she has warmed to you the most. Her mind is a fascinating place, William, and when I explore her thoughts I often find you there. She values you highly."

"How do you know this?"

The doctor smiled, showing a straight row of yellowed teeth. "You don't think we haven't made ways to chemicalize your powers and use them for our purposes? We have produced salves using your DNA for healing, technology using Marcus's power and Fearne has become quite a wonderful tool in testing staff for-"

Will stood to his feet, his chair toppling backwards, towering over the table and Dr. Wolfe who was hidden by his shadow. Will's body quivered in fury. He'd never felt such rage for this sadistic man. How easy it would be to reach over the table and snap his bony neck-

"William," Dr. Wolfe murmured in a low tone as though he were talking to a misbehaving pet. "You've always been so good at controlling your anger and taking the punishment. Don't break your streak now."

"Don't tempt me," he growled.

"I understand your need to protect your friends." The doctor got to his feet, buttoning his coat again, and walked slowly around the table. "It's because you know that you don't have much time left, am I right?"

Will felt the blood drain from his face as Dr. Wolfe reached up and placed a skeleton-like hand on his shoulder. The grip raised the hairs on his neck. Over the years he'd watched many deteriorate. People he learned to care about. Older brothers and sisters, of such. One day they simply didn't come down for breakfast. He was smart enough to learn that Dr. Wolfe had disposed of them, for they were so weak from experimentation and lack of nutrients that they just... died. The others knew it too, and it terrified them all.

"What will my power do to stall my death?" he asked.

"That, not even I can tell you my boy." He nodded sadly and urged Will to the door. "Oh well, it's been a wonderful journey we've had together." Two guards were waiting to escort Will back to the cell block. "I'm interested to see how it ends. And please," he added as Will was taken by the arms again, "I'd like no more trouble from you. Remember, I know what – I'm sorry, *who* – your weaknesses are. Am I clear?"

"Yes Sir," Will muttered, and the door closed softly behind him.

Will marched through the dark halls of the institution with men guarding his way. His thoughts returned, as they always did, to a life he imagined outside. A world where the sun was bright in a cloudy sky over the Thames, where little black cabs and red buses zoomed around him, where Big Ben chimed through the chilly air and there was a sense of possibility. A world in which he could choose where to take his next step, breathe in freedom and simply... be.

It was a wonderful fantasy world, and it was all he had.

NINETEEN

Joshua gripped the steering wheel so tightly, his bones ached. New York disappeared in his rear vision mirror, but that did nothing to comfort him. Even if they were on the other side of America, Joshua would not stop looking behind him. In fact, before two hours ago, Joshua had been checking over his shoulder every day since Hunter's birth.

And yet they had found him. Again. It was history repeating itself, only this time he didn't have a child to protect. He had a teenage boy and a teacher instead.

Neither Jenny nor Eli had spoken a word since Joshua shoved them in his car and sped through New York traffic towards the highway. Joshua didn't much mind whether the kid was alright, but Jenny...

"How do you feel?" he asked her, his voice loud amidst the silence.

Jenny squirmed in the leather passenger seat. "My adrenaline level is kicking pretty high right now, but otherwise... I'm fine."

Joshua nodded. "Good."

"And you?"

"I... I'll be alright once we're a very long distance away from the city, and there's no one on our tail."

"Who were those guys exactly?" asked Eli from the back seat. "You told us there were people looking for you and Hunter, but you didn't say they were murderers."

"They're Agents who work for an institution that imprisons people like us with special abilities. They run tests and research our genetics."

"Like what you do?"

Joshua grit his teeth, trying to be patient. But the boy was already grating on his nerves. "I don't torture innocent people."

"No," said Eli, "you just fake their deaths and put them to sleep in your freezer."

The air in the car dropped to below zero in seconds. Joshua could feel the ice creeping through his fingers, but he had to remain calm. If he lost control, it might draw attention to them again, or he might make more mistakes that could not be fixed.

"Eli, he saved our lives," said Jenny softly.

Joshua glanced at her in surprise. *She's standing up for me.*

Jenny frowned at him. "What? You did."

"I... I couldn't let them kill you."

Her brown eyes filled with warmth, and it was just enough to push the ice back inside him. He almost couldn't take his eyes off her, and looked back at the road.

Eli started snickering. "I *so* knew this would happen between you two."

Clearing his throat, Joshua ignored him. "So I've formulated some sort of a plan. In order to keep the Agents off our tracks, we're going to have to get a new car as soon as we stop tonight."

"Where are we stopping? Chicago?" asked Eli excitedly. "Oo, do you know what we should do? I heard about this place that-"

"This isn't a field trip Eli," Joshua snapped. "We're running for our lives here. We're staying in low-budget hotels, leaving early in the morning and driving all day. We're not doing anything touristy, and we're not talking to *anyone* unless they're serving us food. Got it?"

Eli huffed and sat back against the chair. *Ungrateful little shit, isn't he?* The Iceman rolled his eyes. *Doesn't appreciate that you literally saved his life. Maybe we should have kept him under.* Joshua shook the voice out of his mind, afraid it would turn him into a monster again. He needed to be in control.

"Where are we driving to?" asked Jenny. "Do you have a destination in mind?"

Joshua squirmed in his seat and shot her a sideways glance. He *did* have a destination in mind, and it had come to him out of the blue the moment he started the car.

The Agents had found his secret laboratory, which could only mean they had already found Hunter. It took a lot for Joshua to accept that, but once he came to terms with it, his mind started formulating a plan. In order to get Hunter out of ICE incorporated, he had to go *in*.

But he couldn't do it alone.

"I was thinking… Seattle."

"Seattle?" Jenny gaped. "Why Seattle?"

"I have an old friend there who might be able to help us."

"But that's miles away!" Eli exclaimed.

"Then I'll just leave you back at my apartment where you'll be shot or taken by the Agents for questioning, how does that sound?"

Again, Eli shut up immediately.

Joshua sighed. "Look. Those Agents were literally about to kill you because you were in their way and you had nothing of value that they couldn't get themselves. They're after me because I have abilities and because I have information about my abilities that will be of great use to the people at ICE Institution. But if we don't get as far away from them as possible, leaving no traces behind, they *will* find us again. And this time I won't be able to save you. Now I need to know that the both of you are going to do *exactly* as I say-" He glanced at Jenny and then in the rear vision mirror at Eli. "-And that you're going to cooperate and not complain, or else we're all dead. Am I clear?"

They nodded, and even though he felt guilty for being so harsh, he knew it was for the best.

After a moment of tense silence, Jenny spoke.

"Does it make you worry that they didn't ask us where Hunter was? Do you think they might already have her?"

Joshua couldn't bring himself to answer that question, because in truth, he knew they found her. So instead, he turned on the radio and tried to think of anything but Hunter in the hands of Dr. Wolfe.

TWENTY

A man in a white lab coat stood over Hunter when she woke up. He was quite pudgy around the waist, and his coat was creased at the bottom, as if his closet were too small. Gray hair flowed over his head and a moustache like Mr. Monopoly was perched on his upper lip. His blue eyes were kind and welcoming and he gazed at her with one eyebrow raised, as though she'd been caught with her hand in the cookie jar and it amused him greatly.

"Miss Harrison," he muttered in a gentle voice and the moustache wiggled. "Good evening."

Hunter started to sit up, but her head was pulsing a deep pain and it was too hard to move. It must have been quite a punch Will gave her. She rubbed her jaw and soon found a lump on the back of her head where she hit the ground.

She was sitting in a simple surgery room with only her bed and a chair beside it. Sensing the familiar cold, she soon became aware that the bracelet was glowing blue again, the same spidery veins pulsing beneath her skin sending ice into her blood. The fire had disappeared, frightened of the power entrapment, leaving her shivering on the outside.

"What happened... after I blacked out?" she asked.

He gave her a reassuring smile. "Nothing, really. It was over. You were brought here to my care, and I attended to your injuries." He indicated to a stitched cut on her forehead that she couldn't remember getting. "I'm aware that this place can be very discomforting." He rocked back on the balls of his feet and placed his hands behind him. "How are you finding it?"

Hunter couldn't figure out if this was some sort of test, and if she got the answer wrong or said something smart, she'd be sent straight back into the Orb. "It's... fine."

"Hmm. Unlike our genius Dr. Wolfe, I am genuinely concerned for your well-being."

That's a little hard to believe.

"Who are you?"

"Rosenthal," he replied. "Dr. Albert Rosenthal."

The name was vaguely familiar. She eyed him suspiciously, deciding to be careful of what words she used. Dr. Rosenthal was looking at her in such a way that made it seem like he was waiting for her to say something. Maybe that she recognized him or remembered him from somewhere. Hunter remained completely emotionless.

"That was well played, what you did in the Orb," he said slowly. "What most children do in those situations is save their own necks. I've seen far worse injuries than yours come out of that awful place."

Hunter didn't understand the context of his words. *Is he pretending to be nice and caring, or is it a front?*

"Well," she said, "Will *could* heal himself. That made it a tad easier."

"You still protected him from the rain. And I believe you refused to burn him yourself, am I correct?"

Hunter bit her lip.

"You can talk confidently here Hunter. I promise you that nothing said in this room will be spoken to anyone else. You have my word on that."

His blue eyes were truthful, but could he be lying? Hunter had learned that all the scientists at ICE were heartless. Could this man be different?

"Is there something you need, Dr. Rosenthal? Or may I go back upstairs to bed? I'm pretty tired."

Dr. Rosenthal stepped away from the bed and gestured to the door. "Be my guest."

Cautiously, Hunter swung her legs over and went to the door. Her head swam, but she was eager to get away. The doctor was wigging her out.

"Miss Harrison, I wonder if you might answer a question of mine first."

She turned with her hand on the door handle. "Okay."

"Did Joshua ever go back to the shack?"

Hunter said nothing in reply, but her heart was racing as she clung to the door. *The shack? How does he know about the shack?*

Dr. Rosenthal chuckled. "Oh dear, that boy did *not* know what he was doing. But you're here and you're well, and your powers are marvelous. He must have figured out how to take care of you."

"What are you talking about?" she hissed. "How do you know about the shack?"

Dr. Rosenthal patted his hand on the bed. "I understand you're tired Hunter, and I know that what I have to say might be too much for you to comprehend, but it is important that I tell you now. This may be the only time I have alone with you. If you do sit down, you must promise me this: you cannot tell a single soul in the institution what I am about to tell you. Is that clear?"

Hunter gazed into his old face and glimmering eyes and suddenly knew she trusted him. Her curiosity got the better of her common sense and she ignored the warning radars. Something was pushing her to listen to him.

She sat down. Dr. Rosenthal gave her a grateful smile, the bristles around his lip stretching out as he grinned.

"Thank you, my dear. I appreciate that. Now, to explain myself. In a nutshell, I met Joshua what must be... close to sixteen years ago. You were with him. You were this tiny two-year-old filled with bright color. They separated you from Joshua and put you in the nursery. Back then there weren't too many kids like you. The only other child we had was dear William."

"Will?"

"Yes. For such young souls, you were quite good friends. He was pleased to have some company, even if you were only a toddler. The scientists didn't know how to take care of you, so I took it upon myself. I tried to keep you away from Dr. Wolfe as much as possible. Sometimes I would sneak you back to Joshua so he could see you."

"Why?" Hunter interrupted. Her voice was thick, as though she'd been holding back tears. "I mean, why would you risk that?"

"Because it broke my heart to see him so wrecked. He was only just learning to use his own powers, Miss Harrison, and while he confided in me, he told me how controlling the power inside him was. How it whispered to him at night. How cold he felt. He was in a bad place here, and the times when I brought you to him were the only times I saw him happy. Not only that, but Joshua was terrified you would end up a slave to your own powers... when they breached the surface. You didn't know you had abilities at that age. He couldn't bear the thought of your power controlling you. He wanted to raise you away from the truth."

Hunter wrapped her hands around her waist, staring down at her bony knees, guilt closing in on her heart. A war raged inside her; did she hate him or did she thank him? He was only trying to protect her. *Sometimes people do crazy things for love, right?*

"Now... I've worked for this institution for many years. In fact, I was one of the first geneticists employed here. I was young – well, *younger* – and naïve. To the outside observer, this place is a scientist's paradise. 'Genetically enhanced humans' is something everyone wants to be involved with. Most of the workers here are only in it for the fame, but as you already know, your identities are secret... for now. Once I started, I found myself trapped. I can't stress to you how much I risked when I helped you and Joshua escape."

"*You* helped us escape? But... why?"

"My dear," he sighed, "I may work for the devil, but I can assure you I'm as pure as they come. I've seen a lot in my time, and the pain I saw in that broken man sixteen years ago was something shocking. I didn't care how valuable the both of you were; I had to get you out."

"What about the others? What about Will? Haven't you seen what kind of pain he goes through?"

Dr. Rosenthal grimaced. "I know William has suffered. And one day, I hope to help him out as well. Times will change very soon, Hunter. But back then, young William had nothing. His family abandoned him. He was classed as a freak. This wasn't the best home for him, but Will had no responsibility. He didn't know love. Joshua, however, had you. He struggled with his powers, and he worried that soon you would as well. He wanted to get you away from Dr. Wolfe, and I knew I had to help."

"How did you do it?"

"I will tell you soon. But our time is up for today." He rose to his feet and put a hand on her shoulder.

"But can't you-"

"They will be coming for you if you're not upstairs soon. I just need you to know that you can trust me Hunter. I won't force you to, and I hope you think a lot about what I've said. And remember one more thing-" He urged her to the door. "-Try not to defy Dr. Wolfe. He doesn't like rebels, and he won't be afraid to make you suffer."

"Dr. Rosenthal, I..." Hunter trailed off, not sure what she wanted to say. As she gazed into those warm blue eyes, the sense of familiarity became a sense of comfort. It was a strong vibe and it grew stronger every moment she spent with him. "Thank you for helping me, and for helping Joshua."

Dr. Rosenthal nodded, his eyes crinkling as he smiled. "We'll talk soon, my dear."

The door opened and Hunter headed out of the surgery rooms. As she moved into the labs and veered left down the long corridor with the glass windows displaying a nearly empty lab on her left, two Men in White were coming from the opposite end, half dragging a very disheveled scientist in their arms. His eyes darted to Hunter and quickly looked away. He was covered in sweat and his eyes were bloodshot.

Feeling the hairs on her arms and neck stand up, Hunter pushed on towards the elevator. She passed another corridor beside it and caught a glimpse of what was going on in one of the other rooms just as the door was sliding closed.

Fearne stood over a desk with two scientists behind her. There was no metal brace on her head. She stared at something, a look in her eyes so murderous and pain-filled that Hunter felt her insides start to squirm.

As the door shut off her view, Hunter caught the first of a series of male screams before she heard nothing more.

TWENTY-ONE

"There she is!" called Zac and he waved her frantically over to his table. "The Dragon!"

"Don't call me that," said Hunter as she slid in beside Chantal, her plate full of breakfast. Before Zach even blinked, Hunter was shoveling food into her mouth.

It had been late last night when Hunter returned to the cell block. It was strangely eerie, walking down the corridor on her own in the dark. Even more eerie after what had happened with the guard in the bathroom. Hunter had crawled into bed, and even though her body was exhausted, her mind was wide awake. She didn't sleep well at all, and it showed on her face that morning. She could tell by Chantal's grimace.

"But you can breathe fire, right?" Zac pushed.

"Probably. I've never tried it."

"Why the hell not?" he frowned. "It'd be the first thing I'd try."

"That's because you're a lunatic," said Chantal. "How are you feeling Hunter? I mean about the Orb and everything."

Hunter's eyes roamed the breakfast hall and found that Will hadn't come down yet. He was usually last to arrive. There was a chance he might still be in surgery. Hunter had been so busy trying to process her evening with Dr. Rosenthal – not to mention struggled with the idea that Joshua wasn't all psychotic-killer – that she was surprised to dream of Will again that night. Of his sacrifice for her. Of a small boy in a dark room talking to her as a child as they lay awake and alone in the cold. Her heart softened at the very thought of him. It was something she hadn't felt since... since Eli.

"I'll be alright," she finally said. "It was hard, but we got through it."

"Hell yeah, you did," said Zac through his food. "And it was bad-*ass*. I was almost sad Will knocked you out."

"Thank you for reminding me," she winced, dabbing her fingers against her bruised jaw. "Anyway, what has everyone else been saying about it?"

"Nothing much. After Will knocked you out, he sort of..." Zac looked at Chantal for help with words, but she avoided his eyes. "Well, he just looked at you for ages. Then he... he picked up your head and... and he held it *really* carefully, you know like someone holds a day-old baby, and he bent over and..." Zac's voice softened as he pretended to hold an invisible head in his hands, his eyelids fluttering. Chantal dropped her fork, the sound snapping both of them out of the intense moment.

"Oh my God, Zac!"

"What?" he exclaimed, staring at her crossly. "That's what he did! It looked like he was about to kiss you," he said to Hunter, who found herself caught between a breaking heart and extreme laughter.

"The guards took him away, that's all that happened," Chantal blurted and went back to playing with her food after shooting a sideways scowl at Zac.

"We all went down to the common room after," Zac continued. "Except Marcus and Mosi. They went to the fitness room, as always."

"What are they *doing* in there?" .

"I dunno, bumping ugglies?" Zac suggested.

"You're vile," said Chantal.

"Fearne disappeared. Jet and Mikayla got up to their usual snuggling, but they were separated by the Men in White and sent to their cells. And us... well we sat down for a game of chess with Benji and Ryo and couldn't stop talking about the fight. It was the most excitement we've had since Chevie's escape."

"What?"

Zac's eyes widened. "No one's told you about that yet! Oh man, it's the best story ever!"

"Did you say someone *escaped*?"

"Chevie Pulicover – great name, huh?"

Hunter glared in a way that said 'Zac. Get on with it'.

"Okay anyway, he was pretty much the coolest person you'll ever meet – one of those real indie types. Everyone loved him."

"What was his power?"

"Uh…"

"I'm pretty sure he could fly," said Chantal.

Zac clicked his fingers. "That's it! He could fly. So yeah, Chevie had been here for only… two years, I think, before he decided he needed to get out. We all thought he was joking. One morning at breakfast he said 'guys… I'm going home tonight.' Yeah right," Zac snorted.

"But he wasn't kidding, was he?"

"Nope. The next morning, he was gone. Benji swore he saw him sneak out of his cell in the middle of the night, and he wasn't seen again."

"His time was nearly up," said Chantal. "He'd already reached twenty-one. Gorgeous guy, too."

Hunter stared at the both of them. "How long ago was this?"

"Mmm, about three months I think?"

Chantal nodded in agreement.

"So this guy escapes–"

"Well we don't actually have proof that he did technically escape. He could have been caught and locked up somewhere, or killed, or both." Zac scooped food into his mouth and pointed his fork at her. "But Dr. Wolfe was *really* pissy the next day. And since then, they always have guards patrolling the corridors at night. So we figured he got out."

Hunter felt elated, as if a balloon had blown up inside her stomach. If someone could walk out just as easily as this Chevie guy, maybe it was possible for the rest of them to escape as well.

"So no one else has tried it?"

Zac and Chantal exchanged glances.

"Hunter… Chevie was a genius. I'm not kidding, his power might as well have been intelligence. And he never told *anyone* about his escape plan. He just up and left us."

Thinking of Joshua, Hunter looked down at her plate. "He didn't come back for you, obviously."

"Well," Zac shrugged. "I never pinned Chevie for a dickhead. None of us did. But that's the way life goes, right?" They ate together silently. Hunter found herself falling deep into her thoughts, running over possible escape plans, letting herself dream of freedom as she so often did.

Fearne walked by their table a few minutes later looking drained of all happiness. She limped on one leg and swayed, as if intoxicated.

"Can I ask you something?" Hunter bent her head closer and the two of them did the same with eagerness. "Do you know anything about what Dr. Wolfe does to Fearne? And not just the testing?"

"What do you mean?" asked Chantal.

"Well… last night I saw her down in the labs in this room with a few other scientists. She didn't have her brace around her head." Their eyes narrowed, as if this was news to them. "She was staring at this guy and he was… screaming. She was doing something to him."

"Sounds nasty," said Zac.

"Were they testing her power?" suggested Chantal.

"Maybe they were trying to see if she could make someone's brain explode," said Zac.

"Maybe."

"So anyway," said Chantal, "we never got to hear why you two were even put in the Orb so suddenly."

Hunter looked Chantal in the eye and wondered if the truth would scare her. Then again, nothing in this place was ponies and ice-creams.

"One of the guards tried to take advantage of me in the showers." She watched Chantal's eyes darken and her small smile fall away. "Will pulled him off of me just in time. They beat each other up and I tried to stop it, but I got knocked out of the way and passed out. I woke up in the Orb."

"Those bastards," said Zac.

"Will saved you?" asked Chantal in a small voice. "What a hero."

Hunter frowned at her. The bite in those words made her wonder if Chantal had been through exactly the same thing. She wouldn't be surprised if last night wasn't the only attack on a girl in the bathroom.

"It's okay," Hunter said directly to her. "Revenge is sweet."

Chantal muttered something so quietly, Hunter thought she'd imagined it. With that, she slammed her tray down, whirled out of the bench and stalked away in a huff.

"Damn, that girl always has serious mood swings," said Zac.

Hunter rolled her eyes. "You really can't read girls, can you?"

Zac's mouth dropped as Hunter pushed her tray away and ran to catch up with Chantal. "What did I say?"

Hunter slipped through the door and bumped straight into Will. Her heart leapt in her chest at the sight of his damp brown hair tucked behind his ears and that stoic expression. She had to admit, despite his pale color and disfigured posture, he was very well built and definitely the tortured, handsome type. But her relief went beyond that. He had put his safety at risk when he pulled Jamison away from her in the showers and how did she repay him? She burnt him alive and punched him in the face.

"Will, I need to-"

"Not here," he muttered.

A guard brushed past him, knocking him in the shoulder and forcing him against her. Hunter's back hit the wall and they froze as the guard shot them a crooked smile. Hunter's eyes widened. She'd know that smile anywhere.

Jamison.

The fire exploded within her. Hunter made a move to attack him, but Will whipped an arm around her stomach and held her back. The guard chuckled, his eyes raking her body with malicious thirst, and then he disappeared inside the breakfast hall.

"What are you doing?" Will hissed into her ear. His arm still held her tight, his grip nearly bruising her. "Do you want to get us both put back in the Orb?"

Hunter shoved him away. "What happens if he comes at me again while I'm in the shower, huh? You won't be there watching me all the time."

Will blushed, the color striking against his pale cheeks. He scratched the back of his head shyly. "Look, can we talk about this later? I need to eat and the corridor isn't exactly the most private place."

"But where is-"

"Meet me tonight in the boy's bathroom straight after dinner. That's when the staff eat; there's less security. And there's never any guards."

"Fine."

Will nodded and moved away. The moment he left, a sudden emptiness overcame her. There was no denying that there was something stirring inside her for Will. Even before the Orb, it felt like they already knew each other.

But what about Eli? Had she already forgotten him? Was there so much going on in ICE that it felt like a completely different world to her life in

New York with Joshua and Eli and school and reality? Even if she couldn't escape, even if Eli was dead, it was still too soon.

She forgot about chasing after Chantal and hurried upstairs to her cell. She wanted a shower, but she was afraid to even glance at the bathroom. Instead, she slumped into her cell and sat down on the hard mattress. Tears and emotions drained out of her body. She was tired and upset and angry and confused and just wanted to go back to sleep and forget all of this and dream of a better place.

Moments later, there was a small knock on her cell door.

Fearne stood behind the glass. She smiled warmly, and even though she didn't really want to, Hunter couldn't help but invite the girl inside. It wasn't the first time Fearne had been there to comfort her. Having the ability to read minds meant that Fearne knew a lot about Hunter's life even after she told her everything. She could always sense when her thoughts were not on the present, but her cloudy past.

"You still miss him, don't you?" she asked as the door opened for her.

"It's easier being here than in New York, where I just... moped around. I'm distracted in this place. But there are times..."

"When you're alone?"

"How did you know?"

Fearne sat back against the wall on the bed. "I can't read thoughts directly. This–" She pointed to the metal bar digging into her temples, "– stops me. But I can sense things. It's almost like a premonition. They don't know how to stop it."

"That's probably a good thing. At least you're not completely powerless." She held up her wrist.

"You were amazing in the Orb yesterday. The way you shielded Will from the acid rain." Her bright green eyes lit up. "Your power is very strong. Wait–" Her words were cut and her happy gleam dissolved like smoke. She whipped out a hand and pressed it against the center of Hunter's chest. She froze, waiting, watching the young girl as her eyes darted around in their sockets. It was alarming, but oddly captivating. And yet Hunter knew the girl had sensed her fire.

"It controlled you once," she said.

Hunter bit her lip. That was one thing about her past Fearne did not know yet. But it wouldn't hurt to tell the young girl the truth – especially since she felt better already just being with her. "Almost. When I first

discovered what I could do, I was fragile and didn't know how to use it. I...
I killed someone trying to defend myself."

"You are brave, Hunter."

She blinked in surprised. "Well... I'm not the only one who has suffered
here. Everyone has experienced pain."

"Our pain has passed. Yours is still raw."

"I just can't move on yet. I didn't get to say a proper goodbye, and now
I'm locked up here playing cat and mouse. I still haven't forgiven Joshua
either."

"These things take time," she said, as if it were the simplest answer.

The words toppled out again before she could stop them. "Fearne, what
were you doing with that scientist last night?"

For a moment, she sat there thinking, the smallest frown knitting her
brow. "I'm... I don't remember. What was I doing?"

"You don't remember anything?"

"No," she replied. It didn't look like she was lying. "Was it something
bad?"

Of course, they erased her memory. Hunter leaned forward and wrapped a
wispy lock of hair behind Fearne's ears, trying not to wince at the bald
patches.

"Never mind," Hunter smiled. "Thank you for cheering me up."

"You're welcome," she said and threw herself against Hunter, wrapping
her stick-thin arms around her neck. "I'm very glad you're alright. You were
so good to my Will in the Orb."

Hunter's heart almost broke again. She waited until Fearne had waved
goodbye – not without a light peck on her cheek – to let the tears fall again.
Only this time, they were tears of joy. The first real tears of joy she'd had in
what felt like centuries.

TWENTY-TWO

Somewhere, between her first few days of imprisonment and this new side to inhumanity she discovered in the Orb, Hunter felt a darkness swirl within her. It was black and cold like Dr. Wolfe's soul and it leeched through her, like tar smothering the cracks on a road. The fire cowered from the blackness, because it had never felt anything so dark. Except once: That night in the warehouse, when revenge crept up on her and the fire had brought out an evil side she'd never seen before. It was not quite as silently deadly, but it was just as bad and just as powerful.

The fire didn't know this darkness. It was grief and terror and hurt and fury all at once, and it was spreading in her soul. The only thing that stopped the fire the first time was love. But her love had vanished when she truly accepted Eli's death, and there was certainly no love in her life now.

That was why Hunter didn't seem to care about the black spirit that quietly freed itself inside her. Even if she had love in her life, could she see it then? Or was there a greater love to overpower it? Was the ultimate battle with her inner self still to come?

Voices interrupted Hunter as she pounded her frustrations into her punching bag that evening. Out of the corner of her eye, she watched Marcus and Mosi stroll into the room. For the first time ever, Hunter noticed there were no guards, and the two boys were using that opportunity to talk a little louder than normal.

"I don't mean Jamison," Marcus hissed and sat down on the bench. It was always Marcus bench pressing, Hunter noted. Mosi never seemed to do anything. "You know that, right? It's Steel we should be worried about."

"We should be worried about even discussing this," Mosi replied. He shot Hunter a glance. "People could be listening."

Marcus frowned, and only then did he seem to notice her. After a moment he leaned back on the bench and gripped the bar. "Spot me."

Hunter pretended to reposition the bag and tried to ignore them, but Mosi had other ideas.

"Your boxing wasn't up to scratch in the Orb," he addressed her quietly.

Hunter turned. "If you were in my position, you would know that wasn't the case."

"Yes," he said. "But fortunately, if I was in your position, Will would be dead."

A lump rose in Hunter's throat at the truth in his words. Though Mosi's eyes were soft and burdened, his body was strong and large. He could crush her with one clench of a fist, and she didn't doubt that he'd do it to survive.

"So are you gonna correct me on my technique again?" she asked. "Am I not standing right?"

Mosi inclined his head. "If you turn a little and bend your knees, you'll have a stronger impact."

Hunter snorted and turned back to the bag. "Thanks, I appreciate it."

"Did you punch Jamison when he attacked you in the bathroom?" he asked, hovering his palms under the bar as Marcus lifted.

Zac, you blubbering twat. Hunter sighed and decided if this was question time, she might as well sit down. She started stretching her legs out on the mat beside them.

"It's a little harder fighting a grown man with an extreme hard-on than a sack hanging from the ceiling."

Marcus started to chuckle and nearly lost his concentration.

"I can only imagine," said Mosi.

"I have a question for you guys, if that's alright."

Marcus dropped the bar and exchanged looks with Mosi. "Shoot."

Hunter met his raven-black eyes. "Why are you always in here with each other? Mosi doesn't even need to work out."

Marcus's eyes narrowed. "It's because I'm Jet's brother, isn't it?"

"Not... necessarily," she lied.

"I'm nothing like him," Marcus said, as if that were the only explanation needed.

"And I do not need to lift weights," said Mosi simply.

Hunter suddenly found herself laughing. Even as Mosi stared at her in surprise, Marcus started chuckling too. It felt good to laugh.

Hunter sighed and fell back on the mat. "I need to lift," she said to herself. "My stamina isn't exactly up to scratch."

"You fight well though, Hunter," Mosi said in his deep voice. "You might not be as strong as you once were, but you are smart and you are passionate. That makes a good fighter."

"Please," Marcus scoffed.

"You are a Techno," Mosi snapped at him. "What do you know about fighting?"

"I'm a *gamer*, what *don't* I know about fighting?" Marcus looked Hunter up and down, his eyes glinting like coals. "And anyway, I could beat her in a fight with my eyes closed."

Hunter's eyebrows shot up. *Don't do it,* warned a voice in her mind, but it was just too tempting.

"You're on," she said.

Mosi and Marcus looked at her with frowns.

"What?" asked Marcus.

Hunter backed up a few steps until she was standing on the larger yoga mat. There were still no Men in White around, making her challenge even more alluring. She raised her fists in the basic boxing position, her smile widening.

"Come on, Spazzy McGee. Get your ass up and fight like a real boy."

Marcus breathed a laugh and wiped a hand over his mouth. "You're serious?"

"Better put your fist where your mouth is," she replied. "Or I'll do it for you."

Mosi chuckled beneath his breath and crossed his arms over his large chest. Marcus leapt to his feet and appraised Hunter. Then he stepped onto the mat.

"You're on, Hot Cakes."

After shifting back and forth on the balls of his feet and grinning like the Joker, Marcus made the first move and the fight began.

Hunter didn't realize until she and Marcus were dodging hits and kicks and rolling across the floor how much she actually missed her training sessions with Joshua. As surprising as it was, the man could really dance the deadly art and he taught her a lot about reading the opponents moves and hitting pressure points. Though Marcus's hits were strong and would surely bruise her fragile bones by morning, his gaming skills didn't pull through in a real fight. His reflexes were slow when it came to knowing his own body, and his flexibility was poor.

After ducking under a right hook, Hunter kicked his knee in and caught him around the neck, dragging him down to the floor and pinning one arm under his body. The other one swung heavily up to sock her in the face but she flipped onto his chest and forced the arm under her knee, pressing it down.

Marcus kicked furiously. "Fine! You win!"

Hunter knew she couldn't hold him for long and so she rolled off him, breathing hard. Mosi was grinning and clapped his hands together.

"Well done," he beamed. "I wonder if you noticed we have company."

They spun to face the door, but it was only two small children of no more than five or six hiding behind the door frame, peering in. Hunter relaxed.

Mosi motioned for the children to enter and their faces transformed into wide eyes and grins. They hurried to the edge of the mat and sat down with eager gazes pinned on Hunter. She felt insecure and uncomfortable at teaching children how to fight, but perhaps it was a good thing. And the look in Mosi's eyes told her she might be right.

"Go again," he nodded.

Hunter glanced at Marcus. "Well?"

With his hands clasped around his knees, Marcus made a face that said this was the last place on Earth he wanted to be, but behind that she could see his thoughts ticking. He really wanted to learn, he just didn't want to be humiliated.

"Think of it as practice rather than a lesson," she said. "After all, I'm no martial arts master."

"Someone taught you though," Mosi noted. "And he taught you well."

Hunter raised an eyebrow at him. "What makes you so sure?"

"I... know more than you think."

"You fight her then," Marcus muttered.

"Chicken!" exclaimed Sammy, a little boy with silver blond hair and one glazed blue eye that happened during an operation downstairs. He and Hunter had become good friends in the past few weeks. Sammy could glow brighter than sunlight when he didn't have a power restraint on. "You're just a big fat chicken, Marcus."

"Who asked you, Sparkles?"

The young boy glared and the girl next to him hid a giggle behind her hand.

"Alright, enough," said Hunter. "I think we'd better quit it before the guards come. I don't know why they're not even here anyway."

"There's some kind of shortage today," Marcus said. "None of the guards are upstairs in the cellblock either, just the common room and the breakfast hall."

"Why?" asked Hunter. She remembered her earlier conversation with Will. *He must know that, or he wouldn't have wanted to meet me tonight. But how?*

None of them had an answer. *Perhaps it's something to do with why Dr. Wolfe was so cheerful this morning,* Hunter thought. Then she realized that whatever the reason, she didn't want to know. If Dr. Wolfe was planning something, nothing in the world could be more terrifying.

TWENTY-THREE

Like most of the Institution that evening, Hunter found the lower floor with the boy's bathroom empty of all Men in White. She crept cautiously, expecting to be tasered in the back as she went through the common room to the bathrooms on the other side. She pushed open the iron door and peered in. No one was there.

This room smelt far worse than the girls'. Hunter slapped her sleeve over her mouth and grimaced. The faint sound of dripping taps echoed in her ears. The silence was eerie, and memories of the scene upstairs stirred inside her. She went to turn around and go back when someone cleared their throat and Hunter opened her mouth to scream.

A hand slapped over it and she whirled, expecting to find herself caught in Jamison's slimy embrace again. But there was Will, all tall, broad and anguished. She was so relieved that she felt the urge to hug him, to have him wrap his arms around her protectively. The instinct brought upon her a wave of uncertainty and she pushed him away quickly.

He stared at her with seriousness. "Sorry I scared you."

"Where did you come from?" She glanced at the door and frowned. "I was standing right at the door."

Will nodded his head behind him, a glint of mischievousness in his eyes. "Secret passage."

For the first time, Hunter saw an inconspicuous slit in the tiling. "How the hell did you find that?"

119

"I've been here a very long time. I know everything there is to know about this place. You'd be surprised at some of the things the guards neglect."

Hunter gazed up at Will, at the way flashes of silver light blinked in the deep brown of his eyes half hidden by the dull locks of hair that hung over his forehead. His thin lips were parted slightly, his arm still extended towards her as if he longed for her touch. Though alarms should have been blaring behind her eyes, Hunter felt no fear in following him. In fact, it would be safer wherever she was going if Will was leading her away.

"So," he whispered and pushed the wall inward. It made a soft grounding sound like stone on concrete. "Can we talk down here?"

Hunter stared at it apprehensively, then nodded. "Okay."

"This way to the dungeons," he smiled suggestively. It was small and crooked, but a smile no less. Hunter had never seen Will with anything more than torment on his face, and for a moment she was transfixed and didn't move. Then it disappeared and turned into a frown and he was cautiously reaching out to her. "I'm kidding, it's not... I didn't mean-"

"It's okay," she said and pulled herself together. The voice of the fire in her mind was shaking its head. Figuratively.

"I've been down here a hundred times. You shouldn't worry."

Hunter went behind him into a tiny tunnel. He stopped once she was inside the dank space and eased the wall back into place. It was suddenly pitch black.

Hunter groped around for him, her heart beating erratically, and found his arm. She gripped it tight, marveling at his tense muscles instead of feeling fear.

"Don't worry, I know these hallways like the back of my hand," he said. His voice spoke close to her, and its deep tone was soothing. She longed to light a fire to guide them.

Will gripped her hand as they walked. It had been a long time since Hunter had held a strangers hand that way. It was not the most outlandish thing that had happened to her in the past few weeks, but it was definitely odd. She felt comforted, despite her circumstances. It was unclear to her where she stood with Will, whether they were 'friends' like she was with the others, or whether there was something else, a bridge between friends and more. As she moved slowly deeper into the darkness with Will guiding her, she tried to concentrate on his hand in hers rather than the guilt that was still settling in her stomach.

Will slowed, halted and patted his foot around. Moments later he dipped down and grabbed Hunter's other hand.

"Stairs," he said.

It was so dark that Hunter couldn't even see Will's outline before her. They took it slow, and Hunter gripped Will so tightly she could sense his smile, especially in his tone as he encouraged her further. Since her sight wasn't active, her other senses were on hyper-drive. She could smell wet wood, dust and metal. She heard every creak of the wooden stairs beneath them, every drip of a distant pipe, every breath that blew out of their mouths. Will's hands in hers were cool and soft and strong, as you would expect of immortal skin.

"Where are you taking me?" she asked to fill the silence.

"I'm not exactly sure what it's called," he replied and for the first time she became aware of a very faint British accent. It was only obvious now in the silence. "But from what I've explored, these tunnels were once a part of the institution. Down further is a separate level. It's deserted and some of the walls have crumbled, but there are cells. Old cells." Will stopped immediately and felt in front of him. His hands came to a blockage and he bent down, gripping a door handle and pushing it inwards.

More darkness awaited them, but Will walked confidently forward. She could tell this space was much bigger than the tiny hallway and staircase they'd come through. The reverberations of their voices echoed. She imagined a corridor as he'd described, with cells like theirs stories above, only decayed and in shades of gray, green and black. An old prison. Ruins.

Will moved left very suddenly and opened another door. There was less space there, and he was soon placing her before what felt like a bed. Will pried her hand away and closed the door. She tried to find him again, waving around.

"Will!" she hissed. "What are you-"

"Just a minute." He was ruffling in something and then a match was lit.

His face glowed in the fire light that set the room around them in a golden luminosity. Hunter could have sung with relief to have light – or even better, fire.

They were in what appeared to be someone's old quarters. A bed with a spring mattress was set up against the right wall. Will stood on the other side of the bed, a chest of drawers behind him. He was lighting a row of candles melted down in mountains of dripping wax. Soon the room was glowing and the presence of even a little warmth was enough to relax her. The smell of age still thickened the air, and the candlelight cast shadows as they moved on the walls. A small wooden cross hung at the head of the bed that made Hunter feel as though she were in a scene from *The Exorcist.*

Hunter walked around the bed and joined Will by the drawers. She followed the line of candles with her eyes, waving her fingers through the flames and waiting for the burn. Thankfully, the bracelet seemed to only stop the fire from coming out. Her skin was still immune. The warmth was heavenly after having such a quick reunion with her powers yesterday in the Orb.

"Is that strange?" he asked. His face glowed with an oddly beautiful presence in the light of the candles. "Never being able to feel a burn?"

Hunter shook her head. "I don't know any different. In class, I used to be able to hold my finger through the Bunsen burners and all the guys thought it was the coolest party trick ever." She chuckled to herself and then saw the look of confusion in Will's eyes. She realized he would have no idea what she was talking about. Clearing her throat, she pried a clump of wax away from the cupboard so she could keep the tiny flame close to her.

"I can't believe you come here by yourself." Hunter sat on the creaky mattress, ignoring the ugly stains, her back to the wall that was cold against her. Part of the bed was wet from a leak in the roof and layered with dust.

Will sat himself at the other end, leaning against the iron bars with one leg folded under him. He gave her a tired look. "It's the only place that I can hide from everyone. No one else knows about it... well, except Fearne. But she knows everything."

Hunter snorted, looking around. "We must be pretty far down."

"Not that far," he said. "Sometimes I hear distant voices from the end of this corridor. There's another passage that leads to the labs upstairs, and I think there's something else down below."

"What? Below this?" She pointed at the bed.

"I hear scientists going by the locked door at the end of this corridor. I'm guessing they've kept part of this old institution running for secret experiments and stuff."

Hunter sat forward eagerly. Wax began to dribble down her fingers, but of course, she couldn't feel it. "Can you get down there to see?"

Will sniffed a laugh. The amused glimmer in his eyes caused Hunter's heart to flutter. "Why the hell would I want to do that? Do you know how much trouble I'd be in if I was caught snooping around down there?"

Hunter shivered inside. "I can imagine," she muttered. Her thoughts were racing. There were so many secrets in this place that Hunter would bet her right arm Dr. Wolfe was hiding something, and it had to be down there. But what was she willing to risk to find out?

"You've known Dr. Wolfe a while, right?"

"Almost all my life," he said. "Charming fellow, isn't he?"

"Very pleasant," she replied, equally sarcastic. "Do you ever think he has another agenda besides torturing us for his pleasure?"

"Oh, all the time." Will drew his other leg up and matched Hunter's cross-legged stance, leaning closer to her. She stared into his eyes, almost black in the shadow of the candlelight behind him, shadows defining the shape of his square jaw and length of his eyelashes. "He built this place from scratch, but he's never really *with* us unless it's something important."

"I've noticed that. He stopped seeing me for my checkups almost two weeks after I got here."

Will nodded.

"I wonder what he does every other time." Hunter had the urge to tell Will about Fearne's escapades, figuring he already knew since he was so close to her. "Fearne works with him sometimes, she knows what he's up to right?"

Will's face instantly hardened and his hands clenched tightly together. "Fearne is an innocent girl. Dr. Wolfe is cruel to her."

"He's cruel to everyone."

"She has a special place in his heart, because her mind is so complicated. They haven't figured out how to stop her powers completely yet, and she's been here for six years."

"What is he using her for then?"

Will's brow creased. "Using her? What makes you say that?"

Hunter sighed. Will was like a protective big brother to Fearne. If he ever knew what Dr. Wolfe had her do to those scientists, he'd get himself into a hell of a lot of trouble. So she brushed it off.

"Never mind. What's it like to be immortal?"

He readjusted his legs and grimaced.

"I hate it. I always have. From the moment I knew I could heal myself, my life turned to shit. I was four when I was cast out of my family."

"What happened?"

"Uh…" Will began to shut himself off from her, and Hunter wanted so badly to know what made him so heroic and fragile that she leaned over on the bed and put a hand gently on his knee.

"Hey. Whatever hell you've been through… I was just around the corner."

Glued to her gaze, Will's troubled frown deepened to the point where he blinked rapidly and let out a long sigh. "You'd be a lot more messed up if you went through what I went through."

"And we'd be a lot closer if I knew what it was you went through."

"Fine." He took another deep breath. "Don't say I didn't warn you."

Hunter let a wry smile form on her lips. "Try me."

He looked deep into her eyes, drawing her attention with a tug as strong as the tide. "I was born in Northern London. My parents were wealthy and high up in society. My father was a power hungry man. When I was a boy, he would constantly grain it into me that I needed to grow up fast to get ahead in life. That I should do whatever it takes to be successful and rich. Money is a privilege, he said. You have to work for it. I hardly saw either of them and was taken care of by the housekeeper, Hannah. When I was a boy, I was… in an accident."

Just the way he said it made Hunter sure he was lying. She peered at him closer and couldn't stop the words that fell out of her mouth.

"Your father beat you, didn't he?"

Will's lips were pursed in a tight line and every muscle around his neck tensed. He didn't say a word.

"That's how you got that scar, isn't it? You-"

"*Stop*." He spat the word out and instantly, she was silent. Will threw his legs off the bed and walked to the corner of the room with his back to her. The air was tensely thick.

"I'm sorry," she muttered. "I just… I wanted to know more about your past."

After a moment, Will turned back to her. "The doctors thought I wouldn't live. They gave up on me. But someone noticed my apparent strength as I clung to life in a hospital bed after my father beat me within an inch of my life and decided to experiment with my biology – secretly, I might add. He changed something in me, gave me the ability to regenerate. That man's name is Dr. Albert Rosenthal."

Hunter frowned. "Dr. Rosenthal?"

"You met him?"

"Yeah. I woke up beside him after you knocked me out in the Orb. But what was he doing in London?"

"I've asked him consistently, but he has never told me the truth. I remember the day I first met him in the hospital in London, the day he told me how I survived the accident and what I could do with my body. He said-" Pausing, Will stared at the mattress between them and ran his fingers down one of the seams. "He said 'No manmade formula can ever protect you from the pain of a life without love. Every bruise, every fracture, every slice in your skin will heal, but there are some wounds that never heal completely.'" He stared around at the dark, shadowed room. "I grew up in a family that neglected me, and then I came here, where the nights were cold and dark dreams haunted my sleep and no one ever held me. The only people I let in were Fearne and Dr. Rosenthal. He became like a father to me. A father I never had."

"Why didn't your parents take you back from the hospital?" she asked. "Did Dr. Rosenthal bring you here?"

Will let out a small, bitter chuckle that raised the hairs on Hunter's arms. "After they discovered what I'd turned into at the hospital, they took one look at me and closed the door in my face. They didn't want a 'mutant' son, not when they had a reputation to uphold. A part of me thinks that my father couldn't bear to look at me after what he almost..." Will couldn't seem to finish his sentence. "Dr. Rosenthal brought me here. Later I heard him and Dr. Wolfe talking about my parents, that they told the police I'd run away."

"I'm sorry," she said.

"Why should you be, it wasn't your fault."

"I'm sorry I thought that my life was any worse than yours. There can be nothing more terrible than growing up here." She looked around as he had, at the long cracks in the walls and the dirty stains on the concrete. Then her eyes met his, shaded by loose locks of hair not tucked behind his ears, pained from the memory of his horrible childhood. "I understand now why you're so quiet and... broken."

Again, he chuckled. "So I've not had a very colorful life. I'm still alive, right? I'm strong. Ish," he added. "It's because of my past that I'm able to keep living."

"That makes no sense. If anything, you should be crazy by now. Like Fearne."

"She's not crazy," he growled. Hunter flinched at the ice in his tone, and his eyes fluttered. "Sorry. I just mean there's nothing crazy about her. When I arrived here, I was kept separate from the others. I was young, but not the youngest. You were there, in the nursery, and then one day you were gone." His eyes swum with a memory of the night Joshua took her away from ICE. "For many years I didn't speak to anyone, only Dr. Rosenthal. I ignored the others that tried to comfort me when I was moved into the cells upstairs. I lived for so long without a purpose. Dr. Rosenthal tried to help; he put others up to the challenge of at least having a conversation with me. Some succeeded, but I was just too sad to talk. Until a little three-year-old girl arrived. I was fourteen. She was so fragile, with her big green eyes and the light that radiated from her." He breathed a laugh, shaking his head, his eyes swimming with tears. Hunter didn't realize until her vision started to blur that she was crying too. "She came straight to my table at breakfast, sat down with me, and started talking."

"What about?"

Will smiled at the memory. "I have no idea. Everything that came out of her mouth I didn't understand. But listening to her became one of the best things that had happened to me here. It wasn't a therapist or one of the other kids telling me I needed to cheer up or that everything would be okay. It was just a little girl, talking to me. And it was nice."

Smiling, Hunter finally felt the courage to ask what she'd been thinking since the moment they were alone together.

"Will, why am I here with you?"

"I just... I thought we should talk about what happened. In the bathroom and in the Orb. We hadn't been introduced before we were thrown together into the Lion's Den."

"But you saved me from Jamison," she said. "Why did you do that when you knew you'd get in trouble?"

"Come on Hunter." He smiled and swung his legs off the bed. "Don't look at me and tell me you don't have a hero tendency that comes with your powers. You practically shielded me with your body when the acid rain was falling."

"I couldn't stand there and watch you melt."

"Exactly." He opened a drawer and peered inside it. "I heard a scream as I was passing, and when I saw him on top of you I couldn't walk away."

He has a point, the fire reminded her, its opinion a nuisance to her at that moment. Hunter sighed and let her fingers dance through the flame of the candle. She was sure there was more to it. *He tries so hard to deny his goodness*, she thought, *and doesn't see the signs that prove it. Will is a true hero. And a true hero does not boast of their abilities. They refute it with modesty.*

"You fought back too, you know," he rubbed his arm as he sat down opposite her again, his smile tipping to the side. "I remember."

"Well... when you lose everything, you have nothing left to live for."

Will gazed at her with fire in his eyes. "If you've got nothing left to live for, why are you still fighting?"

For a long time, his stare remained that way. It did not soften or lose its fierceness and emotion. The tension in the room was so strong Hunter felt every muscle in her body freeze in place. The sheer depth of his eyes trapped her and caused the fire to roar and swirl inside her until her breath caught in her throat.

Then, Will reached into his pocket and drew something out of it. He lifted the object, placed it between his lips and slowly lowered his head to meet the flame of the candle she was holding.

Oh God. Her insides melted. *He's found my kryptonite.*

Will inhaled, smoke billowing around him, and frowned at what would have been a very disturbing expression on her face. "Sorry, do you mind?"

"Where did you get that?" she breathed.

He plucked the cigarette out of his mouth and smiled. "I won them in a poker game with one of the guards. Here," he shuffled closer to her so their knees were touching and stuck the cigarette in her mouth before she could protest. "You're practically drooling."

With eyes darker than the sky at midnight, he watched her inhale with his lips stretching into a sly grin. The toxic smoke danced around her and Hunter felt as though she might collapse from relief. Ignoring the glimmer of amusement in Will's eyes, she inhaled deeper. Oh, it was glorious.

"How long has it been since you've had a smoke?" he asked.

"Since I've been here." She blew out a long draft. "I was never addicted, I just did it because the smoke soothed me and it helped me relax sometimes. What about you?"

He pointed to himself with the cigarette. "Immortal. Lung cancer is irrelevant."

She huffed a laugh and coughed, waving the smoke away. Will's smile widened, and it was beautiful. Perfect white teeth, creases on each side and a real glow in his eyes. Eli had a great smile, but Will's was immaculate. Perhaps that was because he rarely smiled, and to see it was just as breathtaking as a clear sky after a storm. Hunter cursed herself for the feelings that stirred inside her, but she was only human. Any girl would be swooning right now.

"Too much for you is it?" he chuckled.

Hunter opened her mouth to retort, but only a cough came out. Will laughed, and it was so loud and surprising and wonderful that Hunter started coughing harder, and then they couldn't stop. Will was laughing at her coughing fit and the tears rolling down her eyes, and Hunter was laughing at how utterly ridiculous and high pitched his laugh was. After a moment, the both of them were wheezing and lying side by side on the reeking bed amidst their cloud of smoke.

For the next five, ten, sixty minutes – or however long it was – she and Will lay there in comfortable silence together, making formless shapes with the smoke.

"Will..." she whispered. "Can we do this again? I like being here with you. It's comforting."

He turned his head and gazed at her. She was sure she saw relief in his eyes, or perhaps it was uncertainty. It could have been both. But whether Will was afraid or not, he said "okay" and smiled.

– PART 4 –

A GREATER LOVE

TWENTY-FOUR

oshua is going to murder me.

Eli rested his forehead against the cool glass of the cab as they passed Lake Johanna outside the city of Minneapolis, trying to still the rapid beating of his heart. The pink slip of paper in his hands was crumpled and torn from how many times he'd scrunched it up on the ride. He was so close now, he could almost see his mother's face when she opened the door.

All it took was one phone call to his grandmother in Chicago. Joshua didn't know, and that didn't matter. Sure, Eli was risking his identity and his safety by leaving the hotel, but he couldn't pass through the city without at least trying to get in contact with the mother that abandoned him nine years ago. Even just to see her face, to ask her why she left.

His fears grew from hills to mountains as the taxi cab pulled up in front of a simple suburban house. The setting sun made the white walls glow brightly and the chime hanging by the front door jingled in the breeze. Eli didn't move from his seat and the meter continued to go up.

Mom is right there, he thought. *Just a few steps away. What if she closes the door in my face? What if she refuses to see me? What if she isn't home?*

All his life, he dreamed of that moment. But it all seemed too good to be true.

"This is the house, kid," grumbled the driver. "You gonna get out or what?"

Eli frowned at him. "Are you sure?"

"Been a cab driver in this city for thirty-two years," he replied. "Trust me, I know these streets. That'll be twenty-seven fifty."

In a daze, Eli handed over the cash and stepped out of the cab. He stood on the sidewalk between two crab-apple trees for what felt like hours. He soon found the courage to force his legs to the front door and knock. He'd come this far. Might as well get his answers.

There were running footsteps to the door and Eli felt his heart leap into his chest. The door opened to no one. Frowning, Eli looked down and saw a small girl of about five wearing a blue princess dress and her blond hair in pig-tails. She peered up at him from behind the door.

Eli couldn't find his voice. *I definitely have the wrong address.*

"Are you the mail man?" the little girl asked.

Eli started to back away. "Uh... I..."

"Sia, honey, who—"

A man appeared in the doorway. He was tall with sandy-blond hair tucked behind his ears. He had chiseled features and a serious country vibe. As he smiled at Eli, he swung the little girl up into his arms and rested her on his hip.

"Can I help you?"

"I'm... I'm sorry," he stuttered. "I think I have the wrong address."

"You're looking for the old Andersons, right?" The man stepped outside quickly, causing Eli to back up against the porch banister. For some reason, he feared the man was about to punch him. "They're down at number twenty-five. Everyone gets us mixed up. I'm Dean Anderson, by the way."

Mom can't be living here. "Yeah, I definitely have the wrong address. I'm looking for a Mary Akerman."

"Mary?" he frowned. "That's my wife. She's upstairs."

Eli suddenly wanted to keel over and die. He gripped the banister for support and Dean rushed forward to help him.

"Woah, are you okay there Bud?"

"She's here?" he croaked out. "Mary's here?"

"Yeah. She's working in the study. Wait... who are you?"

Eli looked up at Dean – his Stepdad – and blurted out, "I'm her son."

"Mary!" Dean called from the front door.

"What?" came the reply that flipped Eli's stomach over. He couldn't turn back now – she was already coming.

"There's someone here to see you!"

"Who is it?" Her voice hadn't changed. Still melodic and silky. It blasted him with memories of his childhood, of when his mother used to sing him to sleep at night or read to him or encourage him to play the violin. He had barely enough time to prepare himself before she appeared in the doorway beside her husband.

She wore a smart pantsuit with an electric-blue blouse underneath. Work clothes, he presumed. She looked immaculate with her hair twisted up into a bun on her head. They made a very attractive couple.

It had been nine years, but she still knew him. Her green eyes, identical to his, widened. He stood frozen in her gaze, his shoulders shaking and tears brimming in his eyes.

"Hey Mom," he muttered.

Her breath caught in her throat. "Eli? What are you doing here?"

He shrugged. "I uh… I was in the neighborhood. So, what happened to you not wanting to live in a city again, huh?"

She sniffed and glanced up at Dean. "Things change when you fall in love."

"Yeah. I noticed."

At that, Mary squeezed between her husband and the doorframe and wrapped her arms around Eli's neck. He melted into the embrace. His heart beat with happiness like charged electrons, the feeling of finally being home taking away all his fears. She still smelled like jasmine. Eli clung to her and never wanted to let go.

"I'm so glad to see you Eli," she said and stepped aside. "Join us for dinner?"

"Oh, that reminds me–" Dean dropped Sia gently and ran into the kitchen. "The pizza is probably burnt!"

Eli felt strange as he entered his mother's home. He walked by the walls filled with photos and memories that were not at all familiar to him. This was the life he could have had with his mother if she had only taken him with her. Instead, he was stuck with a father who had no time for homemade pizza.

They sat down at the island in the bright kitchen.

The smell was overwhelming. Sia sat low and colored in while Dean sliced the pizzas.

Eli kept glancing at his mother, wondering if she was real.

"How did you two meet?" he asked.

"At a conference a few years ago," she said. "I got an internship at a publishing house, and Dean was a writer. We were married a year later."

"And is... is she yours?" Eli nodded at Sia, who had dribbled juice all down her dress.

"Not technically," she replied. "Dean's first wife died when Sia was a baby."

"I'm sorry."

"It's okay," said Dean with a smile at Mary. "Sia is lucky to have this beautiful woman as her new mother."

Mary squeezed his hand, but it made Eli feel sick.

"Why didn't you call? Or email? Or explain to me why you left me with Dad? Was it just too hard to make the effort to see your own son, even if you couldn't stand to be around Dad?"

"I... I'm sorry Eli. My life with your father did not turn out at all like I planned. I rushed into marriage because it was so glamorous. I was young and naïve and I didn't have a plan for my life. I fell pregnant with you, and I couldn't get myself out fast enough. I fell into depression when you were young. Harvey became more and more business focused with the company making millions, and... it just came to a point when I knew I needed to start my life again." Dean rubbed her back soothingly as she spoke. "I wanted to take you with me, but I was afraid Harvey would want to share custody and I just... I couldn't see him again."

Eli snorted. "That's a joke. Dad would have given anything to ship me off to boarding school, given the chance. He was never a good father to me."

"Oh sweetie, no. Your father loved you more than anything. More than his job, more than me. You were the best thing that ever happened to him."

Feeling as though someone had gripped his heart tight, Eli couldn't finish his pizza. His father *hated* him. He ignored him, he pressured him, he tried to make him a businessman and force his life down a path Eli couldn't bear to think about, let alone live.

"He had a shit way of showing it," Eli grumbled. Dean and Mary glanced at Sia, who was completely oblivious of the cursing going on around her.

"Maybe... maybe he didn't know how to be a father alone. Despite being a confident billionaire, Harvey was never good at relationships. He turned to his work to escape the pressure. I can imagine that's what happened to... to you..."

Mary started sobbing. Dean pulled her into his arms, giving Eli a look that said 'you should probably let it go now'. But Eli wanted more. He was finally discovering the truth behind his lonely life, and he wanted some sort of payback for the years he spent in his father's shadow, tied down instead of free.

"Eli if... if there was a way I could take it all back, I w–"

"Too late," he grumbled. "You made your choice years ago."

"Yes," she said. "And now I'm pregnant."

Eli slipped off his chair weightlessly. Everything felt suddenly wrong. The fact that she was pregnant made it official: There was no room in her life for him. She had moved on completely.

He backed away from his mother, wishing he'd never come. Wishing he'd never met Dean or Sia or walked into their perfect life in their perfect house. It was completely wrong, and he wanted no part in it.

"Eli–"

"I'm leaving. This was a mistake," he said through his teeth. *What did you expect, a happy reunion?* The voice in his mind was like a stab through his chest, but it was right. *Your mother moved on the moment she moved out. You're too late for things to go back to the way they used to be. She left you for a different life. A better life.*

"Please, Eli, can we just talk some more?" Mary left her chair and started towards him. Eli was frozen in her hypnotizing gaze. His heart ached to be a part of their home and forget the past nine years, just like he'd forgotten the past ten months. "Sweetie, please?" She trailed a finger down his cheek. Eli melted at her touch. "Please forgive me."

The urge to nod and hug his mother and cry with her and forget was stronger than ever. Eli had grown up learning to please people, to not speak his own mind but to do what's right and expected of him. His father taught him that. *Respect, Son, that's what gets you places. You shut your mouth and give people what they want.* He had been weak from that moment on. He let Benny Layman bully him, let his father drag him to business meeting after business meeting. Eli couldn't remember the last year, but he was sure it had been exactly the same, even with that Hunter girl.

But now, it was time to change. This was his chance to turn his life around and live it the way *he* wanted to. As much as he longed for a mother, he was not going to take the easy road.

Suddenly, words he couldn't remember reading popped into his mind. *The greater our ignorance to something, the greater our resistance to change.* Forgetting what his mother put him through was like sweeping it under the rug, when he could be walking away. *And sometimes, even with the ones you love, you have to walk away. Walk away and live your life and find love somewhere else.*

So Eli gently lifted his mother's hands from his shoulders, gave Dean a nod and said his goodbyes. His mother stood by silently, tears dripping down her cheeks, her eyes longing for him. Years ago he would have killed to see that look on her face. He would have stayed without a doubt. But things were different now. And thanks to Joshua, so was his mind.

But his heart would never change, and as he left his mother's cozy suburban house, he left a piece of him with her. It belonged to her all along.

TWENTY-FIVE

I'M GOING TO *MURDER* HIM!"

"Joshua calm down." Jenny sat on the edge of the stiff bed in their hotel room, watching Joshua storm around and drop icicles on the carpet. "He's not running away, he's just getting some fresh air. What do you expect, he's been sitting in a car all day and now he has to sit in a hotel room."

"I told him," Joshua growled, "not to leave my *sight*. And you were distracting me, weren't you?"

"What? I didn't-"

"You two planned this, didn't you?" He marched over to her and snatched the collar of her sweater. She fell back on the bed, frozen in shock. "Didn't you!"

Jenny had never seen Joshua so furious, his pale eyes hard and menacing, his fingers shooting cold vibes through her chest as he gripped her tight. But she knew the ice inside his heart was only abusing his anger, using Eli as an excuse to release rage. She'd spent enough time with him to know that much.

"Let me go Joshua," she said slowly. "Please."

His eyes flinched, looking back and forth between hers, the room so silent she could hear the cars in the street twenty floors down. Then he unclenched his fingers and Jenny flopped on the mattress.

"I'm sorry. I... I just can't do this." He ran a hand through his slick black hair. "I can't worry about Hunter and worry about *him* too."

Jenny didn't know quite what to say. Yes, Joshua was over reacting. Eli had been gone for only an hour now, and Joshua freaked out as though he should call the authorities. Jenny knew Eli only wanted to get away from the both of them, to explore after being cooped up in a laboratory like a prisoner. The hotel they'd stopped in smelt terrible, and it made her nervous to sleep in her bed, so to be honest, Jenny didn't blame him for running away.

But after nearly being killed by the Agents, she didn't want to leave Joshua's side for even a second. Perhaps she just wasn't as brave.

"Worrying about Hunter doesn't bring her back," she finally said, "and Eli can take care of himself."

"You don't get it. It's been me and her since the beginning. I've fought to protect Hunter since the day I promised her mother I would, and now she's gone and I'm stuck with you two. I just don't know how to... how to *be*."

Jenny nodded, even though she wasn't sure what he meant. But she could see the strain in his eyes. She knew even before he admitted it that Hunter meant the world to Joshua and every day she was out there in the unknown killed him a little more inside. Her heart ached for him, and she wanted to find Hunter just as much as he did. But there was nothing they could do.

"Joshua listen to me." She stood up and walked to him as he leant on the small refrigerator. "I know you want to find Hunter. But there are more important things to do first, like fix your mistakes. Eli needs his memory back. If Hunter finds out what you did, she'll hate you even more."

"No. She thinks he's dead, Jenny. She'll forgive me once she knows what really happened."

Jenny longed to put a hand on Joshua's shoulder, to comfort him, but she wasn't sure he was ready for that. "Forgiveness is a difficult and fragile thing. It takes time. If she and Eli are reunited and he actually remembers who he is and what they shared together, then there's a chance she *will* forgive you. But it will traumatize her when she finds out he doesn't love her."

"He has to love her," said Joshua. "It has to be there somewhere."

So he does see the love, but only when the ice isn't warping his mind. Jenny watched Joshua with pity and fascination. A desire to fix things and make amends was painted across his sharp features. *He truly has faith in Hunter's love for Eli, but when he loses control and the ice takes over, love does not exist anymore. If only he could find some way to block out this split personality from hell, none of this would be happening.*

"It *is* there Joshua," she said. "But right now his mind is fragile. That's why we need to fix his memory. In the meantime, Hunter will just have to wait to be rescued."

Joshua bit his lip. There were tears brewing in his eyes that he tried desperately to hold back. "I just want to know if she's safe. I *need* to know."

Jenny reached out with a shaking hand, very slowly, as though she were about to touch a frightened animal, and placed her hand gently over his. As she expected, it was colder than an icepack. The friction of their grip shocked him and he yanked his hand away, turning his back on her.

"Joshua, I-"

"Thank you, Jenny, for your... advice." He started walking to the door. "I'll let you know when Eli returns."

Jenny wanted to let him go, but her heart wouldn't allow it. She ran after him, grabbed his shoulder and yanked him around to face her. Something in her mind was screaming warning signals, and every muscle in her body was tensing, afraid of where her heart was taking her. But everything, all her thoughts and morals and fears and emotions, blew away in a breath of air. She grabbed him by the collar – just as he'd done moments ago – shoved him against the door and kissed him.

It was by far the strangest kiss she'd ever had – and Jenny had kissed a *lot* of men. None of them had a power like Joshua, and none of them were in such an emotionally traumatic state, but none of them had a heart like she knew he possessed. Why she had these urges so suddenly was a mystery to her, but it just felt... right.

Joshua didn't move at all. He stood stock-still against the door as she kissed him, completely taken aback. But once the surprise was over, he still didn't move. She wondered with her hands drifting down over his chest if this was the first time he'd ever kissed a woman, because he was either still completely flabbergasted or he just didn't know what to do with his hands, or his tongue. It was like pressing her lips against a dead fish.

The moment that thought occurred to her, she broke away and stepped back in such a hurry that she nearly tripped over his pack lying against the wall.

Joshua's mouth was still hanging half open.

Oh my God, what did I do?

"Uh… I think you'd better leave," was all she managed to say. Not 'sorry Joshua, I shouldn't have been so forward' or 'why didn't you kiss me back?' Just a harsh kick in the butt. *No wonder you're not married Jenny*, the new and inferior voice in her mind sighed.

But Joshua was all too happy to oblige. Shock plastered across his pale face, he fumbled with the door and then hurried awkwardly away, leaving Jenny alone in the room to wallow in her embarrassment and hope she could find something that would suffice as a noose.

TWENTY-SIX

Another three weeks passed, and Hunter and Will continued to meet in secret, sometimes late at night and sometimes in the middle of the day. It didn't matter down below, because there were no windows and it was always dark. Nor did security ever pick up, and many of the others were starting to wonder what had happened. Apparently there was 'some sort of shortage of men with no souls in the world', as Zac had said.

She and Will went down to the old quarters whenever they could, and there they smoked and talked in the candlelight about life and their future and where they'd rather be. Most of it was light hearted. Eventually Hunter told Will her story. Will said not a word about Eli and Joshua, but the fury in his eyes was greater than the rage that stirred in her own. He asked a lot of questions about Joshua. Those hours spent in the cold, dark room were what Hunter looked forward to most.

Second in the running was her afternoon gym sessions with Mosi and Marcus that had, since that day, turned into a sort of amateur fight club. Most of the others came to watch as she and Marcus practiced the skills that Mosi taught them – Hunter having covered the basics with Joshua. Mosi never told them where he learned to fight so cleanly when all they knew of him was his work in the mines as a child. But he was a patient teacher, and sometimes other volunteers joined in for a lesson. They were caught several times by a passing guard, but since the numbers grew, he could only close the fitness room and give them a warning rather than send them all to Solitary. The fight club started out of boredom, but became – for Hunter and some others – like a sort of silver lining; if they learnt to fight, then their chances of escaping Death Cave were greater. It gave them all hope, and especially the younger ones who observed with careful attention.

The constant nightmares she'd been having about Eli and Joshua and Dr. Wolfe slowly drifted away the more her friendships grew. Despite still being locked up in a prison from hell, Hunter learned to grasp the positives. After the fight club, she no longer feared an attack from the guards. She grew closer with Fearne and Will and all the others, and found she actually enjoyed getting to know them. Hunter had never really had close friends, particularly in the past few years of her high school life. At ICE, everyone was the same. Sure, they all had different powers and some were a little nuttier than others, but they could get along – minus Jet, who was an asshole to everyone – and soon she was part of the family.

At breakfast, she always sat beside Will at a table with the others. Hunter noticed everyone come together – Marcus and Mosi joined Zac and Chantal, Benji and Ryo sat with them, and Will and Fearne were no longer alone. It made the institution feel much smaller now that they were all good friends, and Hunter knew everyone by name and power. She often smiled and laughed with the others at Zac's hilarious jokes and goofy nature, greedily consuming plates of food after early morning workouts. She and Will decided to start exercising more often to gather their strength back. It was more for his benefit. The weights, boxing and strength training were much harder when Will didn't have enough energy in his system from the surgery he still undertook in the evenings. Often when they spent time together in the secret room, Will was so weak that they would just lie there in silence. She didn't mind though. Helping him recover his energy kept her mind off of other things.

Like Fearne, for instance.

Ever since she saw the young girl interrogating a scientist, Hunter knew it had something to do with the lack of security. The guards were either being fired or killed, and no one had any idea why. Fearne could never remember anything about what Dr. Wolfe was forcing her to do. Hunter was almost afraid to get involved. If she knew Dr. Wolfe, and by now she had a pretty good inkling, he was most certainly up to something sick and twisted.

Dr. Rosenthal was no help on the matter. He was quite good at not giving anything away when Hunter saw him every once in a while for a consultation, but it was obvious he wanted to tell her. She often didn't understand why he couldn't help her escape again when he'd already done it. But above all else, Hunter trusted Dr. Rosenthal. He was kind to her and there was an aura of knowledge about him, as if he knew everything that was going on now and in the future at ICE. He was never afraid of anything. Not even Dr. Wolfe could control him.

Over the past weeks, Hunter's desire to stand up and turn things around tripled. She wanted to escape with Will, to show him the world the right way, to let him live his life. She wanted to get the children away from so much pain and harsh treatment to a loving home with real parents and a life to live. She wanted, especially, for Fearne to be free of the mind controlling device that restricted her powers and turned her insane. Maybe Will was right; maybe she did have a hero tendency, and every day she trained in the fitness room or fought with Mosi or spent time with Dr. Rosenthal or even lay on the operating table in complete agony with Dr. Wolfe leering over her was a day that strengthened her need for some serious payback. Hunter was waiting, waiting for the day when she and the rest of the special kids she now called her family would be free and could inflict their own batch of pain on the guards and the scientists who treated them like aliens.

Then, when she was free, what Hunter wanted most of all was to find Joshua. She wasn't sure why exactly, because the fire hadn't had a chance to really react to her emotions since she'd been bound by the bracelet. It could still be hungry for revenge. Sometimes, when she thought about Joshua before she went to sleep at night, Hunter could feel the dark power of her fire stirring. It longed to burn him until he melted. But Hunter was confident she had control over it. Her *love* had control over it.

But did love still exist? Every day away from Eli was a reminder of how she missed his love. Every day she spent in ICE with the neglected, unloved children with no purpose was a reminder of the parents and families who simply gave them up for being different. Hunter struggled to find love in such a cold place, but she knew it was there. It was in those times she spent with Benji and Ryo playing chess in the common room. It was there when she read *Peter Pan* to the younger children after dinner. It was there when she laughed with Zac and Fearne as Marcus wrestled with Mosi who was unbeatable. It was definitely there when she lay close to Will in the silence of the old quarters amidst a cloud of smoke and burning candlelight. And although there was so much anguish and rage and terror biting down on her heart, Hunter stayed strong. She focused on getting the others out, on the bright sunny skies that lay beyond, of freedom. Of starting life over and forgetting her dark past.

Maybe, even, of saving the world.

"This is bullshit. I'm sick of this food!" Zac threw down his fork in frustration, splatting a large clump of gray goo in Chantal's face. He immediately put his hands up in apologetic surrender. "Oops."

"You son of a bitch," she growled. "I *just* showered."

"Go ask Cook for a cloth to wipe it off," said Marcus in his easy-going manner. The more time he spent with Hunter and the others, the more she realized how completely different he was from his brother.

Chantal stormed off towards the door and the rest of them went back to eating their dinner. Hunter was now used to eating the same food day in and day out, but God, she would kill for a thick, cheesy pizza. Even just a cup of coffee for a bit of variety.

Will nudged her with his knee and she looked up. His lips were pressed together in that way that said something was amiss, and then his doe eyes locked on the door. Hunter turned and saw about six or seven Men in White stalk into the room and take their posts around the perimeter. It was the most she'd seen in one place in weeks.

The others noticed it as well.

"Think the brute squad is back?" asked Marcus.

One of the guards marched straight past their table, and Zac gave him a nod and a smile. The guard rolled his eyes.

"Hey Ryan," he said. "Did you get a haircut?"

The guard didn't answer.

"I will say this," Zac said to the group, "they're touchier than before."

"So what, they were just on break or something?" asked Marcus.

"God knows," Zac scoffed and picked at his dinner.

As they watched the door, two more Men in White entered the room. This time, they were not alone.

Hunter remembered her very first day at ICE like it was yesterday. The first time she entered the breakfast hall, every eye stared her down as though she were a new toy at the toy store. So as the newest member of their mutant crew stumbled into the hall, Hunter stared along with the rest of them and wondered if her face looked just as terrified as his.

"Ooo," said Zac, glee plastered across his face. "Now it's getting interesting! A new person already?!"

"He needs seven Men in White to escort him in?" said Marcus unbelievingly. "What kind of power does this kid have?"

"Shh!" hissed Hunter, for at that moment, the boy passed their table.

The first thing Hunter noticed was his eyes. They were so red and bloodshot, she couldn't even tell if they were blue or green. His blond hair was greasy and stuck up in all directions. He was lanky and tall, about Zac's age, and he walked with heavy feet, his back slightly arched. He stared them down, too exhausted to look away, and made it to the cafeteria line after his guards split off.

"He looks rough," said Ryo. "We should make some room for him."

"He might already be making friends," Hunter said, and they watched as Mikayla and Jet slid in the line right behind the boy and tapped him on the shoulder.

"Oh no," said Marcus. "That poor kid."

The rest of them ate their breakfast and tried to read the conversation between the two snakes of the institution and the very vulnerable new addition. Hunter saw the boy's face pale after Jet slapped him across the back. The word 'faggot' spilled out of Mikayla's mouth. The boy paled even more-so, and Jet and Mikayla laughed.

"I can't watch this," she muttered to Will and got to her feet. There were many things Hunter missed about the real world, but bullying was not one of them. She would not allow the poor boy's first day at ICE to begin with Jet opening his mouth.

"Hunter, don't-"

Ignoring Will as he reached out to grab her, Hunter stormed through the tables towards the cafeteria line.

"So then, you must be one of those quietly sensitive gays, am I right?" Jet asked in a mock-serious tone. "Because I wouldn't have guessed it by the youthful sound of your voice."

Mikayla chuckled behind Jet, but the boy said nothing as he collected food on his plate and moved along.

"Where did you say you were from again Alfie?" he asked. "Sweden? Is gay marriage even legal in-"

"Hey!"

Jet and Mikayla turned as Hunter approached them. Alfie's eyes flicked up and met hers. Instead of throwing her fist into Jet's face, Hunter decided to pretend they didn't exist.

"Hi, I'm Hunter," she said and held out her hand to the young boy. He looked up at her in shock and shook her hand. "Welcome to ICE Institution. Do you want to come sit with us?"

"Uh, thanks?" He picked up his tray and followed her towards the others.

"Hunter," said Jet from behind her. "He's not interested, okay? He only likes *booyyss*."

Hunter spun and glared at Jet's smug face. "I know that you enjoy a little sexual banter as much as the next person," she said with a forced smile. "And maybe one day you'll figure out exactly which team *you* bat for – no offence Mikayla." The girl scoffed. Hunter let her smile fall away as she turned back to Jet. "But I swear to God, you slimy little leech: if you say one more word to him, I'll..."

She trailed off instantly when Jet's face started to fall. And it wasn't because of her threat. His eyes were still on Alfie. There was a crash and a squeal from Mikayla, and Hunter turned to see what exactly had wiped the smirk right off Jet's face.

Alfie was quivering. He stared down at his hands, his chest heaving, his tray of food splattered over his feet. Whatever Jet had said triggered something inside him, and now he was starting to change.

"Alfie?" asked Hunter. "Are you okay?"

"He's changing," said Mikayla from behind her.

"Into what?" asked Zac, who was sitting up on the table only feet from them. "What is he?"

Alfie was breathing hard through his teeth.

"You're about to find out," said Jet.

And then, right in front of the entire table, Alfie seized up and let out a shrill scream like the cry of a banshee that deepened instantly into a roar.

TWENTY-SEVEN

"Well-" said Eli as he slipped into the backseat of the car, coffee sloshing over the rim of the plastic lid, and slammed the door just as Joshua skidded away from the curb. "I don't know about you guys, but I'm pretty keen to put Minneapolis in the rear vision mirror."

He handed Jenny the coffee and she took it wordlessly. Joshua wriggled in the driver's seat, his eyes – as always – glued to the road. There was tension in the air, and Joshua wasn't sure if it was his fault or if it had something to do with Jenny as well.

"Guys?"

"Why, did something happen to you last night while you were out gallivanting around the city behind my back?" Joshua snapped. He remembered hearing the boy sneak back into the hotel room at an earlier hour than he expected, but decided to leave it until morning to get furious.

"For your information," said Eli, "I visited my mother, a mother I haven't seen nor heard from in nine years since she ran out on me and my dad. I'm terribly sorry if that was any inconvenience to you. I'll try to be less *selfish* next time."

The car went instantly cold. Joshua squirmed in the seat and said nothing.

"Are you alright?" Jenny asked him.

Eli shrugged. "I guess so. It wasn't worth the sixty bucks I spent in cab money, I'll tell you that. So did you guys get up to any mischief last night?"

Jenny choked a little on her coffee and wiped a hand across her chin to cover it. Joshua pretended to fiddle with the radio, but his palms were getting clammy. And that *never* happened.

"Okay... something's going down that you two aren't telling me." Eli leaned forward and tapped Joshua on the shoulder. "Is it something to do with this professor guy you're taking us to?"

"It's..." Joshua shot a sideways glance at Jenny, and then he blinked several times. "It's nothing."

Eli must have seen the blush that crept into Joshua's cheeks, for he sat back against the leather seat and huffed a laugh.

"Holy shit. You guys buried the bishop, didn't you?"

This time, Jenny spat coffee all over the windshield. Joshua let out a yelp and the car swerved, jerking all three of them to the right.

"Hey, watch where you're driving!" Eli groaned at the sight of half his coffee sloshed on the carpet floor of the car. "Now I have half a laté. Thanks."

Joshua flicked his wrist at Eli and instantly, his laté turned to ice. Rock solid ice in a Styrofoam cup.

"There. Now you have half a *frozen* laté." Joshua stepped on the gas and they all lurched forward. He didn't have the patience to deal with Eli any more than he wanted to re-live the awkwardly terrifying events of the night before.

"Joshua, I think you need to relax a little." Jenny lifted a tissue and delicately wiped away the coffee dripping down the dashboard. "Do you want to get pulled over?"

Joshua didn't like Jenny telling him what to do, but sometimes her voice was like a cool rush of water that moved through his body and commanded the ice to stop whatever it was doing and listen. He eased his foot off the break.

"You're right. We don't need that kind of trouble." Joshua's eyes sought Eli's in the mirror. "We did not do anything of that sort, for your information Eli."

He coughed a clearly audible 'bullshit'. Jenny hid a smile.

Joshua readjusted his hands and turned onto the highway. "It's about nine hours to Dickinson. I suggest you both... sleep for a while. I'll stop for gas in about an hour and we can eat a real breakfast."

Jenny nodded and opened her book, kicking her feet up on the dash. Joshua didn't even order her to put them back down. He focused on the road ahead, but his thoughts were miles away. Without realizing it, Joshua drove straight into a bump on the road and the three of them were jolted upright.

And just like that, Joshua was taken by a memory. He and Liz were driving through the mountains in Cuba into town to buy some groceries and visit the hospital for a check-up. He glanced at her sitting in the passenger seat, examining some data he'd printed out earlier.

"Honestly, don't you think that sometimes these readings have a mind of their own?" Liz asked, turning the paper upside down as if that helped the data appear regular.

Joshua swerved around another bush, cursing the rough terrain. The heat of the mountains was making him jittery. "Not really, yours look pretty-"

"Not mine; Hunter's. Are you sure you did this right?"

"Liz, that's my first homemade ultrasound in a power-generated shed out in the middle of nowhere. It's highly probable I made a mistake."

Liz groaned and shoved the pages back in her bag.

"What's wrong? I told you, no one will find us out here. I mean we're living here illegally, I know, but after the fire I was sure you just wanted to run and-"

"It's not that, it's the baby."

"I promise you, you're not going to give birth to a demon, alright? Everything will be fine."

"I just don't know Joshua," she sighed. "Everything we've searched for here has only led to more questions. And then there's the heat flushes, the random fires in the shack, the voice, the-"

"The what?" He turned to stare at her and almost swerved completely off the track. "You're hearing a voice now? When were you going to tell me this?"

"Never," she said softly. She was biting her lip. "It's nothing."

"Nothing?" Joshua snorted. "Yeah, because I hear a voice in my head all the time."

"Don't mock me," she sneered. "I just get these random thoughts, okay? Sometimes they come in the middle of the night and I wake up in a heat flush, sometimes I get them when I'm in the shower, sometimes when I'm outside lying on the hammock. They're just... feelings."

"I'm not sure I know what you mean." He leaned forward and checked both ways before turning right on the wider dirt track that led to town. "What exactly does your mystery voice say?"

"It..." she began hesitantly, "it says..."

"Liz, you can tell me. I'm here for you, remember?"

"Fine. It says... 'Take me back to the lake of fire'."

Joshua slammed his foot on the brakes and they both went lurching forward.

"Joshua! Give me whiplash-"

"You heard a voice tell you *that*, and you didn't think it was important enough to tell me? What, so next time you start breathing fire just bring it up over coffee a month later, sound good?"

"You're freaking out," she muttered. Her hand clasped over her belly as she eyed him cautiously. Those dark eyes always made his temper calmer and Joshua told himself to relax, but inside his head was screaming. Should he listen to this? Did it mean anything, or was it just the distorted mind of a pregnant woman whispering psycho things to herself? He decided to remain calm – for Liz's sake, mostly – and investigate later. Whatever it was, it made him feel nervous.

"I'm sure it's nothing," he said and pulled back onto the road. "I think we should just forget it and concentrate on the checkup."

Liz's smile widened. "Thank you Joshua."

"I'm here for you Lizzie," he replied gently.

He gripped the steering wheel and made a mental note to himself: Postpone testing with the formula until further research on side effects has been complete.

Don't want any creepy voices in my head, he thought and dropped his visor to block out the sun.

TWENTY-EIGHT

lfie exploded. And expanded. And transformed before every eye in the breakfast hall into a gigantic, twenty-foot beast with a mammoth mouth opening and closing in slow motion. Slivers of rope-thick saliva stretched from one deadly tooth to the other. He had russet brown scales and crazy black eyes the size of tennis balls. His tiny hands hung limply from his body, and his tail swung back and forth, knocking over tables with a loud crash.

The Men in White were slow to react, because they weren't sure what was going on. Alfie had had a restraint around his neck like Chantal's that stopped him using his powers. How could he have changed?

One of the guards was stupid enough to take a shot at Alfie with the taser, but his skin was too thick for it to do any damage. The dinosaur turned his head and spotted the guard who stood frozen in fear. He stretched his mouth wide open and let out a terrific roar that caused the thick glass across the canteen windows to shatter.

"It's Jurassic Park, people!" Zac shrieked. As he did, the ten-ton tail of a T-rex slammed down on a table just feet away from him. He leapt out of the way, rolled twice across the floor, and scrambled to his feet just in time to yell with incredible calm, "Seriously, does *anyone* have a tranquilizer gun?"

The breakfast hall was in utter chaos. Half the room had emptied, but Alfie the dinosaur was blocking the way out and there was nowhere else to run to. The canteen was jammed with tables that had been thrown against the kitchen glass. An alarm like an alien ringtone was blaring. The Men in

White couldn't contain him because the tasers didn't have any effect on Alfie's skin. The more they tried to take him down, the angrier he became. And there was nothing worse than a pissed off, twenty-foot dinosaur.

"Zac, get down!" Hunter shrieked, and in a matter of seconds they had scattered like petrified rabbits to their rabbit holes.

"We have to do something!" Marcus screamed at the others.

They were all cowering behind upturned tables. A few of the younger kids were holding tight to Hunter's jumpsuit, and if she weren't so preoccupied by the stomping dinosaur, her heart would have broken for them.

"Okay," said Zac, "you grab a rope and lasso him around the neck while I run around and pretend to be a nice juicy cow or something."

Hunter didn't have the time to roll her eyes.

"This is all your fault Hunter!" hissed Jet from behind the next table. "You shouldn't have interrupted our conversation, now he's confused!"

"How can you even *be* that stupid?" she snarled back. "It's because you called him gay!"

"Uh, he *is* gay!"

"Shut up you two!" Marcus waved frantically at them.

A crash and a scream caused them to peer over the rim of the table. Alfie was stomping towards two of the guards who were cowering in the corner. As she watched, her heart beat faster. Alfie's giant tail wagged back and forth and he let out an almighty roar that shook the room. One of the guards pulled out a knife from his belt and managed to run forward and drive it into Alfie's leg. The dinosaur roared it pain before opening wide his mouth and snapping it around the guard's body. His scream was cut off and blood sprayed across the white walls of the breakfast hall. The other guard scrambled away and ducked behind some chairs.

Alfie chewed on the guard, his bones cracking. The terrible sound of blood and entrails falling to the floor with a splat echoed throughout the room. Hunter dropped back behind the table and little Sammy cried and wriggled closer to her.

"Block your ears," said Hunter and she held him tight against her.

Will placed a hand on her shoulder. Hunter turned her eyes to his fear-filled face and furrowed brow. He really had no idea what to do.

"We have to get them out of here," she whispered.

"Yes, but how do you knock out a dinosaur the size of a crane when tasers aren't powerful enough?"

An idea hit her. "They're not powerful enough. But I know someone who is." She nodded to the opposite table where Marcus was crouched down, staring at them both. He frowned as if to say 'what are you looking at me like that for?'

"Hunter," said Will. "He's useless. We all are without powers."

"Then we get one of the guards to disarm our bracelets."

"But they don't-"

Alfie roared again, cutting Will off, and Hunter started searching for someone who could help. Almost instantly, she spotted a man in the white guard uniform lying flat under a bench with his hands over his head. He was too far away to reach. She'd have to run to him. She looked again at Will and ignored the doubt in his eyes.

"You got a better plan?"

For a moment he struggled, knowing there was a chance the guard might not even have the authority to disarm their bracelets, but it wasn't in Will's nature to back out if there was still hope.

"Well then you'll need a distraction."

"No," Hunter said firmly. She knew exactly what he was thinking, and she didn't like it one bit. "No way in-"

Will jumped up, removing himself from the protection of their fort.

"Will, don't-"

But he was running, his back bent low and his footsteps gliding along the floor. He ducked around the table while Alfie nuzzled the ground on the other side of the hall for food, and ran in the opposite direction.

Her stomach curdling, Hunter sprinted as fast as she could and slid down beside Marcus.

"What the hell are you doing?"

"You need to put this dino down," she said firmly. Before he could argue, she grabbed his wrist and gripped the bracelet. "I'm going over to that guard to get him to unlock your bracelet. Once you're free, you have to electrocute it."

"Are you outta your mind? I haven't generated that much power in my entire life! To put down a dinosaur it's gonna take more than just a zap, Hunter!"

"Just… I dunno, draw it from somewhere! A power hub or something!"

There was a shout from the opposite side of the room and Hunter and Marcus peered up and over the table at Will. He was standing on a bench, waving his arms at Alfie and throwing trays at his body that wouldn't have been more effective than hitting a building with a pencil, but the shouting drew his attention. He turned and roared at Will so savagely, Hunter's ears rung.

"Do it!" Will screamed, and Alfie started to charge.

"Can you do this Marcus?"

"Do I have a choice?"

Hunter kicked off from the table and sprinted to the guard lying under the bench. She slid along the scuffed floor and knocked into the man, who turned over and nearly screamed in fright.

"What the hell-"

"Where's the key?"

"The what?"

"The key, you know, to unlock this thing!" She tapped her bracelet.

Alfie chomped down on the bench where Will had been standing and threw it across the room like it weighed nothing but air. Will scrambled away and Hunter started shaking the guard.

"I don't have it!" he whimpered. Hunter moaned, thinking *these guys were such hardasses when their stupid tasers worked, and now they're hiding here like wimps while us kids take care of the raging dinosaur!*

"Listen, we can take this thing down, but we need your help! Give me the key. I know you have it!"

She was bluffing, because she had no idea what they used to unlock the restraints. It could be a machine sealed in the lab for all she knew. She was unconscious when they deactivated her bracelet and put her in the Orb. But it was her best bet, and if it didn't work they had nothing else. *Jeez, where's Dr. Wolfe when you need him?*

But it turned out they didn't need him. The guard finally saw reason and reached into his pocket for a set of keys. On the chain, there was a single card used as his ID, a couple of average keys and a black square with a silver button in the center. He forced the chain into her shaking hands and said, "The black one scans the restraint and deactivates it. That's the best I can do."

Hunter didn't need telling twice. She scrambled out from under the bench just in time to see Will take a running leap over a fallen table. The dinosaur ducked its head and knocked the table out of the way just seconds after Will cleared it. The table flew through the air and collided with Will, throwing him against the wall with a thump. Hunter's heart leapt. The table had crushed him.

"Hunter!" he shouted. "Hurry!"

Adrenaline pumped through her as she sprinted back to Marcus and slid into him. Her hands fumbled with the key as she gripped the black square and pressed hard on the button. A bright, silver laser shot out of the tip. She pointed it at Marcus' outstretched wrist. The bracelet lit up like a firecracker and then became loose.

A split second of wonder passed between them before Marcus shook his wrist and they jumped to their feet.

The sight before her eyes knocked the air out of Hunter. The dinosaur's jaws were clamped around a table that was flung aside, leaving Will to army crawl as fast as he could away from reach. But he was right beneath Alfie, and his legs were crushed. He couldn't move. He was about to be chomped by an extinct predator.

But Marcus was quick. He ran as close to the dinosaur as time allowed before throwing out his wrist and aiming it at the nearest power outlet. It sparked angrily. Marcus started twitching. Just as Alfie's jaws opened wide, a bolt of electricity shot like lightning from the power outlet directly into Marcus's outstretched hand. He seized up and went bright blue like an electric fly trap. Hunter would have shielded her eyes had she not been frozen in fear and amazement.

Marcus extended his other hand towards Alfie. The electricity that shot from the power outlet bolted at Alfie and hit him hard in the neck.

The scream that came from Alfie's gaping jaw was deafening. He jerked backwards, stumbled and twitched just as Marcus had. The power that zapped into him was enough to bring him to an almighty crash on the floor. Marcus let out a sound between a scream and a growl from the effort it took him before he released the electricity and collapsed. A few sparks jumped off his body – and Alfie's huge dinosaur form – and then, there was silence.

Hunter didn't wait another second before she sprinted across the wrecked room to Will's body. She rolled him over, gasping at the blood that stained his legs from where the table had crushed him and the deep cut across his forehead. Why did he do this to himself again?

"Will! Will, wake up!" She shook his shoulders.

A groan escaped his lips and his eyes fluttered open. Hunter resisted the urge to wrap her arms around him and squeeze him half to death, especially when his mouth stretched into an exhausted smile.

"Hello," he said.

"You're the *stupidest* person I've ever met, you know that?" For some reason, there were tears in her eyes as she shook her head harshly. "Do you *always* go sprinting off towards danger without caring for your own safety?"

"I think it's my hero tendency." His brown eyes sparkled up at her, his hand clutching hers without either of them realizing it.

"Yeah… well I'm starting to wonder if you even have other tendencies." She brushed the hair away from his eyes. The simple touch felt almost natural to her, and she was so filled with relief to notice that Will did not flinch at all.

Someone tugged on her shoulder, and Hunter turned where little Sammy was staring fearfully down at her, his bottom lip shaking. He didn't want to look over at the giant form of the dinosaur that was slowly morphing back into Alfie.

"Is it over?"

Hunter reached up and curled her arm around him, bringing him close against her in a tight hug.

"Yeah Sammy," she sighed in relief. "It's-"

"What the hell are you doing?!"

Hunter and Sammy whipped around at Ryo's shriek. Instantly, Hunter's stomach fell at the sight of Alfie's limp, naked body floating in the air just meters from her, dangling like a puppet on strings. His eyes were closed.

And there stood Jet, with his hand raised, his black eyes sparkling and his power restraint gone. The guard's keys were nowhere to be found.

"I'm trying to wake him up again!" Jet yelled. "Oh, come on! It was getting kind of interesting there, you gotta admit!"

"Put him down Jet," said Hunter. "Now."

A fierce pull in her chest caused Hunter to lurch forward. Her feet left the ground and her stomach flipped over inside her. She saw Jet come closer to her and suddenly she was there, right in front of his face, her body immobile and hanging off the ground.

"I can't help but notice," he growled, "that you're a little lacking in power right now and I… well, I don't think I need to paint you a picture of the kind of energy radiating through me. It tingles all the way down to my toes."

Hunter looked around with her eyes – because her head wouldn't move – and saw that the guards were closing in on them, talking into their earpieces, warily approaching the threat. After the attack from the raging dinosaur, Hunter wondered if Jet was even worth the caution, but apparently there was nothing any of them could do but stay back and wait. Alfie lay on the floor, unconscious, and the only other person whose powers were useful was Marcus. He'd passed out after electrocuting Alfie.

"So what are you gonna do?" she asked, trying to keep him distracted. "Now that you have your powers back? Will you escape?"

His smile twisted to the side. "Oh baby, no way. You gotta plan things like that. And you know what they say: keep your friends close–" He grabbed the collar of her jumpsuit and yanked her to within an inch of his face. "–And your enemies closer."

One of the Men in White decided to take action. He took a running leap over a table and dove towards Jet, his arms stretched out as though he were flying. Hunter felt the return of gravity as Jet released her and her legs caved in. She caught sight of the guard just as Jet's arm flew in a wide arc. The guard soared across the room, his back thumping against the wall where he slid to the floor and didn't move.

Jet smiled, but it was only the beginning. More Men in White started attacking, their tasers at the ready and their fists flying. Jet seemed to take it all as a game, ducking under their punches and flicking his wrist, sending them all spinning into furniture and cackling madly. Out of the corner of her eye Hunter saw the other kids start to whisper to each other. They pointed at something she couldn't see from the ground. She hauled herself to her feet and saw Mosi stride forward – a dark shape amidst the white – with a little blond head walking before him.

Hunter tried to call out, praying Sammy wasn't about to attack Jet. But it was too late. A blinding light radiated from him, burning like a spotlight straight at Jet. He screamed and shielded his eyes and in a moment, Mosi had thrown himself against Jet and wrapped his strong arms around his neck. Jet tried to rip at Mosi's skin with his power, but Mosi's diamond-tough skin protected him. After a few seconds of struggling, Jet went limp in his arms.

Hunter surveyed the havoc of the breakfast hall and the unconscious guards. The others were crawling out from behind the upturned tables, fearfully watching as Mosi threw Jet's body to the floor and met eyes with Hunter. *Now it's over,* they said. He looked down at his arms, flexed his wrists and smiled.

Hunter understood that look. He wanted to escape. And now would be the perfect opportunity – at least six Men in White were down and, though there would be more, if they could all remove their restraints at once there might be a chance they could make it out.

She opened her mouth to shout at Mosi when a blaring alarm sounded throughout the institution. It was not at all like the gong of the morning bell that woke her or the alarm that sounded as Alfie turned. Hunter covered her ears and dropped to the ground as everything flashed red. In an instant, she saw Will crawling towards her.

"Hunter!"

The room darkened. A strange smell filled her head and Hunter looked around. A hazy mist came from nowhere and forced her eyes to close.

Stay awake! the fire begged her. *Find a way out!*

The mist was making her sleepy. She felt her cheek press against the cold institution floor. A hand closed around hers and she lifted her head slightly to see a shape falling down beside her; a boy with doe eyes and brown hair. Her world disappeared but his hand did not, and she remembered that as she met darkness once more.

TWENTY-NINE

fter the breakfast hall incident, things at DC went back to the way they were when Hunter first arrived: cold, tense and nasty. Dr. Wolfe ordered her locked up in Solitary for forty-eight hours, along with Marcus and Will and anyone else he thought was involved in the dinosaur attack. Hunter stewed over the injustice of it while she rocked back and forth in a strait jacket like some sort of lunatic. Jet deserved to be in Solitary – and he was, for a whole week – but Will did not deserve it, and neither did Mosi or little Sammy, who was only trying to be brave.

While in Solitary, Hunter had time – a lot of time – to think deeply about what she'd seen over the past few weeks. The secret rooms downstairs, the interrogations, the lack in security and the fact that Dr. Wolfe hadn't been at his most murderous in days felt like puzzle pieces that were trying to form a picture, but all it looked like was one of Picasso's famous paintings. Nothing made sense, but she knew without a doubt that something was distracting the doctor.

Hunter squirmed on the hard cement floor, staring at the blank walls and the shadow of the light in the silent corridor outside, and couldn't get her thoughts to shut up. They were choppy like rough waters and didn't make sense. She argued with the voice in her mind until she dipped in and out of consciousness. At one point she opened her eyes and saw a figure of her own self sitting cross-legged against the opposite wall. Only this figure was on fire, flames dancing lightly over her skin, smiling as though she knew something that Hunter herself didn't.

You're going crazy, she said.

"I am not," Hunter replied, and her voice was hoarse. Her need for water deepened every time she woke up.

Then why am I here?

"I don't know, to keep me sane?" She wheezed a dry cough. "To help me organize my thoughts?"

Go ahead then, lay it on me. You were thinking about that little black key, weren't you?

Hunter rolled over and stared at the roof. "It was there the whole time and none of us knew about it."

And now it's gone.

"What?"

Well Dr. Wolfe isn't going to let them anywhere near you, not after what Jet did. Your chances of ever escaping have just been minimized even more so.

"Great. And what about Dr. Wolfe's secret downstairs escapades?"

I know no more than you do, her double snorted. *But it would be worth a look, right?*

Hunter stared at her. The flames were entrancing and made her sleepy. "If it means getting out of here, then yeah, it would definitely be worth it."

What will you do once you get out? Go back to New York? Leave your new friends?

Hunter found herself dreading ever departing from the wonderful people she'd met in ICE. She longed to be with Will in the old quarters, to sit with the others at breakfast, laughing over Zac's jokes or watching Fearne make strange pictures in her food. Despite her present company, Hunter suddenly felt lonelier than ever, and it was in that moment that she started thinking of Eli again.

Each time she imagined him, they were lying on his bed in the soft glow of his lamps, their legs wrapped around each other, their faces inches apart. Everything was warm and joyful. Eli's glasses were slipping to the edge of his nose, but he pushed them up just in time. He smiled and a dimple formed in his cheeks. His fingers left goosebumps on her skin as he ran his hand up her arm, to her shoulder and her neck and then to her chin, where he guided her toward him and pressed his lips against hers.

But his lips were cold, colder than the cement floor on which her cheek rested. Tears spilled from her eyes and dripped onto the ground. It just didn't feel real anymore. She was forgetting him, and every day she felt emptier and emptier and the only things that filled the hole in her heart were the things that distracted her. But there, in Solitary, she was alone.

Not completely alone, said her other self, and something inside Hunter squirmed with uneasiness at the look the girl on fire gave her.

Hunter fell asleep somewhere between that period, and in her dreams, something strange happened.

She was sitting in the dirty, empty aquarium in front of the giant blue tank where Rose and Halle danced. She watched them not with sadness as she had the weeks that followed Eli's death, but with surprising numbness. And as she sat on the bench, someone came and sat beside her. Hunter turned and saw Fearne. The blue waters glimmered in her wide, knowing eyes. And somehow, Hunter wasn't stunned to see her there.

"I very much like these dolphins," said Fearne. "I've seen them before in your dreams."

Hunter wrapped her arms around herself. "So this is another one of your gifts, right?"

"Dream walking," she nodded. "Dr. Wolfe can't stop it, but it's harmless."

"Can you talk to anyone?"

"So far, it's just the people I'm close to. I talk to Will a lot in his dreams. Some of the others I've visited, but they don't like it much."

Hunter gave her a smile. "I like it. I've been a bit lonely lately."

"Yeah," she grinned, "I know what that's like."

"So, if you can visit dreams, does that mean you can find out what happened to Alfie?"

Fearne looked down at her hands. Her face was painted with sadness. "I can't reach him. It's like there's something blocking his mind, a wall I can't break down. I hope Dr. Wolfe didn't..."

"I'm sure he's fine." Hunter didn't really believe that, but she wanted to reassure her anyway. Lately Hunter had felt herself become very protective over the younger children at the institution. Perhaps it was a quality she'd never had the opportunity to use, having grown up alone.

Fearne reached out and put a hand on Hunter's clenched fist. She flinched, expecting it to be cold like Eli's lips, but it felt like nothing but air.

"You're trying to do too much at once, Hunter," she said softly. "Don't feel like it's your responsibility to hold us all up. With the fighting in the fitness room and rescuing us from Alfie… you're too fragile to carry all of this."

"Someone's gotta do it, if not for you and the others, at least for the younger ones." Hunter breathed a laugh. She'd forgotten Fearne was still a child too, but mature enough to be older than even Will.

"Someone does. But right now, you need to put the past behind you."

Rose and Halle laughed and clicked and nodded, as if in agreement with Fearne. Hunter shook her head. "I have. I've moved on, I'm not even thinking about him anymore."

"You can't lie to a mind reader Hunter," she said. "Just tell me what's wrong."

Hunter bit her lip. She wanted to be strong for her, for the others. She didn't want to cry. But Fearne gave her hand another squeeze, and Hunter knew it was pointless. Fearne knew her now well enough.

"I didn't give myself enough time to grieve for him," she murmured through a clogged throat. "I had a few weeks after his death, and then I was brought here, and the only times I have even a minute to spare a thought for him are at night before I go to sleep, and in my nightmares. So much has happened since then that I've forgotten who he was without having moved on."

Nodding, Fearne stood up slowly and walked towards the tank. There, she pressed a small hand against the glass, her breath fogging the surface as she watched the dolphins.

"You need to find peace," she said.

Hunter wiped the tears from her cheeks. "How do I find peace when I'm stuck in hell?"

Fearne turned, her smile twisted to the side. Her green eyes were as bright as the water. She held out a hand to her. "Start here."

Without a thought, Hunter took the young girl's hand. Fearne pressed her palm against the cool glass and a wave of water washed through her. But it wasn't damaging like ice, it seemed to cleanse her. It calmed the burning fire that was tired of being trapped. The water was refreshing.

But it did nothing to surpass the hurt she still felt inside.

"Sometimes it just takes a small step," Fearne said in answer to her thoughts. "I know you won't forget Eli, Hunter, and he won't forget you. When someone dies, the love they give you will never leave."

Something clicked in her mind and she stared down at Fearne in amazement. "That's what you meant when you said to me 'it never leaves you', on my second day here."

"Yep," she beamed. "I may look mad, but it's all up here." She tapped her temple and giggled. "Just know that it's okay to move on and to forget, because our loved ones are always with us. And maybe... after you've moved on... you can make room for another?"

She fixed Hunter with a strong, meaningful gaze and Hunter blinked in surprise. Had Fearne noticed how much time she and Will had been spending together? It was true that Hunter had feelings for Will, but they weren't feelings of love just yet. More of comfort and the need for a friend. Was that because she still loved Eli?

"Thank you Fearne," said Hunter through blurry eyes. "And you're right. It will take time. Lucky I've got all the time in the world."

"Maybe not all the time."

Hunter frowned at the gloom in her eyes, like a giant charcoal cloud looming on the horizon.

"What do you mean?" she asked, thinking of the time she saw Fearne torturing a scientist. "What does Dr. Wolfe have planned? What's gonna happen?"

Fearne whispered something inaudible. It was as if someone controlling the dream suddenly muted her voice.

"What?"

"Now isn't the time for that Hunter," she smiled reassuringly. "Just remember this... you cannot truly find peace until you have said goodbye."

With that, Fearne stood and backed away into the aquarium, swallowed up by the dark room, and vanished.

Hunter looked back at the glass, at the reflection of her dull, red hair and hollow figure from not enough food, at the bags under her eyes that were slowly turning her into a zombie like the others. But while her body looked weak and unhealthy, her mind was strong. Now she had a goal; to pick herself up, to not be that broken girl still hunted by the ghosts of her past. There were bigger things to fear, things that she needed to be strong for. People she needed to fight for.

In the reflection, a shadow suddenly appeared behind her. He had green speckled eyes, dirty blond hair and an innocent, perfect smile. He waved goodbye to her, and then he was gone.

THIRTY

D r. Wolfe's rubber gloves slapped over his wrists with a bloodcurdling *thwack*. Hunter stared up at him, her eyes near-blinded by the light from the overhead beam, and suddenly wished she was back in her solitary cell by herself, a steel door's width from this lunatic.

"Welcome back, Miss Harrison," he said cheerfully and picked up some gauze with metal pliers. "I trust you had a pleasant stay in Solitary?"

She always loathed his humorless small-talk, but found it better just to go along with it.

"Actually, I rather enjoyed the peace and quiet. And the solitude. I did miss the excitement though. Am I mistaken, or did I detect a roar coming from downstairs one night?"

"You're mistaken," he said sharply and lifted the protective mask over his mouth and nose. "It won't be heard again, I can assure you that."

A chill ran through her spine, a feeling she did not welcome back.

"For today, however, I'd like to show you some of the X-rays we took last week."

He reached behind the steel table she lay upon and pulled on a lever, allowing the back of it to rise up like a reclining chair. Hunter – still strapped to the table – had a clear view of the door. Dr. Wolfe's bright screens on her left showed a long succession of X-rays. Every single part of her body was on full display, all ghostly and skeleton-looking. Everything appeared normal, to her eyes anyway.

"Your blood tests are normal, well to your standards. I've come across some unusual toxins, however, which I have matched with Joshua's DNA. I seem to find myself with an interesting number of unknown substances. Tell me, Hunter, when did Joshua get his hands on Feucotetanus?"

Hunter clenched her jaw and refused to meet Dr. Wolfe's oyster eyes. *So he knows about the drug. So what? It's only half the formula, and even then, the rock is far more powerful than the drug alone.*

Dr. Wolfe watched her closely for a moment, but saw she would not crack. He grunted something under his breath and continued.

"I came across Feucotetanus many years ago. The Swedish people are very smart, very well developed. In fact, most of the equipment we use was manufactured there. I had a sample of Feucotetanus, once. Now I wish I made multiple copies, because all the laboratories in Sweden were destroyed. Unfortunately the test subject we were using our last batch on escaped this facility and went into hiding. The drug was too much for his system and there was no way he would have survived more than a few days before it reached his heart and consumed him. Died of hallucinations, I assume. It's a shame we never got to monitor his progress."

Hunter was seriously tempted to spit on the man, purely because of his selfishness. But then suddenly, she remembered something. Joshua had said that her mother operated on a homeless man the night of the fire that killed her father. Was it too much of a coincidence that this man, the man who passed the drug on to her mother, who then gave Hunter her abilities that night when she was conceived, was the same man who escaped this facility? Was she really so close to New York?

Dr. Wolfe didn't seem to notice that her thoughts were somewhere else, and continued talking. "This other... substance, I am unable to identify."

Stick that in your pipe and smoke it, she thought smugly.

"But what I do know is that whatever has infected your blood, it happened long ago. Around the same time that it happened to Joshua, am I correct?"

Hunter didn't answer, staring at her rib cage on the X-ray board, imagining a hole like the center of the earth burning within her, volcanic lava oozing out. That was where the fire dwelled, the living fire that came from inside the stone. Ravenadium.

"And there's something else I found." Dr. Wolfe's smile widened and crooked teeth protruded from within. He was very much enjoying this show and tell. "I think you already know, Hunter, that this substance – when combined with Feucotetanus in the right chemical mix – is what gave you your powers. When I separated the two, I found something fascinating. This other substance... it lives."

Hunter started sweating. Blood throbbed into her head, reminding her of how dehydrated and hungry she was. It had been over twenty-four hours since she'd eaten. The lack of food was confusing her thoughts, and in a moment of panic, the same figure of fire appeared behind Dr. Wolfe, leering over his shoulder. Hunter stared at her reflection in fright.

He's growing closer, she sighed, shaking her head down at Hunter. *He tortured Joshua into revealing the secret, and all you're doing is sitting there.*

Hunter swallowed hard. *He won't find it.*

What if Dr. Wolfe gets lucky? What if he stumbles upon the location, or even finds the samples hidden in Joshua's lab? Would he try to re-create our powers? Would he use our blood samples to make more of us?

"It's a marvelous thing, Hunter," said Dr. Wolfe. "And I *will* find out what this substance is. By any means, I *will* find it."

Hunter gazed in fear at her shadow self, hoping she had something encouraging to say, or at least a way to distract her as Dr. Wolfe started attaching electrode patches to her chest.

Protect our secret, said the fire, and the figure of Hunter melted away into the shadows, leaving her and Dr. Wolfe alone.

Hunter forced herself to the fitness room after a late lunch, because it was the only way she remained strong and not weakened from Dr. Wolfe's surgery. Even if she felt faint, even if her body screamed at her to go straight to her cell and sleep, she wouldn't. She allowed herself to cringe and walk slowly, but that was it.

Mosi, Marcus Will and Chantal were in the fitness room when Hunter entered, working on their combat skills under Mosi's tuition. She heard Marcus hiss at the sight of her bruised arms from Dr. Wolfe's machine, and the burning rage in Will's eyes hit her like headlights from across the room. She stalked to the bench press and slowly lowered herself.

"You look like someone painted you with purple leopard spots." Marcus poked one of the bruises on her right arm and she gasped and slapped him hard on the shoulder.

"Ow! You asshole, that hurt!"

"Jeez, I'm sorry. What the hell happened to you?"

"Don't ask," she grumbled. "When did you both get out?"

"Only this morning," said Marcus.

"Dr. Wolfe was merciful and didn't call me in for surgery," said Will with grit in his tone.

"Lucky you."

"Guess you're not up for a tussle then Hunter?" Marcus raised his eyebrows and nodded to the mat. "Mosi was just teaching me some new moves. I wish we had something more interesting to fight with though. Like targets or knives."

"Hey guys," called Zac from the door. He came in to join them, followed by Sammy and Fearne. Sammy's smile widened at the sight of Hunter and he sprinted up to her.

"Hunter!" he exclaimed and threw his arms around her middle. She groaned and hugged him back as best she could. "Oo, sorry, are you hurt?"

"Just a little sore," she replied. Marcus and Mosi went back to their training. Chantal joined them, mimicking their moves and nodding along with Mosi's instructions. "Has Alfie come back yet?"

Will, Fearne and Sammy shook their heads. "There's been no sign of him," said Will. "Something tells me it won't be anytime soon."

"Alfie doesn't deserve whatever treatment Dr. Wolfe is giving him," said Hunter. "I know exactly what it's like to not have control over my powers. It takes time to grow in strength and perseverance."

"Maybe they'll make him a bracelet soon," said Sammy. "Maybe-"

The room was suddenly silent. The fight had stopped. Hunter peered around Sammy and her heart thudded at the sight of two Men in White in the doorway, staring at their group with menacing stares and rigid posture.

Jamison and Steel.

Hunter had never been formally introduced to Steel the way she had with Jamison, but she had passed him many times in the halls. The two guards were the most powerful, and Dr. Wolfe let them have free reign within the Institution, handing out punishment where they saw fit. Though she shared no connection with the buff army man whose entire upper body pulsed with veins and chest hair, Chantal knew him all too well.

After the way she reacted to Hunter's attack in the bathroom, she knew on some level that Chantal had been through the exact same thing. Zac eventually caved and told her that it was Steel, and no one was there to stop him.

"Well well," said Steel as he strolled into the room, crossing his arms under his pecks. Jamison's sticky gaze didn't leave Hunter's as he closed the door and locked it tight. "What have we here? A little fight club, eh?"

No one said a word.

"Come on," said Steel cheerfully. "Please continue, we're just here to observe."

"Maybe even instruct a little," Jamison added. His voice made Hunter's skin crawl.

"We're not doing anything," said Chantal. Hunter noticed how completely stiff and guarded her exterior had become. Her eyes were blazing blue hate at the both of them.

"Miss Leférve," said Steel. The name seemed to roll off his tongue and Chantal shrank back. "We're not stupid, okay? And we're not going to tell Wolfe. We're just... interested in what goes on in here all the time. So please-" He cocked his head at Mosi and Marcus. "Continue."

He and Jamison stood against the wall. Nervously, Mosi and Marcus shifted their feet and prepared for a fight. Hunter thanked God she wasn't in their position, nor Sammy or Fearne or even Will. She ran her hands over the material of her jumpsuit and watched the fight.

Mosi's face never gave anything away – no strain, no stress, no fear. He made swift movements and neat, harmless punches. Marcus, however, was much sloppier after the pressure of their guests. Sweat dripped from his forehead into his eyes, and his movements were jerky and hesitant. Hunter drew blood from biting her lip so much. Instinctively, she moved a step closer to Will, only to find him nearer than he had been moments ago.

Halfway through the fight, Steel waved for them to cease.

"Stop, please, this fight is so predictable."

Marcus and Mosi broke apart, heaving as Steel stepped onto the mat.

"You need more competition," he said to Mosi. "But I can see that the only person who would have any chance of defeating *you* would be myself or my colleague." Jamison snorted in agreement. "So let's see someone else take a turn, eh?"

Mosi stepped back, his arms clenched so tightly that the veins protruded from his black skin. Nervous butterflies took flight in Hunter's stomach as she looked around the room, following Jamison's gaze. Who would he choose?

"You," he pointed a stubby finger a Sammy, whose face paled in shock. "Your turn, Sparkles."

Sammy sucked in a breath and stumbled backwards against Hunter.

"No." Hunter gripped the boy's shoulders tightly. "He can't fight Marcus, how is that any more fair? In fact, how is any of this fair?"

Steel frowned in mock confusion. "I'm sorry, isn't this what you were doing *before* we came in?"

Hunter didn't answer. If she told him they were training to fight the Men in White when it came time for their escape, she'd be in a far more trouble than she had been a few days ago. Dr. Wolfe couldn't know of their plans.

"It was just for fitness purposes," she murmured. "This is different. Making Sammy fight Marcus is ridiculous and pointless."

"I think you're missing the fun part," said Steel. "*We* get to watch."

"Don't you get enough of that in the Orb?" asked Chantal.

"Not nearly," he sneered. Chantal shrank back again.

"Alright Steel," said Jamison as he pushed himself away from the wall. "I think that's enough."

Steel turned to him, his eyes glinting with malicious anger. "*What?*"

"Miss Harrison is right. There's no fun in watching a scrawny little kid fight this punk."

Marcus pretended not to hear that.

"Oh isn't there?" Steel sneered.

"No," he said, "what's *fair* is watching a fight where the weaker wants to win far more desperately than the stronger opponent. Where there is true determination in each player. No fear, just anger. Just a thirst for a fight." His eyes swept the room and found Hunter's. She knew he was talking about her. Everyone knew. "Am I right, Harrison?"

Very slowly, Hunter got to her feet. Will tensed beside her. Sammy made a whimpering sound. She ignored them all. She ignored her body too, and how much it begged her not to move. Jamison's words were like a magnet to the fire inside her, and it raged from the tips of her toes through every fiber of her being, controlling her limbs and moving her onto the mat. Jamison glared at her greedily as everyone else stepped back.

"A clean fight," he murmured. "No one but us will know."

"You won't tell Dr. Wolfe if I beat you?"

He laughed, the sound tickling her nerves and making her already start to sweat. "What makes you think you're going to beat me?"

She wasn't. She knew that even before she left the bench. Even at full strength, she could never beat a man of his size and stamina. Her head throbbed just standing up straight with nothing to lean on. After a few punches, she would be out regardless of whether he'd hit her or not.

But if it saved Sammy from being forced to fight, she'd take it. She'd make it interesting, maybe even extract a little revenge of her own.

There was no doubt, however, that she would lose. She ignored that fact. "Just get on with it."

Before Jamison made his attack, out of the corner of Hunter's eye she saw Will. She saw the way his hands curled into fists and remembered the bathroom. Would he step in again and save her from Jamison? This was a different situation – voluntary, to say the least – but he seemed to be straining to hold himself back. She gave him just the slightest nod, telling him she was fine, that she could fight for herself, that she wanted to.

Then Jamison attacked.

Hunter knew that Jamison only wanted some sort of heated connection to her again, therefore she knew what was coming before it happened. He didn't want to knock her out, he wanted to make contact. He wanted what he couldn't have all those weeks ago, and this was the only way he could take it. His huge upper body wrapped itself around her and the two of them went crashing to the floor. Déjà vu hit her almost just as hard as the impact of the floor and she momentarily lost her vision. She smelled metal again and felt bile rise in her throat. All she wanted was to run, to get as far away from this man as possible. His weight pressed down on her. He seemed to linger, as if his intentions were purely to be on top of her again.

But Hunter knew what to do this time. Her hands were free; he hadn't thought that far ahead. She pulled her right arm back, summoned all her energy and threw her fist across Jamison's nose, going for a clean break.

They all heard the crack. Blood sprayed down on her. Jamison rolled off Hunter's body and moaned, clutching his nose with one hand and pushing himself up. Despite being afraid, they all wore grins on their faces, all except Jamison. Even Steel looked somewhat amused.

"That all you got?" Hunter heaved, pretending she was stronger than she felt, when really her wrist was throbbing and her vision blurred. "Or are you going to run and cry to Dr. Wolfe about how a *girl* made you bleed?"

Jamison chuckled, unfazed by her trash talk and his broken nose.

"Make your move," she growled.

"Ladies first," he smiled. There was blood in his teeth.

Mosi had told Hunter never to rush into a fight. To see her opponents moves planned ahead in his eyes was not something she'd mastered yet, but she knew more about Jamison than he did about her. So she faked a kick to Jamison's head and when he reached out to grab her foot she stomped it back down, spun her waist and threw her other foot into his jaw. He roared with frustration and took two steps towards her, snatching her raised arm before she could punch again and twisting it, hard. Hunter squealed in pain and ignored everyone around her, focusing on making the fight last as long as possible. Maybe then, they would leave the others alone.

Jamison grabbed her other wrist and pulled her close.

"You're a slippery one, I'll give you that," he said in her ear.

Hunter breathed hard through her teeth and tried to wriggle away. She stepped on his foot by accident and Jamison lost his balance. The both of them went toppling to the floor.

Hunter lay on her stomach, the world bending and twirling. She could feel Jamison beside her. As she rolled over on her back, he crawled over her. He seemed sick of the fight as well, for his fist was beside his head and she saw it coming. The fight was over, and the last thing she would see was Jamison's hungry, blood-stained face. She didn't want that. She turned her head and found Will with his hand wrapped in Fearne's, his eyes glued to hers, but they weren't afraid. They were pleased.

You did well, they said.

Pain came, and then nothing.

THIRTY-ONE

fter passing out, Hunter woke up in her cell under her rug, afraid to move. She knew there would be more pain, so she wanted to avoid it as long as possible. She turned her head to the glass door and saw that the lights were all on. It was still day.

She stared at the corridor for minutes, thinking about the fight. When would the cruelty end? When would they stop being victims? Would she ever be able to walk the halls without fearing the presence of the man who was so addicted to her, to her body? A cold shiver passed through her. She felt dirty and wanted a shower. She wanted ten showers.

As she watched the lights flicker in the corridor, nothing happened. No one passed. *Where is everyone?*

Hunter told herself to get up. She had a lot to do. She wanted to find the others, to make sure they were all okay and that the fight had ended with her unconsciousness.

When Hunter finally willed herself to stand, she felt as though someone had jabbed her with a stick in random spots all over her body, and they were all aching like giant bruises. Her head swam. She caught her reflection in the glass and cringed. *Why, why do I always look like a beat-up ghost?* She told herself it was just the lighting and stumbled out of her cell.

An empty corridor stretched before her. She glanced behind her, but no one was around. *This is just too weird,* she thought. Hunter started towards the stairs when a cell door opened up ahead and little Sammy hurried out. He caught sight of Hunter and his face immediately lit up.

"Hunter!" He sprinted towards her and, for the second time that day, he nearly bowled her over with a hug. She would likely never get used to the contact of the small boy, but she dared not refuse.

"So things must have calmed down after what happened with Jamison," she smiled down at him. "This place is dead."

"Not exactly," he murmured, his pale face devoid of color. "Everyone's in the Orb."

Hunter's heart dropped. "What? Who's in the Orb?"

"It's not a fight," he replied. His eyes swam with fear, fear of the unknown. "They told us to go there now. Something's happening, I don't know what. We have to go or the guards will get us into trouble."

He tugged at her hand and Hunter followed him to the stairs, instead going up. Hunter's stomach was slowly twisting around and every step they took was a step closer to whatever horror lay inside. She kept thinking *please don't let it be Will in there again, or Fearne. Hell, don't let it be anyone who doesn't deserve it.* Which, come to think of it, was none of them. But Sammy said it wasn't a fight. Then what fresh hell did Dr. Wolfe have in store?

Sammy dragged her to the next floor, and they ran down a corridor longer than the cell block to a double gray door. It opened into a dark room with two doors on the left and right that read 'Seating 1' and 'Seating 2'. She had no time to stop the nausea from creeping up into her throat before Sammy pulled her through door number one and she found herself in an enclosed room much like a theatre, with rows of metal benches on a slope, all looking down upon a giant glass screen. Through that screen, they had a clear view of the inside of the Orb.

It was strange seeing hell from the outside. It appeared much smaller from their view. But the people down below looked like little dolls walking around in the blank space where she had unleashed her flames. Hunter was shocked to see that they weren't kids. They were scientists.

"Hunter!" Sammy scampered to a seat down the front with the others. About five Men in White sat up the back with arms folded over tasers, ready to fire. Jet and Mikayla sat close together a few rows down near the other wall. Hunter sidestepped through the isle and squeezed in beside Will and Marcus near the front.

"What's going on?"

173

"Don't know," said Marcus. "About five minutes ago we were all ushered down here. The guards said nothing, and there was an announcement over the speakers that we had a special screening in the Orb. But no one's in trouble."

"Benji is missing," said Will.

"What?" Hunter looked around and counted faces. He was right; only Benji was missing. Something was wrong, and her stomach didn't agree with it. She hated being there, watching the horror down below.

"He wasn't at dinner." Marcus leant forward and tapped Ryo on the shoulder. "Hey, when did you last see Benji?"

When she turned, Hunter saw that her usually mischievous and glowing expression had fallen completely. Tears streaked her face. "The guards took him from his cell. They didn't say anything. He never did anything wrong!"

Hunter leaned over and put a hand on her shoulder. "It's going to be okay."

"I wouldn't bet on it," said Zac. He was pointing to the glass window, his voice empty. "Look."

Inside the Orb where the scientists were gathering in the center, they could see some sort of machine being rolled out. It was a long black platform rather like a conveyor belt, with two sturdy poles on either side. Behind it was a more lethal device; a wall with silver spikes decked out all over it. Anyone who ran into that would be staked in over twenty parts of their body.

"What the hell-" Zac whispered.

"I don't like the look of this," said Chantal uneasily.

Hunter was literally on the edge of her seat, straining to see who was being dragged out behind the machine, even though she already knew. Two Men in White carried a boy with blond spikey hair, skinny as a runt. He was struggling madly between them. The scientists – about four of them – set up the machine and stepped away. Benji was placed on top of the conveyor belt, his wrists attached to long chains that snaked around the poles. He was heaving, and she wondered if he might faint. He kept twisting his head around and looking at the wall of spikes directly behind him. It was all starting to click together, in his mind and in Hunter's. She turned and glanced at Will, whose face was a mask of hatred, his hands clenched together, his jaw jerking from side to side. He knew as well.

"Welcome, ladies and gentlemen of The Advanced Genetics and Human Exploration Institution, to our first demonstration." Dr. Wolfe's voice rang loud and clear over an intercom. All of them turned to each other with the exact same panicked expressions.

"The Advanced Genetics and Human *Exploration* Institution? Who the hell are they?" asked Marcus.

"They must be some sort of science company," said Mosi. "Like this one, only they probably don't imprison kids against their will. They must be watching."

"What does he mean by demonstration?" asked Zac.

"I think we're about to find out." Hunter wrapped her arms around herself and wished she could take her eyes off the sight down below.

"Today, we'll be starting with subject number 0895," Dr. Wolfe continued. "Benjamin Given, age twelve. Subject has the ability to run at outstanding speeds. Our research thus far has driven this subject to a speed of ten times the speed of sound, or up to 1,000,000 miles per hour. We're attempting today to test the subject's limits using a specially designed treadmill. This will determine exactly how fast the subject can run when faced with certain peril."

"Certain peril?" Zac shouted suddenly. "There's a goddamn porcupine up his ass!"

"Shut up!" one of the guards yelled.

Benji was looking around at the scientists who were getting ready their clipboards, their cameras and the controls for the machine. He was shouting something at them, something that they couldn't hear over the sound of a buzzer. On the glass, they could see the reflection of a timer counting down from ten in large red numbers.

Hunter wasn't sure why she did it, but she needed some sort of support before she slipped into panic. She reached beside her and gripped Will's strong, warm hand in hers, lacing her fingers between his. As the buzzer reached its final count and everyone held their breath, Will wrapped his fingers tighter in hers.

And then, Benji began to run.

THIRTY-TWO

Welcome to Livingston," said Joshua aloud and both Jenny and Eli jumped upright in their seats and stared at their surroundings.

Day five into their travels, and things were starting to get a little chilly. Normally, Jenny would have happily sat in a car and driven across the country. It felt unreal that she was suddenly there, halfway across America, with two complete strangers on a mission to find a crazy scientist smart enough to return someone's memory, a memory lost while frozen at minus 180°C.

Hey, it beats being dead.

Jenny stared at the raging winds, hoping Joshua was as good a driver as he boasted and could get them to the hotel quick. There was a queasy feeling in her stomach.

"I'm starving, can we stop somewhere?" Eli moaned from the back. "I hear there's a really good rib and chop house?"

"We can eat at the hotel," Joshua replied.

Eli leaned forward and peered through the window. "God it's like a cyclone out there," he said. "You'd think it would be at least a little mild, being the beginning of September."

"Livingston is one of the windiest places in America," said Joshua as though he were reading out of a textbook. He turned to Eli and added, "it just feels cold, but really it isn't."

"Not sure I believe that," said Eli, and he stuck his mouth in his scarf. It was attached to a beanie with a bear face and two ears. It looked absolutely ridiculous, but kind of cute. They'd stopped for lunch at a restaurant with a gift shop, and Eli bought it, if not for the chilly weather but to annoy and embarrass Joshua. "And anyway, where are we staying?"

"The Murray hotel."

"I've heard about that place," said Eli. "My dad says it's rowdy."

"I've called ahead and booked a room as far from the bar as possible. We'll get a good night sleep and then tomorrow it's on to Spokane early morning."

"Awesome," said Eli sarcastically. "Just gotta say, guys, this road trip hasn't exactly been the most thrilling of adventures."

"Would you rather be at school?" asked Jenny.

"Yeah, but we're driving across 3000 miles of quality American country and all we see are the insides of hotel rooms and rest stops."

"If you didn't sleep so much, you'd see a hell of a lot more," Joshua snapped at him. "Oh, but if you'd rather be back in New York in the hands of the Agents, that's fine with me."

"You're just grumpy because you won't let anyone else drive and now your eyes are melting out of your skull."

Joshua sighed deeply. Jenny noted that, had he not been concentrating so hard, he would have pinched the bridge of his nose or wiped his hand over his jaw. *Oh God, I'm picking up on his mannerisms now? What are we, a couple?*

The uneasiness in her stomach increased and she curled her arm around it. *Maybe I'm sick because I ate too many of those philly burgers back at the café near Laurel.* But Jenny knew herself better. It wasn't the food. It was something far worse. The pain started off in her stomach, but it always ended up near her heart.

Joshua was staring at her, his eyes darting back to the road. "You okay there?"

She nodded, not wanting to distract him from the road.

The storm started clearing as they drove deeper into the main part of town. Most of the shops were closed off and the street lights guided their way to the motel on the corner. Jenny gathered her things and stuffed them into the bag as he pulled the car into park. Eli wrapped his bear scarf tighter around his neck and gave her the thumbs up, then bravely opened his door.

Screaming winds hit them hard in the chest like a punch from a boxer. Joshua shouted at them to go inside and he would get the bags, but Jenny refused. The three of them threw open the boot, hauled their backpacks over their shoulders and sprinted through the heavy front doors into the Murray hotel lobby.

A tribute to western history, the Murray hotel was a cozy, elegant building with as much charm as the Hilton and even more charisma. Loud country music played in the bar and the lobby was filled with people coming and going from the restaurant and upstairs floors.

Joshua – who would normally storm straight to the receptionist desk to sign them in without caring what the hotel looked like – did a double take himself. Jenny watched him lower his bags slowly and then march over to the nearest fireplace where an array of snow globes were perched on the mantelpiece. Even Eli stopped gaping to frown with her as Joshua picked up each snow globe, examined them closely, and then shook them. A group of people rugged up in coats sitting around the fire were gazing at him, dumbfounded, murmuring and laughing to each other. Joshua returned to them with a smile on his face.

"What was that all about?" asked Eli. "Are you retarded?"

Joshua's grin faded instantly and he huffed. "I prefer the term *obsessive*, if you don't mind. I'm going to check us in." And with that, he headed straight to the front desk before Jenny and Eli could burst out laughing.

"Ooo-kay then," Eli snorted. "I guess we learn more about that freak as we go along."

Jenny laughed and suggested they move to a few empty chairs to release the burden of their heavy bags. Eli continued to stare open-mouthed at the lobby of the hotel.

When Joshua returned, he wasn't happy. "I specifically requested a room on the opposite side, but I'm too tired to care right now," he said. "Come on, let's go."

The moment Jenny stood up, she was hit with a searing pain in her chest, a pain so familiar that she looked at Joshua with wide, fearful eyes and her legs gave way beneath her. Joshua shouted her name and grabbed her shoulders. The look on his face was of pure panic.

"Joshua," she whispered. "Take me… to hospital."

THIRTY-THREE

In his sixteen years imprisoned in ICE institution, Will couldn't remember ever being more furious. There was a time when he saw one of the Men in White beat down a young girl who told him he was ugly, and she was locked in the infirmary for a week to heal. That made him pretty angry, but it hardly compared to his exploding rage at that moment as Benji – sweet, silent Benji – was chained to a treadmill and forced to run.

'Run' was actually a very tame word for what Benji was doing at that moment. Even if he did trip up or stop sprinting, the speed of the treadmill would send him zooming back five feet into the wall of spikes, killing him instantly. There was no way of stopping it. No panic button, no safe word, no hand-up-if-it-hurts. If he made one slip, Benji would be dead.

That's why Will found himself so livid with rage that his grip on Hunter's hand caused her to gasp and tear it away. He turned to her and saw the same look in her eyes. The same agonizing fury. It was easier to stare into the golden, warm depths of her eyes than it was to watch the horror below. So he took her hand back again and held it a little more gently, and when she turned to watch the demonstration, he simply stared at her hair instead.

He could tell by the expression on her face – and the hisses and gasps from the others – that Benji was tiring. He'd been sprinting at an impossible speed for at least five minutes now. Will forced himself to turn his gaze to the race below where Benji had become a blur of white and the scientists were chatting to each other and recording every second. On the glass, there were giant red numbers displaying the speed of the treadmill. Will almost lost his breath.

"I believe we've reached a new record Benji!" came Dr. Wolfe's voice over the intercom and the moment Benji started to come into focus again and the treadmill slowed down, each of them let out a long breath of air. The scientists became jittery, like ants that were afraid of being squished, and when Benji finally slowed to walking speed, his legs were quivering and twitching and his body was drenched in sweat. All of the color was drained from his face, giving him more of a skeleton look than any of them. He collapsed on the treadmill and his body rolled back as far as the chains would allow, and then he was simply being grazed by the conveyor belt until it stopped and he was unchained and dragged out of the Orb.

As Dr. Wolfe spoke up over the announcement – something about the company's goal to test limits and further increase abilities – Will could feel darkness twisting and brewing inside of him. He'd always been a quiet, tortured soul. But seeing this and fearing what was to come made him that much more desperate for freedom, and to free the others as well.

"I can't believe how *sick* that was," said Chantal through her teeth. "I honestly feel like I might vomit."

"Who else has to do that?" asked Zac, genuine fear in his tone as he pointed to the scene down below. "They can't put me on a treadmill, I can't run at all!"

"They're probably going to test all of our powers in different ways," said Marcus. He wiped a hand over his mouth and shook his head. "There's no way they're testing me."

"Or me," said Chantal. "And who would *watch* that? Where do all these awful scientists come from, is there some other institution like this in the world? Has *everyone* turned evil?"

Will listened to them argue, sensing the fear that underlined their anger. Hunter remained silent by his side, and after a few more minutes, he could feel her shaking. He knew she was about to explode. If she didn't have her power restraint, he presumed they'd all be burnt to a crisp.

"Are you okay?" he whispered to her.

Her teeth were clenched so tightly that she didn't answer him. But she said it with her eyes.

Then, Hunter got up and stormed to the door, disappearing behind it.

Will gazed down at the Orb, the others following Hunter's lead and clearing out of the theatre room, but he felt as if his butt were glued to the bench. He was so afraid for the others, dreading the next few days and who would be up next. Most of all, Will wondered if he'd ever get to see anything good in his life. What if he died there? Suddenly, Will wanted more than anything to find happiness. To know that there was something more in his life, something to look forward to. A happily ever after.

Enough of this misery and torture, he decided. *We need to get out of this place.*

THIRTY-FOUR

Y ou sick son of a *bitch*!"

Had the fire not been trapped inside her, Hunter was sure she would have torched Dr. Wolfe to a crisp and happily danced over his ashes. But all she could do was charge at him and be satisfied with the momentary panic in his eyes as he backed up into the corner of the surgery room where he'd been cowering after the demonstration, ducking away from Hunter's raised fist.

Two Men in White grabbed each of her arms and pinned them hard behind her. One of them was Steel. She was angry enough not to be afraid of him, nor did she notice the pain as he stretched her arms almost out of their sockets. Hunter shrugged hair out of her face and growled at the old man who straightened his coat and reformed that trademark wicked smile of his.

"How could you do that to Benji, huh?" she hissed, wrenching her arms from their grip only to be pulled back harder. "What was the purpose of your little death game?"

Dr. Wolfe undid the cuffs of his coat and started rolling up his sleeves. "The purpose, Miss Harrison, was and always is for research. As I said in the announcement, the subject was tested to his limits. And as you saw in the demonstration, he exceeded any test we've ever subjected him to. Benjamin did an outstanding job, and because of his efforts, this company has gathered more scientific minds committed to our operations. Those scientists from The Advanced Genetics Institution were largely impressed."

"So it's about recruiting new staff then, because you're so lacking at the moment." She glared at the two Men in White, but as always, they remained completely obtuse.

"As a matter of fact, we are presently in dire need of staff, Miss Harrison, but it isn't your business to know why. Now I have a lot of work to do in preparing for tomorrows demonstration, if you wouldn't mind-"

"You're having another demonstration *tomorrow?*" Suddenly she didn't feel so brave and relaxed her clenched fists.

Dr. Wolfe switched on a computer monitor and picked up the mouse. "Yes, that was what I meant when I said that Benji was the *first* test subject. The scientists want to see more of what you can do."

"More of... of us?" *Okay... I might just be sick again.* Hunter didn't want to appear weak in front of the man – if he was even human and not the spawn of the devil – so she lured rage from deep inside her and yanked her right hand from the grip of the other guard. He fumbled with her, but not before Hunter was able to twist around and knee him in the groin. The man gasped out a puff of air and bent over. Hunter started scratching at Steel's face, but he snatched her other wrist and brought it around across her chest. She now had one arm behind her and one bent around her front. Steel breathed heavily on her neck and Hunter felt sicker still.

Dr. Wolfe stepped forward, his expression deadly, his eyes as black as his soul. "Might I remind you," he sneered, "that this is *not* vacation camp. This is an institution of *science*, Miss Harrison, and I will do everything in my power to better our knowledge of the limits of mutants like yourself, whether it's testing Benji, or you, or any of the other subjects here. It's not only my job, but it's my life. My passion. It's who I am."

Hunter wanted to insult him, hell – she was even tempted to lean forward and bite his crooked nose off if she wasn't so afraid of being poisoned or acquiring some sort of disease, but she refrained herself. If she didn't know any better, she'd say he was trying to provoke her. To make her miserable. And so far, he was succeeding.

Dr. Wolfe nodded slowly and straightened up. "I'm not going to lock you in Solitary if that's what you're worried about. Circumstances are different now. Things have been somewhat... tranquil around here these past couple of weeks. In fact, it's been rather like vacation camp, if you ask me. But those days are over. Ends have been met-" Hunter swallowed at the tone he implied, making her fear for Alfie and his absence, "-and I'm very pleased to inform you that, as of today… you and the others will experience exactly what it feels like to be a beautiful freak of nature, on a whole new level."

Her blood ran cold and Dr. Wolfe nodded at the guards to take her back upstairs. Hunter was whirled around and shoved to the door.

"Wait!" he called back. "Do me a favor, Miss Harrison, take this to the common room and find a place to tack it up, would you?"

He shoved a piece of paper in Hunter's hand and ushered them out the door. The moment she was alone with Steel and the other guard, she wrenched her hands away.

"I can walk," she snapped. Steel's eyes glinted. They followed close behind her and Hunter flipped the page around and read the list of names under the title 'DEMONSTRATION SCHEDULE: SEPTEMBER 3RD – SEPTEMBER 9TH'.

Day 1 – Benjamin Given (1900hrs)
Day 2 – Mosi Sofana (0800hrs)
Day 3 – William Evans (0800hrs)
Day 4 – Hunter Harrison (1900hrs)
Day 5 – Marcus Slater (0800hrs)
Day 6 – Jet Slater (1900hrs)
Day 7 – Fearne Matherson (0800hrs)

Holy shit.
Hunter turned to the guards. "Is this for real?"
They pretended as though she hadn't spoken.

If Hunter ever thought this place couldn't get any worse, she was clearly wrong. How in hell did Dr. Wolfe find all these people who would willingly sit and watch children be tortured and not do a *thing* about it? Were they all brainwashed?

Hunter immediately considered something she never thought could be possible. Was that what Dr. Wolfe had Fearne doing? Brainwashing all of the new scientists into believing as he did; that this was all some sort of greater-good project and they were just guinea pigs, just cells walking around in a body of skin and bones?

Hunter was hit with a powerful urge to escape. As she was marched back through the long corridor along the laboratory window, she ran through possible plans and came up with exactly zero. With the power restraints hidden even better than before after Alfie's attack in the breakfast hall, their chances would be near impossible.

Hunter's thoughts were so far away that she almost didn't notice a ruckus in the laboratories until an alarm was suddenly blaring.

The guards froze.

"What's happening?" she shouted at them. They exchanged glances and grabbed both her arms, hurrying to the elevator. "Wait, what's-"

A mechanical woman's voice spoke through a speaker system over the alarm. "Warning," she said neutrally, "Terminal One disarmed. All personal please report to DC. Warning. Terminal One disarmed. All personal please report to DC." She continued to repeat the message, and once again the guards were stunned. Scientists in the laboratory were all pouring in from the offices, running in the same direction; to the exit at the back.

"Steel," said the shorter guard. "We need to get down there."

"Shut up Eddie," hissed Steel. "Just get her upstairs, and don't say anything. I'm heading down to-" he stopped himself, shot Hunter a hard look and took off running back to the other end of the corridor.

Hunter was led away from the chaos to the elevator. They waited, and waited, until finally the door opened and six guards spilled out, jogging straight past them to the other end. Hunter's mind was racing. Something bad was happening if an alarm had to be raised, and what did the woman's warning mean? What was Terminal One? And was DC code for something other than the name Zac had used to describe this institution?

The moment the door opened, Eddie shoved her into the corridor and stabbed the down button. Two more guards pushed past her into the lift. Zac and a few of the younger kids were peering out of the common room door. Then, the door slid shut on the guards and the alarm was ceased.

"What the hell is going on?" Zac asked.

"Did you hear the announcement?" Hunter snapped at him.

"Nope, just saw a bunch of guards sprint to the elevator from the breakfast hall. There's, like, no one here. It's empty."

Hunter had no idea what the hell was going on, but it had to be a sign. There were no guards. No security. Despite Dr. Wolfe's warning and his big 'things will be different now' speech, everything had turned around. Wherever the guards were heading, it was obviously going to occupy them, hopefully giving Hunter and the others time to talk about an escape.

Her prayers were being answered.

"Where is everyone?"

Zac shrugged. "I dunno, the breakfast hall, the common room, I think Chantal and some of the other girls are in the shower. Benji is asleep, poor guy, I just-"

"Round up as many people as you can and tell them all to meet in the common room," she ordered. Her blood was pounding in her ears, her mind working like a speeding train. She had to treat this time like precious diamonds. There would likely never be another chance.

Zac opened his mouth to ask questions, but her expression must have been enough to silence him, because he spun and ran to the stairs immediately.

"What's going on?" Imogen, a young girl with auburn curls, pouted up at Hunter.

"I'm not sure Immi, but let's go in here and wait for the others." She ushered the three kids through the door to the common room and found Ryo sitting with Marcus and Mosi on the couches, looking grim.

"Hey, what happened to you?" asked Marcus. They all sat up quickly, sensing something was wrong. "After the demonstration you just took off-"

"I had some rage to vent," she snapped.

"Yeah," he scoffed, "I know what that's like. We were just in the fitness room boxing out a little rage of our own when all the Men in White started disappearing."

"They're all gone, down to the labs," said Hunter. She threw him the piece of paper. "And I hate to bring you more disturbing news, but Dr. Wolfe gave me this."

Ryo, Marcus and Mosi gathered around to read the list. The children scrambled on the couches, waiting like rats for food, having no idea what kind of terror awaited them.

After reading the list, Marcus went to tear it up, but Hunter shouted "stop!" and snatched it from his hand.

"This is complete bullshit, now *we're* going to be tested too?"

"If that wasn't obvious, you're more stupid than I thought," said Ryo, crossing her arms.

Marcus glared at her.

Footsteps sounded outside and Zac entered, followed by Chantal and Mikayla with wet hair, Jet and a sleepy Benji. He leaned against the door frame, his legs shaking with each step he took. He looked worse than Will on Hunter's first day.

"This is all I can find," Zac heaved and collapsed on the single armchair. "I looked everywhere."

"What about Will?" Fearne burst through the door. She stared around at all the faces. "Where is he?"

Hunter wasn't about to give away Will's secret hideout, which was where she presumed he would be, especially after what happened to Benji in the Orb.

"I'll find him," said Hunter. She turned to Marcus. "Explain that list. I'll be right back."

"Wait, what's going on Hunter?" asked Fearne. Her eyes widened as she caught the vibes of panic within her thoughts. "Something downstairs?"

"In the labs?" asked Zac.

"No," said Hunter. "Down further. When I was in the labs, a voice came over the speakers saying something was disabled in Terminal One, and all personal needed to report to DC."

"What?" Jet stared around the room. "But... we're *in* DC."

"Zac, where did you hear that name?"

He shrugged, looking around at all the faces. "I dunno, some guy who was here before me."

"We've always called it Death Cave," said Mosi solemnly.

"It's just a nickname," said Jet, "it's supposed to be funny."

"Well apparently it's a name for something else," said Hunter. "Now stay here, I'm getting Will."

"Why?" asked Chantal. "Why are we all here?"

Hunter sighed, time ticking away, and looked around at each of the worried, anxious, trusting faces all gazing at her. How she – the new girl – had become a figurative leader, she couldn't explain. But she was sure that once she told them of her idea, there would be an uprising.

But then she remembered. Mosi and Marcus wanted the same thing.

She turned to them. "Now's your chance."

Marcus frowned and looked at Mosi, who always knew exactly what to do. He nodded.

"What's going on?" asked Jet.

"Trust me, it's important. Just... hang tight."

With that, she sprinted past Marcus and Mosi to the door on other side of the room that led to the boy's bathroom.

"Where are you going?" called Marcus.

"To find Will!"

"There isn't enough time!" called Chantal.

"I don't care!" Hunter yelled back to them. "I'm not doing any of this without him."

Then she was running, through the door and down the stairs to the secret passageway in the boy's bathroom.

THIRTY-FIVE

It was like something of a dream. The institution felt completely barren as Hunter sprinted down the empty corridor. She took the second door into the boys toilets, taps dripping, no sound but the buzzing of electrical lights. It made her uneasiness rise like dust swept up in a cyclone.

Hunter slipped through the secret door and kept her hands on the wall to guide her as she hurried down the old wooden staircase. She winced at the sounds she made, but knew it was more important to hurry. Once she reached the old quarters and felt along the wall again, she swung open the door to their room and found Will sitting on the bed with a book between his hands.

"Hey, you're-"

"We have to go," she said and grabbed the book.

"What are you-"

Hunter intended to throw the book at the wall, snatch Will and run. But her hands froze when she saw the title 'Holy Bible' written in silver script on the black leather binding.

"You're reading the Bible?" she gaped. "Where'd you get this?"

"In one of the other rooms," he shrugged. Then his eyes narrowed. "Why does it matter?"

Hunter let out a laugh. For some reason she was angry, and she couldn't understand why. Not when there were far more important things to worry about. "Because it's bullshit. If there's a God, why are we all being tortured like this?"

"Don't ask me, I'm not a priest." He reached for the book and snatched it back from her hands, almost protectively. "But I need something better to cling onto in this awful place Hunter, and after what we just saw with Benji, an almighty God is good enough for me."

"Well cling to this then: we're getting out of here."

Will lowered his hands slowly. "What?"

"Come on, we don't have much time. There's something going on in the labs downstairs, literally every single security guard has disappeared. We're completely alone up there, and it's the best chance we've got right now."

"But how?"

She grabbed his hand and smiled. "So far, I have no idea."

"Great," he sighed, but he didn't protest when she started pulling him towards the door.

They crept back into the corridor, the chill sinking deep into their skin and the puddles from leaks in the pipes making their footsteps all the more obvious. But just as they were nearing the door to the stairs, Hunter heard something from behind them and they both spun around.

A light swished under the crack of the other door at the end of the corridor. Hunter and Will could hear voices, soft at first but now becoming louder. Someone was shouting to hurry, and they sped up. More light raced past, as if from a flashlight.

"Who is that?" Will uttered in her ear.

"I dunno," she said, "but I have a feeling it's something to do with what's happening in Terminal One."

"Terminal what? Hunter, what's going on?"

She ignored his questions and snatched his sleeve, dragging him down the corridor and creeping to the door. The voices were dying out to the left. *We'll lose them!*

"Does this door open?" She ran her fingers over the dark steel-trap door with a large latch and no padlock.

"I dunno, I've never-"

Hunter grabbed the latch and pulled hard towards her. It slid aside with surprising ease, and the door creaked in. Hunter smiled, put her hand on the door and pushed.

It led them to another dark corridor, but a little way down the left they could see a faint glow of light on the walls. *This must be an old passageway that the scientists use. The electricity is running, so it has to be useful.*

"This way," she whispered and started creeping down the low-roofed corridor.

"Hunter, I know you're curious and stuff, but I'm not exactly up for more punishment, okay?" She glanced back at him and could just see the crease in his forehead half-hidden by his hair. Light from up ahead danced like candlelight in his eyes. "I don't want to go through what happened to Benji today."

Hunter bit her lip. *He'll find out soon enough.* She kept walking. "I hate to tell you this Will, but you don't have a choice. Seven of us were picked for the demonstrations. Benji was only the first. You're up after Mosi."

Will kept silent as they walked.

When they grew closer to the light, Hunter saw that the corridor was a long underground tunnel lined with fixed light bulbs connected by wiring along the top. The scientists had vanished without a trace.

"I thought you said we were going to escape," said Will as they walked. "What are we doing down here if the others are upstairs?"

"Why do you think that all the guards disappeared? Something Dr. Wolfe has kept hidden is suddenly a threat, and I'd give anything to know what it is. It could be the key to getting out of here."

"Or it could get us into serious trouble."

Hunter didn't reply, even though her heart was skipping beats and her entire body felt clammy with sweat.

The corridor took a bend and there were two doors on their left and right. A flickering bulb in the corner gave them enough light to see the inscription on each door.

"Morgue," Hunter read, "or Cell Block?" She turned to Will. "You pick."

Will frowned. "What do they need a morgue for?"

She peered in through the small barred window. Inside the dark room there was a bank of square hatches like those used for the storage of safety deposit boxes. At the back was a giant black door rather like a furnace for cremation. There were other various objects in the room, but it all looked very morgue-like to her.

She backed away so Will could peer inside. "Do you think this is where he puts the bodies of those who die here?"

Will's face paled and she wished she'd never mentioned it. He could only be thinking that this room would be his death bed sooner rather than later.

He swallowed. "I guess so."

Hunter wrapped her arms around herself. The only thing she could do was put it in the back of her mind and stew on it later. "Come on, let's keep going."

They took the other door marked 'Cell Block'. This corridor was lit also by light bulbs joined with wiring at intervals over cell doors like those in the old quarters. They were so old, they practically blended into the wall. There were faint numbers and letters etched along the top between each light bulb, about two meters apart. Hunter ran her hand down the wall as she went, feeling the moisture. It was danker down there than in the old quarters, if that were even possible.

It's like we're in a cave.

Hunter froze. Will bumped into her back and stopped too. Stretching on her toes, Hunter strained to see what was written near the ceiling and read the number '17' beside the letters 'DC'.

"Death Cave," she breathed.

"What?"

"All this time, I thought Zac was referring to the entire institution as Death Cave, because it's always so cold. But it came from the scientists, from the guards. From here. Look," she pointed to the number on the other side that read '16 DC'. "These are all cells. Will," she turned to him and swallowed down the sickly lump in her throat. "We just found the real Death Cave."

Before Will could open his mouth, there came a very faint sound that raised the hairs on the back of her neck: A moan for help was coming from the cell on her left. Hunter turned her head and a scream fell out of her mouth.

There was a face between the bars.

THIRTY-SIX

J enny?" Joshua shot up in his chair beside the hospital bed. He saw her eyelashes flicker and something of a mumble escaped her lips. "Can you hear me?"

Jenny's eyes fluttered open and she squinted at the bright light. Joshua released the tension he'd been holding ever since she fainted in his arms. Despite ignoring her and pretending he didn't care about the kiss, Joshua still worried, and the only person he'd ever had to worry about was Hunter.

"What happened?" Jenny muttered, her voice hoarse.

Joshua grabbed the plastic cup of water and gently fed it to her. "You had a minor heart attack. You've been asleep for 24 hours, but your vitals are well."

"A heart attack? But I thought everything was fine."

He stared at her a moment, struggling with the truth. It had been hours since he'd found out about her illness, and since then he hadn't been able to get the thought out of his mind.

"Everything is fine," he assured her. "The doctor said it's uncommon for this type of occurrence given your condition."

"My condition?"

"Yes. Because of your cancer."

Jenny went pale and her small hands clenched the hospital rug. Joshua couldn't help but remember the very last time she lay in a bed like this just moments before he almost killed her. "It's true, I... I had lung cancer. I'm not a smoker, I was just unlucky. It was early in the treatment when the fire happened at school, and then the smoke, it… it accelerated the disease. I was pretty close to dying when you came, and when I woke up in the lab I thought I was dead."

"The doctor said the cancer is gone."

Jenny's eyes suddenly filled with tears. "It's gone?" A small chuckle escaped her lips. She reached out for his hand and found it. Joshua flinched, remembering the other night in the hotel room, but he couldn't take his eyes away from her glowing face. "I'm cured. Joshua, you cured me." Joy coated her words and his heart throbbed, a strange and warm feeling he'd never felt before. At least, not in a long time.

"What do you mean?"

"I thought there was some mistake, and so I checked everything over in your lab when you went out. I kept fearing I'd have another episode and pass out, but it never happened. And that's when I forgave you. You had no idea, but you saved my life."

"I did it for selfish reasons though." He took his hand away and shook his head. "I needed you to help me get Hunter back. She wouldn't talk to me after what she thought I did. And I was so lost, I didn't know how it was possible that she'd beaten the fire. And… when I went to the hospital and found you I…"

"What?"

"There was… there was something in your eyes. You reminded me of someone. You were terrified of me, and that's understandable, but you were… happy to go. I thought you'd given up."

Jenny shook her head. "I knew my time was coming, but obviously I was wrong. And now… I don't care where I go. I'm alive for a reason, and it's led me here."

Joshua was speechless, his throat becoming strangely thick.

"Joshua?" she continued. "Can I ask you something?"

"Sure," he said hoarsely.

"Why didn't you kill me? Why didn't the ice inside you make you kill me?"

He grit his teeth. "I guess… I had control all along. Not much, but enough to know I didn't want to be a killer. The Iceman told me it was necessary, that I was doing it for Hunter. But I'm really not that person. I never intended for anyone to get hurt."

194

"Uh…" There was a knock at the door and Eli stepped inside the room with three burrito wraps in his hands. "Sorry to interrupt the chick flick moment but… I brought lunch."

"Thank you Eli," Jenny smiled.

Joshua grumbled his thanks but was in no mood to eat. He wanted to shoo the boy back out the door, because he still had questions to ask Jenny.

"Listen Eli, we-"

"Did you know there's a cop outside the room?" he asked casually and bit into his vegetarian burrito.

Joshua jumped to his feet. "What? He's visiting?"

"Nah," said the boy through a mouthful of food. A piece of lettuce took a dive on his knee and he flicked it off. "He's like right outside our door just… standing there. He wasn't there when I left, so I guess he just arrived."

"Did he say anything to you?"

Eli shook his head. Then his expression fell. "Wait, do you think he's here for *us*? Oh my God, are we gonna get arrested?"

Both Eli and Jenny gazed at him and Joshua wished he had something soft to kick besides Eli. "Jesus, this just keeps getting worse and worse, doesn't it?"

Eli stared at the ground as though he wished it would swallow him up. "I'm going to prison. I'm gonna be someone's bitch."

"You're not, I am." Joshua ran a hand through his hair.

Eli snorted. "Yeah, no offense Joshua, but I think you're a little less marketable to bald, fat men with 'Mom' tattooed on their biceps than I am."

Joshua glared. "You two are supposed to be *dead*, and I'm the only person attached to you. The doctor must've called the cops after pulling up your record." Jenny bit her lip. "It's not your fault," he added, "I was careless."

"You were worried about her, that's what," said Eli. He raised his eyebrows up and down and gave them a smirk, which quickly faded after he caught Joshua's murderous, there's-no-time-for-that glower. "I mean uh… can't we just tell them it was a misunderstanding?"

"It's not gonna go down that easy kid," Joshua rushed over to the window and threw open the curtains. "We can't talk to the cops; they'll separate us and try to pull the truth out, and if that ever happens, we're all getting hoarded to the madhouse. Trust me, I know." He threw Eli his backpack and peered out the window. "We need to get out of here. Can you walk Jenny?"

She sat up slowly, ripped out her IV cords and winced. "Yeah. I think so."

"Good. I'll go out first and grab the car, meet me out the front in three minutes."

The two of them nodded and watched Joshua duck under the open window and drop onto the bed of roses outside. Silently he thanked God it wasn't a two story hospital room and hurried around the back of the building.

First her heart attack and now I've got the cops on my ass? What a day this has been. And if the police know we're here, the Agents can't be far behind.

The howling wind had settled to a wispy breeze as he sprinted to the car park, the lights from the street lamps making the pavement shine around him. For a moment he had the feeling he was being followed and spun on his heels with his hands raised, ready for men in black suits to attack. But the car park was empty.

Joshua put his hand in his pocket to fetch his keys, turned back around and felt his heart leap out of his chest at the sight of a man dressed in a neat suit and red striped tie standing a car length away. He smiled, his hands clasped firmly around the handgun pointed at Joshua's chest.

"Joshua Harrison," he grinned. "Long time no see, eh buddy?"

Joshua gaped, so shocked he didn't think to defend himself.

"Jesus…" he breathed. "Barry?"

THIRTY-SEVEN

T he girl was terrified, dirt-stained and desperate for help as her fingers wiggled between the bars.

"Help!" she croaked again, and Hunter was too shocked to move at all. If she ever thought her appearance was gaunt looking in the bathroom mirror, she was sorely mistaken. This girl's brown hair was shaved nearly to her head, and her teeth were yellow and stained.

Will jumped into action. He reached for her, frantic as he assured her that they would get her out. The door was padlocked, but Will pulled at it anyway. He made a lot of noise.

Run, the fire whispered to her. *Pretend you never saw her. You're going to get caught if you try and get her out.*

Will looked back at her. "What are you doing? Help me!"

Hunter looked from the girl with tears of relief pouring from her eyes and then to Will. He read her mind before she spoke. "Hunter, we have to help her."

"It's locked!"

"Then we find a way to open it."

The girl sobbed. "Please get me out of here, I've been locked up for months, I haven't seen another face in days… I'm starving, *please.*"

Her words made Hunter want to cry. She couldn't look at her.

"Will, we can't even get ourselves out of here, how can we-"

"Is… someone there?"

The voice came from two cells down. Hunter and Will left the girl with her hands hanging out and ran down to the other cell. A man stood behind the bars, the room dark behind him. He was much older than any of them, maybe early thirties. As he begged them to help, more voices came from the corridors, more cries and pleads, more dirty hands dangling from between the bars, and Hunter felt panic bubble from her core.

"What do we do?" she asked Will. He was breathing heavily as his eyes darted to all of the bodies imprisoned around him. It was a nightmare.

"I... I don't know."

"Hey," hissed the man from the cell beside them. "Can you get me out?" He stuck his hand between the bars to reach them, only his hand wasn't there at the end of his arm. It was only a stump.

"What happened to you?" asked Hunter.

"Experiments," the man said. He twitched his entire head to the side and it cracked, making Hunter jump back in fright. "G-get me out, will you?!"

Will's hand curled around Hunter's arm, pulling her back.

"I don't like this," she whispered to him. "There's something wrong with these people."

"Where are you going?!" the man shouted at them.

"Are we really going to leave them?" asked Will. "There's nothing wrong with-"

"*Argh!*"

Hunter shrieked when a man in a nearby cell threw himself against the door, thrusting his arm out towards her and snatching a fistful of her hair. She tore herself away, pain searing her head as he ripped her hair from her skull. Desperate for Will to put his arms around her and make the sounds go away, she fumbled for his arms and he held her from the window and the prisoner. But the sight of the man with no eyes remained glued to her mind even when she turned away.

They ran, passing many more cells filled with people crying and reaching for them. Hunter's stomach rolled over at the sight of a girl who looked normal in the darkness, but when she pressed her face against the bars, her skin was layered with burns.

"Please help," she moaned. "Please help. Please."

"What has he done to them," Hunter hissed at Will. "What are they doing down here?"

Will didn't answer. He started pulling her back the way they came. "Let's get out of here. There's nothing we can do."

"But-"

"We *can't help them.*"

She stared into his eyes, wondering why Will would risk punishment to save her in the bathroom, but not to save the dozen lives that were locked in the cells around them. It was true, there was nothing they could do, but they had to try anyway.

"Hunter?"

She whirled at her name and started running. From down the end of the corridor, she saw a bigger and sturdier cell with an arm hanging out, waving at her. As she grew closer, she knew who it was immediately.

"Alfie, oh my God!" She grabbed his hand and held it tight. It was ice cold in her grip. "Are you okay?"

He looked shabby and dirty and there were blood stains all over him. "It's madness down here," he said. "I haven't left this cell in days, and they hardly ever feed me. And guess what: These people don't have powers."

"What? They're just regular people?"

Alfie nodded. "He experiments on them. He's testing *our* powers, trying to re-create them."

Hunter looked back at the cells and saw the girl with the burns on her face. She felt sick and dizzy.

"Has he tested on you Alfie?" asked Will. "What has he done to you?"

"Nothing but starve me." He lifted his wrists and chains jingled. "I can't turn anymore, not even if I tried."

"We'll get you out," said Hunter and she looked at Will. "That's a promise."

Suddenly there came a crash from behind the locked door at the end of the corridor. A scream followed it, a scream that chilled Hunter down to her bones.

"What's in there?"

"I don't know," said Alfie. "But there's been noise coming from that way for ages now. Guards and scientists ran in there and they haven't come out."

"Hunter, let's leave," Will pleaded her. "Before we find anything else we're not supposed to."

"I can't," she said. "You can stay here if you like, but whatever is in there could be the answer to getting us *and* these guys out of here. Will," she gripped his wrist. "Are you coming?"

After only a split-second of hesitation, he nodded.

"We'll come back for you Alfie," she promised him, and with a breaking heart, she ran. When they came to the door at the end, Hunter took note of the number above it.

"Death Cave 1," she murmured. Her heart was pounding in her chest as the noise became louder. "Here, help me with this latch it looks heavy."

Together, they lifted the metal rod that felt like ice beneath her fingers and heaved it to the right. The latch was oddly soundless, and after unlocking the door, Hunter pulled it open towards them. She ducked her head around the corner and found yet another staircase.

The lower they climbed, the colder it grew. The stairs led down to a smaller door, this one without a padlock on it. It had a simple old handle, rickety with age.

Hunter looked up at Will, but it was too dark to see his expression. Instead, she found his hand. And just like earlier in the theatre room, she squeezed it and he squeezed back. *It will be okay,* he seemed to affirm. Hunter drew in a deep breath, slowly turned the handle and eased the door open. Pearly fluorescent light poured into the stairwell and she pressed her back against the wall beside Will. After she was sure no one saw the door open – because there was too much crashing coming from inside for anyone to hear them – Hunter peered through the doorway.

She saw what appeared to be a circular dark room the size of a small cathedral. The roof stretched further than her eyes could see, enclosed in darkness. The only light was coming from the center of the room, where a glass tank no bigger than her own cell was surrounded by heavy machinery, cords and wiring and equipment like nothing she'd ever seen. There were scientists in white lab coats scattered around the room, hiding behind crates and machines and other various things Hunter couldn't name to save her life. Men in White – dozens of them – were scattered too, though they were grouped in a strong formation around the glass tank in the middle, all with taser guns aimed at whatever was threatening them. Hunter craned her neck to see over a pile of crates and as the guards stilled, she saw that the glass in the tank had shattered on one side. Whatever was trapped had been freed.

Hunter knew then and there that she wasn't thinking logically, because before Will could pull her back inside the safety of the stairwell, Hunter ducked into the room, keeping low so none of the scientists would see, and hid down behind what looked like a bunch of DVD players on a food tray.

Will hurried up behind her, gripped her arm tight and hissed, "Are you barking mad?"

"Shh," she mouthed and pointed at the tank.

From their view, she could really only see the backsides of the Men in White. They shifted nervously, some of their faces clenched in fear as their eyes were trained on whatever was in the tank. Their fingers were fixed firmly on their trigger buttons.

"This is some serious X-Men shit," Hunter muttered.

Will elbowed her to be quiet.

"We can do this the easy way, or the hard way. Your choice," came a voice as soft and commanding as sin and Hunter and Will peered at the right side of the room where two double doors had opened and Dr. Wolfe strode in with an alien confidence that absolutely no one in the room held. Every person moved not an inch as he marched through the crowd of Men in White to the tank.

In an irrational attempt to see who – or what – was imprisoned in Death Cave 1, away from even those trapped in the other smaller cells, Hunter stood from behind the tray, ignoring Will's scrambling hands trying to yank her back, and finally saw him.

The figure was crouched, like a lion taking a few deep breaths before it pounced. He wore a shredded jumpsuit, muscles straining against the fabric, as though he were transforming into some sort of Hulk. He breathed heavily, skin tanned and hair a dark brown. Hunter pulled against Will long enough to see Dr. Wolfe approach the tank. He bent down, whispered something to the figure – a boy her age, she thought – and then the figure rose.

The first thing she saw was rage. Pure, incomprehensive rage. The veins across his chest, throat and face strained against his skin. His eyes were almost pure black, no whites at all. His frame was hunched, everything clenched. Hunter would have bet her left arm that he was preparing to explode, and she realized that's what had happened to the tank. This was why all of the Men in White were called.

The side of the glass tank was labeled in giant bold letters 'TERMINAL 1'.

"Get down!" Will hissed at her and one of the trays rattled threateningly. She worried a scientist would hear them, but their eyes were fixed on the angry boy in the open tank. They all feared for their lives.

Why don't the Men in White just put the creature out or lock him in a cell like they did with all the others?

"You can't kill me!" the boy shouted in a deep tone and Dr. Wolfe stumbled back. Hunter would have liked to give the guy a high five for scaring the doctor, had he not been so terrifying and unstable.

"Now calm down, I know you can't control this rage and we'd like to help you-"

"Help me?" he growled. "You've had me locked up in here for months, shot me with lasers and stuck me with needles and *now* you're offering to help me?"

"Actually, you're here for a far more important reason." Dr. Wolfe threw his arms up and stared around the room. "You're powerful, young man, and I'd like to turn your gifts and abilities into something greater. A weapon."

"A weapon?" the boy shivered angrily. "I'll never do it. You'll create war."

"Oh, dear boy," he chuckled. "War is exactly what I want."

Hunter and Will looked at each other, eyes wide. They were both thinking exactly the same thing: that their situation was much bigger than they originally interpreted. *He's crazy. He actually wants to use our powers as a weapon of mass destruction?* Hunter was almost too stunned to hear the rest of the conversation.

"No way," said the boy, "I'm not helping you. No way in *hell.*"

"You're already in hell. So you might as well cooperate."

In a moment of panic, the figure moved to run to the exit. One of the Men in White took a shot at him with a taser and missed by an arm hair. The boy froze where he stood, turned to the guard and glared with hatred so raw and powerful, Hunter felt the darkness hit her from her hiding spot at the back of the room.

Then suddenly, the guard who opened fire started to quiver. His weapon clattered to the floor. A few of the scientists around him began to murmur to each other. One of the Men in White grabbed the guard's collar and shook him, barking out his name, but the guard looked as though he was having a seizure.

Then, without even a word, the guard exploded.

Blood, skin, bone, organs and whatever else was in his body sprayed over everyone around him.

There was mayhem; the scientists were screaming and running for cover, the Men in White were firing at random at the boy in the tank, having a difficult time in keeping him down, and Hunter swallowed the nausea in her stomach long enough to stare at the figure. Her view cleared as the people disappeared, and the boy stepped out of the tank and started walking towards a cowering Dr. Wolfe who had backed up against a large computer monitor and desk. As he moved, a light beam shot across his face and Hunter saw, for the first time, who the psycho truly was.

Her world spun. She froze, unable to move, unable to blink or take her eyes off him. Everything she'd seen up until that point in the institution could not compare to the horror of what had just occurred before her eyes. Not even the mutant people that cried out for her to help them shocked her even half as much.

It can't be him. It just can't.

But the words didn't change what was real before her eyes.

"Please," Dr. Wolfe begged, scrambling back as far as he could go. He looked around for help but none of the Men in White knew what to do. They stood there, wide-eyed and dumbfounded. Dr. Wolfe continued to beg and Hunter continued to watch, until suddenly there was a crack louder than the sound of fireworks and the boy collapsed on the ground.

Silence fell. Dr. Rosenthal stepped into view, and Hunter couldn't take it anymore. She saw the world tip and fell back against Will, who caught her just as she passed out. It seemed almost like she was waking up again rather than slipping into darkness, because darkness and dreams and nightmares were a billion times more believable than seeing Dr. Rosenthal shoot a murderous Jack Holloway in the back with a shotgun.

– PART 5 –

THE ESCAPE

THIRTY-EIGHT

T he chair was the worst thing. Every time Joshua moved, it squeaked like a plastic chew toy in the mouth of a Rottweiler. So he kept his hands – in cuffs – between his legs and literally sat as still as possible. After all, the squeaky chair gave away his every lie, and he wanted nothing given away. Not to the man who leant on the steel desk and glared at him.

"So why don't you tell me," Barry said in that casual, overly-confident tone all agents have when the criminal is safely behind bars, or – in his case – locked in the Livingston police department, interrogation room two. "What *have* you been up to lately? And don't flake out on me like you always do. We're not in Tappy's bar, old friend. You're in some deep shit here, and only the truth is gonna dig you out again."

Joshua rolled his eyes. Okay, so Barry had caught him off guard. In fact, off guard was a bigger understatement than if he'd started off with "Nice weather we're having" and pointed outside to the raging storm that pounded on the window. But did he really think that the whole threatening routine would work on him? *Not today Barry.*

"You've got all your wires crossed," he said. "There's no need for the FBI to get involved in whatever hoodoo you think is going on here. Those two, back at the hospital, are alive. Always have been, and murder or no murder, you can't prove I was involved at all."

Barry smiled down at the table and stood, loosening his tie. Joshua couldn't help but notice how nicely Barry scrubbed up in a uniform, having been so used to seeing him in tattered jeans, biker boots and bulky jumpers with a case of beer under his arm. He'd shaved, slicked back his thinning hair and actually brushed his teeth.

"You think I'm pulling you in here because you're on a happy little road trip with two supposedly dead missing persons? Jeez, I've underestimated just how stupid you really are Joshua."

"Uh, ouch," he said sarcastically. "So if it's not about them, what's it about? Did I forget to pay a parking ticket?"

Barry nodded, his eyes sparkling. "Very funny, wise ass. You know you're a slippery little sucker. I've been on your tail since the day you started at Colombia. I searched your apartment. I followed you to work and from work. I bugged your house, and all I could come up with is some silly banter between you and Hunter about a fire and some other ridiculous crap."

"And here I thought we were pals," Joshua smiled.

"You think I'm friends with you coz I like you?" Barry huffed a laugh and looped his fingers into his gun holster. "Sorry pal, I just tailed your ass to get info from ya."

Joshua grit his teeth, but didn't retort.

"You see, there's this case I've been working on for… near twenty years now. Missing children have been taken from their families all over the world, mostly in America. A couple from Paris reported their daughter missing a few years ago, saying something about a rehabilitation facility. Two foster boys – who were quite the juvenile delinquents – disappeared from their care center, and all the warden could tell us was that one was bailed out of jail, and the other was adopted that same day. Some families simply… give them up. They won't tell us why. No one can explain it, not until something very interesting came up a couple of years ago." Barry's eyes were glowing, giving Joshua the uneasy feeling that he knew more than he let on. "New evidence arose on a case they re-opened in Sweden. You remember the laboratory explosion, don't you? It would have been just after Hunter was born and you became her guardian. See, those clever Swedish bastards found something: Your prints."

Joshua's chair squeaked. It was almost as if he'd shouted "yes! I did it! I'm Iceman!" Barry chuckled under his breath and sat down opposite him. For a long time he remained motionless, letting it all sink in and hoping Joshua would crack under the pressure. But all Joshua thought about was sticking a thick, round icicle through Barry's heart.

"Do you know this man?" Barry slapped a photograph before Joshua and he tipped his head to the side, avoiding the glare from the lamp above them. The picture showed a man in his late thirties, gray-haired but strong-boned with thin lips and a beaky nose. He faced the camera, and only smiled through his dark, piercing eyes.

Of course Joshua knew that man. He could not forget him. Dr. Wolfe was the only person on Earth that even the Iceman feared, and he had Hunter in his greasy clutches right at that moment, while Barry stood there cracking sly jokes.

But if Joshua told Barry about the doctor, he would not cooperate the way he needed him to. So he shook his head and sighed.

"Nope. Why, is he related to this case you're working on?"

Barry's jaw twitched from side to side. "I shouldn't be telling you this, but what the hell. We believe he has something to do with the missing children. Dr. Winston Wolfe entered our country many years ago – around the time this photo was taken – and we have not been able to find him since. Not only that, but someone in our country has been transferring large amounts of money between here and China, and no one can track the location of this account. The money goes through just before the children are reported missing. Now this can either be a pretty damn stellar coincidence, or a connection. If you know the whereabouts of this man, Joshua, I suggest you give me something."

China? Oh shit. Joshua's knee started shaking and a dark, cold anger stirred inside him. Dr. Wolfe was the definition of evil, and he had Hunter. He had to save her.

The room started to get very cold, but Barry hadn't noticed.

"A lot of strange things have been going on," he said, running a tired hand down his face, "and all point to you Joshua. Someone from your building reported an explosion and several gunshots from an apartment registered under your pseudonym – a Dr. Emmett Brown, I believe?"

Despite the situation, Joshua couldn't help but snort a laugh.

"Hilarious, Einstein. You know that Hunter is missing, right? I assumed so, since you disappeared without her. Some girl put in a missing persons report. Have you seen her?"

Again, he didn't answer, didn't even look in Barry's arrogantly bright eyes.

"Another thing I don't understand is why you are driving to Seattle with Hunter's boyfriend Eli and her psychology teacher."

Joshua's brow furrowed. *How did he know Eli was-*

"How do I know?" Barry sat forward again, typically getting in Joshua's space as all cops do, and grinned. "I know because it's my *job* to know. And part of my job is to get answers from you. So please, make my life easier by telling me what the hell is going on?"

He sighed. "Fine. I'll tell you. But I want my one phone call."

Barry's grin faded. "Are you serious? Who you gonna call?"

"That is just too tempting," Joshua said and rolled his eyes.

Barry snorted a laugh. "Alright. I'm in a semi-good mood tonight, so here-" he pulled out his cell phone and slapped it down on the table, "dial away."

Eyeing him carefully, Joshua reached forward and picked up the phone. The picture on the home screen was of Barry next to a sweet woman with curly brown hair in a waitress uniform. He dialed the number. The doctor's cell phone – which he'd uncovered after a long search through his old contacts – was untraceable, so he didn't worry that the FBI would be able to track it.

As he turned and put both hands up, holding the phone to his ear, the chair squeaked in annoyance. No one answered, so he left a message.

"Hello, it's Joshua," he said, knowing Barry would hear but still trying to protect his privacy. "Listen, I've run into a bit of trouble so... looks like you're gonna have to carry this one out on your own. It needs to be done as soon as you get this message. Take whatever precaution is necessary and make sure she is taken somewhere safe. I don't care what or who it costs. Please, Albert. Get her out of there."

As he ended the call, a single tear dripped from his eye and he brushed it off before turning and throwing the phone back on the table. Barry didn't look so comical anymore when he saw the tears in Joshua's eyes.

"That's it? A distress call?"

He pinched the bridge of his nose and nodded. "Yep. That's it."

"Alrighty then." Barry leant back in the chair and crossed his arms. "Start talking."

THIRTY-NINE

When Hunter woke up, it was dark and cold and silent. She was lying on a far comfier mattress than the one in her cell, and definitely better than the steel table in Dr. Wolfe's lab.

It only took her a second to realize she was in the old quarters, because the candles were blazing and she could smell the sweet, toxic odor of cigarettes. It only took her a second more to remember what had happened before she passed out.

She was so paralyzed she couldn't move. Before today – or whatever time it was – she thought that nothing more in this place could surprise her, but Dr. Wolfe had just stepped into a whole new level of deranged. When did he find Jack? After the warehouse? After he found Hunter? Had he really been locked up in a glass tank all this time?

And then there was Jack himself. Joshua had said he was special, that he was like them. But the Jack she had just seen in Death Cave 1 was not the Jack she used to know. The old Jack studied in the school library and followed after her like a puppy. The old Jack was sweet and innocent and harmless.

This Jack was a cold-blooded killer with a powerful ability: Destruction.

And Dr. Rosenthal shot him.

Hunter turned her head and watched Will blow out a long puff of smoke. He had his eyes closed.

"Hey," she whispered.

He jumped in surprise and relief filled his features. "Oh, hi. Are you alright?"

As she sat up, she rubbed her eyes and reached for his cigarette. She was wet and muddy all over her back, as though she'd been dragged through the sewers. "I really need one of these. Thanks."

"Sure," he smiled. "That was a pretty shocking sight in there."

Hunter nodded and breathed in heavily. As much as she wanted to tell Will it wasn't the sight of the guard exploding like a tomato in the microwave or the horror of the mutated people locked in the dirty cells that made her faint, she wasn't sure she wanted anyone knowing about Jack. Why, she hadn't figured out yet.

"How long was I out?"

"A few hours. Everything is back to normal upstairs. After Dr. Rosenthal shot that guy, they detained him and put him in one of the other cells like the ones filled with people. Apparently the shot wasn't enough to kill him. He must have some sort of power like mine. They're repairing Death Cave 1. I dragged you in here before they could find us, then I went back upstairs and there were guards everywhere. Everyone was quiet. Zac said that they waited for us but we never came."

"We lost our chance," she whispered, rubbing her eyes. "There was no security, we could have escaped. We wasted our time."

"Not exactly. The others thought of a plan while we were downstairs."

"What?"

He pulled out another cigarette from the pack and lit it up. "Marcus and Mosi have been talking about it for months now. Apparently the lack of guards made it easier to carry out the plan. Marcus and Chantal snuck down to Dr. Wolfe's office. That's where he keeps the map of the institution."

"A map?" Hunter's heart was thumping. "Are you serious?"

"Yep. And it seems luck was on their side. Dr. Wolfe keeps the restraint locks in his office as well. Marcus was able to crack the safe even without his powers." Will huffed a laugh. "Wolfe's not exactly on top of things these days, is he?"

"After what we just saw downstairs, I'd say he's a little distracted. What about the security cameras? Doesn't he have those in his office?"

"Marcus took care of it."

"Remind me to thank that guy." She smiled and took the cigarette back, more questions flooding into her mind. "So we've got a way out, but how are we gonna do it when all the guards are back?"

"We need to wait. Especially because the demonstrations mean there are more scientists around. They had a look at the map, and the only way out is through the labs. There's a staff elevator leading up."

"There's no emergency exit through the tunnels?"

"It was blocked off years ago. But there's another problem."

Hunter sighed. "Of course there is."

"It's Jet."

"What?" A funny feeling arose in her stomach. "What's he done now?"

"He's missing."

"Oh." She wanted to say 'who cares' and leave without him, but something in Will's eyes told her there was more to it. "Do you know where he is?"

Will paused and rubbed his hands on his knees. "I think he went to Dr. Wolfe."

"Wh-" It dawned on her the minute she opened her mouth and she sat bolt upright. "That son of a bitch."

"He disappeared before Marcus and Chantal found the map and the key to the restraints, so basically all the little leech knows is that we're planning an escape. It's not as bad as it could be, but it's still bad."

"And Mikayla?"

"Marcus spoke to her. She's not having any part in this. She'll wait for Jet to come back."

"Suits herself," Hunter shrugged. "What about Death Cave 1?"

"I went back through the tunnels and hid in one of the empty cells," he said. There was something snarky in his tone, as if he were proud of his courageous venture to defy Dr. Wolfe. "I heard Dr. Rosenthal and Dr. Wolfe talking. Apparently this guy – they call him Jack – has some sort of destruction power. He can destroy things with his mind; it's like a disease that's taken over him. It started off as objects and now I suppose he can destroy people with a single look. It could turn into buildings and cities and someday the world. That's what Dr. Rosenthal thinks."

"So he wants to put him down," Hunter nodded. *Dr. Rosenthal is a noble man, would he really murder an innocent boy?* "Is he going to kill him?"

"I don't know. Dr. Wolfe won't allow it, he wants to use Jack as a weapon. But that could seriously lead to the end of the world, so I think I'll side with Dr. Rosenthal on the murdering part. If it saves billions of lives, at least."

Hunter swung her legs over the bed and started pacing. Her blood was pumping and everything suddenly felt so real. *You can't worry about saving Jack as well as planning an escape,* said the fire. *It's one or the other.*

But Hunter couldn't choose. Not only did she feel sick thinking of Jack locked up downstairs with all of the other crazy mutant humans, but now she had to worry about the demonstrations that would be taking place in the next couple of days.

"Will, what should we do about the people trapped in the Death Caves? Are we going to try and take them with us?"

His dark eyes swam with pain in the candlelight. "Hunter I don't know. I was dragging you back through the tunnels and they were asking me to get them out, but… something about them gives me the shivers. I feel like they could be dangerous."

"We have to get Alfie out, at least. He didn't do anything wrong."

"Yeah but… he's a dinosaur."

Hunter ran a hand through her hair. "I can't just leave them there to suffer. They don't deserve it."

"Can we think about this later?"

Hunter's heart skipped a beat. "What about Fearne?"

"What about her?"

"Has she been taken down to the labs at all?"

Will raised slowly off the bed and dropped the cigarette on the floor. "What makes you ask me that?"

Hunter pursed her lips shut. The murderous rage on Will's face was blooming like gray storm clouds. His entire upper body clenched, but if he knew the truth, he would explode.

"Hunter," he seethed. "What – has Dr. Wolfe done – to Fearne?"

"Will-"

Will charged at her, put his hand on her shoulder and drove her back against the wall. She hit the cement hard and her jaw rattled from the impact. With his face so close to hers, she could feel the heated anger radiating from his body, from the arm he pressed against her throat that forced her chin up and from his heaving chest, pinning her to the cold cement. A fire burned in his eyes, a fire she'd never seen before. This wasn't the Will she knew, and it reminded her of the blackness inside her soul that used to eat away at her.

"Listen to me Will," she said very slowly and very calmly, as though she were talking to a snake about to strike. He released his grip only slightly. "Whatever Dr. Wolfe has done, he will sorely regret it one day when everything collapses and all the people he hurt will return for their payback. Personally, I'd love to be the one dishing out the revenge, but right now there are more important things to worry about. Like getting all of these kids out in one piece."

Will's eyes searched hers, and after a moment he nodded and broke away. "You're right. I'm sorry. All of the shit that's been happening lately has really gotten to me. And now this demonstration…"

"Do you think we could make it out of here before it's over?"

"As much as I don't want to go through it…" he sighed. "I don't think we have a choice."

"I was afraid you'd say that. It could be weeks before we get another opportunity like we did today."

Will did nothing but stare at her. Then, after a moment, he stepped towards her, put an arm around her back and pulled her in for a hug. She buried her face into his chest and it was as if a wave of peace washed over her. It wasn't strange that this was the first time they'd embraced in this way, because it felt so natural. "It will work out, okay?"

"How can you be so confident of that?" she muttered.

"Because… I have faith." He pulled back and gazed down into her eyes with the smallest smile on his lips.

"And when there is nothing else, there is always faith to cling onto," she whispered. When Will frowned at her, she said, "that's something my mother once said."

"She's right," he whispered.

Hunter was afraid to move. It amazed her that just being in Will's arms helped her forget the mess she was surrounded by. It was like being in the eye of the storm, where nothing could touch her.

And then the moment ended. Will let his arms drop and stepped away from her. "We should get upstairs," he said in an empty tone. "It's Mosi's turn early tomorrow."

Hunter nodded, feeling cold, and went to the door, but not before she turned to the dresser and blew the candles out, leaving them to follow each other in the darkness.

FORTY

The demonstrations continued with Mosi. It was just as ugly as Benji's performance. The scientists tested the strength of his skin by firing heavy machinery at his unprotected body. They sawed at his bones with razor-sharp blades and dropped giant blocks of concrete on his head. Mosi grit his teeth and bore through it all, but eventually the pressure put him into unconsciousness and he woke up a day later.

Then it was Will's turn. Hunter watched them slice and burn and beat and crush his body over and over and she longed to be sick, but there was nothing in her stomach to throw up. His screams still echoed in her mind late into the night. No horror movie she'd ever seen could compare, particularly when it was someone she cared about. Oh, and she knew she cared about him. Because after what he went through, Hunter refused to leave his side in the infirmary until she was dragged away by three of the Men in White.

Her turn came the day after, and she walked into the Orb shaking from head to toe. She told herself to be brave for the younger ones, and having the fire swarm through her skin was blissful enough to give her courage. She wished Will was near, but his body still hadn't reformed.

The Orb was more terrifying when filled with people. In the center of the giant space was a glass box identical to the one Jack had destroyed in Death Cave 1. It stood on a raised platform, four silver gas tanks attached to each corner with tubes running up the glass and into the roof. Hunter swallowed as she was led up the steps into the glass tank that sealed shut behind her. All of the sound made by the whispering scientists and buzzing machinery around her vanished. In a way, it was oddly comforting. The fire blazed inside her and she lit her hands, forming balls of flames that danced around her like jumping rabbits. She smiled, enjoying the moment, before Dr. Wolfe's voice interrupted it.

"Ladies and Gentlemen, I give you subject 0997. Hunter Harrison, age 19. Subject has the ability to withstand impossible heat and – as is clearly demonstrated before you – she can also produce flames from within her body. Today we are going to test the limits of her skin and exactly how much heat she can withstand."

Hunter breathed a laugh and crossed her arms. *That's all he's got?* the fire laughed mockingly. It was easier to laugh than be paralyzed with fear.

"Begin," Dr. Wolfe commanded.

Four men in lab coats approached the corners of the cage. They turned valves on the oxygen tanks and Hunter heard a very faint, high pitched whistle. Then suddenly, fire burst from the ceiling.

It was warm and wonderful, like walking into a heated restaurant after spending so long in the cold. The fire burned through her jumpsuit almost immediately and Hunter felt sick again, knowing that the guards – Jamison in particular – would be up in the theatre room watching. *Don't forget Zac and Jet and Marcus.* Hunter groaned.

She soon lost sight of the scientists as the fire swarmed around her, which made it easier to imagine she was completely alone and no one was watching. Just to piss them off, Hunter put her hand to her mouth and yawned. She imagined Dr. Wolfe sneering. The heat began to build.

Joshua had never done anything like this with her in the lab back in New York, so in a way she was curious to see how much heat she really could take. After so much research on the stone – which came from a volcano – she was pretty sure she could withstand anything, especially something created by chemicals and some stupid gas tanks. What she couldn't determine was the strength of her skin after living in darkness and near-starvation for so long.

Hunter looked down at her hands. They were slowly turning as bright as the flames around her. Her veins glowed a luminescent orange again. Her hair whipped around her face and the roaring of the fire increased, but still she didn't burn.

Hunter would have given anything to see Dr. Wolfe's face.

After a few more minutes, the fire ceased and she stood completely naked in the glass tank. She covered herself as best she could, thinking, *he can't get me a towel or something?*

"Subject has withstood a temperature of 2000°C. Impressive, Miss Harrison," he added.

She took a bow just for the hell of it and waited for the 'but' she knew was coming.

"But-" *There it is.* "-You must know the three elements of the fire tetrahedron. Fuel, heat and oxygen. You need oxygen to produce your fire."

Hunter's heart stopped. *Don't you do it, you bastard.*

"Judging from your pale complexion, I think you know where I'm going with this Hunter."

Is anyone listening to him? She stared around at the scientists who were scribbling notes, oblivious to her torture. *So it's true. He's brainwashing them.*

"Subject will now be tested in the same way, but without oxygen. I will start with a very low temperature, just to be safe. Are you ready?"

She stuck her finger up at him.

"Very well," he chuckled.

Hunter looked up at the valves, waiting, her heart about to leap from her chest.

"Begin," he said.

This time, no flames appeared. The floor quivered and Hunter looked down to see the ground beneath her feet start to split. Vents were opening and something was hissing. Hunter wobbled unsteadily on the uneven floor, praying for courage and strength as a feeling as if someone were pushing down on her lungs hit her hard.

He's taking away my oxygen.

Immediately, she forced her breathing to slow. There wouldn't be much left in a matter of seconds, and it was already burning her lungs. Through blurry vision, she saw the scientists approach the silver tanks, turn the valves and fire burst from the roof.

The heat was immense, and it scared her to death.

I could try breaking the glass cage, she thought desperately, *but then that would put everyone outside at risk. As much as these scientists deserve some pain, they don't deserve to die. And then what would Dr. Wolfe do with me? Put me in a Death Cave? I'd never get to help the others escape.*

I don't have a choice. She grit her teeth and thought harder.

A technique she'd taught herself in a hotel room a long time ago came to mind. Using her hands, she pushed the fire away from herself, trapping the chemicals of the flame and forming a protective shield. But the oxygen in the air was slowly fading. She fell to her knees, gravity caving in on her. Her eyes were watering and it blinded her. She could no longer see anything but bright light. The fire inside her roared, protective of her, but it could do nothing. And for the first time, it felt real fear. The fire was afraid of itself.

Hunter couldn't hold the flames back anymore. She never thought she'd see the day when fire would take her life, but it was only seconds away from happening. She didn't get to see the others escape, didn't get to save them, didn't get to tell Will she-

Blackness came for her, but it wasn't quick enough. Just as her lungs collapsed, the fire dove on her and she released the shield.

Then, Hunter burned.

FORTY-ONE

D r. Albert Rosenthal was a gentle man. He had lived through some unspeakable horrors during his childhood, and after the war he decided to dedicate his life to becoming a scientist of the mind and the body, a biologist and a doctor. In his lifetime he studied hard, moved from the very bottom to the top of his classes and was even offered a job in one of the most prestigious hospitals in England.

But Dr. Rosenthal wanted more. He believed he was destined for greater things, for more challenges, and that was when he met Winston Wolfe.

They studied the same course for a number of years, and became close friends, both with a dream to explore human genetics. Dr. Rosenthal often thought Dr. Wolfe was a little too eccentric – he would join many groups and socialize with a lot of the professors, whilst Albert stayed in his dorm to study and could often be found in the library. They were like chalk and cheese, and still they became good friends.

Then one day, Winston came to him with an idea, a dream to move to America and start a revolutionary company that studied human genetics. At the time, Albert was considering a profession in a similar area, and though he was not very adventurous, Winston's enthusiasm had him hooked. He followed the doctor all the way to Seattle, and that was when it all began.

Dr. Rosenthal remembered the first few years. It was messy, and he saw another side to Winston that had never come out. A manic side. He saw his friend go to great and dangerous lengths to get what he wanted. He often sent Albert to locations around the world to find people with special genetic gifts. Albert went only to get away from Winston's craziness.

He should have seen the signs earlier, should have backed away before it became impossible. But the more humans he found with special gifts, the more he wanted to learn, and working for Winston was just a sacrifice he had to make.

It wasn't until thirty or so years ago that Winston started to mistreat the subjects. It was done behind his back, but of course, Albert knew. He always knew what was going on. Call it a special gift of his own. He pretended to be blind to it, and that was his biggest mistake. When his back was turned, it was easier to ignore it, and that was how it remained.

Until Joshua arrived. Albert saw in that man a love stronger than anything he'd ever come across. It was a tortured love, a desperation to keep young Hunter safe, a disappointment in his failure and a grief for Hunter's mother whom he cared about so deeply. Albert knew this would be his chance to turn things around. To change. To start doing *good*. And so he helped Joshua escape.

Fortunately, Winston never suspected him. They were still friends, much to Albert's reluctance, but he could not leave the institution or more horrors would unfold and Winston would fall off the deep end. The institution needed someone who was not completely crazy to run things behind the scenes. Albert continued doing good; finding people with gifts, enhancing their powers, encouraging them. Will was one of his proudest experiments, and though the child grew up in a terrible place, he would have died at the hands of his father. Now, he had a chance to live.

But enough was enough. Winston never informed him of these demonstrations, and putting them through such unspeakable torture simply to gain attention from other scientists – most of which were not at all horrified – was the last straw. Something needed to be done.

"Hello Albert," said Dr. Wolfe as he knocked on his office door only hours after Hunter's demonstration. He was so shaken up that the doctor frowned at is appearance. "Is something wrong?"

"I cannot believe what this has come to Winston," he grumbled. Normally, he could keep his anger better controlled, but suddenly Dr. Rosenthal was seeing his long-time friend in a different light. "Do you realize what a terrible man you've become? What evil lies in your heart?"

"I don't understand, I thought this was our dream Albert." The doctor shook his head and sighed, tidying his papers. "I was afraid this day would come, when we would reach a crossroads and each go our separate ways."

"Oh we've been on separate paths for a very long time, Winston. And you can no longer use the excuse 'for science'. Science has *ethics,* and what you are doing is no better than the experiments performed on the Jews."

At that, Dr. Wolfe leapt to his feet and slammed his fists down on the desk, his eyes so menacing that they nearly burned holes in to Albert's. But he was not afraid of the doctor. He stood his ground, mirroring his hard, fiery gaze, ready for what he knew was coming.

"How dare you be so hypocritical, Albert," he growled in that low, slippery tone. "If I recall, you have been by my side from the very day this company existed. So why, now, are you suddenly pretending to be so moral? So righteous?"

"I have always been there for you," he replied, equally fierce but not nearly as cruel. "I left the country when you requested, I protected your secrets and your identity. But this has gone too far. I cannot let you treat them any less than what they are; people. Children. Don't even get me started on those poor people you've imprisoned in the Death Caves."

"And what are you going to do about it, Albert? Help them escape, like you helped Joshua Harrison escape all those years ago?"

For a moment, Albert was stunned, and that was not something that happened often. He had no idea Dr. Wolfe knew about that.

"Yes, I know about your little midnight getaway. You do realize what the punishment might have been if you were caught, don't you?" the doctor sneered at him. "And shooting Jack Hollaway in the back with a shotgun certainly did not help our operations."

"He was going to kill you," said Dr. Rosenthal.

"He wouldn't have killed me, he doesn't know how to kill. He's a child."

"It doesn't matter, some powers outweigh a person's humanity. Especially someone as weak as Jack."

"That's not the POINT!" Dr. Wolfe roared and he slammed his hand down on the desk again. He raised his bony white fingers, wrinkly just like his own, and pointed it at Dr. Rosenthal's face. "I kept my mouth shut for you. I went against my every rule, I protected you. I gave up everything. And now here you are, acting like you're the better person. It makes me *sick.*"

Dr. Rosenthal felt his heart sink in sadness. It was true that things could have gone a completely different way, but the demonstrations were under his control. And he was too drunk on power to notice.

"You need to stop this, Winston. Please, for the sake of this institution and our dream, stop this. I don't want to see you go down the path of destruction."

Dr. Wolfe turned his back on him and his shoulders sunk in a tired sigh. "It may already be too late for that, old friend." In his tone, there was a hint of a smile, a smile of old memories and a lifelong journey together. "But I will not back down until my dream is fulfilled. And you are either with me, or against me."

Dr. Rosenthal's heart broke. This was the moment he had been dreading. He had faith in his friend, and now that faith was shattered.

"I'm sorry it has to end like this," he said softly and walked to the door.

As he left the office, he was sure he heard his friend mutter a broken, "I'm sorry too, Albert," before he turned away.

FORTY-TWO

She dreamed it was raining. The water was crystal clean and perfectly cooled and it hammered down upon her hard and heavy. But, like everything good in life, it never lasted. As soon as the rain was done and the blackness cleared and Hunter woke up in a dimly lit room, she felt the pain as though she was being burnt all over again.

Hunter didn't know where she was. It was white and cold like the institution, but she wasn't in a cell or a surgery room. Then suddenly, she remembered: This was the infirmary where she visited Will a day ago. Her bed had a plastic mattress and metal bars on the side. Thin curtains were pulled across both ends and directly opposite her was an identical empty bed. She could hear soft voices from somewhere in the room, and they echoed.

As soon as she tried to move, she let out a shriek of pain. Her entire body was heavy and thickly coated in bandages. Someone heard her cries and a moment later, a nurse was fussing over her, telling her to relax and take deep breaths and try not to move. Hunter was so confused and she tried to speak, but the woman inserted a tube into her mouth and trickled cold water down her throat. Hunter swallowed it greedily and almost choked.

"There there dear," said the woman. Her face was becoming clearer now. She was old with saggy skin and frizzy gray hair twisted in a bun on top of her head. Her eyes were kind but blank, like a ghost. *Perhaps she is a ghost,* Hunter thought. "Everything will be alright. You've been unconscious for a day and a half now, but your skin is patching up quite nicely. I'm pleased to tell you that it won't be a matter of days until you're up and healthy again."

Hunter didn't care about that; all she wanted was more water. "Please…" she breathed.

The nurse smiled and fed her more. As she did, she kept talking, telling her it would be alright and the world was all sunshine and lollypops. The whole charade was far too forced for Hunter to believe. She expected Dr. Wolfe to arrive any second now to gloat of his successes.

But it wasn't Dr. Wolfe who arrived. It was Dr. Rosenthal.

That night, he came to visit her. She was drifting in and out of sleep. The infirmary had grown darker and someone down the way was snoring. She heard his footsteps and saw him appear at the end of the bed. He looked almost as worse as she imagined herself to be.

After a moment in which he leaned on the post at the end of her bed and stared in the dim light from the back of the room, Dr. Rosenthal shook his head and wiped a finger under his eye.

"Joshua would kill me… if he saw I'd let this happen to you," he muttered. She could have sworn his old voice broke in a sob.

Hunter wished she could see him clearer, even sit up and comfort him if that's what he needed, but she literally could not move on the bed.

"Dr. Rosenthal, it's not your fault," she croaked. "It's that bastard Dr. Wolfe who did this."

"I know," he replied. "I've tried to put an end to it, but it's like provoking a serpent; I've only made him angrier and more reckless. These demonstrations, they're not for our benefit. They're for his. He wants to feel in control, to show off. And those new scientists, they're… they're afraid of him."

"So the recruitment isn't going so well then?"

Dr. Rosenthal removed his glasses and wiped them on his coat as he took a seat in the chair beside her bed. Painfully, Hunter turned her head to face him.

"Not at all. That scare in Death Cave 1 had most of them running for the hills."

Hunter's heart started pounding. "Wh… what scare?"

He fixed her with a knowing look. "You're not as sneaky as you think, you and William. I know you were there when Jack broke free. I know

William was listening in on mine and Dr. Wolfe's conversation about destroying him."

"How-"

"It doesn't matter. What's important right now is getting you away from here. Things are becoming far too dangerous. I should never have let him go this far. When you are well, Hunter, I need you to lead the others out of this place."

Hunter sighed. "Dr. Rosenthal, I'm with you one hundred percent on the escaping part, but... I just don't see how."

"That's where I'm going to help you," he whispered. "The nurse has given you a lotion I made with some of William's DNA in it. You should be completely healed within a matter of days. And then the demonstrations will be over, Dr. Wolfe will be busy with the new recruitments – or what's left of them – and I will provide a suitable distraction for you and the others to scurry out of here. You have the map, you have the key to your restraints should you run into any trouble. I need you to step up and get them out of here, *all* of them, before it's too late."

Her mind was throbbing from so many 'but's and 'how's. Dr. Rosenthal didn't seem to be in the arguing mood, however, because he reached out and gently ran his finger down her cheek. The touch made her flinch, but she felt no pain. It was just a memory, and it faded quicker than the tingling sensation that ran through her.

"I want to tell you Hunter," he said and again his voice was wavering. Seeing this wonderfully gentle old man on the brink of tears was enough to bring them to her own eyes. The salt ran into her burns and it stung. "I'm proud of the woman you've become. We don't know each other as well as I wish, but the day I said goodbye to you all those years ago was the day I realized that I had made too many mistakes in my life. I couldn't change the past, but I could work towards a better future. And when you returned here, I knew this madness with Dr. Wolfe had to stop. Even if..." he took a shaky deep breath, "even if it's the last thing I do, Hunter, I will set you free. But you need to be a hero. For the others, understand me? You will start a *revolution*. And with revolution comes war. But you are already prepared, my dear. You are strong and you have courage, I have seen it numerous times already. You are prepared to fight the evil in this world, because you have *love* flowing in your veins. Not an evil flame, Hunter, but love." Ever so gently, Dr. Rosenthal rested a hand over her heart and dropped tears on her bandages.

Hunter sniffed, wishing she could sit up and hug him tightly. His words bound firmly to her heart and she knew, with dreadful sorrow, that they would be the last she ever heard from this man.

"It seems I'm not the only one who believes so," he sniffed and reached for something on the bedside table. When he sat back, Hunter saw it was a leather-bound book. Will's Bible. "Dear William was here several times, when the guards weren't watching. He so badly wants to believe in love, but I don't know if he's ever truly experienced it. It is a sad thing, to live without love. But when you have it," Dr. Rosenthal raised one eyebrow at her, "it needs to be shared with another."

Hunter couldn't take her eyes off the Bible, feeling warm inside again knowing that Will had not only woken up, but visited her even when it was forbidden.

Dr. Rosenthal opened the Bible. His eyes sparkled as he read the words, "'Greater love has no one than this: to lay down one's life for one's friends.' That does sound very much like William, doesn't it?"

Hunter responded only with a small nod. It sounded exactly like Will.

The doctor smiled and placed the book back beside the nurses' salves and fixed her again with his shimmering blue gaze.

"Promise me, Hunter, that you will leave this place as soon as the opportunity presents itself and never look back."

"When?"

"The day you're released from this infirmary," he said.

"But where do we go? I have no idea what continent we're on."

"You'll know once you're outside. Go to this address—" He slipped a piece of paper into her bandaged fingers "—and go nowhere else. It is safe, I can assure you."

"But... then what?"

He blinked through the darkness at her. "That, my dear, is up to you. You'll find anything you need at this address and instructions as to what I *advise* you do next, but you are free from then on. Now do you swear you'll do as I ask?"

Hunter nodded, her breath coming out in sobs that made her chest ache. "Yes sir."

"Good." Dr. Rosenthal stood slowly on his feet, wiping a hand over his beard and smiling down at her, his eyes like twinkling stars. "Good girl."

"Dr. Rosenthal, wait. What about the others down in the Death Caves? What about Jack?"

A sadness settled over the old man's face. "I'm so very sorry Hunter. I'm afraid Jack can't leave with you. Or Alfie, or any of the others. They are too unstable, too dangerous. It's too risky."

"Why?" she said through her teeth, angry but at no one in particular. "I thought you were going to work towards a better future. Jack is not a killer, you just need to give him a chance."

"No, dear, I can't. Because Jack cannot be helped."

"But I can't just leave-"

"You *must*." His voice pleaded with her. "I am sorry, I know how you cared about him."

Once again, Hunter opened her mouth to ask how in hell he did know, but Dr. Rosenthal whipped up a hand.

"There's one more thing I'd like you to do for me Hunter."

She bit back a sob. "I'll do anything."

Dr. Rosenthal smiled, dipped his head and whispered, "Forgive him," before slowly blending back into the shadows.

FORTY-THREE

So let me get this straight," said Barry through a mouthful of the burger clamped in his hand, "You brought both Jennifer Smart and Eli Akerman back to life from a cryonics state, and now you're travelling across the country to find a man who can help you get Eli's memory back when it was *your* fault he lost it in the first place, is that right?"

Joshua sighed. *I'd kill for a time machine right now.* "That's pretty much the gist of it."

"And how in God's good name did you get your hands on the technology to actually revive someone from the dead, or at least from a coma in sub-zero temperatures? None of this shit has even been invented yet Joshua."

"I have connections, okay?" Joshua lifted his cuffed hands onto the table and rested his head on his palms. "Look, are you going to wrap this up or not? And also, I need to use the bathroom."

"Well you're just gonna have to hold it," he picked up his jacket, took another bite of his burger and opened the door. "I'll be back."

"Wait! Where's Eli and Jenny?"

Barry grinned at him, and Joshua winced at the sight of the food squeezing through his teeth. "They're in exactly the same tricky situation you are, only they're supposed to be dead. Hang tight."

With that, he was gone and the door locked behind him.

You should just tell him, the Iceman coaxed inside him. *It will make your life easier.*

"How?" he said aloud, not realizing that he was probably being watched from the other side of the glass. But the people behind the glass wouldn't be able to see the blue Iceman sitting in the chair opposite him. "It goes against every fiber of my being to make my powers known, and to this guy? This man of law and logic? No way."

He's human, said the Iceman. *I'm sure if you laid out the basics he'd probably believe you. Hey, make him a popsicle. That ought to sweeten things up.*

Joshua snorted. "What good would it do?"

Think about it. If Barry knows the truth, he'll go the FBI. He flicked his thumb in the direction of the door. *The FBI will find ICE, probably arrest all the scientists there – including Dr. Wolfe – and Hunter and all the other kids trapped inside will be free. Now tell me that's not a good plan, huh?*

"But he's not going to believe me, even if he knows about my powers. First of all, showing him my abilities is basically a confession because Eli and Jennifer were killed by ice. Second of all, he'll laugh at me if I tell him an evil scientist has kids locked up in a secret lab somewhere, including Hunter." He sunk down on the table, the cool steel numb against his cheek. "It's completely pointless."

You just need to prove it to him. And I have a plan for that.

"What is it?" he asked, sitting up fast.

The blue Joshua smiled. *Take him there.*

"You're crazy! Can you imagine what could happen to those kids if I brought the FBI to ICE? What Dr. Wolfe might do?"

But if Dr. Rosenthal has done his job, the kids won't even be there. Look, this Barry guy has been searching for the missing kids for half his life. If you lead him to them, this whole investigation will be over. It'll probably open up another box so big, Barry will completely forget about your little 'crimes'. You will save lives.

Joshua frowned. "Okay, since when do you care about the greater good? You're completely evil."

He chuckled. *Just think – you'll find Hunter, reunite her with Eli after restoring his memories, the FBI will take care of ICE and you'll never have to worry about the Agents hunting you down again. Life can go back to normal, for you and for those poor kids under Dr. Wolfe's knife at this very moment.* He leaned back on the chair and put his hands behind his head. *I'm telling you, this plan will solve everything.*

Staring at the Iceman, Joshua was feeling very convinced. So far, he couldn't see a loophole in the plan dangling before him. If Barry didn't believe him, there'd be worlds of proof if he took them directly to ICE. He could save lives, be a hero, get Hunter back, reunite her with Eli and sweep this entire mess up under the rug and pretend like it never happened. He could turn his back on ICE forever and start a brand new life.

But what if the world found out about them? Could he live with the guilt, knowing that he was the one who blabbed to the FBI?

That's just a sacrifice you have to make. Think of Hunter.

Joshua nodded. "Okay. I'll do it."

The Iceman smiled wickedly, giving Joshua an uneasy feeling as though he had some hidden agenda, but Joshua had a mind of his own. And so far, this plan was looking pretty damn good.

The only problem, however, was whether or not Dr. Rosenthal had managed to get them out.

Joshua's Iceman vanished and almost immediately he was taken back into his memories. Normally, any memory of that cold prison was not allowed to enter into Joshua's mind, but tonight he was so consumed with anxiety over the terrible turn of events in his present that almost any memory of the past was a relief.

And this particular memory was one of his most treasured.

He was sitting in Dr. Rosenthal's office in ICE Incorporated. It was late at night and Joshua had been woken by the scientist who told him to dress hurriedly. He was to go down to the labs, collect Hunter from the nursery and wait in the doctor's office. Joshua worried that the guards would discover him walking around at night, but there was a look in the kind doctor's eyes that made Joshua trust him without question.

He was all too happy to collect Hunter, and raced quietly down to the labs through the dark corridors to the nursery at the opposite end of the surgery rooms. His heart pounded in his chest, expecting to be tasered in the back at any second, but the place was deserted. It was almost as if everyone had vanished.

Hunter was sleeping in her crib beside a small bed in which a young boy lay curled and breathing deeply. Joshua knew the boy as William, the Immortal Child. He never spoke, but he enjoyed Hunter's company, and every once in a while, Joshua thought he saw joy in the boy's eyes.

Joshua crept to Hunter's crib and gently lifted her into his arms. She was warm and uncomfortable against his skin, but that didn't matter to Joshua. At only two years old, she was big enough for him to carry her without feeling as though she might break and young and sleepy enough not to

232

make too much noise. She yawned when he gently smoothed down her silky tufts of red hair and looked up at him with those beautiful eyes just like Leo's.

"Hello, Hunter," he whispered. "Sorry to wake you, but I think we might be going home."

Hunter fell straight to sleep again, not making a sound. Joshua wrapped her rug tighter around her and lifted her so her head rested on his shoulder.

"You're going?" came a small, empty voice behind him and Joshua stopped.

William was sitting up with his legs dangling over the bed, his small blanket wrapped tight around him, his brown eyes glimmering with tears. Joshua didn't have the heart to lie to him, but leaving the boy behind was possibly one of the hardest things he'd ever had to do in all his life. William's sad face was still taped to the back of his mind years after escaping.

"I'm so sorry William," Joshua whispered. "I don't have a choice."

The boy, of course, said nothing. But he did not take his eyes off Joshua as he took Hunter and left.

Tears dripped from Joshua's eyes as he hurried to Dr. Rosenthal's office. There, he waited for what felt like hours. He rocked a sleeping Hunter back and forth, tapping his foot on the linoleum floor, staring at the doctor's things but feeling so sick to his stomach that he had no desire to pry.

And then, the door swung open and Dr. Rosenthal hurried inside. He carried a briefcase in one arm and a thicker blanket in the other. He practically threw it at Joshua and started packing the briefcase with papers.

"We must go now, we don't have much time."

"We're really leaving?" Joshua gasped. "How?"

"I will explain everything later. She'll need that; it's freezing outside."

Joshua didn't argue and wrapped Hunter in the blankets. Dr. Rosenthal put a hand on his back and guided him to the door. They made their way cautiously through the corridor to the back entrance of the lab, through two double doors and towards another marked 'STAFF EXIT'. Dr. Rosenthal scanned an ID card in the slot and entered in a seven digit code. Joshua almost laughed at how easy it was to get out, but they weren't clear of the battlefield just yet. They had a long flight of stairs to climb, and then they came to a heavy bunker door with another coded lock. Joshua felt the cold air before the door swung inward and he clung tighter to Hunter, praying she kept herself warm, as Dr. Rosenthal urged him into a giant dark space. He couldn't even make out the walls, it was so large. A high-pitched whistle came from the wind outside. Fear and excitement filled Joshua's stomach like a meal he couldn't digest. But Dr. Rosenthal strode confidently to the other side of the room, Joshua trotting after him, and climbed a short flight of stairs where he yanked on a giant red lever and a loud grinding sound broke the deathly silence.

The entire front wall was opening like a bunker hatch. An icy wind blasted into the room. Fresh, freezing, snowy wind. Joshua couldn't believe it. Dr. Rosenthal had opened the gate to freedom.

The kind doctor waddled over to him and yelled over the howling, "There's a bit of a hike ahead of you, but you should reach the main road if you follow the trail! There's a van waiting in the shrubs with the keys in the glove compartment! Drive until you run out of petrol, then fill up with this money!" He shoved the briefcase in Joshua's other hand. "Go to the address I've marked on the map in the front seat of the car! Wait for me there. I'll be with you in a few days."

"Dr. Rosenthal, I can't begin to-"

"No time for thank you's, my boy! I will see you again soon. Oh, and here-" the doctor grabbed Joshua's wrist and scanned the chunky bracelet with a small remote that flashed blue. He then pulled a pair of pliers from a pocket in his coat and pinched the metal until it snapped. Joshua felt it slip off his wrist. Dr. Rosenthal did the same for Hunter's power restraint and she started crying. "You won't be needing these anymore."

"Wait!" Joshua gripped the man's arm. For the first time in a long time, a pang of happiness went through him, and he owed it all to the kind doctor who was most likely risking his career and his life for him. "Tell me why! Why are you helping us?"

Dr. Rosenthal touched a cold hand to his cheek. "Because I have faith in you Joshua. You need to take care of this special child you hold." He gently patted Hunter on her head and smiled. "Your actions will one day save lives. And I believe in that."

"Really?" Joshua murmured.

"Really," said the doctor. "Now go! And good luck! I will see you again soon."

Joshua nodded and turned to the storm, clutching young Hunter tightly in his arms.

FORTY-FOUR

After a couple more nights in hospital, Hunter was given the all clear by the nurse and escorted back to her cell late that evening. The others were all sound asleep. The guard gave her a tray of cold food which she devoured greedily and lay on her thin mattress, staring at the long spider-crack in the ceiling, listening to nothing in particular but her thoughts. She was fresh and sleep seemed so far off that Hunter was afraid of being alone with her thoughts for another night. She sat up in her bed, deciding to take a shower. Even if she was caught by the guards and given a warning, it would be worth it.

But there was someone waiting outside her cell.

Little Sammy stood behind the glass with one hand up in a wave, his rug dragging along the ground. Hunter smiled, crossed to the door and let him in.

"You're better!" Sammy whispered. Once the door was closed, he wrapped his arms around her waist and hugged her tightly. "I'm so glad you're better."

"Hey," said Hunter as she wrapped her hands around his head and peered down at him. "If the guards find you, you'll be in deep trouble Sammy. What's the matter?"

The look in Sammy's one good eye was so beautiful and pure that Hunter wanted to pick him up and hold him tight and never let him go.

"I was having bad dreams and I wanted to see if you were here," he replied. "Hunter?"

"Yeah?"

"Can I stay with you for a bit?"

Hunter would have rather pulled off her arm than say no to a face like Sammy's. His bright eyes widened with his smile and he ran over to her bed and wriggled under the thin blanket. Feeling a little nervous, Hunter slid in beside the small boy – who practically had to lie on top of her, the bed was so small – and stared at the ceiling again. Only this time, she was a little warmer.

Sammy's head rested between her shoulder and her ear. He closed his eyes and breathed heavily. Hunter listened and found it oddly soothing.

"Hunter?" Sammy whispered.

"Yeah?"

"Why do bad things happen to good people?"

Hunter resisted the urge to answer with 'Shit Happens', instead opting for her own personal answer to that question. It was something she often thought about while lying in her cell. She used to believe in Karma – that this was her punishment for the man she killed by accident in the alleyway, or for being so reckless with her powers and not listening to Joshua's advice. But after meeting so many innocent and good people in this place who had done nothing wrong in their lives, she knew that there must be another explanation. And perhaps it wasn't to punish them, but to help them grow.

"Everyone has to go through bad times, Sammy," she said. "It's what makes us stronger. It opens our eyes, gives us the courage to fight and the heart to forgive. If we didn't go through bad stuff, we wouldn't be grateful for the good things we have. Like each other." She squeezed him a little and he squeezed her back.

"Hunter?"

"Yes Sammy?"

"Did your mommy ever sing to you when you lived in the real world?"

A lump wriggled into Hunter's throat. No one had ever asked her such a simple question and reduced her to tears. "No Sammy," she said. "I never had a mommy. She died giving birth to me."

"My mommy sung to me once. I remember because she sung about angels. I really miss my mommy."

"You're very lucky to be able to remember her. Does that help you sleep better?"

"Sometimes," he said. "But sometimes I forget. Hunter?"

"Yeah?"

"Can you sing it to me? The angel song?"

Hunter squirmed on the bed. "I don't know the angel song."

"That doesn't matter," he replied simply. "You can make it up."

"Oh." Hunter swallowed, suddenly feeling very uncomfortable. *No way I could ever be a mother, I'm a terrible singer.* "How about I sing something else?"

"Okay."

Hunter scrambled through her brain for something – anything – to sing to a boy without a mother. She wasn't sure she believed in a happy ending to their story, but she definitely believed – as Will did – that there was a higher power watching over them. Maybe it really was an angel.

And then she remembered.

It wasn't a lullaby; it was a poem she'd studied in school. Hunter had never been musically gifted, but she always imagined a tune to go with the lyrics. Now seemed the perfect time to test them.

She took a deep breath and began.

"There is someone who cares for you,
Who watches you sleep so sound,
Who holds you in their warm embrace,
Who helps the lost be found.

An Angel watches over you,
With comfort and with love.
An Angel carries you away,
To heaven up above."

Hunter sniffed away the tears in her eyes and swallowed the lump in her throat. The sound of her song echoed in the dark cell room, the words still thumping inside her heart. And for a moment, it felt like a prayer being lifted to the heavens, to whoever was watching over them. A prayer for their survival in the escape tomorrow.

Carefully, she twisted her head and looked down. Sammy was asleep.

FORTY-FIVE

The demonstrations were over. They electrocuted Marcus in almost every way possible. He took a day to recover in the infirmary; the moans Hunter had heard the other night were from him. Jet's was a little trickier; to test the limits of his Telekinesis, they threw knives at him from every angle at impossible speeds. He dodged many with his mind, but came out with a large slice in his arm and on his forehead. Fearne was last, but her demonstration was different from everyone else's. Instead of putting her life at risk, Dr. Wolfe did nothing at all to harm her. He simply asked her to read the mind of a volunteer scientist and that was it.

"It was seriously spooky," said Zac at the breakfast table the morning Hunter returned. She sat beside Will – whose eyes filled with warmth when she appeared beside him – and Sammy, who disappeared in the early hours of the morning back to his own cell.

"But it's over now," she said. "It's time to talk about the plan."

"Yeah, uh, about that," murmured Zac uncomfortably. "Are you sure we're actually ready? I mean you just got out of the hospital and-"

"It has to be done today," she snapped, looking at each of them in turn. Their eyes were filled with uncertainty. How could she assure them that everything would be okay when even she didn't know? "I know Dr. Wolfe probably has wind of our escape plan, hell he might have even blocked the way out." Chantal made a small whimper of panic and some of the others exchanged fearful glances. "But hey, we're super-powered freaks of nature.

238

We have power here that none of them can measure up to. If we can't do this, how do you expect to survive in the real world? What's the point in being special if we don't even *try*? It's now… or it's never."

There was silence at the table. Hunter caught a small smile from Fearne and knew she would follow them all to the ends of the earth. Marcus and Mosi were nodding – they already had their game faces on. Chantal was with Hunter long ago. But the children were still unsure.

"First thing I'm gonna do when I get out," whispered Benji suddenly and everyone stared in surprise at the quietest member of the group, "is go to the zoo."

"Hoping you'll find your family there?" Zac chuckled.

Chantal whacked him. "You're a douche, you know that?"

He glared at her. "I suppose the first thing you'll do is walk into the nearest Chanel store and buy yourself a season's worth of shoes, huh Barbie?"

"Why would I do that when I can just *ask* for it?" she replied, batting her eyelashes devilishly.

"I'm going straight to the nearest fast food joint, because this shit-" Marcus shoved his tray of food away, "-is horse piss."

"I want to watch a movie," said Ryo. "A really good one."

"Oh yeah?" Zac nodded. "Watch Die Hard. The first one, not the others."

Chantal scoffed. "How the hell would you know that, you got here when you were seven."

"I happened to be a very young movie buff," he replied. "And I watched them with my older brother."

"I dunno, I prefer-"

"Guys," Hunter interrupted. "As wonderful as your excitement is, we need to be focused. Can you do that?"

They nodded.

"Now, when I give the signal – or whenever the distraction begins – deactivate your restraints. Marcus, do you have the key?"

He nodded and patted the pocket on his hip. "I don't take it off me."

"Good. You all have very useful, very defensive powers. I'm sure you can figure out a way to run from the guards. Hell, some of you will be gone in seconds-" she nodded to Ryo and Benji, "-but what's more important than anything is this: to stick together. I don't want to lose any of you in this escape. We've already lost some."

They grunted complaints and even Hunter had to admit she didn't give a rat's ass whether Jet the snitch and his psycho girlfriend came with them or not.

"Please, *please*, I'm begging you not to run. There's a place we have to meet if something goes wrong. It's the safest place I know." She pulled out the address and started passing it around the group. "Memorize it. It's our rendezvous."

"How do you know it's safe?" asked Ryo.

"Because the person who's providing the distraction gave it to me."

"You trust this person Hunter?" asked Chantal.

"With my life," she nodded. "Mosi, you have the way out right?"

He shot a glance at the door. A few of the Men in White moved around the room and Hunter felt jitters in her stomach. *We have to hurry, the distraction could happen any minute now.*

"It's a little complicated, and we'll make ourselves known as soon as we hit the elevator, but we've got Marcus to shut off the security and get the elevator running. If we can find the right exit in the labs, there's a staircase that leads above ground. If not, there's a sewer system directly above us. After that, I've got no idea what's up there."

"I'll take care of that," she said to reassure them. "Remember to stick together, okay? Use your powers in any way you possibly can, even if you have to use them offensively. Do everything you can to get out."

Slowly and unsteadily, they agreed. She tried smiling in encouragement, but it felt like a grimace, so she put her game face back on.

"We'd all better eat, who knows how long it'll be until we get a decent meal like this."

Zac snorted, and some of them chuckled at her sarcasm, and the mood was lifted. Uneasiness still flowed between them, but the thought of what awaited them in the outside world was well worth the gamble.

"Can we get our powers back now?" Zac moaned. "I'm itching again."

Ryo and Benji nodded in agreement. Hunter glanced around at the older ones. Will gave her a nudge at the table, and she turned to the door.

Steel had just stationed himself by the entrance. He muttered into his earpiece as his eyes shot daggers at their table. He raised two fingers to signal to the other Men in White, who immediately sped to the door and were out in a flash.

Something wasn't right. Hunter waited, feeling the gazes of the others burn into her skull, but she wasn't sure it was time yet. Dr. Rosenthal said she would *know* when the opportunity arose.

Then it happened; a rumble beneath their feet. The trays and cutlery on their tables started quivering.

And from somewhere deep down in the pits of the Death Caves, there came a tortured, infuriated, hair-raising roar.

Hunter looked at the group, nodded to Marcus, steadied her beating heart and smiled, feeling more alive than she had in months. "You heard the dinosaur," she said. "Time to go."

FORTY-SIX

e's crazy. Bat-shit, out-of-his-mind, dingo-ate-my-baby crazy.

H
No matter how many times Jenny repeated that in her mind, it didn't change their situation in the slightest. She was still under 'observation' by the FBI. She was still aching all over from her recent heart attack. And they were still in a chunky SUV driving across the country with a federal agent in the driver's seat.

Jenny glanced at Eli on the opposite side of the car. He was staring out at the dark night, his eyes drooping shut every few seconds then snapping open again. After Joshua's FBI friend – *since when did he ever have an officer of the law as a friend? Since when did Joshua have* friends? – took them out of the interrogation room and told them to pack up their bags and jump in the back of his car, Jenny knew Joshua was up to something. He wouldn't just get arrested for the sake of helping the Feds out. He had a plan; she could see it in his eyes. But in showing this guy all of the secrets he'd fought to keep, what good did that do but get them into more trouble?

Jenny's mind was buzzing, and it made it that much more difficult to sleep. Not to mention the pain in her chest every time they drove over a stone or a dip in the road. It was nearing three-am, and despite the fact that she needed sleep, she simply couldn't do it.

Agent Barry Sanders took his hand off the wheel and pressed his fingers against his ear. "Copy that Arthur. We're about five miles outside of Spokane. I'll need to refuel, call you when we're at the motel."

"What motel?" she asked.

Barry turned the heat up and Eli stirred in the backseat. He had a line of drool down his chin. He didn't answer her.

"Okay, that's it-" She leaned forward and stuck her head between the two front seats. "Joshua, what the hell is going on? Where are we going, and how is bringing the FBI helping our situation?"

Joshua gave her a warning look and the car turned instantly cold. "Jenny…"

"It's helping your situation by not arresting all three of you for fraud and kidnapping," Barry grumbled. "And shit, Edward Cullen, you might not be able to feel the cold but we're all losing valuable body parts here. Turn it off!"

Joshua went rigid and immediately released the cold temperature of the car. Barry shot him a frown and went back to concentrating on the road.

I really don't like this guy, Jenny thought to herself, though she admired Barry's confidence with a man as powerful as Joshua. *He reeks of arrogance.* "Okay, so once we complete this little mission of yours, what happens to us? To Eli and I, at least?"

"Hmm?" Eli sat up fast at the mention of his name. "What?"

"We'll cross that bridge when we get there," Barry replied. "But I believe we have a bigger problem on our hands, am I right Jennifer?"

Jenny grumbled under her breath and heard him snicker. What was the point in arguing with this man? Whatever Joshua told him, he was intent on getting there and nothing she could say would change his mind. Jenny knew she should trust Joshua but something about getting involved with the government – particularly the FBI – made her uneasy. Was she going crazy? Did Joshua really know what he was doing?

Jenny tried to relax in the tight leather seats as the SUV plunged further down the highway into the dark night, but her stomach didn't settle even after they parked in a motel outside of Spokane. Jenny spent longer than usual in the shower and glanced through the peep-hole in the door where a local policeman had taken up guard of her door. The room was on the third floor, so there was no way she'd have any hope of escaping.

This is stupid. What am I doing here? Suddenly I'm a criminal, and we've lost hope of getting Eli's memory back or rescuing Hunter because now we have some agent breathing down our necks, and there's no way Joshua would ever take him to the doctor's house, or risk the doctor's identity.

Or would he? Was that what Joshua had come to?

Jenny towel-dried her hair so vigorously that her head throbbed when she flicked her hair back. She was relieved she had her own room, and flopped in dry clothes on the bed where she tried to imagine that she was completely alone, and there was nothing stopping her from walking out of the hotel and… moving on.

In the middle of her wonderings, there was a knock on the door.

"What?" she groaned.

"Jenny?" came Joshua's familiar voice. He was nervous. "Am I able to come in?"

Jenny hauled herself to her feet and dragged her legs to the door. The hotel had a strange smell, like cherries in the summer only cold and damp. The door was so thin she could almost hear Joshua muttering to himself as he so often did, and for a moment it made her smile.

She unlocked the latch and opened it to see him still in the same shirt, tie and black pants as he'd worn two days ago when they left Dickinson. His expression was full of the usual anxiousness, and his eyes drooped tiredly from the long week of driving. She was surprised he hadn't passed out yet.

"Yes." She stepped aside to let him in.

"Um." Joshua stared at her empty room, not sure where to put himself, and turned to her. "I just wanted to speak to you about what's happening. I feel it's unfair to you, after all that you've done to help, that you know nothing about what Barry and I plan to do next."

"What *Barry* and *I?* So you're working together now, and Eli and I are just tag alongs?" She crossed her arms and glared through narrowed eyes. "Do you still even *care* about Hunter?"

Joshua frowned, hurt. "Of course. Finding Hunter is all I care about."

"Yeah, right. I should have known this would all go pear-shaped. What was I thinking?" She walked to the bed where her backpack lay open and zipped up her vanity bag, shoving it back between her shoes. "That we'd be successful in getting Eli's memories back, and finding Hunter would be easier than finding the nearest McDonalds? That we'd all fly back to New York and life would return to what it used to be?"

"I don't want to go back to what it used to be," he said softly.

"Why not?" She whirled on him. Her anger was building from a hole inside her she never knew existed. "You won't have to constantly watch Eli and I. You can forget everything that happened after you froze me in my

244

hospital bed. Hunter can graduate and you won't ever have to see me again."

"But I want-" Joshua caught his words before they could jump out of his mouth and his eyes seemed to grow wider. He was about to say something that terrified him, but Jenny saw the word form on his lips. She felt her entire body seize up.

"You *want* to?" she breathed.

"No." His tone was harsh, but his watery-blue eyes gave away the truth. He was lying, and he knew it. He was simply afraid to believe it.

"You want to," she said again, this time as a statement of fact. Her next words came out in a breath.

They were only a foot apart, Jenny with her back to the bed and Joshua standing awkwardly near her. A thousand emotions flashed across his face. He was struggling internally, raging a battle with the ice inside him. A magical, invisible force was pulling them closer until suddenly she was staring up into those endless, weightless, wonderfully pale blue eyes and she couldn't control it any longer. The urge was too strong and too tempting.

This time, Joshua didn't freeze up.

"I do," he said. Then he closed the distance between them.

Jenny flung her arms around his neck and forced her lips to his. His hands spread across her back and electricity sparked through her. Joshua's lips moved hesitantly, as though he feared he might make a mistake, but Jenny traced her fingers down his strong cheekbone and pressed harder against him, letting him know she wanted more. In response, Joshua clung tighter and lowered his hands. She forgot about his awkwardness and the fact that he was terribly cold and instead, she found herself lost. There was only warmth inside her. Warmth in her lips and her fingers and her desire for him. Jenny had never felt anything like it.

"You once asked me..." she said between soft kisses as he breathed down upon her neck and melted her knees, "why... Hunter could overpower the fire..."

"Mmm," he murmured as he trailed kisses down her neck, chilling and glorious.

"Now do you understand? She drew power from her memory of love, Joshua." Jenny felt a shiver go through her body and she clung to him tighter. "That's all you need."

Joshua pulled away. He met her gaze with confused eyes, his hands still wrapped around her back. "Wait a minute... you think I don't *love?*"

Jenny frowned. "No... well, I just thought you didn't *understand* the power of love. If it's strong enough, you can overpower the ice. That's the answer."

His hands dropped and he stepped back and Jenny knew the moment was over. She killed it, with her big mouth and false assumptions. She suddenly wished she could take it all back as Joshua regarded her with painful confusion.

"What, you think I'm some monster Jenny?" His face was a mask of hurt. "You think I have no emotions at all?"

"No, I-"

"I took care of Hunter's mother when she was pregnant with my best friend's child because I *cared* for Leo like a brother. I took Hunter in when her mother died in my arms because I *loved* Liz more than anything in this world, and it killed me to see her die!" As Joshua's voice rose, the temperature in the room dropped. His eyes filled with tears. Jenny was so paralyzed with shock that she couldn't think of words. "I *threw* away my life for Hunter, and I grew to love her like my own daughter, feeding her and sheltering her and going to fucking parent-teacher meetings and piano recitals because she *needed me there!*" He stabbed at his own chest, his blue eyes blazing. "I love that girl with every fiber of my being and I spent so much time trying to protect her that I have no strength left inside me to fight this *evil, disgusting* power that clings to my soul every single day of my existence. I lose control because I can't *stand* the thought of her hurt, or in pain, or on the brink of death. Now she's trapped in an institution that I pulled her away from when she was a child and it's *all because of me!*"

Joshua's face was streaked with tears, and Jenny's heart was breaking very slowly and very painfully in her chest watching him crumble before her. Joshua sobbed, wiped a hand under his nose and shrugged his shoulders.

"She thinks I killed him," he said. "The love of her life. She thinks I'm a monster. She is out there, *alone* and *grieving*, and for the first time in her life I am not there for her. I promised her mother I would protect her, but I love Hunter so much, I lost sight of what it is to sacrifice everything for someone, because I was too selfish to let her go, to let her love another." He looked up into her gaze and suddenly, he fell to his knees and cried.

Jenny could not stop herself from dropping to the ground beside him. She had never seen a man cry, not since her father anyway, and to see someone like Joshua – who was usually so stiff and emotionless and formal – crumpled and defenseless on his knees before her was oddly freeing. She had been so unsure of him for the past few weeks, but suddenly she couldn't believe she hadn't seen it before. Joshua was not without love. In fact, Joshua had so much love inside of him that it physically hurt him in everything he did.

And the only thing she could do was be beside him. So she carefully took both his hands away from his face.

"Hey," she muttered and let joy fill her words. "I'm sorry I thought that. It turns out I was terribly wrong about you Joshua."

He gazed at her like a small child, afraid and helpless. Her heart ached for him.

"But you're wrong," she said. "You didn't lose sight of how to protect Hunter, because you didn't ever stop loving her. And love is more powerful than anything in the world. You didn't kill me because you are caring. You didn't kill Eli because you knew on some subconscious level that Hunter loved him. And now you are sitting here, so worried about her, so angry with yourself, when you should be *proud*. Your love for that girl is what carries her." Jenny lifted her hand and brushed away a tear that rushed down his cheek. "You *showed* her love, Joshua. She would never have beaten the fire if she didn't have you to guide her."

Joshua's thin lips spread into a smile. "Thank you," he said, his voice thick from the tears. "I'm sorry for ruining your life."

She pulled his head towards her chest and held it there, stroking his hair gently. "It's okay," she said. "I forgive you. Now you just need to forgive yourself."

"I'll try," he whispered, gripping her arms and breathing against her chest. "I promise."

FORTY-SEVEN

The fire was stronger this time. Maybe it was the probability of never being trapped again that fuelled the flame. Maybe being free of her restraint in a place where she was not confined and forced to fight another mutant made it easier to believe there was hope. That escaping was actually possible.

Regardless, the fire had never felt more alive as it swarmed within her. It was hungry for flesh to burn and it gave Hunter a sense of power.

The others were deactivating their restraints in secret, except Fearne who had to turn away from Steel and disarm her head brace privately. The moment their powers were returned to them, it was as if a heavenly light had broken through the oppressive storm clouds. Suddenly, her friends were glowing, pumped and ready rather than gray and sunken and full of defeat. Only Will looked the same.

It's time to raise hell, she thought with a grin and led the group to the door.

Almost immediately, Steel stepped in front of their exit. He crossed his arms under his pecks and grinned down at them all.

"Where do you think you're going?"

"Back to our cells," Hunter said innocently.

"There's a problem downstairs. Everyone needs to remain in this hall. Doctor's orders."

Hunter opened her mouth to answer back, but Chantal had moved through the crowd and put a hand on her shoulder.

"Let me handle this," she said sweetly.

Steel's cocky smile dropped away the moment his eyes fell upon her neck collar. It no longer poisoned her veins and hung there like a chunky necklace. His eyes moved from hers to Fearne gathering the other children and deactivating their restraints. His hand went to his taser.

"Not so fast," said Chantal in the softest tone, but it was commanding enough to make Steel freeze and stare down at her as though she were a giant bowl of strawberries and ice cream and everything good that ever was. "Drop the taser."

The weapon slipped out of his hands and clattered to the floor. Marcus scooped it up fast and pointed it at his head.

"Should we give him a taste of his own medicine?" he asked, his finger hovering over the trigger.

"*Please* make him sing," Zac begged her.

"We don't have time." Hunter shoved Steel away from the door and nodded for everyone to pass. "Hurry!"

But Chantal hadn't finished. As everyone ran by Hunter, she saw the beautiful blond girl slide closer to Steel. Her eyes were murderously happy. Hunter could just hear her whisper, "I've waited a long time for this Steel. You're gonna regret ever taking advantage of me-" Her gaze met Hunter's and a glimmer of understanding passed between them, "-you *all* are. So I want you to grab hold of your little *friend* down there... and pull as hard as you can until he comes *off*. Can you do that for me?"

Hunter's stomach churned as Steel — whose stoic face went whiter than his uniform — reached with an enormous struggle slowly to the zipper of his pants. The spark of justice in Chantal's eyes was almost poisonous as she gave him a pat on the back and met Hunter in the doorway. They both watched Steel as he turned to them, his pleading eyes filling with tears, every muscle straining and his whole body shaking as he fought to disobey her. But Chantal's power was too strong for him to refuse.

"You were right," Chantal said as they turned to the corridor and walked away from the breakfast hall. "Revenge is sweet."

Steel's screams followed them even after they ran to catch up with the others.

It seemed luck was on their side, because there were no guards on the bottom floor. The elevator opened up completely empty when Zac stabbed the button. They all scrambled inside, Ryo hit 'down' and the door slid closed.

"Everyone okay?" Hunter turned to the group.

Their faces were a mix of anticipation and excitement. The energy in the small elevator buzzed as they stood squished together like sardines.

"Ryo, any way you can check ahead and see if we'll run into trouble?"

She peered up at Hunter with a pained expression. "I don't know. I haven't used my powers in years, I don't remember how. I could end up in a different dimension."

"That's okay," said Hunter, "looks like we're going in blind."

"Maybe not completely blind," came Fearne's small voice from the back corner. As everyone turned to her, she shut her eyes and concentrated hard. After a moment, she lifted her head and stared directly at the door. "There's trouble in the labs."

"Specifically?"

"Someone's waiting to trap us."

"We have to go through the labs to the other side," said Marcus as he stared at the map in his hands. "There's no other way."

"We'll just have to face it," said Hunter. She stepped into the corridor and carefully peered around the corner. "It's clear. Follow me."

Heart pounding, Hunter crept down the walkway followed by the others, their footsteps padding lightly on the linoleum floor. She went straight for the double doors that led into the lab. She didn't hesitate when she opened the door, only because she was surrounded by ten super powered kids. Whatever they faced, it couldn't stop them.

But as soon as they entered the giant laboratory she found a greater bump in the road than she'd ever expected.

At the other end of the room, standing before the door they needed to get through, was Jet and Mikayla, flanked by at least twenty Men in White. Their tasers were aimed and ready to fire.

"Leaving without us, are we?" Jet said loudly. His voice echoed around the brightly lit room, reverberating off the glass windows and steel ceiling.

"You didn't give us a choice," Marcus seethed. Hunter had never seen him with such a homicidal expression. "You ratted us out, didn't you?"

Jet chuckled. "Come on, bro, lighten up! I wanted to get out of here as much as the rest of you, but I'm not an idiot. You're making a huge mistake and it's only gonna make things worse for you in the end."

"Bite me," Marcus spat. "Or get out of my way, *now*."

"I was hoping it wouldn't come to this," said Jet.

In one swift movement, he signaled to the Men in White.

Their taser guns fired. Hunter went to duck when something incredible happened. Bright lights flashed before her eyes as the electricity from the tasers hit an invisible force field protecting them. Hunter looked around and spotted Imogen, her hands raised and shaking, her eyes focused. The others whooped in encouragement.

All of a sudden, the Men in White's tasers were jerked from their hands and launched around the room. Petrified, the guards did nothing until, one by one, they were knocked down with their own guns by a force strong enough to send some of them into unconsciousness. A blur of papers blew up around them and a second later, Benji appeared beside Hunter. He gave her a grin.

"Nice work, Benji!"

The Men in White scrambled to their feet and stared searching the room for their tasers, looking back at Jet for instructions.

Marcus had suddenly had enough. He shot his hand out and Hunter expected to see a bolt of electricity shoot from his fingers, but nothing happened. Marcus frowned, stared at his palm and turned back to the group.

"My power is gone," he whispered.

"Technical difficulties, Marcus?" shouted Mikayla. "Guess my power isn't as useless as you all think."

Marcus's rage consumed him. He clenched his fist and started charging straight down the walkway towards them. But Jet wasn't going to let him get that far. Marcus took no more than three steps before he was flung five feet into the air and crash-landed on a desk, glass from test tubes shattering around him. He groaned and rolled over, slowly getting to his feet.

Hunter wished more than anything that she could throw balls of flaming fire at them, but it seemed her power – and those of everyone else around her – had vanished too. Benji could no longer move fast. He gave Hunter a panicked look.

I underestimated Mikayla's power, she admitted to herself. *But this has to end now. We don't have much time.*

"If you're not coming with us," she called to them, "why are you stopping us?"

"Because you're an idiot," Mikayla snapped back. "You're all idiots. You can't win this fight, and I'm not just talking about getting out of here. I'm talking about the fight of good and evil."

"When did this get so freaking biblical?" Zac whispered from behind her.

"We just want to be free," Hunter called. "What's wrong with that?"

"You're making the wrong choice, that's what," said Jet. "Sometimes it's not about doing what's right, but doing what's necessary. You go against Dr. Wolfe, there'll be consequences. There's *always* consequences for people who break the rules."

"Well I think we've made our choice," she replied, sick of the banter. "Now let us go."

"We're trying to help," Mikayla pouted. She turned to Jet and said, "why don't they understand that?"

"Cut the bullshit Mikayla," said Will. Hunter shot him a glance and suddenly realized one of them was missing. She turned slowly, her eyes darting everywhere, and panic rose in her when she spotted a small head of blond hair ducking behind the desks, making his way towards Mikayla and Jet.

No. Sammy, no!

Desperate to keep their attention on her and not the small boy who was growing closer and closer to the opposition, Hunter stepped away from the group and raised her hands.

"Fine. You guys want to stay here and kiss Dr. Wolfe's ass for the rest of you lives?!" she shouted. "Go ahead then!"

"Easy there, Hot Stuff," Jet chuckled. "Dr. Wolfe will be here any moment now to set things right with you, and then everything will be back to normal."

"Isn't he a bit preoccupied with, oh I dunno, a giant prehistoric monster?"

"They've developed a way to stun the queer long enough to sedate him," said Mikayla. "I just hope that this time they'll learn their lesson and put that fugly creature down."

A rumble of rage rippled throughout the group. Most of the younger ones looked ready to pounce. But Mikayla and Jet were grinning, completely confident. Unaware of what was going on around them.

That was their biggest mistake.

Sammy's power was beautiful. He could radiate a blinding white light from his body, making his appearance completely angelic – if you had a long enough look at him before your eyes started to burn. Mikayla's power seemed to act as a force-field against whomever she directed her gaze at, because suddenly Sammy had leapt out from behind a desk and dove on her. It was like seeing a shooting star flash by in slow motion. Mikayla screamed and the moment she broke concentration, their powers returned.

Sammy wrestled with Mikayla and Jet threw his arm up to shield himself the light. Benji disappeared and zipped to the back of the room, attacking the Men in White from behind. Hunter charged directly down the walkway, the others right on her heels, and Marcus recovered quick enough to direct a lethal current of electricity at Jet from a power plug a few feet away from him. Jet seized up and every muscle clenched as he twitched to his knees.

The others went into fight mode. Zac, Chantal, Ryo, Will and even the younger ones applied the skills Mosi had taught them in their gym session. The Men in White put up a good fight – ignoring the fact that they were fighting children and using their most brutal methods – but against super powered kids, the Men in White didn't last very long. Zac found a taser and started firing at random. Hunter didn't have time to ensure that they were winning; she had to get them all to the exit before more guards arrived.

Sammy released Mikayla from his blinding light and smiled at her cowering form beneath him. She was sobbing and groping around for Jet beside her with her eyes squeezed shut. Hunter slid to her knees besides Sammy and held her arms out to scoop him up.

"Did you see what I did?" he grinned at her proudly.

"You were so brave, Sammy," she whispered into his hair. "So brave."

Then, a scream came from behind her.

"No!" Fearne shrieked, but it was too late.

Jet was on the floor just feet away, his arm outstretched, a psychotic look in his eyes. Sammy jerked and went limp in her arms. Time slowed. The room fell eerily silent.

Hunter pulled Sammy away and felt his body slide to the floor. She lifted the boy's head – his neck loose like a spaghetti string – and rested it in the crook of her arms.

Sammy's one lifeless blue eye stared up at the ceiling, the other glassy iris just as blank. His mouth hung limply open, a line of blood dripping from his lips. And the light, the beautiful, heavenly light, around his body faded into oblivion.

Oh God. Not Sammy.

Hunter grit her teeth and whipped her head around. Carefully, she lowered Sammy's body to the floor. Jet chuckled softly but said nothing as he glared at her. Most of the Men in White were out for the count, but even the ones left standing stopped fighting. The entire room was still.

"Oh no," Chantal sobbed, putting a hand over her mouth.

Fire burst from Hunter's wrists. Jet's smirk hardly faded, but Hunter was all too happy to burn it off for him. *Screw doing the right thing*, she thought with poison clouding her mind. *The fire can have this leech.*

"You killed him." Her voice shook with rage. "YOU – KILLED – HIM!" She screamed so loudly that she felt as if her throat might fall apart. Will snatched her around the waist before she could tackle Jet as she continued to yell, "YOU'RE DEAD, YOU SON OF A BITCH!"

"There's no time Hunter!" Will shouted in her ear.

"No, he deserves it Will! Let me go!"

Jet didn't stop laughing, not until his face suddenly screwed up in intense pain and he began to shriek. All of them froze in shock, even Hunter.

"Stop it!" Jet squealed. When he looked up, his eyes met Fearne's. "Stop it please!!"

Everyone looked at Fearne. Her face appeared hardly human. Her hands were shaking by her sides. Her eyes were wide, her pupils nearly as big as her irises. The corner of her mouth twitched. She looked demonic and Hunter knew it was her torturing Jet's mind, just as she had tortured the scientists.

Will's arms fell away from her and she stumbled weakly against a desk. He ran to Fearne's side and shook her, trying to break her eye contact with Jet whose ears were bleeding through his clenched fingers. Even his nose was dripping red. He rolled around on the floor in agony.

"That's enough," called Chantal. "We have to go!"

Hunter was so transfixed by Fearne's power and the intense aura she was protruding that she didn't hear shouts coming from somewhere in the distance. The Men in White were almost upon them.

"Fearne!" Will clutched the young girl's chin and squeezed, forcing her gaze to his. Drops of red were falling from her nose. "Listen to me, you have to *let go.* Come back to me okay?" He shook her harder. "Fearne, *please!*"

"Make – her – stop!" cried Jet.

"Will, hurry up!" called Zac.

"Will!"

"Fearne!"

"*ARGH!*"

And finally, Fearne's eyes rolled back into her head and she fell into Will's waiting arms. Will whispered into her ragged hair, rocking her back and forth like a baby.

"Is she okay?" asked Hunter.

"There's no time to tell," said Ryo. "Look!"

Men in White appeared outside the glass in the surrounding corridor. Benji flashed to the door and twisted the lock before they could burst through, trying with all his might to shove furniture in front of the door. It only took him a moment before there were piles of desks blocking the entrance.

He flew back to them. "That won't hold them for long. Let's go!"

"You won't get far," Jet sneered, his face smeared with blood. He looked drained and unhealthy. "Dr. Wolfe will find-"

Marcus bent down and threw his fist under his brother's jaw so hard that Jet flipped backwards and lay spread-eagled on the floor. "Go fuck yourself, Jet." He turned back to the group, who stared at him incredulously. "What the hell are we waiting for, let's GO!"

Before they took another step, Imogen collapsed.

"What happened?" cried Ryo.

The Men in White pounded on the door.

"Her bracelet, look, it's flashing!" Hunter waved at Imogen's wrist. Indeed, her deactivated silver bracelet was glowing red. Mosi instantly grabbed her hand and ripped apart the metal bracelet.

"They must be stunning us," said Marcus.

"But they're deactivated!"

"Doesn't mean they can't still be controlled," he snapped at Chantal. "Quick, get your bracelets off!"

Scrambling to find something to tear open her bracelet, Hunter's heart thumped like the beat of a drum. It was a time game; any second now her bracelet could zap and she would be knocked out and likely slow the group down, meaning they'd all be caught.

But fortunately, Mosi worked quick. Everyone's bracelets lay on the floor in a matter of seconds. All except for his own.

"Mosi hurry!"

"I can't," he growled. "It's attached to my heart. If I rip it out, I could pull apart my own chest."

"Let me," said Marcus. The two of them stared each other down. Mosi's tight jaw made it obvious that he didn't trust Marcus's technical abilities with something as fragile as his life support, but there was no time: any second, the Men in White could burst through the door or his restraint might knock him out as well.

"Trust me," said Marcus almost gently. "I can do this."

Mosi nodded. He ripped open his jumpsuit, baring the flashing red device implanted into his skin and grit his teeth hard.

"Then do it," he said.

Everyone held their breaths as Marcus lay a hand on Mosi's chest and closed his eyes.

The room was deadly silent. Hunter tried to breathe and steady the pumping of her blood. She almost wanted to reach over and grab hold of Will's hand, if he didn't have his arms full with Fearne. She moved her gaze back to Marcus, then at Mosi, listening to the hissing of the electricity being forced into his heart-rate monitor.

Mosi jerked suddenly. Chantal squealed and jumped back. Then Marcus stepped away and they stared at Mosi's chest and the little device that was black and emitting smoke. It was still attached, but no longer did it control the steady beating of his heart.

Zac whistled in awe. "Holy shit Marcus. You are *so* lucky you didn't kill him."

Marcus was about to snap at Zac when the lights went out, replaced by a red glow and an alarm that was all too familiar to them all. It was the alarm that sounded after Alfie had been detained and Jet took his powers back.

"Oh no," said Chantal and she covered her mouth. "The mist!"

Hunter started to panic. They had no time to run back; the Men in White were seconds away from breaking through the door and attacking with their tasers.

"Guys here!" called Benji from the left. Through the glow, Hunter spotted him across the room standing by a bank of shelves. He was tearing out boxes and throwing things at them. One of the objects hit Hunter in the chest and she fumbled with it. It was a rubber gas mask.

"Put them on!" she shouted at the group. The moment her face was covered, she heard the sounds of the mist spraying down upon them. They managed to guard themselves before any of them were knocked out by the gas. Then, it was time to run.

Hunter looked back for only a split second and felt her heart tear open at the sight of Sammy's dead body on the ground. It looked like a scene from a horror movie as the red light flashed over his broken body. She wished to God she could carry him out, to take him to see the sun again. To return him to his mother that he missed so much.

A heavy darkness fell upon her. She didn't even hear the blast as the Men in White exploded into the lab and sprinted towards them. It took all her strength not to collapse on the ground beside Sammy's body and she had to cling to Marcus as he dragged her away from the lab, shouting at her to move.

As she left, Hunter prayed for the small boy, that he would fly away to a better place.

She prayed for an angel to carry him, and then she ran.

FORTY-EIGHT

They were so close, Hunter could almost smell the fresh air and feel the hot sun burning her skin. The exit door was ahead, and Marcus reached it first, slamming against the handle.

"Locked. And there's no security panel." He searched the door and slapped it with his palms. "Dammit!"

Mosi passed Imogen to Will – who now had his arms free when Fearne jolted awake as they ran – and pushed through the group. Hunter felt the ground rumble with each of his footsteps. Everyone fell back.

As Mosi threw his fist against the door, Hunter felt the bite of a taser as it fired past her arm. She whirled, her heart leapt into her chest and then a fight began.

The dimness of the hallway splashed with red light made it difficult to see, and the gas masks weren't much help. Benji zoomed between the guards, knocking them over with his speed. An explosion shook the walls around them. Hunter glanced back and saw that Mosi had caused the entire door to crumble in. But it wasn't enough; behind the rock-solid cement, a steel emergency door blocked their path. It must have activated when the alarms switched on. They couldn't get through.

"Watch out!" screamed Chantal.

An electric blue bullet zipped past her head and barely missed Will's shoulder.

"Marcus!" yelled Ryo. "Duck!"

A guard grabbed her collar. Using moves she'd learnt in her training, Hunter dropped under a right-hook and twisted the guards arm behind him, taking the taser and shooting him in the back. A blow to the head sent Hunter down and she screamed in pain when someone crushed her fingers. The corridor was so packed with children and guards fighting that there was no room to move. In the red haze, everything seemed blurry.

What are we going to do, the way out is blocked!

Chantal let out a cry that made her stomach flip. Hunter rolled away from a falling guard and bumped against the wall. Ryo took a hit to the stomach just beside her, so Hunter grabbed the ankle of her attacker and forced heat into her hands. His ankle caught fire and it burned like a twig up his leg.

They weren't prepared for such a fight. Even though their powers far outweighed the Men in White, it would be useless if there wasn't another way out. Hunter forced herself to her feet and threw a fireball at a guard charging towards her. He screamed and ducked out of the way.

"Mosi!" Hunter shouted.

Mosi's large form was dancing back and forth in swift movements between two Men in White. He thumped one on the head so hard that Hunter was sure his spine had split in two. The other he threw against the wall.

Hunter felt a hand snatch her hair and she fell back against the guard that held her. His grip was so tight, he would surely rip her head off if he pulled for much longer. But after only a second, he seized up and passed out at her feet. Chantal stood behind her with a taser.

"What's the plan?"

"The only way out is up, otherwise we have to find our way to the sewers," said Mosi.

"Then we have no choice," said Hunter.

Benji zipped past her and skidded to a halt, nearly tripping over an unconscious guard. "I've been everywhere," he said. "Mosi's right: the only way out is through the sewer, but it's blocked by some sort of coded door."

"I'll be able to unlock it if we hurry," said Marcus. His nose was gushing blood.

"Then we'd better-"

Hunter was cut off when an ear-piercing alarm blared throughout the institution.

Over the alarm, there came a voice.

"WARNING. ALL SYSTEMS DISARMED. PLEASE EVACUATE IMMEDIATELY. WARNING. ALL SYSTEMS DISARMED. PLEASE EVACUATE IMMEDIATELY."

The monotone woman's voice repeated her message, just as she'd done when Jack had tried to escape. Hunter wondered for a moment if it was a sign that she should try to run down to the Death Caves and rescue her friend. But was it worth the risk?

"Are we going to explode?!" shouted Zac over the noise. "What do we do?"

"Follow me."

Mosi charged past her. Hunter quickly did a head count, thanking God they were all conscious and alive. Imogen must have woken up during the fight. She was breathing without the gas mask, which meant the mist had vanished. Mosi led them past the surgery rooms and back to the elevator.

"We're going upstairs?" called Chantal. "What if there's more guards?"

"Then we have to fight them, don't we?" snapped Marcus.

As Mosi slammed his hand against the elevator door, a chill went up Hunter's spine the moment the alarm stopped and silence fell. There came a crackle of static over the intercom, and then another voice spoke up.

"Children."

They all froze, even though the elevator door had opened.

"I know what you're planning to do," said Dr. Wolfe. "Your efforts are wasted: I have every exit secured, and more guards waiting on level 1."

"He's bluffing," said Zac.

"Shh!"

"Save yourselves the punishment and stop this fight. You dare not even *dream* what I have in store for you if you continue to resist restraint."

Imogen whimpered and clung to Chantal's arm. Hunter looked around at the group, their fears accelerating with each word the doctor spoke. *It's what he wants. To put fear in their minds. It's working.*

"Let's go, get in the elevator!" Hunter shouted.

They were hesitant.

"We've made it this far, now come on!"

Mosi moved first and the others hurriedly followed. Will stood close to Hunter in the small box as it shot up, and Hunter's blood pumped in her ears.

After the door was sealed shut for only a second, the elevator went pitch black and came to a grinding halt. Several of them screamed. Hunter pushed the fire to the edge of her skin, letting her veins glow bright like the sun and give them some light. Their faces were pale and terrified. She removed her mask and breathed in the clean, confined air. The rest of them followed.

"Marcus, can you power it up again?"

Sweat dripped from his brow as he nodded and pressed his palm against the power box. The elevator rocked back and forth.

"He's doing everything he can to stop us," said Hunter. She looked at each of their faces and realized that she had become their leader. She had to be braver than all of them. And at that point, as the fire surged through her skin and emerged from the dark pit it had been hiding in all those months, she felt truly brave. Brave enough to lead them to freedom. "You've all lived so long in this place that the idea of escaping seems impossible. But we're already halfway there. He knows that we have our powers, and that scares him. He can't stop us. The most he can do is throw obstacles in our way. We have to keep going, or our fears will weigh us down."

Light burst to life inside the elevator. Marcus breathed hard through his teeth and suddenly the electricity switched on and they shot up so fast, Hunter's stomach dropped.

Zac and Ryo cheered.

Hunter wondered what Dr. Wolfe would try next. She had no time to prepare herself for what might lie on the other side of the door, for they slid open seconds later and the corridor lay empty before them.

"Go!"

They sprinted to the staircase, Mosi in the lead. He burst into the common room with such force that the door was knocked off its hinges. Inside the room were three Men in White waiting, their tasers raised. They opened fire. One hit Mosi, but his skin could not be penetrated. Again, Imogen raised her hands and protected their group with a giant forcefield. Mosi stalked forward and swung his fists, no mercy given. They were at the door in seconds.

"How do you know there's a way out here?" asked Zac as they entered the boy's bathroom.

Mosi looked around, suddenly confused. "I don't."

"I do," said Will. He ran his hand down the crack on the left hand side and slid the secret door – their secret door – aside. The others gazed at him in surprise. "Follow me."

Hunter gave him a smile and entered first. It felt so good to summon the flames and light their way. For the first time, she saw exactly what the staircase looked like; a muddy, cemented corridor with stains of green and gray running down the walls. They followed her light in silence until they reached the door that led to the guard's quarters.

"What is this place?" asked Zac after Will had closed the door behind them. The corridor was tall with old lamps dangling from the ceiling, the walls made of decayed brick and the doors labeled with scratched-out names. The one above the room that she and Will used to sit in read 'Alistair Barnes'.

"We need to go right at the end of this corridor," said Mosi. "Then there should be a stairwell and an emergency exit."

Hunter nodded as they walked. Her heart was pounding in her chest. All she had to do was tell the others to meet her outside, then go left and find Jack. But could she get him out? Had he woken up yet? And what about Alfie? There were no roars coming from the Death Caves, which meant that Dr. Wolfe must have sedated him. Could she get him out too?

Will slid the latch on the door aside, and they moved into the next corridor. Hunter stopped and glanced left at the dimly lit passage, clenching her fists. She couldn't move her feet.

"Hunter," said Will by her side. "Let's go."

She looked up into his shadowed face. At once, her choice seemed easy. Find Alfie, find the prisoners, find Jack. Free them all.

But it was not that simple, and a part of Hunter knew that. She knew it was stupid and reckless and completely against the fire's guiding voice that urged her to run with the group and not back to the dark caves of death.

And yet something was pulling her. A force so powerful, it seemed to be a power of its own.

The power of a hero.

"I can't," she said to him. "I have to get them out. I have to try."

Will's eyes filled with ferocity. "No. Hunter, don't."

"What are you doing?" called Mosi.

"There's people down there," she said to the group. "Why should we get to escape and leave them in this place?"

"Uh," said Marcus, "because they're crazy? You said so yourself Hunter! We can't risk it!"

"They're still *people*." Hunter started backing up the corridor. "I want you all to run."

"Hunter-"

"Listen," she snapped at Ryo. "If I get caught, so be it. At least you'll all be out. You've been here too long, it wouldn't be fair. You guys go ahead without me." She slipped from her pocket the address Dr. Rosenthal had given her for a house somewhere outside of Seattle. She didn't know how far it was from ICE, but it was a safe house and she'd memorized it already. She handed the paper to Marcus. "Go to this address and stay together. I'll meet you there."

"What happened to sticking together?!" called Chantal. "You can't just leave!"

"I'm sorry."

She turned to run.

"Hunter, wait-"

Will came jogging up to her. As the others hurried down into the darkness towards the sewers, Hunter's spirit soared. He stayed with her.

Will took her hand. A connection buzzed between them. For a split second, Hunter felt a flame burst to life inside her, a flame she hadn't felt in a long time. It was ecstasy and excitement and bravery all at once. It was pure warmth.

"You're not doing this alone," he said. "Come on."

FORTY-NINE

T here were footsteps behind them, and Hunter and Will made it to the end of the corridor before they were attacked by three Men in White.

The darkness made it hard to fight, but Hunter threw her fire anyway. She wasn't afraid to hit Will – his power let him heal. Bright fire blinded her attackers and while they dodged the balls of flaming heat, Hunter shot forward and took them out.

"Where did they come from?" asked Will as he tried to catch his breath.

"Dr. Wolfe probably sent them after us." She yanked on the hatch of the door marked 'Cell Block'. "Hopefully there aren't many left after Alfie got loose. Maybe they're-"

Her words froze in her throat as the door swung inward and they faced the Cell Block corridor – or what was left of it.

Alfie had destroyed the place. Clouds of dust still floated in the air. There was rubble strewn across the walkway. Cells were blow apart, the walls crumbled in and the doors lying open. Beams of light from the broken ceiling were scattered right to the end. The bulbs were flickering on and off and buzzing with detached electricity. An eerie silence wrapped its claws around Hunter's heart and for a moment she wished they'd never come back. But a part of her knew this was the right thing to do. They had to rescue Alfie. And she had to at least try to find Jack.

Will glanced down at her in the dim light and nodded, his jaw clenched. "After you," he said.

With her eyes wide open, Hunter started to creep down the Cell Block. Each step was louder than a scream in her ears. She was shaking from head to foot, praying that Alfie was in his cell – alive, at the very least – and it helped motivate her.

She stepped unsteadily over a pile of broken stone–

And something grabbed hold of her ankle.

Hunter shrieked. She groped for Will as she struggled to tear her foot from the grip of someone lying under the rubble.

"Will-"

The figure moaned. Hunter lit her palms on fire and pointed them at the debris. Her stomach turned over inside her at the sight of a woman coated in dust, trapped under heavy slabs of concrete with dirty blood dripping down her face. Her eyes were closed but her hand moved slowly, begging them for help.

"Oh my Go-"

"There's nothing we can do," said Will. "Hurry, before-"

Something jumped out of the shadows and collided with Will. A high-pitched screech fell out of Hunter's mouth as Will and the attacker – a man in torn clothes – tumbled over a pile of fallen rocks. Hunter swore she heard Will's ribs crack and break. The man looked about to rip Will apart as he growled and raised dust in the struggle.

Hunter didn't waste a second. She grabbed the man's neck and dragged him back. He kicked at her, and when his head whipped around and a light flashed over him, she saw a mutated face with black and malicious eyes. Hunter felt just as much shock when he raised his hand and slashed across her stomach with his fingers.

Pain seared her. Blood began to seep through her white jumpsuit and she stumbled against the wall of a cell. The man had razor-sharp blades for fingers.

"Go Hunter!" Will shouted, and the man jumped on him again. "Find – Alfie!"

Hunter didn't want to, but her choices were few: Stay and free Will who could heal himself anyway, or continue on her suicide mission that was becoming more and more impossible the deeper she dove into the caves.

Leaving him tore her apart, but it was what Will wanted. She scrambled to her feet. No longer did she care about staying quiet. The corridor loomed before her, the possibility of more psycho mutants hiding behind the walls, ready to jump out at her, filled her mind with fear. So she thought of Jack, and that helped her run.

Her fingers were slick with her own blood. She twisted her ankle on a loose slab of stone but she kept moving anyway. Her eyes were on Alfie's cell, but her heart was taking her to Death Cave 1. She tried to ignore the grunts and screams of Will and the mutant and banished images of more of them piling onto him and tearing him to pieces like cannibals, because that slowed her down.

She came to where Alfie's cell once was. A gaping hole in the roof and torn-down walls where he had transformed lay before her. No Alfie.

Why did Dr. Rosenthal choose to let Alfie run loose and kill half if not more of these innocent people just to set us free? Where is he? Where is Dr. Wolfe?

Hunter buried her questions in the back of her mind and stepped back. Her heart thumped in her chest as she watched Will struggle. Out of the corner of her eye, she saw a girl standing in a slash of light, her figure silhouetted by shadows. She watched Hunter for a moment, then raised a hand and waved slowly. Chills ran through her and all she wanted was to get away.

So Hunter ran to Death Cave 1. If Dr. Wolfe was keeping Jack alive, he would be there. Hunter felt strangely responsible for the horrible things that had happened to Jack, and that only made her run harder. Her chest burned from the slices the mutant had made, but she didn't care. She nearly tripped in her haste to get to the bottom of the stairs and threw open the door that led to hell.

Everything had been repaired; the glass tank, the broken equipment, and even the blood stain from the guard that exploded. The room felt much bigger without all the scientists and Men in White crowded around Terminal 1. Hunter hurried forward without checking the shadows that bordered the room. If there was anyone hiding, she didn't see them as she pushed her way around a machine to the front of the glass tank.

There was a bed inside. On the bed was Jack. She was surprised to see him look exactly like he used to; no more black veins, no more Hulk-like exterior or complete anger radiating from every muscle in his body. He was asleep, hooked up to at least three different monitors. She found herself standing on the platform with her hands pressed to the cold glass and tears spilling from her eyes.

"Jack," she whimpered. "I've come for you, okay? I'm so s-sorry."

How do I get him out? Taking him away from the machines would kill him. Hunter searched the tank for a way inside but couldn't find the button. She began to panic. She forgot about Will and the others and whether they'd escaped or not. All she cared about was getting Jack away from the institution and back to Clare and the real world where he only dreamed about superheroes and never thought he was one. Where there was no pain or torture and he could be normal again.

But he was not normal. He never would be.

"It's no use trying," said a voice from the shadows behind her and Hunter spun.

"Who's there?" she asked, even though she knew.

Dr. Wolfe stepped into the light. He was covered in dust and blood and looked more physically exhausted than she'd ever seen him. But that didn't stop his gaze from sending chills through her body.

"If he leaves that tank, he dies." Dr. Wolfe walked towards her and the Men in White started to bleed from the darkness with their tasers aimed at her. She felt sick and angry at her own stupidity that she'd let herself get caught for no reason but to see Jack. "You should have known better."

"He's alive, right? Dr. Rosenthal didn't kill him?"

"Of course not. He will heal in time."

"Then what? You're going to train him to become a killer? To destroy the world?"

"No training needed, my dear." Dr. Wolfe was only feet from her and it was all she could do not to burn the smirk off his filthy face. "Jack is already a killer all the way to his core."

"You don't know him like I do," she said confidently. "Jack is selfless and brave and he would never join you."

"Oh, it won't take much. Just like your fire, Jack's darkness and destruction eat away at his soul. He doesn't have anyone to help him overpower it. I only want him to nourish that darkness. Jack will become one of the most powerful beings on the earth, and there's nothing you can do to stop that."

A crash at the back of the room made all of them turn. One of the Men in White started dragging something from behind a desk. Hunter's heart shattered at the sight of Will's bloodied and bruised body.

No.

Why had he followed her? Why didn't he run to get away from the mutants? Why did he have to get caught like she did?

Because he said he wouldn't let me do this alone.

"Ah William," said Dr. Wolfe. "I should have known you'd be here to save the day."

Will spat blood onto the floor and slouched in the grip of the guards. As usual, he said nothing.

Hunter clenched her fists so hard, her bones throbbed and her fingernails pierced her skin. It was her fault they'd both been caught. But at that moment, it was easier to be angry at the doctor than feel guilt for her actions.

"I must say; I'm not entirely surprised that you two found each other here. You had a very special bond when you were young. I suppose that bond has rekindled." The doctor turned to her and smiled. "It's a pity you will never get to see each other again."

Something exploded inside Hunter. She launched herself off the platform and set her hands on fire as she fell through the air. All she wanted was to rip him apart and wipe that sadistic smirk off his withered face. The doctor moved out of the way, but she managed to catch his arm mid-jump. She pulled him down with her and they went rolling on the floor. The Men in White hauled her to her feet, but they couldn't stop the fire. It was out of control. Molten-lava oozed from every pore in her body. She raged and screamed and burned anything that tried to hold her back from revenge.

Then a white-hot pain stabbed at her side and she felt her entire body jar from the electric shock of the taser. Her vision blurred. She jerked on the floor in agony. It must have been set on a low dosage, for it didn't knock her out.

"Hunter!"

Will called her name. It cut deeper than the slices the mutant had made in her stomach.

Dr. Wolfe leered over her. She could hear Will struggling in the background. Her head flopped to the right and she saw the guards beating him mercilessly, each punch like a gunshot in her ear.

"I know it was not you that initiated this escape Hunter," said Dr. Wolfe, his breath blowing hot against her face. "But I will make you *suffer* for leading them out of here, of that you can be certain."

They got out. I did it, they're free. Despite the throbbing aching of her body, she managed a small smile. But the smile – the thought, even – was not enough to wash away the fear that rose within her at the doctor's next words.

"You will never leave this place. You will never see another soul outside of my staff. And you will hear of Jack's destruction as we work together to bring havoc to the world. I promise-" He grabbed her chin and forced her eyes to his. They were black with rage as he sneered down at her and spat out his words, "-That you and William will listen to each other *scream* in pain and misery every day and every night until you take your very last breath."

The taser jabbed into the side of her neck. This time there was enough power to send her into complete darkness where she prayed to God she'd never wake up again.

FIFTY

T he barrier between reality and unconsciousness fell apart and Hunter broke through the surface. She wasn't aware of the space she was in. She couldn't feel anything, but she knew on some level that wherever she was, it was cold. Everywhere was dark and blurry, the shapes outlined in a thin glow as they bobbed around her. Suddenly, she was grateful not to feel pain.

Through the numbness, Hunter started hearing voices.

"Keep her under. Dr. Wolfe doesn't want her gaining consciousness just yet."

The voice was not familiar to her.

"I'm at fifty milligrams," said another voice. This one sounded fuzzy.

"Add another ten. The cuts are deep. She lost a lot of blood."

Help! Hunter begged in her mind for her tongue wouldn't move. *Help me...* She was too sleepy and hazy to move at all. Even her mind started to drift again. *What's happening to me? What is Dr. Wolfe doing?*

Hysteria surfaced inside her. The faint beep of a heart rate monitor increased and the shadows around her moved quicker, waving at each other as they tried to make the beeping cease. The sound was suddenly a scream. Was it her own? *Make it stop... please...*

She drifted, and then she woke again, and there was silence and darkness around her. She squirmed and felt her fingers clench.

A shriek of pain from a room nearby filled her ears. It was Will, she knew it. Her chest heaved as she thrashed on the bed Dr. Wolfe had her strapped into. There were tubes sticking into her arms that doused the fire and made Hunter remember the chair Joshua kept her in, the chair that fed ice into her bloodstream. No matter how she struggled, she couldn't get away. Nor could she block the sound of Will yelling in agony.

You and William will listen to each other scream in pain and misery every day and every night until you take your very last breath...

Dr. Wolfe's words were so loud in her mind that she suddenly believe he was standing right beside her, repeating them over and over. It had begun: The eternity of suffering he promised her.

No. Please no.

She tried to imagine the others reaching the outside world, finding their families and living their lives again. She searched her mind for their faces, but they no longer existed. Fear seized her in a grip so tight that at once, she was gasping for breath.

I'm alone, she thought. *Forever and ever.*

A faint light started to glow around her. Hunter opened her eyes wider, blinking. She saw the fire of her reflection standing over her, looking grim.

You're not alone, she said. *Not while I'm here.*

Then, Hunter slept.

Dr. Wolfe stood over her. Hunter had never been more afraid of a man in her entire existence. Even her nightmares about Joshua and his pale eyes as he cackled over Eli's dead body did not compare to the terror that slithered under her skin.

He said nothing – just watched her, just smiled with yellowed teeth. She wished she could get up and run or even close her eyes. But this time, she was wide awake.

"I like this much better Hunter," he finally muttered. "Now I have you and Will and Jack together, and I don't ever have to leave. The only thing that would make this ideal would be if Fearne was still with us. Oh, and Joshua of course."

Hunter's heart pounded like a drum. She was surprised at how much that thought pained her.

"I will find him soon, I promise."

271

"What will you do with me, with us?"

"Well, since I now have less test subjects in my Death Caves as I began with, Hunter, I am in desperate need of your assistance. You see… I have studied Will for sixteen years. And I have studied you enough to know exactly how your body works. I no longer need your DNA – I have plenty of samples. And there are no more demonstrations either. My next project is much bigger, and much more complex." He grinned down at her. "I need you and William to be my new mutants along with those that survived the cave-in."

For a moment, Hunter wasn't afraid. Because in the doctor's eyes she saw anger and disappointment, as if he had failed only himself. So much loss had occurred in his institution and he had no one else to blame.

But the satisfaction was momentary, for now he had a real reason to cause her pain and no desire to keep her alive. He got what he wanted and now it was time for revenge.

Perhaps she deserved it. She was stupid enough to separate herself from the group when she could have easily followed them out to safety. Instead, she had to play the hero and run blindly back to imprisonment.

But Will did not deserve this. Furious guilt swarmed inside her. It was because of her that he would suffer, and that was worse than any pain the doctor could imagine.

FIFTY-ONE

unter regained consciousness not on an operating table, but in a cell. It was so dark she could hardly see her own hands. Her lungs were dry and itchy with sawdust and her body ached from lying so long on the damp, concrete floor.

Everywhere was silent. It took her only a second to realize she was behind the bars of a Death Cave and again, she panicked. Her heart thumped in a tired beat. She picked herself up slowly, dizzy and sore, and hobbled to the door of the cell. Her stomach was patched up with bandages, but the movement made the wound throb. As her eyes adjusted to the darkness, she became aware of what was outside her cell.

Rubble. So it hadn't been repaired yet, meaning it could only be days – hours, even – after she and Will were captured. Either that, or Dr. Wolfe didn't care for the architecture of the underground prison.

Only days ago, Hunter voluntarily walked the halls of the Death Caves. Now she was locked inside one. Which number was it? How close was she to Jack?

And the most pressing question of all: Where was Will imprisoned?

She stood with her hands on the bars for a long time, listening to the silence and thankful that her thoughts, too, were silent. Sometime later, Hunter heard a female sobbing far away from her cell. The sound was like poison in her ears and she stumbled back until she hit the wall and slid down to the ground. She curled up in the fetal position, even though it hurt like hell.

Then she, too, was crying. Heaving. She cried so much that her tears dried up and her chest ached. The fire tried to warm her, but it couldn't reach her skin. Once again, a bracelet circled her wrist and she was back where she started.

"Hunter?"

His voice broke through the darkness, hoarse and wonderful. Hunter lurched upright and looked for him in her cell.

"Will? Where are you?"

"Next to you. There's a crack in the wall."

Hunter scrambled to the left side of her cell where his voice was coming from. She pressed her body against it, desperate to be close to him. She scratched at the concrete with her fingers until they ached.

"You're the stupidest person I've ever met, do you know that?" he said from his cell. "Do you always go running off into danger without any concern for your safety?"

Smiling, Hunter remembered saying those exact words to him when he lay on the floor of the breakfast hall after the dinosaur attack. "You came with me, you know."

"Yeah. I guess it's my hero tendency again."

At that, Hunter found she couldn't control herself anymore. The tears bubbled up in her throat as she muttered, "Will, I-I can't – I'm so sorry – it's my fault you're–"

"Stop it Hunter," he snapped at her, but his tone was soft. "You're being ridiculous. It's not your fault."

"But it is. We should have just left with the others. Why did I have to run down here to save crazy people who only attacked us and Alfie, who could be dead too and Jack, who was-"

"You went back for *Jack*? Why?"

Hunter wished more than anything that she could see his face. She put her hand against the cold, crumbling wall and sighed. She owed him the truth.

"Because it's my fault Jack is here in the first place."

Will paused. "Hunter, you're delusional. Not everything is your fault."

"You're right. I am delusional. Delusional that I thought I could make everything right and save the world. That I could bring my friend home to his sister, to a life in New York where my guardian kidnapped him from his own home and studied him like Dr. Wolfe himself. I'm delusional for not making sure he left the warehouse safely."

"Okay, now you're not making any sense at all. Tell me what you're talking about and start from the beginning."

So Hunter told him. If not for his benefit, but at least to keep her mind occupied. It felt good to talk about things and to hear her own voice and not the dark thoughts. Occasionally Will mumbled a response, and that helped remind her that she wasn't talking to herself alone in the cold.

He didn't seem angry. But then again, she couldn't see his face.

"Why didn't you tell me this earlier?"

"I... I guess I was selfish." It was the honest truth, and it stung worse than the gashes across her gut. "When I saw Jack in Death Cave 1, he was... he wasn't the sweet and normal boy I left in New York. He was a monster. And I felt responsible because I bought him into this mess. If it weren't for me he wouldn't even know he had a power."

"You're wrong. The only person to blame is Joshua."

The bite in his tone made her frown. "Are you still upset about Joshua?"

"I have good reason to be. He left me here sixteen years ago and took you with him. And after leaving this place, he didn't tell a single person about it. Instead he raised you and went about his life as if nothing had changed while soul after soul died here within these walls, tortured because of something they couldn't control. It also sounds like he wasn't the best influence towards you either. He did kill your teacher and your boyfriend and kidnap your friend, right?"

"He was doing that to protect my secret."

The words just fell out of her mouth. She had defended Joshua. Hunter couldn't believe it, and yet it was true. Joshua only ever wanted her to be safe. He went crazy because he cared about her.

A deep ache erupted in her chest. She missed him. She missed Joshua more than anything.

"Hunter..."

"I'm okay," she sniffed and wiped her eyes.

After a moment, Will said, "I wonder where the others are right now."

"Free?"

"Yeah." She heard him sigh. "Free."

275

They sat in silence again, but it wasn't so terrifying knowing he was just a few blocks of cement away. Hunter closed her eyes as she lay slumped against the wall. If she fell asleep, it didn't feel like it, for next second she had jerked awake at the sound of several footsteps in the corridor.

Her heart leapt into a familiar rhythm, pounding fast and hard. Keys jingled and a cell door opened.

"Good morning, William."

Dr. Wolfe's voice brought ice back into her soul. She leapt to her feet and pressed her face against the bars, desperate to see what was happening, desperate to see Will.

And there he was.

"Let go of me!" he exclaimed to the guards that dragged him from his cell. "I can walk myself, let go!"

"Will!" Hunter called.

In a split second, he turned and met her eyes. He was dirty and covered in dried blood stains, but all she saw was his face. She stretched her arm out of her cell and reached towards him. Will shrugged out of the grip of the guards and his hand grabbed hold of hers. It was strong and cool and so familiar that her knees felt suddenly weak. The touch lasted only a moment, until the guards shoved him hard in the shoulder and he stumbled forward, out of sight.

"No, *Will!*"

"It's okay," he called back. "Don't worry about me!"

She rested her forehead against the iron bars with her hand still slumped out of her cell, her fingers tingling with the ghost of his touch. She listened to his footsteps fade away, horrible thoughts of where they were taking him forcing the guilt further into the pit of her stomach.

When she looked up, Dr. Wolfe was a foot from her face. Hunter gasped in fright and fell back.

"Look at yourself Hunter," he sneered. "So afraid. You're not even going to insult me?"

The fire burned in outrage, but the doctor was right. She had nothing left inside her but fear.

He shook his head. "So easily broken, and I don't see a fire in your eyes anymore. Your embers are dying out."

With that, he was gone and she was alone again. She rocked back and forth, flinching at every sound no matter how small or distant and waiting for Will to return. Waiting, endlessly, waiting.

First came the anger. She picked up broken rocks from the ground and threw them at the door. She screamed and tore at her hair and kicked the wall until her stomach ached too much for her to move. Then, she crawled up against the wall next to the crack, forcing herself to sleep until he returned.

And when the silence came, so did the sobs of the woman in another cell and the mumbling of a man who had surely gone crazy and the sounds of someone scratching against the walls. All of it echoed in her mind louder than the pounding of her heart.

This was hell.

FIFTY-TWO

Hunter heard footsteps hours later. She scrambled to her feet and threw herself against the door, praying it was Will. But to her utter shock, the guards were not dragging a mutant with them. They were dragging Dr. Rosenthal.

She could not believe the state he was in. It looked like someone had run over the doctor with a monster truck. He could hardly put one foot in front of the other.

The guards threw the doctor in the cell directly opposite hers. She heard him gasp in pain. The Men in White stalked away and she waited a few more seconds before she called to him.

"Dr. Rosenthal?"

There came no response.

"Dr. Rosenthal, are you alright?"

He grumbled through the silence.

"What did you say?"

"Hello... Hunter."

His face appeared between the bars – or, what she could see of his face. Most of it was covered in blood and ugly bruises. His right eye would not open.

"What did they do to you?"

"Oh," he sighed, "most of this wasn't the guards. It was a struggle to set Alfie free and... I didn't get out in time."

"You were here, under this chaos, while a dinosaur stomped around? How are you alive?"

"Karma, I like to assume," he smiled. How he managed to be humorous, she could not understand.

"Where is Alfie now?"

"I don't know what they did with him Hunter, but I'd be surprised if he made it what with all the chaos he caused. Then again, Dr. Wolfe likes to keep the unstable ones in case they're needed, so there's no way to know."

Hunter hoped Dr. Wolfe had mercy on poor Alfie.

"And what are you doing back here? Did I not risk my life to assure your safety? Did I not explain myself clearly when I said you *must* escape?"

Hunter felt her stomach turn over. More guilt crushed down on her harder than a rockslide. Yet another person she had disappointed, another life that was over because of her selfish decisions. She had forgotten Dr. Rosenthal's sacrifice.

"I'm so sorry," she said blankly, no more tears left to cry. "I wanted to leave with the others, but it felt wrong to go without the people trapped down here. Will… volunteered to come with me to rescue them."

"Hunter." Her name fell from his mouth in a sigh. "I told you they could not be helped."

"I know. I'm sorry."

He looked at her through the bars. She couldn't tell if he was angry or not; it was too dark. But the heat of his gaze felt as though it had stabbed her in the chest.

"I'll be honest, a part of me knew you'd try," he said. "You've changed a lot these past few months Hunter. Your fear does not consume you."

"What do you mean? I've never been more afraid."

"Not of yourself. Of others. Selflessness led you back to these caves to rescue the mutants, and Jack I presume. Qualities of a true hero. And heroes have no time for themselves."

If he was trying to make her feel better, he was not succeeding. The only way Hunter would be able to flush away the darkness in her soul was to right the wrongs she'd created. If she didn't save everyone, she did not succeed.

"I know it's not right of me to ask you this," she said as she rested her forehead against the cool bars. "But is there any escape for us now?"

His words came out pained as he said, "If I know Winston, we'd be lucky to remain alive for much longer."

Nodding, Hunter stepped away from her cell door.

"But Hunter-"

She stopped and went back to the window. "Yes?"

"There is always hope."

Smiling a little, Hunter returned to her place by the wall to wait for Will. Someone came back for Dr. Rosenthal what felt like hours later. They dragged him away, and Hunter did not see the doctor again.

"You awake?"

Hunter rolled her head to the side and put her cheek against the wall. Her eyes stuck together as she opened them.

"I'm not sure," she mumbled. "I could be dreaming."

"You're awake," said Will.

"When did you get back?"

"Just now. You must've been pretty deep asleep not to hear me. I insulted one of the guards and he punched me."

"Why would you do that?"

"Well... he tried to touch my ass."

"You're funny," she said sleepily. Then she frowned. "Wait, why are you funny?"

"I'm not allowed to be?"

"I just don't see how."

After a moment, he said, "cheer up Hunter. I know it sucks right now, but we'll get through this. We'll escape soon."

"I think we've run out of chances to escape. I think we're here to stay."

He didn't answer. She realized then that she was letting the darkness cloud her confidence. She was only trapped in ICE for a few months when she formed an escape plan. Will had been there his entire life. Telling him that they'd missed their chance at escaping would crush him.

"Well," he sighed. "I guess that's it then. I don't have much time left do I?"

"What do you mean?"

"I'm fading away. Just like every other mutant who died within these walls, I'm getting too old to keep living here."

"What are you, eighty-nine?" she scoffed. "Don't be ridiculous Will."

He said nothing.

"Will?"

"Yeah?"

"You won't die."

"I know I'm immortal, but that won't stop it from happening. Dr. Wolfe said-"

"Who cares what he said. *You. Won't. Die.*"

He paused.

"How do you know?"

"Because," she said as she ran her fingers down the dry wall. "I have faith."

Silence fell, but it was a comfortable silence. For the first time, a small amount of warmth filled Hunter from somewhere deep in her core. It was a fire that began as a flame, a fire of assurance and hope.

"Okay," said Will eventually. "I believe you. Goodnight Hunter."

"Goodnight," she said.

FIFTY-THREE

J et Slater truly believed he made the right choice. Dr. Wolfe gave him a tempting offer, his power was better than any of the others and he always felt he had the guts to be a bad guy, a villain. There was a darkness flowing in his veins, and Dr. Wolfe noticed it. He called it potential. Jet was proud to be noticed, and ever since he came out of the Orb with the mental girl, his creative juices flowed hard and fast inside his mind. Being bad just felt natural to him. He was born that way, unlike his idiotic princess of a brother. Jet was destined to do great things with his power, to make men, women and children fear his name. And he had Dr. Wolfe to thank for giving him a chance to prove himself.

But after the others escaped, Jet felt a little less sure of the choices he'd made. The adrenaline died down after the fight, and Jet was left to face the small, dead body of the boy he killed. Sammy was his name. He looked like a little angel asleep on the ground. Only his eyes were open and Jet was sure he'd never forget the look of astonishment and pain there, and the glass eye that gazed into nothing. It felt good to kill, sure, but the feeling afterwards wasn't so appealing.

Mikayla stood beside him in Dr. Wolfe's office days after the escape. She had been quiet for a long time. He knew her well enough to see past her stoic appearance. She, too, was doubting her choice to remain, to join Dr. Wolfe's side. But she trusted him. She said nothing.

Jet faced the room that felt much smaller now that it was almost crowded with people. He and Mikayla had their backs to the wall beside the desk where Dr. Wolfe sat with his hands folded on the desktop. Jet felt on edge just looking at the man. He appeared to be holding back a cyclone of rage. Even though not all of them escaped – Hunter and Will were still in his clutches – the doctor was furious that he'd let them go so easily. He seemed to believe his security was enough, and without their powers, there was no hope. Clearly he needed to keep his office better secured.

But Dr. Wolfe held it together in the company of two official-looking men dressed like generals. Jet guessed they were Chinese, but he couldn't be sure. They were completely robotic, emotionless men with pursed lips, clean-shaven faces and eyes as hard as stone. They wore medals and badges that flashed in the fluorescent lights. Dr. Wolfe put on his I-have-everything-under-control expression and cleared his throat.

"Welcome Gentlemen," he said, all official-like. "Thank you for attending this meeting today. I trust you had a pleasant flight?"

The men glanced quickly at each other and nodded.

"Wonderful… well, as you may know we had a little accident just a while ago with-"

"You let out those mutants, didn't you?" the taller one snapped. "The ones in your little circus act demonstrations?"

Jet grit his teeth hard, tempted to throw his fist into the man's face. *Who's he calling a mutant?*

"Yes," Dr. Wolfe said thickly, "Only eight escaped. We still have two very powerful subjects here, and two others in secure lock up. Those that ran away were practically harmless and have nothing to do with our operations in Death Cave 1."

"I heard you also had some difficulty with a raging dinosaur," said the other in a much thicker accent. One of his eyebrows shot up, as though he was amused to even speak the words. "And several other test subjects were killed in an explosion?"

Again, Dr. Wolfe nodded forcefully. "That situation is completely under control now. But as I was saying, Gentlemen, the escapees will be caught and detained again. That, however, is not our main project."

"Dr. Wolfe," the taller one said.

"Yes, General Cheng?"

"We aren't here to babble with you all day long. What we want is a full status report on your weapons project. Do you have a prototype available?"

Dr. Wolfe's face paled. Jet had never seen him look so vulnerable.

"I do, but I'm afraid he's not ready yet."

"And why is that?" Cheng spat.

"I'll let the person responsible explain that to you himself," said Dr. Wolfe and he pressed a button on his desk intercom. "Send him in," he said to the machine.

A moment later, two Men in White carried a bloodied, bruised and weary old Dr. Rosenthal into the room. His hands were cuffed in front of him. The Men in White shoved the doctor into the chair before the desk and backed out of the room.

Jet felt Mikayla tense beside him. She always liked Dr. Rosenthal. He used to tell her that she would one day have one of the strongest powers in the universe if she strengthened it with practice and never abused it. Abusing it could be dangerous, he'd said. Jet thought he was a complete fool, and a compulsive liar on most occasions. Jet wasn't surprised when he heard the doctor was the one who let that stupid queer out of his dog kennel and provided a clear escape route for the others. He sneered at the man who slumped over in the chair.

"Hello Albert," Dr. Wolfe smiled. "I'd like to introduce to you General Cheng and Officer Wu. Gentlemen, this is our very own Dr. Albert Rosenthal, leading biologist and one of my old friends."

Dr. Rosenthal didn't have the strength to look up at the officers, who stared down at him as though he was a fleck of manure on their perfectly scrubbed black army boots.

"Dr. Rosenthal," said Dr. Wolfe as he stood up slowly, crossed his arms behind him and walked around his desk to level with the weak doctor. "Would you like to explain to everyone in the room why you unlocked a very dangerous creature from a coma and set him loose in the Death Caves to help the majority of our test subjects escape this facility?"

Dr. Rosenthal looked up with a great deal of effort and grumbled something under his breath.

"I'm sorry, I didn't catch that?" said Dr. Wolfe.

"I said… I didn't have a choice," he heaved.

"You didn't have a choice? Between what, recklessness or insanity? Do you know what you cost this institution?"

Dr. Rosenthal sighed deeply and started coughing as though there was something large stuck in his throat. After a moment he pulled his cuffed hands away and a string of blood joined his lips to his palms.

"You also shot my weapon, Albert."

The old man said nothing.

"You have made my associates very unhappy. They were hoping the weapon would be ready by now. The royal family who are funding our entire institution are impatient people. And though the American government have been scratching their heads trying to find me here, I'm afraid it won't be long until I am caught, which makes all of us very uncomfortable. So unfortunately, I'm going to have to tell them to come back another day when their weapon isn't recovering from a hole in his chest. You can imagine how happy they are about that, right Gentlemen?"

The officers glared at Dr. Wolfe, wondering just like Jet what point Dr. Wolfe was trying to make.

"Well Albert, whatever you were trying to achieve, it won't stop my plans for Jack. And it certainly won't stop me from carrying out my mission."

Dr. Rosenthal nodded. "You're starting a war, aren't you Winston?"

"Very good," Dr. Wolfe grinned. "In a few more months, I'll have enough weaponry to empower the entire Chinese army. We will declare war on the American Embassy, who think they are so patriotic and mighty. And you, my friend, won't be able to stop me."

Dr. Rosenthal let out a long and painful sigh. "I was afraid of that," he croaked. "So I'll warn you now while I have the chance." The doctor lifted his head and looked Dr. Wolfe directly in the eyes. "When the wicked thrive, so does sin, but the righteous will see their downfall."

Dr. Wolfe's manic smile widened and seconds later, he began to chuckle.

"Your God tell you that, did he Albert?" he asked. "I wonder where he is now."

"You knew this day would come."

"I didn't want to believe it," he said sadly.

Dr. Rosenthal gave the man a pitying glare but replied with nothing.

The officers cleared their throats, suggesting Dr. Wolfe get on with it, and so he clasped his hands behind his back and walked around the desk. His oyster eyes sparkled venomously.

"Let us address one final issue, old friend."

"What might that be?"

Dr. Wolfe's grin widened. "How would you like to die?"

The officers broke their tough façade for the first time since they entered the room. They frowned quickly at each other before resuming their positions. Mikayla made a small squeak beside him, but Jet had been expecting this. In fact, he was prepared for it.

Jet stepped away from the wall and met eyes with Dr. Wolfe.

"I'd like to do it, Sir," he said.

"Oh, Jet. Of course, be my guest." Dr. Wolfe stretched a hand out and then sat himself down at his desk casually, as though Jet were about to perform a presentation on the current stock market.

Blood pumping in anticipation, Jet stepped around Dr. Rosenthal and looked down at the hunched, sick man who was once a great mentor to him. In fact, Dr. Rosenthal was kind to everyone. But if there was one thing Jet had learnt from living in a place like ICE Incorporated, it was that rule breakers and betrayers were to be punished. And what Dr. Rosenthal did was punishable by nothing less than an execution.

And so, it was an execution he received.

Jet raised his right hand and pointed a finger at Dr. Rosenthal's neck. The old man met his eyes, and even though he knew he was about to die, he appeared almost relieved. He took a deep breath, let it out slow, and gave Jet a small nod.

"There is still forgiveness for you Jet," he wheezed. "Don't let evil steal your soul."

"Too late old man," Jet replied.

And he drew his finger across the air, envisioning a clean blade slicing right through the neck. There was a terrible squelch and a splash of blood fell upon the desk. Red liquid spilled down the doctor's chest as his head slid sideways, toppled into his lap, bounced off his knees and landed face-up at Jet's feet.

There, his wise, compassionate eyes gazed up at Jet, at peace with death.

EPILOGUE

In the room was a bed. The bed had real blankets and real pillows. The room itself was sterile and bright, unnatural for the Death Caves. Someone had placed a single sunflower in a vase on the bedside table.

Lying on the bed was a man. He could have been asleep, but it was difficult to tell because his face was so mutated by burns that no expression he made could ever be clear. Hunter looked at the man and felt the fire squirm.

"What is this?" she muttered to Dr. Wolfe who stood beside her. They looked in at the man through what she presumed was one-way glass from a dark room with a desk and control panel. Behind her was a table covered in a black cloth and two chairs.

It was only a day after the last time she saw Dr. Rosenthal. Will returned while she slept. They were fed a few hours later and taken to a room at the end of the corridor that served as a bathroom. Guards hosed them down to get rid of the blood and dirt and gave them fresh jumpsuits – they smelled clean, but they were splashed with dark stains.

She and Will talked on and off about things that kept them sane, like whether the others made it to Dr. Rosenthal's house in Seattle or if they decided to split up and go home to see their families. She fell asleep with Will's voice filling her mind.

Sometime later, Dr. Wolfe came for her. Expecting to be taken to a surgery room, Hunter was surprised when he led her to a separate part of the Death Caves. It did not look like a cave at all. It was cleaner and Hunter felt dirty just being in it.

For a moment, she wondered if the sight before her eyes was the result of her powers. Was she was responsible for this man's injuries? Was the doctor trying to shove more guilt down her throat?

It was too much to handle. She stepped away from the window. "Why are you showing me this?"

"I've had some spare time on my hands in preparation for the beginning of our experiments. I assume you've been wondering why I haven't taken you from your cell since I put you there. Please, have a seat."

He indicated to the chair. Hesitantly, she sat down opposite him and couldn't stop herself from glancing to her right at the man through the window.

"Will says you changed your mind about experimenting on me."

"More or less," he shrugged. "I may still need you as an extra body, but now I have something much bigger in mind."

She turned her head and gazed at the doctor, fear filling her faster than water in a dam.

"Does it have anything to do with Dr. Rosenthal?"

In the dim light, Hunter could still see the hurt appear on the doctor's face, and at once she knew that he was gone.

"You killed him, didn't you?"

"I did not," he said and cleared his throat. "But Albert is no longer with us, yes."

"Why did you-"

"That's *enough*."

Her throat closed up instantly at the harsh snap of his tone. She clenched her fists in her lap and avoided his eye, and all thoughts of the kind doctor as well.

He sighed. "I couldn't allow Dr. Rosenthal to live after he betrayed me for the second time – this time costing me just as much as shooting Jack Holloway in the back. He was my life-long friend, yes, but... I had no more chances to give him."

Even though he was clearly heart broken, she still felt no pity for him. I *should not be the only one in this hellhole feeling guilty.*

Dr. Wolfe pulled from his coat pocket a tiny silver bell. The sound of the chime rang painfully in her ears. A moment later, two Men in White entered carrying trays of food. It was not the regular gray goo Hunter was used to – this was real food: Mashed potatoes, roast beef with gravy, steamed vegetables, bread rolls and cubes of butter, even a bottle of red wine from the south of France. It was dark in the room, so one of the guards lit a long candle and placed it in the center of the table.

Though the food smelled overwhelming, Hunter couldn't look at it. She wanted to vomit.

"Please, eat." He held out his hand and indicated to the meal.

Hunter didn't move.

"Wine?" He poured them both a glass.

"Dr. Wolfe, what is this?"

"I pride myself upon my ability to remember my patients, Hunter." He put the glimmering glass in front of her plate. "But that patient beside us I never cared too much about. We found him before even Joshua arrived. He doesn't have any special abilities that we were able to uncover, and he used to look much worse. Thanks to Will's ability, we were able to heal the worst of the burns. I'm afraid he won't ever be rid of the scars, but he is alive at least."

The doctor sliced through his tender beef in smooth motions. Hunter thought for a split second about stabbing him with her own knife, but she was too distracted by the patient lying in the bed.

"I did this, didn't I?" she breathed in disgust. "I burnt him."

"Oh, you definitely had something to do with this. But that's not the reason he is here."

"Why then?" she asked.

"I once thought that he might develop abilities after the accident he was involved in. There was an existing element that you are already very familiar with – you remember Feucotetanus, don't you?"

She stared in shock, the pieces starting to click together.

"Yes. Feucotetanus protected this man from dying that night. I didn't realize how much it truly influenced his survival until you returned to ICE. One of my scientists recently found traces of something very interesting in his blood flow."

"What?"

"You," he said.

Hunter looked from the doctor to the man and back to the doctor. What he was saying didn't make sense.

"I don't understand. How is that possible?"

Dr. Wolfe smiled at her through the luminescent glow of the candle. "Because," he said. "That man is your father."

Isabella was born in Adelaide, South Australia. She finished school, travelled Europe and went to work in Canada. Her first book, Rouge, was published in August, 2013 and began as a conversation on the school bus.

www.isabellamodra.com

www.ingramcontent.com/pod-product-compliance
Lightning Source LLC
Chambersburg PA
CBHW031253170626
46807CB00001B/118